Praise for

PANDEMIC

"When there's a scientific breakthrough, Robin Cook doesn't just stand up and cheer. He uses his fertile imagination and writes a novel about its possible perils. . . . By graphically showing what could happen were CRISPR/Cas9 to fall into the wrong hands, the author rings a much needed warning bell about gene-editing technology."
—Associated Press

CHARLATANS

"Cook has been cranking out best-selling medical thrillers since the mid-1970s, and he long ago worked out a formula that works for his fans. [*Charlatans*] is no exception, proving once again that there is comfort and entertainment to be found in the familiar."
—*Booklist*

"Cook fans will keep turning the pages. . . . Makes readers think with long passages about how medical training needs to adapt and how technology is reshaping not only the practice of medicine, but also what it means to be a doctor."
—*Chicago Tribune*

"Tantalizing."
—*Publishers Weekly*

"In addition to elegant use of language, the carefully planted medical details throughout the book and in dialogue make the plot credible and joyful to read. Cook is aware that the world is quickly changing thanks to the new Internet-based technologies and his plots are evolving as well. . . . A great pick for all thriller fans."
—*Mystery Tribune*

HOST

"Spellbinding . . . *Host* is Robin Cook at his very best."
—*Suspense Magazine*

"Engrossing . . . Cook does a good job of making the medicine intelligible."
—*Publishers Weekly*

"A witch's brew of weird science and unbridled greed, Cook's newest medical thriller will boost the blood pressure of anyone facing hospitalization."
—*Kirkus Reviews*

"Brutally intense . . . A medical thriller cannot get any better than *Host*."
—Associated Press

CELL

"Cook, ever the master of the medical thriller, combines controversial biomedical research issues with critical ethical concerns and gripping suspense. This outstanding and thought-provoking thriller will attract a wide readership."
—*Library Journal*

"Cook has found a formula that keeps readers coming back for more."
—*Booklist*

NANO

"Excellent . . . *Nano* is one of Cook's best."
—Associated Press

"Robin Cook, MD, truly is the master of the medical thriller, having pretty much invented this literary genre. . . . *Nano* is one of [his] best."
—*Naples Daily News*

"The scientific details are fascinating."   *—Booklist*

DEATH BENEFIT

"Rewarding . . . An intense read that raises thought-provoking questions."   —Associated Press

"Exciting."   *—St. Louis Post-Dispatch*

CURE

"[A] soufflé of a thriller from Cook."   *—Kirkus Reviews*

"A fascinating tale that never slows down."
     —Library Journal

TITLES BY ROBIN COOK

ROBIN COOK

G. P. PUTNAM'S SONS
NEW YORK

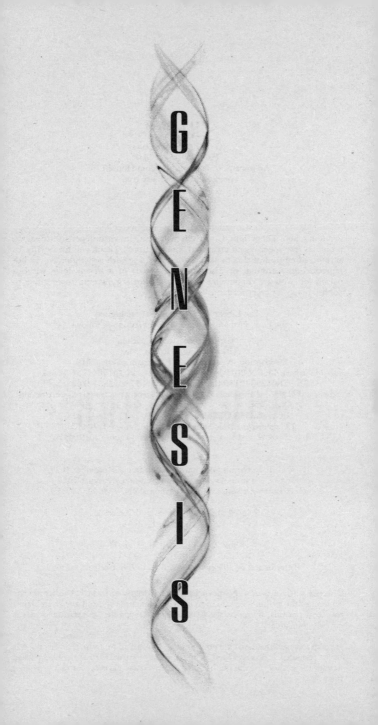

GENESIS

PUTNAM
— EST. 1838 —

G. P. PUTNAM'S SONS
Publishers Since 1838
An imprint of Penguin Random House LLC
penguinrandomhouse.com

The Library of Congress has catalogued
the G. P. Putnam's Sons hardcover edition as follows:

Names: Cook, Robin, author.
Title: Genesis / Robin Cook.
Description: New York : G. P. Putnam's Sons, 2019. |
Identifiers: LCCN 2019041760 (print) | LCCN 2019041761 (ebook) |
ISBN 9780525542155 (hardcover) | ISBN 9780525542162 (ebook)
Subjects: LCSH: Medical fiction. | GSAFD: Suspense fiction. | Mystery fiction.
Classification: LCC PS3553.O5545 G46 2019 (print) |
LCC PS3553.O5545 (ebook) | DDC 823/.914—dc23
LC record available at https://lccn.loc.gov/2019041760
LC ebook record available at https://lccn.loc.gov/2019041761
p.   cm.

First G. P. Putnam's Sons hardcover edition / December 2019
First G. P. Putnam's Sons premium edition / August 2020
G. P. Putnam's Sons premium edition ISBN: 9780525542179

Printed in the United States of America
3   5   7   9   10   8   6   4   2

Book design by Laura K. Corless

Interior art: double helix © John Weiss/Shutterstock.com

GENESIS

PROLOGUE

March 6th
11:15 P.M.

It was a cold, raw, windy, and heavily overcast March night on the Lower East Side of Manhattan. Although the spring equinox was soon to arrive, winter had not given up. As evidence, a few wayward snowflakes swirled down out of the low cloud cover, which was churning like a witch's brew. With the temperature hovering in the mid-thirties, these microscopically intricate and strikingly beautiful crystalline structures were immediately metamorphosed into mere droplets of water the instant they touched any terrestrial surface. In sharp contrast to this wanton destruction of nature's handiwork, the situation was the opposite inside a cozily decorated one-bedroom fourth-floor apartment on 23rd Street. Within the literal and figurative indoor warmth, a cascade of cellular events had begun that was ultimately the absolute antithesis of the dissolution of the snowflakes. Here there was to be a progression of vastly increasing order and complexity initiated by the forcible ejection of more than 100 million eager sperm into a vaginal vault.

The individuals involved in this amorous event were blissfully unaware of the miraculous drama they had initiated and of its ultimate dire consequences for both of them. Thoroughly intoxicated by the passion of the moment and forsaking contraception, they had given no thought to the possibility there would be an almost simultaneous release of a receptive ovum from the female's right ovary. Nor did they consider how determined sperm are in fulfilling their singular desire to fuse with a receptive female equivalent.

Two and a half hours later, when the woman was contentedly fast asleep and the man likewise in his own abode, the fastest-swimming sperm, following a perilous and Herculean marathon from the depths of the vagina to the internal end of the right fallopian tube, collided head-on with the passively descending ovum. Powered by an irresistible reflex, this winning sperm rapidly burrowed between the cloud of cumulus cells surrounding the ovum to hit up against the ovum's tough covering. A moment later he injected his pronucleus into the ovum to allow his twenty-three chromosomes to pair with the ovum's twenty-three, forming the normal human cell complement of forty-six. The ovum had now become a zygote.

Thus, on this nasty New York night, one of the most

astounding miracles of the known universe had been initiated: human *genesis*. Although such episodes of fertilization currently occur in the staggering neighborhood of 350,000 times a day on a worldwide basis, which clouds people's appreciation by its repetition, it begins a process of truly wondrous, dumbfounding complexity. As a single cell that can barely be seen by the naked eye, the human zygote contains all the data and instructions in its microscopic DNA library necessary to form and operate a human body. That means without any additional informational input, the single-celled zygote is capable of orchestrating the origin of some 37 trillion cells of two hundred different varieties as well as several billion extraordinarily specific, large-molecule proteins that must be formed according to exacting standards at just the right time, in just the right amount, and at just the right location. The human brain alone, with its 100 billion cells and more than 100 trillion synaptic connections, might be the most complex structure in the universe.

By March eleventh, five days after the lovemaking that initiated this particular ongoing miracle of human genesis, the rapidly developing conceptus reached the uterus to begin its implantation in the uterine wall. Soon it would make its presence known, proclaiming that a pregnancy had begun. From then on, all that was needed for the birth of a human infant in approximately nine months was maintenance of basic nutrients, the removal of waste, and physical protection. Unfortunately, that was not to be the case . . .

May 5th
10:05 P.M.

Taking a shower was a Zen experience for twenty-eight-year-old social worker Kera Jacobsen, especially after a tense day, which Saturdays were not supposed to be. Being careful not to fall since her bathtub's curved, porcelain-coated bottom could be treacherously slippery, she stepped in, yanking the shower curtain closed in the process. She had already adjusted the water temperature to the near-scalding heat she preferred. After wetting her body thoroughly, she began to scrub herself with the help of a fragrant gel and a long-handled shower brush, washing away the stresses of the day and calming her general anxieties. She'd been experiencing more than her share of both lately.

Kera had been in New York City for just under eight months. Coming to the Big Apple had been a rather sudden decision. She'd grown up in Los Angeles, obtained her master's degree at UCLA, and had held a position in social work at the UCLA Mattel Children's Hospital. Her specialty was working with children with complex medical needs and their families. It was demanding work and often emotionally draining, although ultimately fulfilling. There was no doubt that her efforts made a big difference and were an important complement to the work of the doctors and nurses who were understandably focused on curing and alleviating immediate symptoms of the disease process rather than the bigger picture of how families and individuals coped. In this capacity she'd been content and professionally satisfied. What ended up rocking her world was the sudden and unexpected end the previous September of a long-term relationship with a medical student named Robert Barlow. Over the course of the two and a half years they had dated, they frequently spent the night at the other's dwelling. With similar interests, including a shared liberal political orientation, they were never at a loss for conversation, which occasionally included discussions of future plans with the standing assumption it would be together. His intention was to take a surgical residency at one of the well-known academic medical centers, preferably there in LA or, if not, possibly San Francisco. As a particularly dedicated student, he was hopeful he'd have his choice. Kera had assumed that she would follow if he was to head up to San Fran. With her sterling credentials she was confident she could get a job at any academic medical center.

But it wasn't to be, and Kera still had no idea of exactly what had happened, although she had heard through the UCLA Medical Center grapevine that Robert had been seen frequently in the company of one of the surgical department's first-year female residents. Nonetheless, and with zero warning whatsoever, Robert had informed her one hot, smoggy LA afternoon that their relationship was over.

Having suffered a big blow to her self-esteem, she felt the urgent need to fly the coop. Mutual friends kept asking what had happened between her and Robert, pretending to be sympathetic but actually loving the drama and gossip. Besides, there were just too many chances of inadvertently running into Robert in and around the medical center. On top of all that, Kera had always had a soft spot for New York City, coupled with being tired of the monotony of Los Angeles weather, its uptick of annual forest fires, and the ever-present threat of San Andreas Fault activity. A few weeks after Robert's shocking news, she decided to turn an emotional whammy into something positive and made the cross-country move.

After rinsing the soap off her body, she squeezed a dollop of shampoo into the palm of her hand and began to wash her hair. This was the part of the shower that she liked the best, and she used considerable force as she worked up copious suds to massage her scalp, trying to blank her mind.

At first the move to New York had been positive in all respects except for the continued disappointment voiced by her mother and sister, who claimed they missed her terribly. Kera had managed to get a commitment for a social work job at the NYU Langone Medical Center— specifically with the Hassenfeld Children's Hospital— before leaving LA, so employment hadn't been an issue. As for an apartment, she lucked out by responding to an ad on one of the Langone Medical Center's bulletin boards that had been posted by a nurse who had opted to join the Peace Corps. The listing was for the sublet of a furnished, rent-controlled one-bedroom on 23rd Street just off Second Avenue. More important, from the standpoint of her self-image, she also found herself involved in a whirlwind affair with an attractive, highly accomplished, and older and more mature man than Robert, whom she met over the December holidays.

Unfortunately, her life had taken another unexpected

and unpleasant turn, and she had begun to question her judgment as well as her gullibility. Once again, she was experiencing disappointment and self-esteem issues—perhaps not as precipitously as with Robert, yet she was disturbed enough to have started seriously to consider returning to Southern California. As she expected, her mother and sister were absolutely thrilled with the possibility when she'd called them that evening to broach the subject, even though both had immediately questioned what seemed like a sudden change of heart. Only a month earlier in a similar phone call Kera had impressed them with how deliriously happy she was living in the Big Apple. Unprepared to share any details, she merely carried on about having come to the realization of how important close family connections were to her. She felt a twinge of guilt at not having been forthright, but the truth was that she hadn't completely made up her mind. There was still a vestige of hope that things might improve, although the chances weren't good.

Kera turned off the shower after making sure all the soap and shampoo had been completely rinsed. With her bath towel in hand, she stepped from the tub. Bending at the waist, she rapidly towel-dried her thick, moderately long hair, which she considered the only contribution her emotionally unavailable father had provided her. As she straightened, she subconsciously glanced at her profile in the full-length mirror attached to the back of the bathroom door. When it occurred to her what she was doing, she laughed at herself. It was far too early to see any change.

Finished with drying herself, she was about to hang up her bath towel when her buzzer sounded in the other room, announcing that someone was downstairs at the building's front door. The sudden raucous sound cut through the quiet apartment like a hot knife through butter, shattering the peacefulness Kera had been experiencing. Tossing her towel over the edge of the bathtub and grabbing her robe from the clothes hook, she dashed out to the tiny kitchen where the ancient intercom was mounted on the wall. As she pressed the talk button and asked who was there, she noticed the time on the microwave oven. It was 10:23. Since she hadn't ordered any takeout and there was only one person who would possibly ring her bell at such an hour, although never without a text or call and rarely on weekends, she was reasonably sure who it was. The possibility didn't thrill her. She'd been trying to calm herself prior to getting into bed.

"It's me," the expected masculine voice said.

"What are you doing?" Kera questioned. She leaned close to the speaker. She had to press the vintage device's talk button each time she spoke and then let go to listen.

"I'm sorry about the hour, but I need to talk with you."

"I'm just getting out of the shower. How about tomorrow around lunchtime?"

"I need to talk with you tonight. I've had a change of mind, and I want to share it with you. I *need* to share it with you."

Kera paused even as her pulse quickened. After everything that had happened and everything that had been

said over the previous month, there was no way she could
be at all certain what he meant by "a change of mind."
She could guess. But was it wishful thinking? After all,
he had been painfully and consistently clear over a period
of weeks. Still, if he meant what she thought he might, it
would change everything.

"What kind of change of mind?" she asked finally,
lowering her guard. She didn't want to get her hopes up
only to have them dashed on the proverbial rocks all over
again.

"I've realized you were right all along, and I was
wrong. It just took me some time to figure it out. We
need to celebrate!"

"Celebrate?" Kera questioned, to be sure she'd heard
correctly.

"Yes, celebrate. And I've brought the makings."

Trying to contain her excitement, she hit the door-
open button. Then she fled back to the bathroom, pulling on her robe in the process. She had been standing
naked, clutching the robe to her chest the whole time
she'd been on the intercom. Once in the bathroom she
grabbed her hairbrush and tried to tame the wet mop on
top of her head. It wasn't working. She felt she looked
dreadful, but there was no time to do anything about it.
Cinching the tie on her robe, and with a final desperate
pat to her hair, she was back out to the door to begin
disengaging the panoply of locks and chains the renter of
record had installed. Just as she'd finished, there was a
furtive knock.

With a final check through the peephole, Kera pulled

open the door. Her visitor was wearing a dark fedora and a dark overcoat she'd never seen. Before she could greet him, he swooped into the room, closed the door, and enveloped her in an embrace that took her breath away. Only then did he put down the shopping bag he was carrying and remove his hat and coat, which he tossed onto the couch.

"As I said, we have to celebrate," he announced with great fanfare. He then proceeded to take out several impressive cut-crystal fluted champagne glasses, followed by a chilled bottle of rosé prosecco nestled in a thermal sleeve, and finally, a small package of cocktail napkins. "Check this out!" he said, showing the bottle to her as if he were a sommelier.

"Okay," Kera said while reading the striking black label. "Bortolomiol Filanda Rosé. I've never heard of it."

"It's fabulous," he said proudly, "and remarkably hard to find."

"What exactly are we celebrating?" she asked hesitantly while he struggled with the wire securing the bottle's cork. This kind of response from him was what she'd hoped and had expected when she'd originally broken the news. She'd been crushed when it hadn't happened.

"We're celebrating everything," he said triumphantly. "The fact is, you were right, and I was wrong. What's happened is truly a miracle that was meant to be. I just didn't see it in the heat of the moment."

Kera could have pointed out that he'd taken far longer than a moment to come to the realization; in fact, there had been nearly a month of confrontation. But she didn't say anything for fear of breaking the spell his enthusiasm was creating. She heard a resounding pop when the cork came out of the bottle. A bit of foam with a pink blush appeared at the bottle's mouth.

"As you said, life is too precious a miracle not to embrace." He poured two glasses of the bubbly wine.

"What about your wife?" Kera struggled to question.

"History," he said simply, as he handed one of the glasses to her and then hoisted his and extended it toward her.

A melodious clink resounded in the otherwise silent room as the glasses touched. Following his lead, she took a healthy swig of the prosecco, which tasted better than any other wine she had ever had. Almost a month earlier she'd decided to avoid alcohol, but this moment was special. They had had several unpleasant arguments about the future over the previous weeks, and she'd reconciled herself to their being hopelessly miles apart. His sudden 180 elated her. It was most definitely a time for celebration.

"Let's sit and enjoy the wine," he suggested while gesturing toward the couch. He moved his coat and hat to a side chair. "The company that makes this wine is from the Veneto part of Italy," he added as he tugged on the sleeve of her robe, urging her over to the couch and to sit.

"It is tasty," Kera said. She had no idea where the Veneto was but assumed it was somewhere near Venice. She didn't ask for more of an explanation since she didn't care. As for the taste of the wine, she was being truthful.

As she sat down, she took another healthy swig, enjoying the effervescence as well as the smooth and subtle taste. She'd never been particularly fond of champagne and had always questioned the fuss and the cost, but this was different, making her wonder how much was from the wine and how much from her joyous mindset. Whatever it was, she was savoring the totality of the experience. Of course, she had a million questions, but for the moment they could wait.

While he rambled on about prosecco and the Veneto of Italy with no appreciation of her lack of interest, she took another drink of the wine and held it in her mouth for a moment before swallowing. It was truly a delightful experience, and she luxuriated in the wonderfully relaxing feeling that spread over her, a far cry from the depressive thoughts she'd struggled with over the previous month. But then a dizziness intervened that wasn't so pleasant. Although he was still talking, his words stopped having any meaning. At the same time her vision blurred. Blinking repeatedly to clear her eyes, she put her glass down and tried to stand, but her legs wouldn't work.

"Are you okay?" he asked while putting his own glass down.

"I'm okay, I guess," she managed, but her words were mumbled. "I'm just suddenly so tired . . ."

Kera's voice trailed off as she slowly sank back with her head resting against the back of the couch. Her eyes had closed, and with her mouth agape, her breathing slowed.

CHAPTER 1

May 8th
5:49 A.M.

Laurie Montgomery-Stapleton's eyes popped open much earlier than usual and without Jack Stapleton repeatedly nudging her shoulder. She couldn't remember the last time she'd spontaneously awakened at such an hour. But her mind was churning because it was going to be an exceptionally busy day. So busy, in fact, that she was going to have to talk Jack, who was still blissfully sleeping next to her, into standing in her stead for at least one of her obligations, and that was not going to be an easy task. A week previous she'd agreed to go into John Junior's school and meet with his fourth-grade teacher, Miss Rossi, and possibly the school psychologist about JJ's supposedly recent disruptive behavior. Apparently there had been some aggressive incidents on the playground during recess and other impulse-control episodes. Knowing Jack's impatience with such issues and his tendency to be less than diplomatic, Laurie hadn't even broached the subject with him, preferring to handle it herself as she was certain there was nothing wrong with JJ. Now Jack was going to have to deal with the situation on his own because Laurie had newly arisen, pressing work-related obligations down at City Hall that conflicted.

By lifting her head and gazing out of the two large, north-facing sixth-floor bedroom windows, Laurie could tell that the sun had just peeked over the eastern horizon. Although there were closable window treatments and even blackout shades, neither she nor Jack bothered to use them. Several blocks away on the top of a significantly taller building, she could see an old water tower. At the moment it was totally awash with early-morning sunlight, giving the illusion that it was made of gold.

Next Laurie's eyes turned to glance at the digital clock. It was even earlier than she'd suspected—just a smidgen past 5:50—yet she was totally awake. Laurie had never in her life been a morning person and always struggled to wake up and get out from under the warm covers. It had been particularly true since she'd married Jack, because Jack insisted they keep the bedroom cool, almost cold from Laurie's perspective. But the real reason Laurie had trouble getting up in the morning was that she was a night owl beyond any doubt. On occasion she'd been known to sleep through an alarm only feet away. When she'd been younger, she'd loved to read fiction far into the night, with a predilection for late-eighteenth-century and early-twentieth-century novels. That began to change once she had become a doctor and needed to keep up with the ever-expanding professional literature. These days, she was obsessed with reading not only the current forensic articles but also all the material she was expected to be familiar with as the chief medical examiner of the City of New York. As the first woman to hold the title and thus a pioneer of sorts, she felt particular responsibility to be the absolute best she could be. To that end she'd had to learn how to read spreadsheets and budgets and all the appropriate reports coming out of the New York City Council, from its various committees, and from the New York City Department of Health and Mental Hygiene. She still sometimes found herself shocked at the sheer volume of documents that landed in her in-box.

Despite Laurie's commitment to doing her job well, the jury was still out in terms of how she personally felt about having accepted the position. Only now did she have a true idea of the extent of the political aspects of the job. It had been her general understanding that the Office of the Chief Medical Examiner, known as OCME, had fought and gained its independence after its founding in 1918, so that it could speak unencumbered for the dead. Although that was mostly true, she was learning the hard way that the mayor, who had appointed her, and the City Council, which held the purse strings, could exert considerable power, which she had to struggle to resist. It was especially hard since the OCME's $75,000,000 yearly budget was a tempting target in a city continually starving for funds for other worthwhile obligations. On top of that, the morgue itself, where all the autopsies were actually done, was in need of a multimillion-dollar replacement. At one time it had been state of the art, but that was no longer the case.

Apart from the political headaches of the job, Laurie found that she missed the intellectual stimulation of being personally immersed in the actual forensics, with the responsibility of determining the cause and manner of death. Objectively she recognized that it was best for her to let the nearly forty highly qualified medical examiners handle all the cases—otherwise, as her predecessor, Dr. Bingham, had learned the hard way, every district attorney, police higher-up, fire chief, city bigwig, and mayor would want the chief to do any case they were interested in simply because she was the Top Dog. But for Laurie, it was a sacrifice to take a step back and settle for frequent, unofficial morning rounds down in the morgue, looking over people's shoulders and asking questions. The closest she came to being intimately involved was Thursday morning, when she regularly assisted one of the forensic pathology fellows on an autopsy. In partnership with New York University Medical School's Department of Pathology, the OCME trained a handful of fellows to become board eligible forensic pathologists.

With a sense of excitement and no small amount of trepidation, Laurie threw back the covers and stood up. She shivered as her warm feet made contact with the ice-cold floor. Hastily she wiggled her toes into the slippers she dutifully kept at the bedside and pulled on her robe. She always kept both handy in case she had to get up during the night. Jack had not moved a muscle. He was on his back with his arms outside of the blankets, his hands clasped over his chest, and his mouth slightly ajar, the picture of contented repose. Knowing him as well as she did, Laurie had to smile. Jack was not the calm person he appeared at the moment, but rather someone whose mind never stopped and who had little patience for what he called red tape, meaning rules and regulations he didn't agree with. He didn't abide fools, or mediocrity, and he was never one to hide his feelings. From where Laurie was standing, she could see the scar on his forehead and his chipped left front tooth, both remnants of his determination to do what he thought was right despite putting himself at risk and getting pummeled for it. Although she loved him, she knew he was a handful, especially now that she was technically his boss. Although Jack was by far the most productive medical examiner on the entire staff, he was also the one who required the most corralling. Laurie knew, because she'd been rather similar in her day.

Closing the door silently behind her, Laurie tiptoed into Emma's room, which was considerably darker than the master bedroom, thanks to the shades being drawn. Like Jack, Emma was fast asleep on her back, and appeared angelic in the half-light as only a four-year-old girl can look. Laurie had to restrain herself from reaching out and giving the child a hug. After the initial scare and distress evoked by a diagnosis of autism more than a year ago, Emma had been doing surprisingly well in response to thirty hours of behavioral therapy, five hours of speech therapy, and three hours of physical therapy weekly. It was a complicated, intensive schedule that had all been arranged and monitored by Laurie's mother, Dorothy, who had turned out to be a lifesaver. After she'd initially caused difficulty between Laurie and Jack by camping out in their home after Emma's diagnosis, Dorothy had truly stepped up to the plate to take on Emma's situation as her life's work, shunning all her previous philanthropic commitments. After corroborating the diagnosis with several acknowledged specialists, Dorothy had researched all the best therapists in the city, interviewed them, hired them, coordinated their schedules, and monitored them. And the effort proved worthwhile. After several months there were some positive signs. Emma's inclination for repetitive movements appeared to lessen, and she began to lose interest in her compulsion to align her stuffed animals. Perhaps most promising, she showed increased ability to interact with JJ with even a few appropriate words. There was still a long way to go, but Laurie and Jack both were optimistic that Emma might prove to be in the group of children diagnosed with autism that do make considerable headway in achieving typical developmental milestones.

Being even quieter than she'd been when she'd entered, Laurie left Emma's room, closing the door without the slightest sound. Emma was generally a good sleeper and usually didn't wake up until after seven, but she could be a bear if disturbed, and sometimes it didn't take much. On cat's feet Laurie continued down the hall to JJ's room. Like Emma, JJ was fast asleep in the room's semi-darkness, but unlike Emma, he looked as if he'd been running a marathon in his bed. His covers and sheets were hopelessly twisted around his nine-and-a-half-year-old body, but with his legs and feet out in the cold. Laurie couldn't help but smile. Even in sleep the boy was a ball of action, although at that particular moment he was totally still. Without fear of waking him, as he was the opposite of Emma in that regard, Laurie extricated the knot of covers and then spread them back over him, including his legs and feet.

Satisfied with what she had accomplished, Laurie turned with the intent of heading downstairs to the kitchen to get some breakfast. The plan was to use this bonus time in her day to go over the material she'd laboriously prepared the night before and would be presenting during her command appearance that morning at a recently scheduled meeting of the City Council's Committee on Health. It was this meeting and her long-term anathema to speaking in front of groups that had awakened her so early. But she didn't get far, and an involuntary yelp escaped her lips as she collided with Jack, who had come into JJ's bedroom behind her and was about to tap her on the shoulder. Even Jack jumped at Laurie's apparent shock.

"My God!" Laurie managed in a forced whisper. "You scared the hell out of me."

"I can say the same." Jack pressed an open palm

against his chest in the stereotypical sign of distress. In contrast to Laurie, his feet were bare, and he wore only pajama bottoms to ward against the chill. "Was something wrong with JJ?" He looked around Laurie at the sleeping child.

"No, he's fine. I just covered him up."

"What are you doing up out of bed?" he questioned with obvious concern. "I can't remember the last time I saw you up and about before six. Are you all right?"

"I'm fine. I'm just a little worried about this morning's City Council Committee meeting," she said. "I want to go over the material I was working on last night. I told you about it."

"Yeah, I remember," Jack said with a dismissive wave of his hand. "That's so much to do about nothing. You shouldn't waste your time and emotion on a little mix-up just because a handful of politicians are up in arms."

"I don't see it that way, not when the City Council has oversight over the OCME budget," Laurie said. "Keeping them happy is one of my main responsibilities, especially when we're in dire need of a new Forensic Pathology building and a new autopsy suite."

"But the little body switcheroo was an understandable mistake. No one was hurt, and it was easy to rectify."

"It's easy for you to say no one was hurt. I heard both families were pretty damn upset and at least one of them is thinking of suing. Dealing with death is hard enough without having to experience the emotional shock of confronting the wrong body in an open-casket wake."

The origin of the problem was the near-simultaneous arrival at the OCME of two cadavers with the same first and last name, Henry Norton. Even though they received unique accession numbers, the night mortuary tech just checked the name and not the number when the first body was released, meaning both bodies ended up at the wrong funeral homes. To make matters worse, the mistake wasn't discovered until the family arrived for the first funeral service.

"I truly don't know how you find the patience for this kind of crap," he said with a shake of his head. "So what are you going to say to the committee?"

"I'm going to tell them that I personally apologized to both families, which I did. And then I'll explain the changes in protocol I've made in how bodies are released to make sure it doesn't happen again. I've also asked IT to update the case-management system to call attention to similar-named decedents."

"Well, it sounds like you've got the situation well under control."

"Unfortunately, the problem spread. The funeral home where the mix-up was first discovered is on Staten Island. The director added to his complaint that it takes too long for him to get bodies now that we've closed the Staten Island morgue and do the autopsies here in Manhattan."

"Yikes! So this mix-up of too many Nortons now forces you to justify closing the morgue on Staten Island?"

"It's worse than that," Laurie said with a sigh. "One of the Health Committee members is from the Bronx, where the morgue was also closed. She's claimed that funeral directors in her district have complained about long delays, too. I've had to rush together an extensive report on the turnaround times for bodies from all five boroughs. It's a PowerPoint presentation, and you know how much I detest talking in front of groups."

"You've told me, but it's a mystery because you always come across like a pro."

"That's because I overprepare," she said. "Hey! Aren't you freezing? I'm cold, and I'm in a robe and slippers."

Jack briefly hugged himself and pretended to shiver. "It is a bit chilly."

"Get your robe and come downstairs," Laurie said. "I'll make some coffee. There's a favor I need to ask you to do for me this morning."

"Favor?" Jack questioned as he paused at the door to the hallway. "I'm not sure I like the sound of that. What kind of favor?"

"Something I was going to do this morning, but now because of this impromptu meeting down at 250 Broadway, I need you to go in my place."

"Was this something you were scheduled to do as the chief medical examiner? I don't need to remind you that I'm not good at politics."

"No, it's something I was scheduled to do as a mother. You'll go as the father, which is totally apropos."

"How long has this been scheduled?"

"About a week."

"Are you sure I can handle this?" Jack asked, only half-teasing.

"No, but there's no choice," she said with a short laugh. "Get your robe before you freeze to death, and I'll explain."

Laurie followed him out of JJ's room and watched him sprint down the hall toward the entrance to their bedroom. With all his pickup basketball and bike riding, he was shockingly fit. Laurie wished he'd stop both and constantly tried to convince him that the family needed him injury-free, but she had to admit that he did look good and wished she had half of his stamina. The trouble was that being the chief medical examiner, a mother, and chief household engineer left her scant time for herself or any kind of exercise routine.

A few minutes later and even before Laurie managed to get the coffee water boiling, Jack swept down the stairs and into the kitchen dressed in his white summer robe. His feet were still bare.

"Okay, out with it," he said, pretending to be already irritated.

"You have to go to JJ's school and meet with Miss Rossi and possibly the school psychologist. The meeting is scheduled for eight, prior to classes. I certainly don't condone your commuting to the OCME on your bike, but it will make it easy for you since the Brooks School is on your way."

"I already don't like the sound of this," he said.

"I suspected as much. That's why I intended to just handle it myself unless it turns out a decision has to be made. I'm of the opinion it's just a temporary misunderstanding. I mean, kids go through phases."

"JJ is not going through any phase," Jack said, becoming serious. "What's this all about?"

"I can't remember the entire litany," Laurie said. "But there's been some aggressive behavior on JJ's part at recess and difficulty sitting still in class, allowing other children to take their turn, and impulse control. That kind of stuff."

"Oh, for Chrissake," he snapped. "There is nothing wrong with JJ except he has a Y chromosome, meaning he has a developing male brain that's trying to prepare him to go out of the cave and hunt mammoths."

"You know that, and I know that. But it behooves us to listen and be supportive of the teacher who has to handle eight young male brains all at the same time."

"That's what she's being paid for," Jack said.

"I'm sure it's not that easy," she said. "I give teachers all the respect in the world. I don't think I could do it."

"I know I couldn't do it," he said. "But that's neither here nor there. What do you think they're suggesting?"

"Obviously they're concerned about attention deficit hyperactivity disorder." Laurie concentrated on pouring the boiling water into the coffeemaker.

"Did they say anything about drugs?"

"Miss Rossi raised the issue," she said. "That's all."

"Good God." Jack stared off into the middle distance for a few moments as the smell of brewing coffee enveloped the room.

Laurie poured two cups and handed one to him. She could tell his mind was going a mile a minute, and it wasn't hard to guess the direction.

"My plan was just to go and listen," Laurie said. "I ask you to do the same. You won't be required to come to any conclusions today for certain. Just hear what they say and maybe ask a few questions, so you understand their perspective. Mostly listen! Then tonight we can talk about it. It will only take you fifteen or twenty minutes, tops."

"I don't know," he said with a shake of his head. "This overdiagnosis-of-ADHD situation is the kind of nonsense that could turn me into a conspiracist. It certainly seems like the pharmaceutical industry and the elementary education industry are in cahoots. There are just too many school-age kids, mostly boys, being prescribed speed to make them easier to corral. And then we wonder why the same kids take drugs as teenagers. I can tell you now, JJ's not taking any Adderall. No way."

"That's certainly my feeling at the moment," she said. "But I also know medication can be helpful under the right circumstances. And we need to show some respect for the school's position, whatever it is. It's not rocket science that we need to stay on friendly terms."

"I'm not the natural-born diplomat you are," he said. "I know that about myself, and I don't want to alienate the school, which I might do by being honest. Why don't you go after your Health Committee meeting?"

"I'm sorry, but I've got a jam-packed day ahead of me. I've got back-to-back obligations all day, including an emergency meeting with Chet McGovern even before I go down to 250 Broadway."

"What on earth kind of emergency meeting are you having with Chet?"

"Ever since I appointed him director of education at the OCME, he's really taken on the position with inordinate seriousness, to the OCME's benefit. He's upped the level of all our teaching efforts across the board."

"I'm sorry to sound negative," Jack said with a roll of his eyes, "but my guess is he took the position just because there are so many young women applying and being accepted as forensic pathology fellows. He's an incorrigible Lothario. Chasing women is a sport for him." Jack went to the refrigerator for fruit and milk while Laurie retrieved the cereal from the pantry.

"Maybe that influenced his motivation initially," Laurie said, knowing Chet's off-hours inclinations and social history from Jack, "but he's really put heart and soul into the role of head of education in a way I wouldn't have expected. This emergency meeting he's requested is a case in point. He believes one of the NYU pathology residents isn't acting appropriately on multiple levels. He calls her the Phantom because she isn't taking her month's forensic pathology rotation seriously, ignores advice, and often can't be found."

All anatomic pathology residents at NYU Medical School were required to spend one month at OCME during their four-to-five-year curriculum. Under the supervision of the OCME director of education, they would assist the medical examiners and learn in the process, but couldn't sign death certificates. The goal was to introduce them to forensic pathology rather than train them as forensic pathologists. Forensic pathology fellows, on the other hand, had already completed their pathology residency and were required to do autopsies, determine the cause and manner of death, and sign the ultimate death certificate even though officially they were still in training.

"What's the resident's name?" Jack asked. He occasionally had pathology residents participate on his cases, although he didn't go out of his way to encourage it. Jack had a reputation of doing the most autopsies by far of any of the medical examiners, which gave him the opportunity and excuse to cherry-pick interesting cases. As a result, many of the more motivated residents sought him out even though Jack hated being slowed down for any reason. Being a workaholic was one of the ways Jack dealt with his demons.

"Her name is Dr. Aria Nichols," Laurie said. At that point Laurie and Jack were both eating cereal while standing and leaning their hindquarters against the kitchen countertop.

"I don't think I've met her. But if Chet is interested in her, she must at least be attractive." He laughed to indicate he was half kidding.

"I think you're being unfair," she said. "I don't think Chet is being personal in the slightest with this woman. My sense is that he's sincere and truly concerned about her. He even questioned if she should be a pathology resident or even a doctor."

"Wow," Jack said around a mouthful of cereal. "She must have brushed him off big-time."

Laurie waved away his attempt at humor at Chet's expense and rinsed out her bowl. "I'm impressed that Chet is as concerned as he apparently is, and I'll be interested in what he has to say. Under Dr. Bingham's tenure, there was never much attention paid to the NYU anatomic pathology residents. I think that's got to change, and Chet seems to be doing just that. I want to be supportive."

"Whatever." He followed her to the sink. "If this school meeting is only going to take fifteen or twenty minutes, are you sure you can't tackle it? What about you looping back to the Brooks School immediately after your Committee meeting? I want to support you and JJ and pull my weight, but sending me is a risk. I'm worried that I'll screw everything up by ruffling feathers. I mean, I feel as strongly about this overdiagnosis of ADHD as I do about the anti-vaccination movement."

"I already told you I won't have the time," Laurie said. "As soon as I can get back to the OCME I've got a meeting with the chief of staff, the director of human resources, and Bart Arnold about medical-legal investigators' pay. It's an important meeting the four of us have been trying to schedule for weeks. The OCME is falling too far behind compared to what physician assistants can make in the private sector, which is making our MLI recruitment almost impossible. And following that, I'm meeting with the architects about the new morgue building. Actually, I'm even going to have trouble fitting both of those in because at eleven I'm scheduled to be over at the Tisch Hospital for my annual breast-cancer screening." After Laurie's mother, Dorothy, had been diagnosed and treated for breast cancer a number of years previously, Laurie had had herself checked for the BRCA gene. When it was determined she, too, was positive for the BRCA1 mutation, she'd adhered religiously to regular screening.

"Okay," he said, raising his hands in a gesture of surrender. "Now, that's important! Why didn't you just say that right off the bat?"

"It's not my favorite subject," she admitted. "Actually, I hate it, and I suppose I indulge in a little denial. At least I hate the mammogram part. The MRI I can tolerate because it's not uncomfortable or painful. Worst of all, the whole screening process makes me terrified all over again. I'm always afraid they are going to find something suspicious and put me in a tailspin. I'm way too busy to have a serious medical problem."

"You're also way too important to me and to this family to have a serious medical problem," Jack said. "Your health comes first. Leave the school meeting to me. I'll try to be my normal diplomatic self."

"Thank you," Laurie said. "Despite your sarcasm, I'm confident you can handle it." She gave his shoulder a reassuring squeeze.

At that moment Caitlin O'Connell, their live-in nanny, materialized as she came up the open stairs from the floor below. She was as Irish in appearance as her name sounded, with dark hair, fair skin, blue eyes, and a ready smile. She, too, was in her robe.

"Good morning," she called out, as she approached the granite-topped central island. "What on earth are you two doing up this early, especially you, Laurie? I've never known you to be a morning person."

Laurie smiled and took one last sip of coffee. "Apparently I am one today."

CHAPTER 2

As Laurie mounted the front steps and entered the aged and admittedly ugly OCME building on the corner of First Avenue and 30th Street, she realized it was approximately the time that Jack liked to arrive to allow him to pick through the night's ME cases and choose the most interesting. Although Laurie wasn't planning on following suit and arriving this early as a matter of course, she could already see the benefits. The biggest by far was that the trip from their home on West 106th Street had taken less than half the time it did during her normal eight A.M. commute. There had been monumentally less traffic. She also didn't have to greet and make conversation with so many people since she was probably the first of the day shift to arrive.

Laurie nodded to the night security person manning

the front desk where Marlene Wilson normally held court. Laurie had never met the man, but he certainly recognized her and said a cheery hello before buzzing her into the building. Coming into her windowless outer office, Laurie was surprised at how dark it was. Cheryl Sanford, her secretary, sat out here and always turned the lights on but had yet to arrive and wouldn't for another hour. Laurie went to the wall switch and turned on the overhead illumination.

Within her inner office, there was more ambient light since there were windows, yet it still wasn't nearly adequate. The windows were high, faced north, and were only feet away from the NYU Medical Center building. Laurie turned on the lights as she entered. She loved her office since she and Jack had painted it. When Bingham had occupied it, it had been dark and gloomy, with gray walls, dark trim, and heavy mahogany furniture. Now the walls and trim were white with a pink blush, and to jazz things up even more, brightly colored drapes and a matching sofa had been added. Although Laurie still used Bingham's ponderous desk, the dark library table and dark glass-fronted bookcases had been removed. Also, all the dark paintings of black-suited brooding old men had been moved to the neighboring OCME conference room and replaced with framed, colorful impressionist prints.

Laurie put her backpack on the floor next to her desk chair before hanging her spring coat in the closet. She briefly thought about heading into the ID room, where the communal coffeepot lived, as the caffeine from her first cup had worn off, but she guessed that Vinnie Amendola, who was tasked with making the morning coffee, was most likely not in yet. Instead, she sat down at the massive desk, took out the presentation she'd prepared for the morning City Council Health Committee meeting, and started to go over it all yet again. As she did so, she felt her anxiety ratchet upward. It was hopelessly clear to her that she would most likely never get over her aversion to speaking in front of groups, just like she was likely never to get over her fear of authority figures thanks to her emotionally distant and domineering father.

The first person who interrupted Laurie's concentration was Cheryl, who gently knocked on the partially open door just after 7:30. Stepping in but maintaining a hold on the doorknob, she said, "Lordy, what in heaven's name are you doing in here so early?" Cheryl, a buxom African American woman, had been working at the OCME for centuries, or at least that was the way she described it. She'd been the chief's secretary starting with Dr. Bingham's predecessor before becoming Bingham's secretary for his entire tenure. Laurie was glad to have her, as she had made Laurie's transition to being chief infinitely easier. She'd also become somewhat of a family friend. She and Jack had taken a liking to each other during the countless times Jack had been called on the carpet in front of Bingham for his inclination to ignore rules and regulations in his dogged determination to solve forensic cases. Jack had also gotten Cheryl's son, Arnold, to play on the neighborhood basketball court.

"Trying to prepare for the early-morning meeting down at 250 Broadway," Laurie said.

"Pardon the pun, but you'll knock them dead," Cheryl said with a wry smile. Then she added, "Usually Mr. Amendola has the coffee ready by now. Can I bring you a cup?"

"That would be terrific," Laurie said. "Thank you."

Cheryl nodded and started to back out of Laurie's office.

"Wait, Cheryl," Laurie called out. "I'm expecting Dr. McGovern any minute. Would you send him right in when he appears?"

"Will do," Cheryl said. "And I'll have the coffee back here in a flash."

As it turned out, Chet arrived just as Cheryl was delivering Laurie's coffee. Graciously she asked him if he would like some, but he brandished his cup, saying he'd already been to the communal pot.

Laurie gestured toward the couch and then followed Chet, bringing her coffee. She often preferred sitting there instead of remaining behind the imposing desk. She felt the latter was more appropriate for confrontations than for discussions.

"Thanks for seeing me on such short notice," Chet began. "And I'm sorry I'm a little late."

"That's okay," Laurie said reassuringly. "But we might have to cut our discussion short, as I have a morning meeting down at City Hall. I'll need to leave here in about twenty minutes."

"That should be plenty of time," he said. He had been with the OCME just a tad longer than Jack. They were hired the same year and ended up sharing an office. Consequently, they'd become such good friends that Laurie knew more about Chet than she knew about the other medical examiners. He was about Jack's size, with a similar skin tone and athletic build, to the point that they appeared almost like brothers. In Laurie's estimation, which she admitted was biased, both were seriously attractive men. The main difference was that Chet was experiencing a receding hairline, and to compensate he'd grown a mustache and a goatee. Laurie wasn't a fan of facial hair but appreciated that Chet kept his well-trimmed.

"Before we start, I'd like to pay you a compliment," she said. "You have been doing a bang-up job as director of education. Everything on the education front at the OCME has improved since you took over, even the conferences and lectures. Thank you."

"You're welcome," Chet said, obviously pleased with the recognition. "I do think education here at the OCME is important and deserves equal attention at all levels. The Forensic Fellowship Program has always been given a lot of emphasis and has been consistently top-notch. It's the pathology resident rotation that's been relatively ignored from an educational standpoint, and for good reason. First off, the residents are only here for a month out of a four-year NYU pathology residency, and second, the idea is just to give them a sense of forensic pathology without any real responsibility."

"This is all true. Are you suggesting we change the program somehow?"

"No," he said without hesitation. "Just more supervision. Generally, the program works as is. What's really brought this issue to my attention is an isolated situation with a particular resident named Dr. Aria Nichols."

"I remember you mentioning her name when you asked to speak with me," Laurie said. "I had Cheryl check. Miss Nichols has been with us since the beginning of the month."

"That's right," he said. "She and a Dr. Tad Muller rotated over here May first as part of their fourth-year anatomical pathology program, and there can't be two more different residents. It's like they're from different planets. The program is clearly not working for Dr. Nichols."

"Can you be more specific?" Laurie asked. She put her cup down on the side table and turned to look more directly at him. "What do you mean by 'not working'?"

"After she'd been here almost a week, it occurred to me that I hadn't seen much of her whereas I'd run into Dr. Muller all the time. When I checked, I realized she's often been skipping the cases she's been assigned. Following my predecessor, here's how the system is supposed to work: every morning I check all the scheduled cases, figure out which ones might be good for the residents, and then ask the assigned medical examiner if it would be okay if the resident observed and participated to whatever degree the ME was comfortable with. Invariably the MEs say yes, so I assign the residents two cases a day, usually. In the past, that was generally the end of it, meaning there wasn't any follow-up to make sure the resident actually participated in the autopsy, mainly because they were not responsible for filling out and signing the death certificate."

"They're not allowed to sign death certificates," Laurie interjected.

"Yes, I know," Chet said. "But the problem is they have no real responsibility. When I realized I hadn't been bumping into Aria Nichols, I talked to the MEs on the cases I'd assigned her and found out that she'd go into the pit in the morning, hang out for a time, maybe even ask a few questions, apparently good questions, since she's no dummy, but then leave. Other cases that I had assigned her later in the day, for the most part, she just ignored."

"That's rather brazen," she said.

"That's only half of it," he said. "When I approached her to call her on it, she just out-and-out lied to me, saying she'd stayed for all the cases she had been assigned. Several days ago, when she left the first case after about a half hour, I followed her out of the OCME without her knowing."

"Where did she go?" Laurie asked. She wasn't sure what surprised her more—a resident assigned to the OCME leaving in the middle of the morning or the director of education following her. The thought went through her mind that perhaps Jack could have been right about Chet's motivation.

"Next door," Chet said. "She went into one of the Pathology labs and started reviewing the day's frozen sections. I couldn't believe it."

"Did you say anything to her?"

"Of course," he said. "How could I not? I was appalled. I went up to her and asked her what the hell she thought she was doing."

"And what was her response?"

"She said that if I didn't know what she was doing that I was dumber than I looked."

A slight laugh escaped from Laurie's lips, although she regretted it the moment it happened. Chet had clearly been offended by the resident's cheeky response. Quickly she said: "So, she made no attempt at explanation or any type of apology?"

"Hardly," Chet said. "She then told me to fuck off and leave her the hell alone."

"You're kidding," Laurie exclaimed. It was obvious to her that this woman was a far cry from being a typical pathology resident. In her role as the chief medical examiner, Laurie couldn't help but see dealing with this behavior pattern as a potential problem in relation to the NYU Department of Pathology unless it was decided to kick the can down the road and let NYU worry about her. Good relations between OCME and the NYU Department of Pathology was a high priority for a multitude of reasons, including the Forensic Pathology Fellowship Program. The fellows trained at the OCME but got their certification from the NYU Medical School. At the same time there was an ethical issue involved.

"I don't know how she got into medical school, wherever she went," Chet added, "or how she got selected for a residency at such a high-powered institution. I couldn't believe her audacity. So, I came back here to the OCME and sought out Tad Muller, who's been behaving just the opposite. I was hoping for some perspective. I didn't tell him exactly what had happened, but I did say that she seemed to be a unique individual and mentioned she was shirking responsibilities. His response was to laugh and admit she was one of a kind. Without any further provocation he said she was not very well liked by her fellow residents, although she was respected for her intelligence and encyclopedic knowledge of pathology. He said that some people thought she was so bookish that she comes across as somewhat of a sociopath."

"Being a sociopath seems like an extreme diagnosis for a pathology resident," Laurie said.

"I agree," Chet added. "I said pretty much the same thing. I thought it had to be an exaggeration. But then Dr. Muller elaborated. He said she's pretty damn manipulative and not all that empathetic when it comes to the on-call schedule. He even said that one time while having a conversation with her about dogs, she confided that she didn't like them and that there was a yappy dog that lived in her building that she'd thought about doing in because it barked all the time."

"Oh, people say things like that that they don't really mean," Laurie said.

"My feelings exactly," he said. "But Dr. Muller swore that she said it and that she didn't bat an eyelash."

"Do you know if she's married?" Laurie asked, still wondering if Jack could have been right about Chet's motivation.

"She's not married," Chet said without hesitation.

"All right, what do you think we should do?" she asked while inwardly sighing. With everything else going on trying to keep the OCME on an even keel, she didn't need another problem, which this was beginning to sound like Aria Nichols could become. She checked the time, feeling her anxiety rising again.

"I was hoping you'd tell me," he said. "I could try reading her the riot act and say that if she doesn't take this OCME rotation seriously, we'll have to say she failed. To be honest, I don't know whether that would mean she wouldn't get her Pathology certification, since the month over here is more or less a survey course just to give them an idea of forensics."

"I don't know, either," she said. "As far as I know, such a situation has never come up before. In all the time that NYU Department of Pathology residents have been required to spend one month here during their four-year residency there's never been a problem."

"What about if you talk to Dr. Henderson?" Chet suggested. Dr. Carl Henderson was chief of the NYC Department of Pathology. "I would think that he or the head of the pathology residency program would be able to talk some sense into her and get her to take her OCME rotation seriously. I mean, if nothing else, it's damn disrespectful."

"You know, maybe I should talk to her first," Laurie said. Suddenly the idea that she could possibly prevent a problem between the OCME and the NYU Department of Pathology before it developed had a lot of appeal. Prevention was always vastly superior to cure.

"That's probably the best approach," Chet said. "The way she has responded to me makes me sense she's not all that fond of men."

"On second thought, better than just talking with her, maybe I should do a case with her. There's a chance I could get her excited about forensic pathology. I've had some luck in the past. Our own Dr. Jennifer Hernandez is living proof." When Jennifer was a teenager and having problems, Laurie arranged to have her come to the OCME as an extern. Not only did the experience turn her around, she ended up going to medical school and becoming a forensic pathologist.

"Now, that's an idea," he said. "If anybody could motivate her, you could. But I thought you didn't do cases now that you're chief."

"This could be an exception," she said, warming to the idea. It was only this morning that she was ruing the fact that she didn't get to do forensics. Here was a good excuse to rectify that for a good cause, and she'd make sure it wasn't publicized. "Tell Dr. Nichols when she comes in this morning that she will be working with me this afternoon and that I'm looking forward to meeting her. And check with the day ME to make sure I have a case to do, preferably an interesting one. And mum's the word."

"Got it," he said. "About what time do you think you want to do this?"

"Let's say, middle of the afternoon," Laurie said, remembering all her commitments. It was also the time that the autopsy room was generally vacant.

"I'll see that it happens," Chet said.

CHAPTER 3

Madison Bryant watched the three-member Pierson family file out of her small office. Marge Pierson was the last out the door, and she paused briefly to smile back at Bryant and wave before disappearing up the hallway. It was one of those "happy ending" cases that gave Madison the fortitude to soldier on with her career as a social worker at the Hassenfeld Children's Hospital. After a number of bone marrow transplants, Wayne Pierson, eight, was doing remarkably well, with his leukemia now in complete remission. With everything going so smoothly, including Wayne's experiences at school and the family dynamics getting back to normal, a session scheduled for an hour and a half had taken only fifteen minutes. As a result, Madison had some free time, especially since her next appointment had been canceled.

Putting the Pierson file on her desk, Madison walked out of her windowless office. As usual at that time of the day, the clinic was jam-packed with people and kids of all ages. Thanks to the acoustic-tiled ceiling, the din was bearable. After skirting the reception desk, Madison walked into the staff lounge and then on to the women's room. At that time of morning, it was like an oasis of solitude. As she dutifully washed her hands, she eyed herself in the mirror. Recently her hairstylist had talked her into a straight asymmetrical bob, claiming the sleek look was modern glamour at its best. Madison wasn't so sure, as it was a quantum leap away from her previous short Afro, plus it took a lot more work, but it did frame her face rather nicely.

A tall, light-skinned black woman with a splash of freckles across her nose and cheeks, Madison was from St. Louis but had always dreamed of eventually moving to New York City. She had gotten her wish eight months ago and had been having the time of her life. One of the reasons things had worked out so well was that she had met Kera Jacobsen, who had arrived in the city within days of Madison to work at the same hospital in the same field. As a consequence, they had been introduced and had shared their orientation experience. Being close to the same age, having had similar educational backgrounds, and conveniently free of current romantic involvement with men, the two women bonded. Their friendship thrived, thanks to their similar interests in everything New York, such as theater, ballet, modern art, and bike riding along the Hudson River.

But then, after the holidays, things had changed. With no warning or explanation, Kera suddenly became less available for the numerous activities they had so enjoyed together. When Madison finally built up the courage to question this change, Kera denied it, explaining that starting in January she just preferred to stay in her warm apartment. She said that having lived her whole life in LA made dealing with the NYC winter weather an unpleasant ordeal.

During January and February, Madison accepted this story, especially since on occasion Kera would still be available, particularly on a Friday or Saturday night. The problem was there was little notice, and it had to be Kera calling Madison rather than the other way around. Still, Madison took it all in stride. But things hadn't changed with the arrival of spring and much warmer weather, which called into question Kera's original explanation.

Eventually Madison had given up trying to understand and had made it a point to concentrate on developing other friendships, including several new male friends. Over the past several months her social schedule returned to a semblance of normal, and when Kera called, she was less likely to be available. Gradually it was only in the hospital that they saw each other, either between patients or even more frequently for lunch. It was a source of continued amazement for Madison that Kera pretended everything was entirely normal, as if nothing had changed. And then something truly abnormal happened; yesterday Kera failed to show up for work. Madison had found out because all Kera's patients had to be either canceled or seen by other people, including Madison.

Since Kera had never been so irresponsible as to not show up for work without calling in sick, Madison had become immediately concerned, especially when coupled with the fact that Kera had been acting strangely for months. That was when Madison had started texting Kera to ask if she was okay. When there had been no response to several texts, she tried calling and left several voice messages over the course of the day. Today was the second day and still no Kera.

Madison took her phone from the pocket of the white medical coat that she was encouraged to wear by her department head and placed yet another call. She listened to it ring and intuitively knew that Kera wasn't going to answer. The moment the ring was interrupted, and Kera's outgoing voicemail began to play, Madison disconnected. There was no need to leave yet another message. Instead Madison made a snap decision. With the hour and a half she had before her next appointment, she would go to Kera's building and ring her buzzer. Her hope was that even though Kera wouldn't answer texts or phone calls, it might be harder for her to avoid responding to an actual visitor. It had suddenly occurred to Madison that maybe Kera had been caught up in a mad, passionate romantic affair these months and that perhaps her lover had dumped her. This scenario seemed to match the facts. In that case, maybe Kera was in dire need of a friend. It also helped that Madison was familiar with Kera's apartment since she had visited prior to the holidays. Kera liked to cook and had insisted on making dinner on several occasions, so Madison knew exactly where it was.

Exiting the hospital onto First Avenue and still wearing her medical jacket, Madison intended to quickly walk down to the main entrance where she knew she could easily catch a taxi. But it turned out she didn't need to go that far. Almost immediately she hailed a free cab coming north in moderate traffic, telling the driver to take her to Second Avenue and 23rd Street.

Kera's building was three in from the corner heading west. It was a nondescript brick structure that mirrored the surrounding buildings. Before entering, Madison looked up to what she thought were Kera's windows. They were closed, whereas a number of other windows in the façade were open. The weather was particularly mild for an early spring day.

At that moment a well-appointed middle-aged businesswoman emerged from the building. Like all New Yorkers, she seemed in a rush, but Madison called out to her and brought her to a halt. Madison asked if by any chance she knew Kera Jacobsen, who lived on the fourth floor.

"Sorry," the woman said quickly with a shake of her head. In the next instant she was off toward Second Avenue as if she was a power walker.

Undeterred, Madison went into the building's foyer, where there was a large group of metal mailboxes that covered the wall to the left, each with a button and a nameplate. There were also three marble steps up to the locked front door. To the right was an ornately framed mirror and a hastily constructed wooden wheelchair ramp.

From her previous visits, Madison had a good idea where Kera's mailbox was located. When she found it, she pressed the buzzer button for Kera's apartment, holding it in for five to ten seconds. Above the mailboxes was what looked like a speaker grate that had been painted over multiple times. She stared at it, as if by doing so she could entice it to come to life. But it didn't. Outside she could hear the distant undulation of a diminishing siren, an omnipresent background sound in New York City. Then there was the brief blaring of a car horn, but not a peep from the speaker.

She tried pressing the buzzer again, this time keeping pressure on it for nearly half a minute. She felt there was no way Kera could avoid hearing it no matter what she was doing. But the speaker above the mailboxes stayed frustratingly silent.

"Come on, girl," she said as she pressed Kera's buzzer for the third time. She kept it pressed for more than a minute out of frustration, yet she knew it was hopeless. Just then the inner door opened and a nattily dressed, tall, thin-faced Caucasian man appeared. Like the previous woman, he seemed to be in a hurry, yet when he saw Madison holding down Kera's buzzer, he stopped short. Behind him the inner door clicked shut.

"Is something wrong?" he asked.

Madison released the button. "Actually, there is," she

said. "By any chance do you know Kera Jacobsen? She lives in 4B. She's a woman my age."

"I don't believe I do," the man said. "Why do you ask?"

With obvious concern, Madison told the story of Kera's unexpectedly not showing up for work at the hospital and not answering her phone or responding to multiple texts. "Plain and simple, I'm worried about her," Madison added. "And she's not answering her buzzer, either. Of course, I can't be entirely sure the buzzer is working."

"Mine's functioning," the man said. "But they can be finicky. Do you work at the same hospital as she?"

"Yes. We are both pediatric social workers."

"Maybe you should go up and knock on her door," the man said. "Just to be sure."

"I'd like to do that," Madison said.

The man got out his keys, unlocked the door, and then pushed it open for her.

"Thank you," she said. She smiled before walking inside and to the elevator.

Once she'd arrived at 4B, she took a deep breath, then pressed the doorbell. When nothing happened, she pressed it again. When she couldn't hear any doorbell ringing within the apartment, she raised her hand and knocked on the metal door. Then she listened intently but heard nothing, even after putting her ear against the door. With a disappointed shake of her head, she knocked again even louder. She tried the door, but it was locked, as she suspected it would be. With a sense of frustration, she shook the door. Since it was old, it rattled in its metal jamb and that was when she detected a whiff of a foul odor. It was very slight but disturbingly rank, even nauseating. With some trepidation, Madison rattled the door again and hesitantly put her nose closer to the separation between the door and the jamb. The smell was more intense although still slight, and it keyed off a memory. She had experienced a similar smell when she was a young teen. She and some friends were walking in the woods and came across a dead woodchuck. It was the smell of putrefaction, the smell of death.

Stunned, she backed away from Kera's door. She wanted to flee, but willed herself to pull out her phone instead. With a trembling finger she punched in three numbers.

"This is nine-one-one," the call taker said in a practiced monotone. "What is your emergency?"

"I'm at my friend's apartment door," Madison began.

"What is the problem, ma'am?" the operator interjected.

"She doesn't answer when I knock and hasn't answered her phone for a couple of days. She also hasn't shown up for work."

"Do you think she is in need of assistance?"

"There's a bad smell," she managed. "When I shook the door, I could smell it."

"Is the door locked?"

"Yes, of course it is," Madison said, feeling impatient. "Otherwise I would have gone in."

"What kind of smell is it?"

"It's the smell of death," Madison said. She didn't

quite know how else to describe it. Another mild wave of nausea spread over her as her mind recalled the noxious odor.

"Are there animals on the premises?"

"Not that I know of," she snapped. "I don't think so. Listen, I think you'd better send somebody over here."

"What is the address, ma'am, and your friend's name?"

Madison struggled with her anxiety as she gave Kera's full name, the address, and the apartment number. She had never called 911 before and had imagined it would have somehow been easier. She didn't want to think about what the police may find behind Kera's door.

"And what is your name, please?"

She gave her name. Then she had to give her address and her phone number. She couldn't believe it was taking so long. She was worried about Kera—and a smaller, more selfish part of her realized her free time between appointments was rapidly running out.

"The police have already been dispatched," the operator assured her. "They will be there shortly. When was the last time you saw Miss Jacobsen?"

"Friday at work," Madison said.

"Did you or anyone else that you know speak with her over the weekend?"

"I didn't," she said. "I have no idea about anyone else. Listen, I hate to say this, but I have to get back to work."

"I'm afraid I have to ask you to stay to talk to the patrol officers," the operator said. "Your assistance will be needed."

"I have patients that are scheduled," Madison said. She was paralyzed by ambivalence about remaining where she was. With the smell of death seeping out of the apartment she was terrified of what was going to be found.

"Perhaps you should call your supervisor and say you're involved in an emergency. It shouldn't be much longer. I'm sure the patrolmen are getting close. While we wait, I want to ask you if your friend had any serious medical issues."

"Not that I know of," Madison said. She leaned her back up against the hallway wall. She changed hands with her phone since her palms had become sweaty. She felt claustrophobic.

"Does your friend have family in the area?"

"Not that I'm aware of," she said. "She's from LA."

"Does the building have a live-in superintendent?"

"I don't believe so," Madison said, but she wasn't a hundred percent certain.

The operator asked a number of additional questions before interrupting herself by saying: "I've just got confirmation that the patrolmen are at the front door of the building, but it's locked. Can you go down and let them in?"

"Yes, of course," she said. In truth, she felt relieved to disconnect from the 911 operator and get in the elevator. As soon as she got out on the ground floor, she saw the uniformed police patrolmen peeking through the door's sidelights. There were two. Both appeared to be rather young. The fact that one of the cops was African American made her a bit more comfortable. She'd never had the opportunity to interact with the New York Police Department, but as a woman of color, she'd heard stories.

The moment Madison opened the door, the taller, black officer asked if she was Miss Bryant. When she said yes, he introduced himself as Officer Kevin Johnson and his partner as Officer Stan Goodhouse. It was Madison's sense they were rather new to the job but making an attempt to pretend otherwise. She thought they were somewhere around the same age as she.

"We understand that you're concerned about your friend and a bad smell," Officer Johnson said. "Let's go take a look."

As they rode up in the elevator, the officers quizzed Madison on the information provided by the 911 operator, in particular about Miss Jacobsen not having been seen or heard from since Friday.

"That's true as far as I know," Madison said. "And I've tried to call and text her multiple times over the last two days."

On the fourth floor, Madison led the policemen down to Kera's door. Officer Goodhouse went through all the motions Madison had already tried. He rang the doorbell and then knocked loudly. Next, he tried the doorknob, but it was clear the door was still locked. He even put his shoulder to it to give a hesitant try to force it open, but it held solid.

"Do you smell the bad odor?" Madison asked.

Officer Johnson put his nose close to the crack between the door and the jamb. Quickly he straightened up. "It would be hard to miss that," he said with a grimace.

The two officers looked at each other.

"What's the protocol?" Goodhouse asked.

Madison rolled her eyes. It was even more obvious to her these policemen were relatively new to the job.

"I think it best we call ESU," Johnson said.

Goodhouse nodded and unclipped his handheld radio microphone from his shoulder. As he put in the call Madison asked what ESU was.

"It stands for Emergency Service Unit," Johnson said as Goodhouse talked in the background. "We can't go bashing in doors unless we think we're intervening in an acute emergency. Detecting a bad smell doesn't qualify. But the ESU guys are used to this kind of situation, and they're the best."

"Will they be here soon?" Madison questioned. Every minute they lingered outside the door was a minute when they weren't helping Kera. And there was still the issue of her looming appointments. She looked at her watch. She'd been gone for well over forty-five minutes.

"Should be," Johnson said. "ESU has REP vehicles out on patrol twenty-four-seven. REP means Radio Emergency Patrol. There's probably one in the neighborhood as we speak."

"I have to get back to work," Madison said, still feeling conflicted.

"I'm afraid we have to ask you to stay," Johnson said.

"Okay," Goodhouse said, interrupting. "A REP car is en route. They'll be here in five."

"I want to stay and find out what's going on with Kera," Madison said. "But I've got patients scheduled."

"Are you a doctor?" Johnson asked.

"No, I'm a social worker at NYU Medical Center."

"In a worst-case scenario, we may need you for identification purposes," Johnson said. "As the nine-one-one caller and a friend of the apartment's occupant, we have to ask you to stay. Maybe you should make a call to let people know you will be delayed."

At that moment the door to 4A opened and a middle-aged, frizzy-haired, mildly overweight woman in a housedress appeared. Her expression was one of shocked disdain. "What's going on?" she demanded.

"We've been called to check on your neighbor, ma'am," Goodhouse said as he hooked his radio microphone back to its shoulder loop. "Have you seen her over the last couple of days?"

"No, not for several days," the woman said. "I saw her Friday. Is she in trouble?"

"We hope not," Goodhouse said. "Have you noticed anyone visiting lately, anybody at all?"

"No," the woman said. "But she does have frequent late-night visitors, or she used to have them. But I don't pay any attention. I got my own problems."

"Thank you for your help," Goodhouse said.

The woman eyed the people in her hall and then shut the door without another word.

"She's a sweetheart," Johnson said. "I'll go down and wait for ESU to let them in the building."

Madison was beside herself, wondering what to do.

She wasn't even sure who she should call. What made the situation worse was that the department was already in disarray because of Kera's unexpected absence.

"How well do you know Miss Jacobsen?" Goodhouse asked. "It is 'Miss,' is it not?"

"She is unmarried," Madison said. She thought it best if she called her immediate supervisor rather than the head of the department and took out her phone to make the call.

"I know her reasonably well," she added as she pulled up the number in her contacts. "But, to be truthful, I hadn't seen much of her for a few months."

"Did you two have a falling-out?" he asked.

"Not to my knowledge," Madison said. "She just became less available as far as I was concerned."

"Any steady boyfriends that you knew of?"

"No," she said without hesitation. "At least not here in New York. She had a steady boyfriend in LA, where she grew up, but they broke up before she came to New York."

"Do you know if she was in contact with this former boyfriend?"

"I don't think so," Madison said. "But I don't know for sure. What I do know is that he was the one to break off the relationship."

At that moment the elevator door opened, and Johnson stepped out, accompanied by two additional uniformed police officers. Although their uniforms were blue, they were somewhat different from Johnson's and Goodhouse's, with less paraphernalia. They also had ESU emblazoned on their backs. Madison pressed against the wall of the hallway as they passed. These two new policemen were more obviously seasoned than Johnson and Goodhouse in both appearance and comport. The first one, a heavyset African American, was carrying a tool that Madison had never seen before. It was a weird-looking crowbar with a right-angled point and a narrow shovel-like extension at one end and a claw at the other.

Without the slightest hesitation, the officer stepped up to the door of 4B and with lightning speed popped the door open. Madison blinked at how easy the man made it seem. In the next instant a whiff of the putrid smell drifted out into the hallway while all four policemen disappeared into Kera's apartment. She could hear them talking but couldn't make anything out. She heard a window being opened, followed by an increase in the smell of decomposition. Madison felt a new wave of nausea spread over her, which she struggled to suppress.

A few minutes later the two ESU officers came out of the apartment. Neither spoke as they passed Madison, although they both acknowledged her with a nod. Madison didn't respond. She felt numb. Although she still didn't want to admit it, in her heart of hearts she knew what she was facing. Somehow it didn't seem possible that someone she'd gotten to know and like, who was in the prime of her life, might actually be gone forever. For a time, she felt paralyzed and overwhelmed. She couldn't even cry.

All at once she became aware of the phone still clutched in her hand. She needed to make the call to her supervisor, but before she could initiate the call, Johnson came out of the apartment. His expression told her what she didn't want to hear.

"I'm sorry to have to tell you that your friend is deceased," he said, confirming Madison's worst suspicions. "Did you know she was a drug user?"

"I had no idea," Madison said. "Is that . . . what killed her?"

"Looks like an overdose, which we cops see too much of on a daily basis. It's an ongoing tragedy."

"Am I going to have to see her?" she asked, horrified at the idea and dreading it. She didn't even like seeing dead rabbits on the side of the road, much less a dead human friend.

"We're going to need identification," Johnson said. "Normally we call EMS to come and pronounce, to be absolutely sure, but in a case like this where the victim's been deceased for a couple of days, the lieutenant at the precinct had us call the medical examiner directly. Their investigator will be here shortly. The ME will certainly need an ID, and I understand your friend has no family in the area."

"So, I *will* have to see her," Madison said reluctantly.

"The MEs often use photos, which would be a good idea under the circumstances."

Madison slapped a hand over her mouth to try to suppress a sudden urge to vomit.

CHAPTER 4

May 8th
2:35 P.M.

t was a beautiful spring day with a startlingly blue sky as Laurie walked along First Avenue, heading back to the OCME from the NYU Medical Center complex. Normally she would have enjoyed the short walk just to be outside for a brief time. Unfortunately, on this particular day she was oblivious to her surroundings, her mind in overdrive. The previous three hours had been totally unsettling. Up until then the day had been going well, including her presentation at the City Council's Health Committee meeting. She had been able to overwhelm them with actual statistics showing how the turnaround time for bodies at the OCME had significantly improved under her watch despite rumors to the contrary. As for the regrettable mix-up of the two Henry

Norton bodies, Laurie had been able to say that the OCME IT department had already made changes to the computerized case management system to make such problems much less likely to occur in the future. The only complaint Laurie was not able to completely quash was the concern about closing the morgues in Staten Island and the Bronx. The fact that significant money was being saved and the quality of the forensics had actually improved fell on deaf ears with the City Council member from the Bronx who sat on the Health Committee. This individual took the closing personally, as if the Bronx was somehow being denied appropriate service, which clearly wasn't the case.

When she had returned to the OCME, her meeting to consider raising the salaries of the medical-legal investigators also went well. Everyone unanimously agreed a significant salary increase was absolutely necessary for recruitment purposes. To fill vacancies, the OCME had to be competitive with the salaries that certified physician assistants and paramedics could get on the outside. So, when she had rushed over to the NYU Medical Center for her annual breast-cancer screening, she was feeling smug enough to assume the rest of the day would be smooth sailing as well. Unfortunately, that turned out to be disturbingly not the case.

The worst part of the screening from Laurie's perspective was the mammogram. Each year she wondered if she was being injured in the mildly painful process of having her breasts forcibly squeezed between two firm, unforgiving surfaces, and today was no exception. The experience was as uncomfortable as usual, but at least when the ordeal was over, there wasn't any bad news.

As chief medical examiner, Laurie held a position of Associate Professor of Pathology at NYU Medical School and Head of the NYU Department of Forensic Pathology. Consequently, she was recognized as a VIP and treated as such, meaning the Radiology Department was aware of her presence. Today, like her previous sessions, one of the ranking radiologists was present to read the digital images as they were produced. He even went over them with Laurie, who was rather adept at reading them herself.

The next part of the screening process was the MRI, which she found to be much easier than the mammogram because she wasn't claustrophobic and didn't mind lying prone within the narrow tube-like opening in the massive machine. Usually she was even able to relax during the procedure, and today was no exception.

It was after the test that her day had gone drastically south. Another ranking radiologist came in and looked at the slices. Unfortunately, the MRI picked up a problematic lesion that the screening mammogram missed, requiring a second diagnostic mammogram that was even more uncomfortable. This test, too, confirmed a disturbing abnormality, meaning the MRI finding was not artifact.

Laurie entered the OCME building in a kind of daze as her mind struggled to put in perspective what she had just learned over in the NYU Medical Center, and its implications. Marlene Wilson buzzed her into the building. She could tell the woman wanted to chat, but Laurie was in no mood for small talk. Instead she made a beeline into the head office area. She even passed Cheryl Sanford without stopping, which was certainly abnormal as Laurie was a gregarious person sensitive to other people's feelings.

Once inside her office, she hung up her coat before sitting down at her desk. With unseeing eyes, she merely stared ahead. The problem was simple. She didn't have the time to have a medical issue foisted on her, especially one of this type of potential consequence. She had a thousand employees at the OCME to worry about, and two children, one with a diagnosis of autism and the other with a newly announced potential behavioral problem at school.

A furtive knock followed by her door opening brought Laurie's attention back to the present. Cheryl was standing in the doorway, note in hand.

"Are you okay?" Cheryl asked, clearly concerned.

"I've been better," Laurie said. She didn't elaborate.

"Is there anything I can do?"

"Not at the moment," Laurie said. "I need some time by myself."

"I understand," Cheryl said. "Detective Lou Soldano called. He asked you to call him back as soon as you can. He said he tried to call Dr. Stapleton, but he was in the morgue. The detective seemed upset." Cheryl stepped over to Laurie's desk and put a yellow Post-it Note on the corner. She then quietly left.

Laurie pulled the note up off the desk and looked at

the number. She could tell it was Lou's mobile, which meant he was out on a case, possibly at a scene. As he was a dear friend and an extraordinarily committed Homicide detective who truly valued the contribution of forensic pathology, Laurie felt an irresistible urge to call him back despite her mental turmoil. Since there was a chance the call might have a personal aspect, she used her mobile. Lou answered immediately.

"Thanks for calling, Laur," he said straight off. *Laur* was a name one of Lou's children gave her way back when Lou and Laurie had first met. "I'm over here at the Manhattan General ED with one of my detectives who managed to get himself shot. It's not a life-threatening injury but bad enough. By accident I happened to become aware of one of those cases that makes you sick."

"Can you give me a bit more background?" she asked. There was little or no inflection in her voice, and she hoped Lou wouldn't notice or question. She was trying her best under the circumstances to sound normal.

"Sure," Lou said. "It's a two-and-a-half-year-old Latina girl named Camila Ruiz, who supposedly fell into a hot tub and scalded herself. It reminded me of a case I had years ago, which I hope doesn't repeat itself, because it gave me nightmares for years."

"Is this child dead?"

"I wouldn't be calling you guys if she wasn't. I was hoping that Jack could look into it. I mean, this should be a medical examiner case, right?"

"Certainly, as an accident it's a medical examiner case."

"All right, that's good to hear," he said. "The kid was

brought in by the mom's boyfriend, which is exactly what happened in the case I mentioned years ago. It turned out in that case it was no fucking accident. Pardon my French. Anyway, this case needs a good look as it's keying off my sixth sense that all is not right in never-never land."

"I'll let Jack know," Laurie said. After a few more pleasantries, she disconnected. Then she called Bart Arnold to make sure Camila Ruiz would be posted and asked him to let Jack know when the child arrived.

With that small, sad dose of reality, she felt a bit less paralyzed and began to make some preliminary plans with how she would emotionally adjust to the positive breast-cancer screening result. Obviously, a positive screen didn't necessarily mean she had breast cancer. It just meant that something had to be done to determine whether she did, and as far as she was concerned, it needed to be done immediately, the sooner, the better. But she didn't get far with this line of thinking. Within minutes there was another quiet knock on her office door, followed by Cheryl reappearing. Cheryl never liked using the intercom.

"I hate to bother you again, Dr. Montgomery," she said. "But Dr. Carl Henderson is on line one, and he says it's urgent."

"Okay, thanks," Laurie said. Reluctantly she recognized that dealing with the emotions of her positive cancer screening would have to wait. Being chief medical examiner was far too demanding. As she picked up the phone, she felt mildly irritated that Chet must have taken it upon himself to speak with the chief of the NYU Department of Pathology about Dr. Aria Nichols even though Laurie had told Chet that she preferred to speak with the resident before speaking with her boss. Although Laurie had met Carl Henderson at several NYU functions, she had never spoken with him on the phone. He was relatively new to the NYU Medical School community, having been recruited from the University of Pittsburgh just two years earlier. She remembered he was a tall, slender, worldly-appearing man who dressed particularly nattily, in contrast with so many of the other male pathologists that Laurie knew.

"Dr. Montgomery," she said into the phone in lieu of saying hello. As she had done with Detective Soldano, she struggled to sound normal.

"Thanks for taking my call," Carl said with a certain urgency. He had a deep, commanding baritone voice. "I needed to talk to you about a developing problem. One of our own, a pediatric social worker named Kera Jacobsen, has apparently overdosed and will be coming into the OCME shortly if she is not already there."

"I'm sorry to hear that," Laurie said. Opioid overdose deaths were disturbingly common in NYC, occurring at a rate of one every six hours on average.

"As you know, the NYU medical community has been making a big effort to do something about this terrible, ongoing tragedy in our neighborhood and city," Carl said. "Having one of our own succumb is hardly an appropriate advertisement for our efforts. As I'm sure you are aware, we have been spending considerable resources polishing our image in the city, as has Columbia-Cornell. It's a dog-eat-dog world in medical academe."

"I'm well aware of the competitive hospital environment," Laurie said, wondering where this surprising conversation was going. She thought for sure it would be about Aria Nichols, not an overdose victim.

"I just got off the phone with our hospital president, Vernon Pierce," Carl continued. "He thought that it would be a proper gesture to handle any autopsy that might need to be done here in-house rather than at the OCME. The idea would be to sort of bring her home since she is part of our community. I thought the idea has some merit even if it is a little unusual. I offered to do it myself in our autopsy theater in the Bellevue Hospital, which the president thought would be appropriate."

"This is a rather strange request," she said. She tried to keep her voice neutral, but she was shocked at the suggestion as it was unprecedented as far as she knew. The NYC OCME did not outsource its mandated autopsies, which an overdose was.

"I know it's unusual," he continued, "but Mr. Pierce also thought this might be a way of preventing the episode from possibly appearing in the tabloids. On occasion in the past the tabloids have seemed to have an inside source as to what's going on in the OCME."

"I'm sorry, Dr. Henderson, but we are required by law to do the autopsy, and it will be done here." She was aware there had been rare OCME leaks, as it was difficult to prevent them with as many employees as they had, but they certainly weren't a justification for having an autopsy done elsewhere. She had tried to think of a diplomatic way to make this point clear, but nothing had come to mind. Instead she thought it best to be blunt.

"I see," Carl said. By the tone of his voice it was apparent he was disappointed.

"But there is a way we could perhaps partially satisfy your president," she added as a sudden idea occurred to her in an attempt to appease NYU's fears. "We could have one of your pathology residents who is currently rotating through the OCME assist on the case. And I could make it a point to be involved personally. This would keep it in the family, because, as you know, I am officially part of the NYU family."

"That's a creative suggestion and very nice of you, Dr. Montgomery," he said. "I'm sure Mr. Pierce would be pleased, especially if we can keep your in-house gossip to a minimum and, more important still, keep it out of the papers. Do you know offhand the name of our resident?"

"I do," she said. "Dr. Aria Nichols. By coincidence I was scheduled to work with her this afternoon. What I can do is arrange for us to do the case together. What was the name of the victim?"

"Kera Jacobsen," Carl said.

Laurie wrote the name down on the Post-it note alongside Lou Soldano's number. As she was doing so, she heard another knock on her office door. She looked up, expecting to see Cheryl, but instead it was Jack, dressed in scrubs. Laurie pointed to the phone pressed against her ear. He nodded, closed the door behind him, and went to the couch, where he sprawled out. He looked annoyed. Still, she was glad to see him to share the bad news about the MRI and mammogram.

"Okay," Laurie said into the phone as she struggled with herself, trying to decide if she should bring up Dr. Nichols's less than exemplary professional behavior during her OCME rotation.

"I'd personally like to know if anything abnormal is found on the autopsy," Carl said. "And to emphasize, I'm sure Vernon Pierce will be pleased that it's being kept quiet, particularly in regard to the media."

"With as many overdose cases as we handle, I can't imagine there would be any particular media interest," Laurie said. "But I will let our public relations department know of your president's wishes. Of course, Kera Jacobsen's family will have the last word. As for anything out of the ordinary I might find during the case, I will personally let you know."

"That would be terrific. I appreciate your help, Doctor," Carl said sincerely. "Let me give you my mobile number so you have it if you need to get in touch with me after hours."

Laurie dutifully wrote down the number although she doubted she would need it.

"Again, I appreciate your cooperation and understanding," Carl said. "If I can be of any help to you in the future, please let me know."

Laurie kept the receiver in her hand even after she'd disconnected the call. Ultimately, she had decided not to say anything about Aria Nichols's odd behavior as it

would complicate an already mildly complicated situation. Instead she turned to face Jack. "You won't believe
the call I just had."

"Who was it?"

"I'll tell you in a minute," she said as she placed a call
to Bart Arnold, the head of the Medical Legal Investigator Department. The MLIs were the physician assistants
or paramedics who did all the investigative work for
every death in New York City, which was a lot of effort,
considering that between a hundred and a hundred and
fifty people died in the city every day. Of those, about ten
percent were judged by the MLIs as needing to be
brought to the OCME for further review, and of that ten
percent a bit more than half ended up being autopsied.

"Has a Kera Jacobsen been brought in yet?" Laurie
asked when she had Bart on the line.

"Let me check," Bart said. She could hear the click of
his keyboard. "Yes," he said after a pause. "She arrived
just after noon."

"Anything abnormal in the MLI's report?" Laurie said.

"Nothing noteworthy," he said after another pause.
"Seems a straightforward opioid overdose. Death must
have been rapid because the syringe was left in the vein."

After thanking Bart, Laurie put in a call to Chet Mc-
Govern.

"What's going on?" Jack questioned impatiently. He
was still reclined on the couch but careful to keep his
shoes from touching the upholstery. He'd made that mistake in the past.

She held up her hand, mouthed that she had one more

call to make, and motioned for Jack to be quiet. As soon as she had Chet on the line she said, "Have you spoken with Dr. Nichols about working with me this afternoon?"

"I certainly did," Chet said. "And I made sure she understood it is a command performance. And I found an interesting teaching case for you two, which will demonstrate the value of forensics and possibly pique her interest."

"I appreciate your efforts," Laurie said. "But there's another case I want to do with Dr. Nichols instead of the one you picked out. I'm sorry for the change. The name is Kera Jacobsen. Your case is most likely a better teaching case, since Jacobsen is apparently a routine overdose. Nonetheless, we're going to do this one."

"Okay, fine by me," Chet said agreeably. "Do you want me to get it all prepared?"

"I'd appreciate it," she said. "And see if Marvin Fletcher is available?" Back when Laurie did almost daily autopsies before becoming chief, she liked to work with Marvin for a variety of reasons, mainly because she thought he was possibly the best mortuary tech at the OCME and a pleasure to work with. And today, not knowing what to expect from Aria Nichols, she preferred that the general logistics went smoothly. She knew Marvin would guarantee that.

"What kind of time frame are we looking at?" Chet asked.

"An hour from now should work for me," she said, glancing at the clock on her desk. "Are you expecting any difficulty locating Dr. Nichols?"

"We'll see," he said. "She said she would be in the library, but I do have her number just in case she's left the building. I offered to have her come up here to my office and go over histology slides with me, but she blew me off big-time."

"What exactly did she say?" Laurie couldn't help but remember the woman's mildly bawdy response to Chet's having caught her over at the Tisch Hospital when she was supposed to be in the OCME.

"Do you really want to know?"

"Try me," Laurie said.

"She told me that she would prefer to be run over by a herd of buffalo in heat," Chet said with obvious disgust.

"Sounds like a charmer," she said, smiling in spite of herself. Once again, the idea of Jack's being right about Chet initially trying to make time with the woman went through her mind. Particularly in the current social environment, any suggestion of sexual harassment of any form often evoked a significant response. Laurie told herself to keep an open mind when it came to Aria Nichols.

"If you have trouble finding her, let me know immediately," Laurie said. "Otherwise, I'll expect to see her down in the autopsy theater within the hour."

"You are going to do an autopsy on an overdose?" Jack asked with disbelief as she hung up the phone. "I thought you'd decided not to do autopsies on general principle. And why an overdose?"

"This is a unique situation," Laurie said. "I don't have time to explain completely, but it is going to be with the problematic resident I mentioned to you this morning. I'd arranged it with Chet before I went down to City Hall, but then there's been a new development. When you first came in here, I was talking with Dr. Carl Henderson."

"The chief of NYU Department of Pathology?" Jack asked.

"None other," Laurie said.

"I've never met the man," he said. "Wait! I take that back. I have met him briefly. A tall, good-looking guy, for a pathologist, with a sense of humor to boot, which is why I remembered him."

"I've only met him on a few occasions," Laurie said. "He's relatively new."

"What does your conversation with Carl Henderson have to do with the overdose case you're doing with the resident? With as many overdoses as we process, it doesn't sound so exciting to me."

"The case itself most likely won't be exciting or challenging," she said. "There's a political angle that's developed, which is why Carl was calling. But the main reason for my doing it is an opportunity for me to get a feel for this problematic NYU pathology resident. Still, I'm looking forward to it. I know that sounds pathetic, but I do truly miss doing autopsies. But we are not going to advertise that I'm doing it. Okay? I'm going to tell anyone I run into down in the pit to keep it under wraps. Hopefully, because of the time there shouldn't be too many people down there."

"Okay, fine by me," Jack said, pretending to zip his lips closed.

"Oh, by the way," she said. "I spoke to Lou briefly a few minutes ago. He wants you to give him a call about a case. Do you need his number?" Laurie held up the Post-it note.

"No, I've got it," he said.

"Now tell me what happened at the Brooks School," Laurie said. "You did go, didn't you?"

"Of course I went," Jack snapped. He sat up and put his feet on the floor. "And it turned out to be a disaster like I feared. I'm sorry, but I didn't make us any friends at the school. I tried to just listen as you said, but they were telling me such nonsense, I couldn't restrain myself from letting them know exactly how wrong I felt they were. I even accused them of colluding with the god-damn pharmaceutical industry. That was right after Miss Rossi actually said that she felt strongly JJ needed Adderall. That's when I flipped out."

"Oh, God," Laurie said with frustration. With her elbows on her desk, she closed her eyes and rubbed her temples firmly while her mind did somersaults, trying to think of what they would do if JJ was asked to leave the school. She also realized as much as she wanted to share what she had learned over at NYU Radiology, it would have to wait as it would surely provoke a serious discussion. After a deep breath she said, "Maybe you better tell me exactly what happened, provided you can do it in fifteen minutes. I've got to get downstairs and get into some scrubs."

CHAPTER 5

May 8th
3:35 P.M.

Through the small, wire-mesh window outside the autopsy room, Laurie could see Marvin busily laying out specimen jars, instruments, and other paraphernalia. On table #1 there was a corpse of a woman that was slightly bloated, with significant livor mortis of the lower limbs, suggesting to Laurie's analytical brain that the victim had died in a sitting position.

As she gazed in at the familiar scene, Laurie felt her anticipation build at the prospect of finally being able to do again what she loved. Like she had on so many off moments, she found herself questioning whether she'd done the right thing by accepting the offer to become the chief medical examiner. She shrugged, reminding herself there were no easy answers, before pushing open the door. With a full view of the pit, as the room was called by all who worked there, Laurie could see there were no other personnel present. She wasn't surprised. Not only did most of the activity in the autopsy room happen in the morning, but every afternoon at 3:00 P.M. there was an informal meeting up in the conference room to go over the day's cases. Chet revived the event to great acclaim, having made it fun, interesting, and worthwhile from a continuing education standpoint. It was one of the reasons Laurie chose this particular time to do the case, as she preferred not to have to explain herself to too many people.

"Hello, Marvin," Laurie called to get the mortuary technician's attention. "Are you almost ready?" She could smell a mild amount of decomposition odor, which the powerful evacuation fans were keeping under control.

"Just about," Marvin replied.

"Have you seen Dr. Nichols?" Laurie asked. She was mildly disappointed not to see the woman. Since she had not heard anything from Chet, she assumed all was in order.

"You are the first," Marvin said. "By the way, Dr. McGovern already had me do a rapid fentanyl test on the powder found on the victim's coffee table. It was positive."

"I'm not surprised," Laurie said. Obviously, it was going to be a run-of-the-mill case. "Thanks."

"No problem," he said.

"Where's the case file?" Laurie asked. Her autopsy technique was to go over all the material available on a case before she did the autopsy, to limit the chances of missing something. This modus operandi was just the opposite of Jack's. He liked to do the autopsy as cold as possible, as it was his thought that preconceived ideas of what he would find might cause him to miss the unexpected. It was one of those differences that Laurie and Jack liked to tease each other about with the assumption that they were right and the other wrong, even though both knew they were both right. It was just a matter of choice.

"I put it on the gurney out there in the hallway," Marvin said. "I assumed you'd want to look at it before you started."

Before letting the door close, Laurie gave Marvin a thumbs-up to let him know how much she appreciated the benefits of working with an assistant who knew her routine. Laurie located the file and leafed through all the pages until she came to the MLI's summary, which had been done by David Goldberg, one of the more recently hired MLIs. Reading quickly, she got a good sense of the case. The victim had been found by a friend and coworker, Madison Bryant, in the victim's apartment and had been identified by the same individual. The MLI estimated that the victim had been dead for two or three days and gave the evidence he used to come to this conclusion. The MLI then described the drug paraphernalia that had been found on the victim's coffee table as well as the partially empty syringe still embedded in the victim's left antecubital fossa, or the front side of the elbow. Other important facts were that the victim was not known to have any medical problems, according to the family. It also was written that no one, neither the family nor the identifying friend, had any knowledge that the victim had been using drugs. She was always thought to be a stable, well-adjusted, happy person.

Laurie was still reading the MLI's report as she pushed into the women's locker room and found herself confronted by a woman around thirty in rather fancy and expensive-looking lingerie. At that very moment the woman was reaching into an open locker in the process of hanging up a designer blouse. Contemporary, distressed jeans were visible hanging in the locker, as was a resident-style short white coat.

Assuming she was Aria Nichols, Laurie scrutinized this individual who reputedly had a questionable reputation among her resident colleagues, who'd been verbally brazen to Chet, and who, most important from Laurie's point of view, was not taking her forensic rotation at the OCME seriously. She was about Laurie's height of five feet five, slim but muscular like a ballet dancer, with cold black hair cut in a longish pixie bob. Her eyes, which she turned on Laurie, were a striking cornflower blue while her complexion was rather dark, as if she'd been in the sun. In Laurie's immediate estimation she wasn't traditionally eye-catchingly attractive, yet she exuded a kind of animal sensuality and youthful beauty that Laurie could still admire and guess might appeal to men, at least some men.

"Hello," Laurie said, trying to sound more chipper than she felt. "I'm Dr. Montgomery. Are you Dr. Nichols?"

To Laurie's surprise the woman didn't respond immediately, but rather stared back unblinkingly with a slight, frozen Mona Lisa smile that Laurie found irritatingly provocative. It seemed there was a hint of arrogance, even unprovoked, suppressed hostility. Although Laurie fought against making a rapid value judgment, she recognized that there was something about this woman that she instinctively didn't like. She wasn't sure what it was but guessed it had something to do with an implied entitlement, as if this individual had been born with a silver spoon in her mouth. Laurie had met a number of girls who fit that definition in the private high school she'd attended.

"*You* are the chief medical examiner?" the woman questioned, as if she couldn't believe Laurie could be the head of the OCME. She also spoke in a contemporary "vocal fry" to emphasize her disbelief.

It was Laurie's turn to hesitate as she fought the urge to merely turn around and walk out and give up on this woman. Recognizing she wasn't in the best of moods after Jack's revelations of his behavior at the Brooks School and her own discombobulation from what she learned from her breast-cancer screening, Laurie figuratively counted to ten, took a breath, broke off from the juvenile staring contest she'd been indulging, and went to one of the open lockers. She took off the long white medical coat she generally wore while in the OCME. After hanging it up, she turned back to the woman, who had continued to stare at her with the same impudent smile. "Yes," Laurie said finally, struggling to speak as normally as possible and without emotion. "I am the chief medical examiner. And you?"

"I'm Aria Nichols," the woman said. "I'm surprised. I thought you'd be a hell of a lot older, and frumpy. You don't look like a forensic pathologist to me. You look too normal."

"Is that supposed to be a compliment?" Laurie said as she began to slip out of her dress. She had made a point from the first day she'd worked at the OCME to wear reasonably stylish clothes. Now that she was the first female NYC OCME chief, she felt it was even more appropriate. If nothing else, she wanted to contravene stereotypes like Aria was implying.

"I'm just being honest," Aria said neutrally. She went to get scrub pants and a top. Laurie watched her go, amazed at how nonchalant the woman was about her near nakedness. Laurie had gone to a high school where the girls had separate cubicles to change for gym. It was also true that she had never quite gotten used to a thong.

"I heard from Dr. Chet McGovern that you are not particularly fond of your rotation here at the OCME," Laurie said.

"That's the understatement of the year," Aria said. "To be honest, I think it's a waste of my time."

"You don't think what we medical examiners do is significantly beneficial to society and our community?" Once again Laurie was taken aback by the striking disrespect this woman was willing to project, and it grated on her.

"Hey, I didn't say that," Aria corrected. "I just said it was a waste of my time, not yours. Sure, I know you guys do a lot, especially for law enforcement and such, but it doesn't interest me."

"We do a lot more than help law enforcement," Laurie said. "Medical examiners have also been responsible for a number of safety innovations. As an example, significant electronic equipment design changes to minimize electrocutions have come from medical examiner work. Even low-voltage swimming pool lights are another example. I can't imagine how many lives such innovations have saved."

Aria returned to her locker and began pulling on the scrub pants. "Yeah, that might be true, but as I said, it's not something that interests me. The idea of this rotation is to give me a sense of what forensic pathology is like. I got the message. I like autopsies but only anatomical autopsies that teach us about disease processes. From my perspective, forensic autopsies are disgusting, what with the smell and all."

"They can be distasteful on occasion," Laurie admitted. "But from my perspective they are inordinately challenging. It's an opportunity to listen to the dead tell their stories in order to help the living. It is a medical specialty that offers the chance to learn something every day."

"Please," Aria said. "Give me a break. That's just a bunch of self-justifying bullshit. But fine, you like forensic pathology. Good for you."

"I find your disrespect disturbing," Laurie said, trying to maintain her composure. With everything else that had happened over the past few hours, dealing with this unpleasant woman was a severe test of her patience.

"What am I disrespecting?" Aria said, making an exaggerated expression of confusion. "I'm giving credit where credit is due."

"I heard you were remarkably disrespectful to our director of education, Dr. McGovern."

"Oh, really?" Aria drawled. "Let me tell you something. Old Doc McGovern got what he deserved."

"What do you mean by that? Are you implying he'd been disrespectful to you?"

"Obviously," Aria said.

"What did he say that was disrespectful?"

"It was the way he looked at me and his syntax. The man is a hopeless womanizer. It's written all over his face. Of course, it didn't help that after he'd been talking with me for five minutes, he suggested we should have a drink sometime. I'm not all that fond of men, particularly the Dr. McGovern type. I've had to deal with them all my life."

Once again Laurie found herself staring at Aria, who impudently stared back. As the head of an organization with a thousand employees in an era of heightened workplace sensitivity to issues of sexual harassment, Laurie wondered if beneath this woman's brassiness, she might be communicating something important. The question arose in her mind whether sexual harassment could be nonverbal and merely implied. Thanks to Jack, she'd known for years that Chet McGovern was a philanderer on his own time, but could that reality affect his behavior in-house? Laurie didn't know but stored the thought to examine later. Currently she had to deal with the woman in front of her, who was enough of a conundrum.

"Dr. McGovern followed me all the way over to the Tisch Hospital," Aria said. "As far as I was concerned, that raised a red flag. I didn't want him following me back to my condo some night."

"He followed you because you had failed to make an appearance at an assigned autopsy," Laurie said.

"Big deal," Aria said. "That's easy for you to say, but who's to know. Besides, I'd already stood around and watched one forensic autopsy for the day, and as far as I was concerned, that was enough."

"That's not for you to decide," Laurie said, struggling to control herself.

"Yeah, whatever," Aria said. "I'm learning enough about forensics to satisfy myself, which is the point of this rotation. I'm sure as hell not going to become a forensic pathologist."

"What attracted you to medicine?" Laurie asked, to change the subject. Aria's lack of respect and basic empathy was difficult to weather.

"Whoa . . ." Aria voiced. "This is getting personal."

"Do you mind?" Laurie said. "As I'm sure you are aware, or would be if you thought about it, it's our responsibility to certify that you spent your rotation here at the OCME appropriately. So far your behavior of skipping assigned cases makes us question that."

"Okay, that's not unreasonable," Aria said. "I went

into medicine to get away from the family business. Also, in college everybody seemed to be premed, so I was, too. I really didn't think much about what it would be like being a doctor. I was caught up in the competition, which I enjoyed."

"What was the family business?" Laurie asked.

"My father, the asshole alcoholic, was a very successful NYC venture capital, hedge-fund guy who knocked me around a lot when I was a tween."

"I'm sorry to hear that," Laurie said, meaning it. "Was your father at least pleased you chose to become a doctor?"

Aria laughed derisively. "He never knew, the selfish bastard. He committed suicide when I was just barely in my teens."

"My goodness," Laurie managed. She was appalled. "It certainly sounds like you didn't have the best childhood."

"You could say that," Aria added. "Especially considering the stepdad my screwy mother ended up marrying. He was worse than my real dad in just about every category. But I managed to blackmail him into putting a lot of my mother's money in my name."

"How did you end up in Pathology?" Laurie asked. She wanted to get away from Aria's lurid and depressing family history. Laurie had sometimes felt sorry for herself growing up because her father had been emotionally distant. She couldn't imagine what it would have been like to be physically abused.

"That's a good question," Aria said. "It was by elimination. Maybe I should have given more thought to becoming a doctor, because during medical school I was quick to learn that I hated seeing patients. I mean, it's pretty pathetic when you think about it. But what can I say? It was what it was. Anyway, pathology is the only real choice if you hate patients. It's also intellectually stimulating."

"Well, it's encouraging to hear you were at least challenged," Laurie said. She tried to gird herself for an unpleasant afternoon. "Let's talk about the next hour. My intent here is to get a sense of what you have learned about forensic pathology in the little more than a week you've been here. We have an overdose case, and I want you to essentially do it. Are you up for that?"

"I can tell you this: It sounds a hell of a lot more interesting than me just standing around emptying the wastebasket."

"I hope you find it stimulating," Laurie said. "Maybe we can even excite you a bit about forensic pathology."

"That would be a stretch," Aria said, reverting to her disinterested voice. "Let's not let expectations get out of hand."

CHAPTER 6

May 8th
4:15 P.M.

As far as Laurie was concerned, the first part of the autopsy went rather well, and she began to relax and even enjoy to an extent the nostalgia the experience evoked. Although Aria initially mentioned her disgust related to the mild putrid odor and the ghoulish facial appearance of the deceased, she didn't dwell on it. And Laurie was relieved that the attitude Aria had displayed in the locker room had seemed to melt away once she focused on the actual tasks at hand—Laurie quickly agreed with Chet that she was no dummy.

"The full-body X-ray can potentially help the identification process and will also pick up any foreign bodies that might have contributed to the cause of death," Aria had correctly said in answer to Laurie's question of why the film had been taken. Such a response made Laurie feel that Aria had been listening when she'd observed the forensic autopsies, after all.

Laurie had Aria conduct the external exam verbally and was impressed with Aria's description. Aria talked about why it was best to leave the clothes on the victim, as Kera Jacobsen was still attired in her bathrobe, exactly the way she had been found. She also talked about why the syringe, still embedded in Kera's left arm, had been left in place and why it had been carefully covered with paper and tape so that it could be examined for DNA and fingerprints. She also mentioned two other significant findings that Laurie herself had noticed—namely, that there wasn't much evidence of dried foam around Kera's mouth and nostrils and that although there were signs of other venous puncture marks, they all seemed relatively new.

"My sense is that she had not been a drug user for long," Aria had said, and Laurie agreed.

After they had removed the bathrobe and examined the livor mortis of the lower extremities, Laurie had quizzed Aria about livor mortis, rigor mortis, algor mortis, and other methods of estimating time of death and why the time of death was important. Laurie also talked about various signs of the body having been moved, which clearly had not been the case with Kera. In all these arenas, Aria displayed reasonably competent knowledge. Although she might have skipped some of the autopsies she'd been assigned, of the ones she had observed, she'd absorbed a considerable understanding of the forensic process.

It wasn't until they were ready to begin the internal part of the autopsy that Aria's personality reverted back to what Laurie now feared was her normal inconsiderate self. What seemed to set it off was Laurie merely asking if Aria was familiar with the difference between the forensic or Virchow autopsy technique, which they used at the OCME to determine the cause and manner of death, compared with the clinical or Rokitansky en bloc method that was done to study the pathological effects of disease.

"Yes, for fuck's sake!" Aria snapped in a loud, irritated tone of voice. She was holding the scalpel, ready to make the initial incision. "Hell, I've been a pathology resident for nearly four years. I'd have to be a dumb ass not to know the difference."

Laurie was shocked and found herself back to having a staring contest with Aria. They were both wearing surgical masks with plastic eye shields, so Laurie couldn't see much of her face. The transformation in demeanor had been so sudden that Laurie was momentarily speechless. The only thing that had changed prior to the outburst was that Marvin, who had been hovering in the periphery ready to fetch whatever might be needed, had now joined Aria on the right side of the corpse. Since Laurie had intended for Aria to do the case, she had allowed her to be on the right side while Laurie had gone to the left, where she preferred her assistant to stand.

Before Laurie could reboot her brain, Aria broke off staring at Laurie to direct her attention to Marvin. "I don't like you standing this close to me," she snapped.

Marvin appeared as shocked as Laurie. He backed up a step and raised his hands, palms out. "Sorry," he said.

"What's the problem?" Laurie demanded, finding her voice. "He was just going to lend a hand if needed."

"I don't like men I don't know crowding me," Aria said.

Shocked anew at this obviously gender-discriminatory tantrum, Laurie was again speechless.

"It's not personal, it's just how I feel," Aria added.

Laurie was dumbfounded and switched her attention to Marvin. "I'm sorry," she said. "That was uncalled for, inappropriate, and will not be tolerated."

"As I said, it's not personal," Aria repeated. "I need space, is all. Let's not make a big deal out of it. Maybe he wouldn't like it if I crowded him."

"It's okay, Dr. Montgomery," Marvin said magnanimously. "I didn't realize I was crowding anyone."

"You were," Aria insisted. "You actually touched up against me, and I responded. Now it's over. Let's get this case finished. Go over on Dr. Montgomery's side if you want to participate!"

Laurie and Marvin exchanged a prolonged glance. They had worked together on so many occasions in the past that they often didn't even need to talk to be on the same wavelength. Nonverbally they decided that it was best to get the case over with and deal with the incident later.

Meanwhile, Aria started the case by making a modified Y incision from the point of both shoulders, meeting in over the sternum, and then extending down to the pubis. She handled the knife with confidence. It was quickly apparent she was a skilled anatomical pathologist.

Dismayed at the unpleasant and inappropriate personality that Aria was again demonstrating, Laurie said little as Aria worked although she was prepared to intervene if Aria did anything out of the ordinary. But there was no need. Within minutes Aria had both the chest cavity and the abdominal cavity open with the internal organs in full view. Following Aria's suggestion, Marvin had moved around to the other side of the table to stand next to Laurie.

"I'm going to do the thorax first," Aria said. Her voice had reverted to the mild tone she'd used at the beginning of the case. Laurie merely nodded at Aria's announcement, questioning how this woman got accepted to medical school and then a prestigious Pathology residency with that mercurial temperament. If nothing else, she had to have been a hell of a student.

Aria worked quickly, adroitly, and with great surety. Within minutes she had the heart lifted and angled up toward the head, exposing the left auricle. "Syringe for a blood sample, please," she said, reaching out with one of her gloved hands while continuing to inspect the underside of the heart. Marvin handed her the syringe he had prepared, and Aria took the sample. Next, she turned her attention to the lungs. First, she carefully felt their surface using the pads of her fingers, then she grasped a lung between her thumb and fingers to feel the consistency.

"Not much pulmonary edema," she said, knotting her brow in surprise. She looked up at Laurie. "You take a feel."

Laurie did as was suggested, palpating the lung tissue between her thumb and fingers. "I see what you mean," she said. The lungs were indeed light and fluffy, meaning full of air and not fluid. Normally overdoses had fluid in the lungs, forming what was called pulmonary edema.

"This might have been a cardiac death, not a pulmonary death," Aria said. "I wonder if the patient ever had an ECG."

"It wasn't mentioned in the medical-legal investigator's report," Laurie said.

"Maybe it's a cardiac channelopathy," Aria said, referring to a relatively new class of heart disease that interrupted the heart's rhythm. "That could make this an interesting case."

"I wouldn't count on it," Laurie said. "Cardiac channelopathies are rather rare, especially in an otherwise healthy young woman."

"Yeah, but it's a fascinating area genetically," Aria said. "With the terrific DNA lab here at the OCME, this could be one hell of a case. I happen to be interested in channelopathies."

"When you hear hoofbeats, think of horses, not zebras," Laurie cautioned.

Aria laughed. "Of course, you're right," she said. "Everybody knows fentanyl suppresses breathing, but hell, maybe it also selectively exacerbates channelopathies. You never know. I'd like to know if this patient ever had an ECG or any history of cardiac problems or fainting spells."

"It will be interesting to learn," Laurie said. When Aria removed the heart and the lungs from the body, the lungs seemed to be entirely normal, as she'd surmised earlier from feeling the lung consistency. Both together weighed only two point eight pounds, which was well within the normal range.

"Obviously very little edema involved in these babies," Aria said, taking them out of the scale. "I'm thinking channelopathy all over again."

"Let's look at the coronary arteries before we jump to conclusions," Laurie said. She was again beginning to relax after Aria's outburst and was once more enjoying herself being back in the pit doing an autopsy. For a few minutes she was able to forget all the stresses of being the chief medical examiner on top of her personal problems.

With the heart out on a cutting board, Aria skillfully traced all the major coronary arteries, confirming they were entirely normal in configuration and patency. When she finished inspecting all the heart's chambers and valves, she looked up at Laurie, who was watching her every move. "Miss Jacobsen obviously didn't have a heart attack or a valve prolapse, and she didn't have pulmonary edema. I'm stoked. The channelopathy idea is starting to sound better and better."

"Perhaps," Laurie said. She still thought the chances were pretty small, yet inwardly she was pleased that Aria was raising the possibility and acted enthused. Laurie's goal with Dr. Nichols had been to first find out if she had learned anything after she'd been at the OCME for a week, which she obviously had, and second, to possibly get her interested in forensics so she'd take her OCME rotation seriously. It seemed that this case, even though most likely a garden-variety overdose despite the lack of pulmonary edema, might do the trick. Laurie could well remember when she'd stumbled onto the attractions of forensic pathology when she was a pathology resident.

Finished with the chest, Aria now turned her attention to the abdomen. She worked quickly, to Laurie's satisfaction, as it was now going on five o'clock. Within minutes Aria had the entire bowel out of the body. Marvin offered to take it and rinse it out, but Aria said she preferred to do it herself. At one of the sinks lining the far wall, she flushed it out, opened it with dissecting scissors, and then began to carefully inspect its nearly thirty-foot length.

At that moment, Jack and Lou Soldano entered the pit, laughing about something. Laurie wasn't surprised to see Lou. He was a frequent visitor to the autopsy room. Both men were dressed in scrubs in preparation to do a case. Immediately behind them Vinnie Amendola appeared, pushing a gurney. On it was a toddler whose tiny body made Laurie shudder. Autopsies on children, particularly young children, never failed to bother her even though she'd hoped by this time in her career to have learned to take it in stride.

While Vinnie navigated the gurney next to a neighboring table, Jack and Lou came to Laurie's. Jack leaned toward Laurie and asked sotto voce if Chet's resident bête noire was as bad as he claimed.

"Worse," Laurie whispered back.

"Really?" Jack questioned with surprise.

"We'll talk about it later," Laurie said as she saw Aria leave the sink and start back in their direction. "I take it this is the suspicious drowning death Lou called me about earlier?" Laurie asked, even though she didn't really want to know.

"That's the one. A scald case and drowning with extensive third-degree burns," Jack said. "Lou must have told you he's questioning whether it was an accident as the mother's boyfriend contends. His gut is telling him it was a homicide."

"And his intuition is usually spot-on," Laurie said. She avoided looking at the tiny body as Vinnie moved it over onto the autopsy table. Instead she said hello to Lou, who returned the greeting.

"I'm Dr. Stapleton," Jack said to Aria when she returned to the table.

"I know who you are." Aria gave Jack a cursory glance before putting down the bowel she was carrying. Ignoring him further, she proceeded to take samples from various portions of the intestines and place them in specimen bottles.

Jack watched her for a beat, shrugged at being summarily dismissed, and then led Lou to the autopsy table where Vinnie had placed the toddler.

"The bowel is clean," Aria announced. "Time for the pelvic organs." Returning to the corpse and using mostly blunt finger dissection with a bit of help from blunt-nosed dissecting scissors, she quickly freed everything up. Then, using a scalpel, she expertly transected what needed to be cut and lifted the pelvic organs including the uterus, the fallopian tubes, and the ovaries out of the pelvic cavity.

"I have to say, you are a talented prosector," Laurie said, and meant it.

"I'm glad you noticed," Aria said in a tone of voice that made Laurie wish she'd not made the compliment. After taking a sample of the cervix, Aria forcibly inserted a long-bladed and very sharp scalpel into the cervical os and proceeded to fillet open the uterus to expose the uterine cavity.

"Holy shit," Aria said. She bent over the specimen to take a closer look. "Do you see what I see?"

CHAPTER 7

For several beats, the two women were transfixed by their unexpected discovery. Nestled inside the uterus was a tiny embryo. Although both women were professionally accustomed to death, one more than the other, discovering that the dead woman was pregnant momentarily yanked them out of their comfort zone.

"Oh, dear," Laurie said. "This makes this overdose a double tragedy."

"Has this ever happened to you?" Aria asked. "I mean, discovering a pregnancy during an autopsy when you had no clue whatsoever?"

"Yes, once," Laurie said. "It was similar to this case. Yet we shouldn't be all that surprised. As medical students we were all taught that whenever you are confronted with a female patient ranging in age from menarche to menopause, you should consider them pregnant until proven otherwise. It's to avoid doing anything untoward to the pregnancy, like a simple X-ray or an inappropriate medication."

"It's different with a live patient," Aria said.

"I know what you mean," Laurie said. "The beginning of life is so different than death."

"How old do you think it is?" Aria asked. She looked closer at the tiny fetus huddled against the wall of the uterus with its bulging, oversize forehead and tiny hands.

"Marvin, get us a ruler, please," Laurie said. To Aria she added: "My guess is in the ten-to-eleven-week realm. The hands are quite well developed." She took the small ruler that Marvin handed her and measured. "Thirty-eight millimeters, or an inch and a half," she said. "So yes, I'd estimate ten weeks, meaning it had just changed its designation from an embryo to a fetus."

"Was the victim found by her boyfriend?" Aria asked while continuing to stare at the fetus. Her tone had changed yet again. Now she sounded irritated, almost angry.

"No, she was found by a female coworker," Laurie said.

"That doesn't compute," Aria snapped.

"I'm not sure what you mean," Laurie said. "What doesn't compute?"

"She should have been found by the boyfriend," Aria said emphatically. "The bastard, whomever the hell he is, gets this woman pregnant and then lets her sit around and rot for two or three days. That's not right."

"That's a mighty big leap of faith," Laurie said. "At this point there's no way of knowing the relationship between this woman and the father. For all we know it could have been donor sperm."

"Give me a break," Aria commented derisively. "This wasn't a sperm-donor pregnancy. Some bastard had his way with this woman and then abandons her. I can just feel it. Hell, he might have even supplied the drugs or been the reason she decided to take them."

"Those are rather wild assumptions," Laurie said. "In forensic pathology we have to stick with the facts and avoid value judgments. We also have to finish this autopsy. Let's continue."

Going back to work, Aria followed Laurie's directions for dealing with the fetus and the ovaries. As they expected but hadn't noticed, there was a sizable corpus luteum in the left ovary. For a time, Aria was quiet as she dealt with the rest of the abdominal organs, but it didn't last. Soon she was back to railing against the unknown boyfriend. Laurie listened but didn't respond as she was nonplussed at Aria's apparent anger, making her question if there had been some similar pregnancy event in her life.

Finally, Aria said: "You know, coming across this fetus has really caught my attention. I never expected this kind of surprise twist. I think it deserves to be looked into."

"I would encourage you to do so," Laurie said. "But I need you to do it for the right reasons and with an open mind. I don't want to think that it's your apparent animus toward men or personal history that's motivating you."

"In the locker room you bragged that forensic pathology provided an opportunity to listen to the dead tell their stories. I'm hearing this woman," Aria said, "and she's telling me loud and clear that something is not right in Camelot, and I mean to find out what it is. Someone has to find and talk to the father."

"Okay, I'll encourage it with a couple of caveats," Laurie said. Despite Aria's inappropriately emotional carryings-on about the woman's boyfriend, Laurie couldn't help but be pleased something had caught her attention. "First, you must keep me fully apprised of what you're doing and what you're learning on a concurrent basis. I need this for a variety of reasons but mostly because I am responsible for the death certificate, so be sure to leave me your number so I can get in touch if need be. And second, you do your investigative work under the supervision of our MLI who is already involved with the case. His name is David Goldberg, and he has legal clearance to investigate. As a pathology resident rotating through the OCME, you don't. Is this all understood and agreed to?"

"I suppose," Aria said without a lot of enthusiasm about being forced into a collaboration. She couldn't have cared less whether she had legal clearance. If the boyfriend had been the one who'd found the body, she wouldn't have been so suspicious.

"Those are the stipulations," Laurie said. "Can I get a more definitive reply than 'I suppose'?"

"All right, whatever you say," Aria answered.

"And there is another restraint you have to be aware

of," Laurie said. "Because of HIPAA there are restrictions about the patient's pregnancy until fifty years after the individual's death. It's privileged information. I want to be sure you understand. We will not be telling the family even though it will be part of the autopsy record, which the next of kin can request."

"Yeah, yeah, I know," Aria said.

"Okay, good," Laurie responded. "Let's do the neck and the brain quickly and finish up."

The rest of the case went rapidly, with no more surprises. There was no cerebral edema or swelling of the brain. Laurie continued to be impressed with Aria's technical skills even if she found the woman's personality a hard pill to swallow. Toward the very end of the autopsy, Laurie began to sense that Aria was becoming progressively eager to leave and seemed to be rushing, which was a recipe for disaster. Thoughtful and careful progress during the autopsy was the way to avoid accidents like cuts or puncture wounds with instruments. When Laurie mentioned it, Aria dismissed her concern by saying she was always careful.

As Aria was finishing the final labeling of the specimen jars, Laurie snapped off her gloves and said: "Well done, Dr. Nichols. That was a terrific forensic autopsy, and I'm impressed with your technical skills. Now, before you dictate the case, I'd like you to help Marvin clean up and get the body into the cooler. As for me, I need to get up to my office."

"Sorry, but I don't have time," Aria said. She imitated

Laurie by snapping off her own gloves, but unlike Laurie, she tossed them on top of the closed corpse.

"What did you say?" Laurie asked, even though she had clearly heard.

"I said I don't have time," Aria repeated. She was already walking away from the table, heading to the door to the hall. Calling out over her shoulder, she added, "Besides, it's not my job. And I want to see if I can catch David Goldberg before he leaves for the day."

Dumbfounded, Laurie watched the swinging doors that led to the hall close after Aria had passed through. Laurie shook her head in disbelief at Aria's insouciance.

"I'll give you a hand," Laurie said, turning back to Marvin, who'd overheard the exchange.

"It's okay, Dr. Montgomery," Marvin said. "I'm sure you have better things to do. And Vinnie's here. He'll help me get the body on a gurney."

"Are you sure?" Laurie said. In the past she'd always made it a point to help after autopsies.

"No problem," Marvin said.

"I'm sorry about Dr. Nichols's behavior," Laurie said. "Any kind of discrimination, gender or otherwise, has no place here at the OCME and won't be tolerated."

"She's something else," Marvin said, as he gathered up all the specimen jars to take them out of the autopsy room. "I wasn't all that surprised. I'd heard a few of the guys have had run-ins with her."

Although Laurie was eager to get up to her office, she took the time to detour over to Jack's table. Her morbid curiosity had gotten the better of her. The toddler's body, empty of its organs, lay prone on its shiny stainless steel surface. As efficient as Jack was, he, too, was essentially done with his case even though he'd started well after Laurie's.

"Chet's favorite resident sounds like a real pistol with a mind of her own," Jack said.

"You have no idea," Laurie said. "She's one of the most unlikable residents I've ever met. Apparently, she's not fond of men, or so she said to Marvin. But enough about her for the moment. What did you find on your case?"

"He found just what I feared," Lou said. He was still at Jack's table, staying until the bitter end. "It wasn't an accident that this poor kid fell into a tub of scalding water as we were told."

"That's for sure," Jack said. "There are third-degree burns over most of the child's body except for the ankles and the feet. She didn't fall in, but rather she was held by the ankles and thrust in headfirst."

"Good God," she said. She shuddered. One of the difficult aspects of forensic pathology was having to be a witness to some horrific examples of human beings' capacity for inhumanity.

"I couldn't help but notice your resident helper beat it out of here," Jack said. "Come on, fill us in! What's the story?"

"We'll talk about it later," Laurie said. Vinnie had returned with the gurney, and she preferred her impressions of Aria Nichols not be common knowledge. "Now

I have to get up to my office. I'm certain I'll have a slew of phone calls to return. What time are you going to head home?"

"As soon as possible," Jack said. "I'm psyched. Both Warren and Flash texted me they're going to be out on the basketball court tonight."

"That's unfortunate," Laurie said, half in jest. Now that the weather was improving, Jack was back to playing pickup basketball much more often than she would have liked. She was always fearful he'd injure himself as he'd done a few times in the past. "I'll try to get home as soon as I can. We need to talk about a number of things, so don't stay out there on the court too long. And don't get hurt!"

"Aye, aye, Captain," he said, and mock-saluted.

CHAPTER 8

May 8th
5:35 P.M.

As Laurie expected, Cheryl had departed for home but not before leaving a carefully written note of all the calls that had come in while Laurie was down in the pit. Sitting at her desk, she scanned the list. Two of the calls concerned the Health Committee meeting that morning, and one of those was from the City Council member from the Bronx. Remembering it was well after five P.M., she decided to put that call off until the morning. Not only was it after business hours, she guessed it probably involved more complaints about the closure of the Bronx morgue.

Several of the other calls Laurie felt she couldn't put off, especially the one to Twyla Robinson, chief of staff, about several employees who Twyla intended to terminate. Laurie had made a point with all department heads that she wanted to be notified prior to all termination proceedings. As it turned out, Twyla had more than enough reason to fire the individuals involved and had actually acted with great restraint. Laurie gave her approval without reservation.

With the required calls out of the way, Laurie searched for Dr. Carl Henderson's number. At the time she'd written it down, she thought the chances of her needing it were slim. But since there had been something out of the ordinary found at Kera Jacobsen's autopsy, she thought it would be appropriate to let him know as she had promised. She also thought she might ask a few questions about Aria Nichols, as she still wasn't sure how she was going to deal with the problematic resident even though she felt somewhat positive about the woman's renewed interest in forensics. After searching in vain in her center drawer, she found the number right on top, tucked into the corner of the desk blotter pad.

As the call went through, Laurie pictured the man from the few times she had seen him at New York University functions that she had been required to attend. On one occasion after Dr. Henderson had been recently hired following an extensive search, she'd been formally introduced by the dean of the NYU Medical School, and she remembered him as having light-brown hair, and being slender, tanned, and unapologetically dapper. But even more than his appearance, she remembered him as gregarious, humorous, and quick-witted. In short, she had been impressed.

"Carl Henderson here," he said in the baritone voice

Laurie clearly remembered from speaking with him earlier. His faintly upper-crust accent reminded her of her
father, Sheldon.

"I'm sorry to bother you," she said. It was approaching six P.M., and she knew that many people had already
started their evening activities by that time. She could
imagine him at an elegant, old-world New York club enjoying a cocktail.

"Absolutely no bother, Dr. Montgomery," Carl said,
recognizing her voice. "I'm glad to hear from you, but I
hope this isn't because there was something out of the
ordinary found during the autopsy of Miss Jacobsen."

"I'm afraid there was," Laurie said. "But not terribly
out of the ordinary. It was more of a surprise than anything. Kera Jacobsen was about ten weeks pregnant."

"Oh, no," he said with obvious distress. "That makes
it a double tragedy."

"That is exactly what I said when we found the embryo or fetus," Laurie said.

"It also makes it more important to keep the media
from knowing about the case," Carl said. "That's the
kind of lurid detail the tabloids thrive on. They'd hype it
up big-time."

"I suppose you're right," she said.

"Anything else of note?" he asked. "I'm assuming it
was a typical overdose."

"Seemed reasonably typical," Laurie said. "There was
a very positive rapid screen for fentanyl, which we're unfortunately seeing in far too many of the overdose cases.
The only other somewhat surprising thing was that there

wasn't as much pulmonary edema as usual. It will be interesting to get the toxicology results and see what the blood concentration of fentanyl is. My guess is that it's going to be sky high, meaning it depressed the patient's breathing very rapidly instead of over time like usual. Your resident raised the possibility of a cardiac channelopathy being involved, which is an interesting idea but probably not the case. But we'll rule it out. It's one of the benefits that the OCME has perhaps the best forensic DNA lab in the world."

"That answers my next question," he said. "I was going to ask if you did the case with Dr. Nichols as you suggested earlier?"

"I did indeed," Laurie said.

"Is it normal for the chief medical examiner to do a case with an anatomical pathology resident?"

"No, it isn't," she admitted. "Far from it, and thank you for noticing. When you called earlier, I was tempted to ask you about this particular resident. It had been brought to my attention by our director of education that Dr. Nichols wasn't taking her rotation over here seriously. There was also a question about her attitude. I wanted to see for myself, so I had already scheduled to work with her."

"That's a very generous way to put it," Carl said with a short laugh. "I've had more than a question about her attitude. She's been one of the most disruptive residents I've had to deal with. Actually, it's been Dr. Zubin, our residency program director, who has had to deal with her, but he keeps me up to speed. She's not a team player.

In fact, she's rather antisocial and is not popular among her fellow residents. But, on the other hand, she's extraordinarily bright, and a few of our attendings think she is the best resident they've come across. I've been told that her skills with surgical pathology are exceptional. It's like she has a sixth sense."

"She certainly isn't social," Laurie said, remembering some of Aria's comments, particularly to Marvin. "She freely admitted to me that she does not like men or patients. With that kind of attitude, it makes me wonder how she managed to get into medical school or get a residency here at NYU."

"I wondered the same thing," he said. "When I went back and read the interviews in her application, I got the impression that my predecessor thought she'd be particularly sensitive to patients' needs from having suffered through a difficult childhood. I think she managed to turn her history to her advantage."

"I'm not surprised," she said. "She's obviously smart and clearly manipulative."

"Smart or not, I'm not sure I would have voted for her. Needless to say, she was accepted into the program prior to my becoming the head of the department."

"Personality notwithstanding, I do have to give her credit where credit is due. She's hardly likable, but she did a superb forensic autopsy today, so my reservations in her technical abilities have been lessened. It's amazing how much basic forensics she's apparently picked up from just observing a few cases over a little more than a week. And the finding of the unknown pregnancy seems to have kindled at least some interest in the field. I've gotten the impression she's seriously committed to following up on this particular case. It seems almost like she's emotionally invested, which is what happened to me on my first forensic autopsy."

"Well, that's encouraging," Carl said. "Maybe some good will come from this double tragedy."

"It would be nice to believe," Laurie said.

"I personally want to thank you for all your help in this affair," he said. "And I assume any investigating she does will be under your close mentorship."

"Completely," she said. "Although I let her do the autopsy, I was there for the entire procedure and would have intervened if necessary. Legally the case is mine, and when the death certificate is filled out, it will be my signature on it. I specifically told her that she has to keep me informed of any and all progress as it happens, and she has to do it in close conjunction with one of our medical-legal investigators."

"Perfect," Carl said. "And can I ask you to keep me updated as well? Also, I would like as much input about this resident as I can get, particularly favorable information like you are suggesting. After all, ultimately it will be up to me whether she is certified as a board eligible pathologist."

"I'll be happy to keep you updated," Laurie said. As she hung up the phone, she only hoped she'd be able to send favorable reports—with Aria, she was quickly learning, one just never knew.

CHAPTER 9

Flashing her temporary OCME card for the guard manning the front desk, Aria pushed through the turnstile at the relatively new OCME forensic science high-rise at 421 East 26th Street. Compared with the old OCME Forensic Pathology building up the street at 520 First Avenue, it was akin to being in a different universe. To Aria it was new, modern, and cold compared with being old, dilapidated, and cold.

She had been given a tour of this impressive structure on her first day of her OCME rotation, so she knew where she was going and how to get there. The medical-legal investigator team occupied a spacious area on the fifth floor immediately adjacent to the bank of elevators.

When the elevator door opened, Aria was greeted by David Goldberg holding open the door separating the glass-enclosed elevator lobby from the MLI common office. He was short, shorter than Aria's five-six, and appeared mildly overweight, with rounded facial features, moderately long brown hair, sleepy eyes, and a heavy five-o'clock shadow. His clothes consisted of a white shirt open at the collar, a loosened dark tie, and a brown, baggy corduroy jacket. On his head was a black-and-white yarmulke held in place with a hair clip. Aria guessed he was somewhere in his thirties and had not been captain of the football team in high school.

"Dr. Nichols?" David asked.

"No other," Aria said.

"Welcome," he said as he gestured for her to step out of the elevator lobby. "My desk is over yonder a bit beyond the pale." He chuckled at his own humor as he pointed to one of the desks against the far wall, one with a lamp illuminated despite the overhead fluorescent lighting. The room was a sea of identical metal desks, each with a chair on casters. Some were neat while others were messy, reflecting their occupants. Only a few were occupied with people working. Aria guessed the evening shift had begun.

Leading the way, David took Aria to his desk, which he had seemingly partially organized as there was a clear corner on its surface. His definitely belonged in the messy category. Next to the cleared-off corner was a straight-backed metal chair, obviously for her benefit.

"Please." David gestured for her to take a seat. He sat down in his own chair and pulled himself in to the desk. "So, you're a pathology resident with the OCME for a month, and you are interested in the Kera Jacobsen case."

"That's my story," Aria said.

"How can I help you?"

"I read your MLI report," she said. "There is something missing."

"Something missing?" he questioned with a hint of offense. "I don't think there's anything missing. What exactly do you mean?"

"I've been warned about who I can tell this to, but I assume you are legally in the loop. There was a surprise finding at the autopsy. The woman was ten weeks pregnant, give or take a week. That means around the first of March there had been some hanky-panky going on, which I have to assume was consensual. Nothing in your report talks about a boyfriend or lover."

"No one said anything about a boyfriend," David said defensively.

"Did you ask?"

"I don't remember," he said. "Possibly. Wait, the mother might have mentioned something. Let me look at my notes."

After clearing off his keyboard, David brought up the Kera Jacobsen case on his monitor.

"Okay, here we go. I remember speaking with the mother and a younger sister, both of whom had no idea Kera was using drugs. When I asked them if Kera had experienced any emotional problems or physical pain that might account for the drug use, they both told me no. But then the mother admitted that Kera had broken up with a long-term boyfriend over the summer, though she added that Kera had taken it in stride, using it as an excuse to move to New York, which had been a childhood dream. The mother did say that Kera sounded a bit down on the phone over the last few weeks and just a few days ago, for the first time, talked about possibly moving back to Southern California. She said this took her completely by surprise. But other than that, the mother thought she was a happy, well-adjusted woman who was enjoying New York."

"Did you get this long-term boyfriend's name?" Aria asked. She knew from experience that old boyfriends could be like a bad penny and turn up when not expected. In her senior year at Princeton, she thought she had fallen in love with a fellow student named Brian Higgins. It was the first time, and turned out to be the last. When things had advanced to the brink of being consummated, she interrupted their lovemaking to make sure he understood that it might not be the best time for what they were doing since she was smack-dab in the middle of her cycle. Brian's response was that there was never a bad time to make love with the right person. Unfortunately, that turned out to be false on both counts. Not only did she get pregnant, but he denied responsibility, claiming there was no way he could be the father, and if he was, she had seduced him against his will. Then, a year later, when she was in Boston in her first year of medical school and he in law school, he showed up, tail between his legs, hoping to patch things up. Aria had told him, appropriately enough, to go fuck himself.

"Yes, his name is Robert Barlow," David said. "He's a fourth-year medical student doing a sub-internship at Ronald Reagan UCLA Medical Center."

"Okay, that lets him off the hook," Aria said. She had a good idea of what surgical sub-internships were like since she had made the mistake of doing one. "What about this more recent depressive episode? Any clarification on that?"

"As far as they knew, it was only that Kera was homesick. I sensed from the mother that she was a homebody and very close to both the mother and the high-school-aged sister, who still lived at home. You'll be able to check all this out yourself. The mother is on her way and will be here tomorrow."

"What about this Madison Bryant, who was also mentioned in the report?" Aria asked.

"What about her?"

"You described her as a friend and coworker," she said. "Did you get the impression they were good friends or more like acquaintances?"

"Close friends was my take," he said. "At the same time, she said that since the holidays they hadn't seen as much of each other as they had during the fall. Miss Bryant's sense was that Kera was struggling with New York winter weather and preferred to stay in her warm apartment."

"Did you ask her about Kera having any current boyfriends?" Aria said.

"I didn't, but one of the patrolmen said he did prior to getting the apartment door open. The answer was no."

"I guess you have investigated quite a few overdose cases," she said.

"Tons," he said. "We average about four a day, meaning one every six hours or so, twenty-four-seven, and I get my share."

"Was there anything about this case that made it different from the usual?"

He stared off into the middle distance for a beat and then said: "Not really, but we don't see cases where the syringe is still in the vein all that often, although it does happen, especially now that fentanyl has become so prevalent. The other thing I noticed was that she had quite a lot of drug available, meaning a full sack. My guess was that she'd gotten a recent delivery. That started me thinking that maybe the batch had a lot more fentanyl than she expected. We've seen that problem before, where the drug user assumes the new stuff is the same as the last batch. We'll get a better idea if this played a role when the toxicology report comes back."

Suddenly Aria's phone sounded, indicating she had just gotten a text message. "Hang on," she said as she got her phone out to look at the screen: Dr. Nichols, please give me a call as soon as possible. I need to see you. It's urgent. Dr. Henderson.

"Now that's big-time weird," Aria said. It was her turn to stare off for a moment. She'd never gotten a text from the chief of the NYU Department of Pathology before, nor could she remember even speaking with him.

"Excuse me?" David said.

"Sorry," she said, returning to the present. "Something has come up so we need to wrap this up for now. What I'd like is Madison Bryant's contact information."

"I'm not sure I should provide that information." David knitted his brows as he turned to look off toward Bart Arnold's desk for help. Bart was head of the MLIs, but his desk was vacant. It was obvious he had already left.

"Listen to me, Mr. Goldberg. I'm looking into the case under the direct orders of the chief medical examiner, Dr. Laurie Montgomery. You are to supply me with all the help I need, or you will be hearing directly from her. Do I make myself clear?" Aria was never troubled by exaggeration or white lies.

"Of course," David said. He turned back to his monitor to get the information. While he was writing the address and phone numbers, Aria asked another question.

"Did you manage to talk to any of Kera Jacobsen's neighbors?"

"Yes, I spoke with the woman who lives in apartment 4A, across from Kera Jacobsen's 4B. Their entrance doors face each other. Her name is Evelyn Mabry. I remember because her surname is the same as my mother's maiden name. She apparently was the last person to see Kera Jacobsen alive, which, by the way, is the best way of determining the time of death, contrary to all the forensic TV shows."

"And when was that?" Aria asked.

"Friday late afternoon."

"Did you get the feeling this Evelyn Mabry was good friends with Kera Jacobsen?"

"Not at all," David said. "My impression of Miss Mabry

is that she's a mildly paranoid recluse and a hoarder. There was barely room to stand in her apartment."

Aria could understand the recluse part but not the paranoia or hoarding. "Did you ask Evelyn Mabry about whether Kera Jacobsen had many visitors, particularly boyfriends?"

"I was thinking more about possible drug dealers, not boyfriends, but yes, I did ask her. She said that in the past Miss Jacobsen had late-night visitors once or twice a week, usually midweek, but that had dropped off of late."

"Men or women?"

"She couldn't say for certain because she never saw them, just heard them arrive and occasionally heard them leave."

"What about Friday night?" Aria asked. "Did you ask her if Miss Jacobsen had any visitors then?"

"Of course I asked her about Friday night," David said with mild offense. "She said she went to bed early and didn't hear anything."

"Do you expect the police to be doing any investigation?"

"I don't," he said. "The precinct's detective squad wasn't even notified. What's to investigate?"

Plenty, she thought, but didn't say.

"Listen," David said. "The police don't want to make work for themselves, especially with all these overdoses that we're seeing. Just notifying the detectives means a lot of paperwork. You have no idea." He handed her a three-by-five card. She took it but then immediately handed it back.

"Dr. Montgomery says we have to do this investigation in tandem," she said, purposefully avoiding the word *supervision*. She had no intention of being supervised by anyone, much less by a physician assistant, yet she knew how to make it look like she had. "How about your number along with the names and contact info for the cops that took the nine-one-one call. And what's Kera Jacobsen's address?"

He added the additional information to the card.

"All right," Aria said, taking the card and standing. "I'll be in touch."

David started to respond, but she was already weaving through the gaggle of desks on her way to the elevator.

CHAPTER 10

May 8th
6:42 P.M.

Aria walked north along the east side of First Avenue, passing the famed and busy Bellevue Hospital on her right. Although it was almost seven P.M., sunset wouldn't come for an hour or so. Despite wearing only a cotton blouse, her favorite pair of jeans, and her resident jacket, Aria wasn't cold in the slightest although she knew things would change after the sun went down. Overhead, the sky was shockingly clear with only a few puffy clouds. To her right, the tops of the tall buildings were bathed in a golden glow of late-afternoon sun.

As soon as she had exited the OCME high-rise, Aria had placed the call to Dr. Henderson as he had requested in his text. As she did so, she had felt her pulse mildly quicken. It was rarely a good sign to be contacted by the front office, particularly after hours. Adding to her unease, she'd never had any dealings with the head of Pathology despite lots of dicey run-ins with the director of the pathology residency program, Dr. Gerald Zubin. Aria was well aware she was not considered a team player and accordingly had been continually balanced on a knife edge from the first days of her residency. Right out of the gate she'd bucked the system by refusing to do tasks dictated mostly by men and only because that was the way it had always been done. Her argument was that rules had to make sense. Even more disruptive, she'd made it a point to do as little scut work as possible, particularly during that first year of residency, when a lot of nonsense trickled down to those on the lower rungs of the totem pole as a kind of hazing. Yet through it all, here she was, poised to make it to her final year of residency in a little more than a month, provided the chief of the Pathology Department hadn't been looking for her to try and suggest otherwise. Still, she was confident she could handle just about anything at this point, since she had proved she was significantly smarter than most of the male authority figures occupying the front office.

Although she'd been a tad anxious when the chief of the department had answered the call, the anxiety had quickly evaporated as his tone was congenial from the get-go and the conversation turned out to be remarkably benign. Instead of him being pissed that she'd violated some old, senseless rule or tradition of academic medicine like not taking the Forensic Pathology rotation seriously, he'd been surprisingly gracious, even indulging in a little small talk about how nice the weather was before getting to the reason for the call. "I would very much like to talk with you, preferably right now if you are available," he'd said. Asking to see her right away was mildly ominous, but his tone wasn't accusatory and in truth she was more curious than concerned.

As she passed the old, squat, and crumbling OCME Forensic Pathology building on the corner of 30th Street, she thought about the conversation she'd just had with David Goldberg. She'd not learned much, but what she had learned supported her intuition that the unknown father certainly needed to be found to learn of his possible role in the fatal dose of illicit drugs. She had almost laughed that afternoon at Dr. Montgomery's flowery paean of forensic pathology as "listening to the dead tell their stories." It was so hokey. Yet now, Aria had to admit that Kera Jacobsen seemed to be communicating with her on some level via the mother's describing Kera as being recently "down," and through the neighbor who said that Kera had been having late-night visitors once or twice a week. All this meant there was covert sex going on, meaning one of the couple or both didn't want their liaison to be public knowledge, which was mildly suspicious in and of itself, and that the potential arrival of a little one didn't bring joy to one or both of the participants. From Aria's experience, it had to be the mysterious father who was less than enthused, ergo the tragic outcome.

Just beyond the OCME building loomed the multi-block New York University Medical Center. Cars were backed up while attempting to get into the parking garage. Aria had to squeeze through the waiting autos to continue north until she could enter the building that housed the Department of Pathology. Although she'd never been in Dr. Henderson's office, she was familiar with its location since it was down the hall from the director of the pathology residency program's office, where she'd been called on the carpet on far too many occasions.

As soon as she stepped off the elevator, it was apparent that most everyone in the department had left for the day. The only people present were two of the medical center's janitors busily vacuuming the wall-to-wall carpeting and who ignored her as she passed. Dr. Henderson's private, corner office was down at the far end. The door to the inner office was open. Aria walked in without bothering to announce herself. Rules of etiquette and kowtowing to supposed superiors were not of her concern. Thanks to her fashionable spring-inspired pink leather sneakers, she didn't make a sound.

Pausing just inside the door with the realization she'd not been seen, Aria took the time to glance around at the office's interior. It didn't give her a good feeling as it reminded her of her father's home office in their Greenwich, Connecticut, mansion overlooking the Long Island Sound. For her the décor had the same hackneyed male ambiance, with its dark wood, lots of books supposedly attesting to intellectual and cultural prowess, and framed photos of the occupant indulging in various sports or posing with celebrities. There was even a signed football in a Plexiglas case to complete the similarities.

Still unnoticed, Aria directed her attention to the chief's profile. He was sitting at his desk staring intently at his monitor, which was angled away such that she could see the screen. Although she had never spoken to the man in person, she'd seen him at a multitude of departmental functions. As a resident she was required to attend a bewildering number of conferences, seminars, case presentations, and meetings of all types, and the chief came to a fair number of them, often eloquently introducing the various speakers, especially the famous doctors or researchers from particularly prestigious institutions. He was always dressed in a long, shockingly white and highly starched doctor's coat over a wrinkle-free white shirt with a carefully knotted, brightly colored—but usually pink—tie. As a mild clotheshorse herself, Aria appreciated this aspect of the man's persona. At the same time, she couldn't help but see him as the entitled, chauvinistic male authority figure that he undoubtedly was, and for that Aria was on guard despite his graciousness on the phone.

Moving closer, she was a bit surprised she'd not been seen or even heard. She imagined it had something to do with the hypnotic sound of the vacuum cleaners drifting in through the open door, progressively getting louder, suggesting the janitors were approaching this end of the floor.

Reaching the desk and still undiscovered, she was suddenly seized by a mildly devilish way of making her presence known. With the flat of her palm, she reached out and slapped the surface of the desk several times in a row.

The result was almost as comical as it was predictable. The man leaped to his feet with such suddenness that his desk chair tipped over backward. Aria did all she could do to keep from smiling.

"My God," Carl said while pressing his palm against his chest. "You scared the daylights out of me."

"I'm so sorry, Dr. Henderson. I called out several times but couldn't get your attention," she lied, while laughing inwardly.

Carl righted his chair. For a moment he seemed mildly addled and stared at her as if trying to recover. Aria noticed he somehow managed to look as fresh as if he'd just put on his shirt and tied his tie. She also noticed he wore cuff links, which was not common for a doctor in her professional experience.

"Ummm, let's see! Can I get you something? Coffee? A soft drink?"

"I'm fine," Aria said. "Actually, Dr. Henderson, I'm a little busy. On the phone you suggested there was something you wanted to talk to me about immediately. Maybe you could just tell me what it is, so we can both go about our business."

"Of course. But please, call me Carl."

"If you'd like," she said, but her guard went up a notch with the implied and questionable familiarity.

"I would like," he said, regaining his usual poise. "I'm sorry that you and I have never met on a personal basis and hope that can be changed in the near future. I've tried to make it a point to personally meet everyone who is part of our Pathology team over these past two years.

To that end, my wife, Tamara, and I have been inviting the staff over to our home in New Jersey for dinner, and we're just now getting to do the same with the residents." He smiled. "Do you mind if I call you Aria?"

"I suppose not," Aria said. She couldn't think of anything she'd like less than to go to the Henderson manse for dinner. She hoped the reason for this impromptu meeting wasn't merely to extend a dinner invitation.

"How about we sit over on the couch," Carl said, pointing across the room to a dark, tufted leather sofa, similar to what Aria's father also had in his study.

"I suppose," she said, even though she wasn't wild about the idea as it added to her unease.

Carl came around his desk, stepped over to the sofa, and gestured for her to sit. As soon as she had, he joined her. She purposefully sat at the very right end of the sofa next to a side table. On the table was a small Eskimo statue carved in black stone. It gave her peace of mind to have a heavy, blunt object within reach if she needed it.

"I have heard quite a bit about you from Dr. Zubin," Carl said as he crossed his legs and folded his arms across his chest.

"Don't believe everything you hear," Aria said.

"The part I want to believe is about your exceptional forte with surgical pathology."

"That's my major interest," she said. "But could you get to the point here? As I said, I'm busy."

"Yes, of course," he said. "First, I'd like to be perfectly open with you."

"That's a start," Aria said. Now that she was sitting

reasonably close to the man, she realized that his projected persona reminded her of her father. It had nothing to do with the similarities of the respective offices nor their personal appearances, but rather it was a sense of male cockiness that she despised. The self-satisfied way he had his arms folded was exactly a posture her father would often assume before giving her unwanted advice, and it rubbed Aria the wrong way. She had to resist standing up and walking out.

"First, I want you to know I spoke with Dr. Montgomery twice today. On one of the calls, I'm sorry to say, she implied that your attitude and performance at the OCME had not been up to standard. Are you surprised to hear that?"

"Not at all," Aria said. "I was open with her. I told her I felt I was wasting my time at the OCME. Forensic Pathology should be an elective, not a requirement. In just a few days over there, I believed I had gotten all that I wanted or needed, so I chose to come back over here in the afternoons to go over the day's surgical pathology cases. The OCME's director of education had the nerve to follow me back here one day and bawl me out, the creep."

"That's unfortunate," Carl said. "But Dr. Montgomery also had some good things to say. She told me that she did a case with you this afternoon and was extremely complimentary about how you handled it."

"It wasn't difficult," Aria said. "And in my experience, forensic autopsies are a hell of a lot easier than clinical autopsies. But then again, I haven't done any gunshot wounds yet, which I'm told can be a bear."

"She also mentioned that there was a surprise finding," Carl said. "The patient was about ten weeks pregnant."

"That's correct," she said. The sound of the vacuum cleaners through the open door reached a crescendo and then began to fall off.

"Dr. Montgomery also said that this finding seems to have turned your attitude about forensics around a hundred and eighty degrees. She told me that you are seriously committed to look into it almost on an emotional level."

"She said that? 'On an emotional level'?"

"Yes, she did," Carl said. "And this is why I felt I needed to talk with you. The president and CEO of the hospital, Vernon Pierce, and I are concerned about this case, as is the dean. You do know that the patient, Kera Jacobsen, was part of our NYU Medical Center family?"

"Yes, I'm aware," Aria said.

"And I assume you are aware that our community has made a big commitment to doing whatever we can to stop this opioid overdose scourge."

"I suppose," she said. From her perspective it was more lip service than commitment.

"Even before knowing about the pregnancy, we were concerned enough to offer to do the autopsy here in our theater to make sure that it doesn't become fodder for the city's tabloids. As you undoubtedly know, they love this kind of lurid stuff because it sells papers and encourages conspiracy theories in an age when conspiracy theories are in vogue. If this story does come out in the tabloids, it could put the medical center in a very bad light and negate advertising efforts we've been making over the last couple of years. Are you aware that on occasion privileged information has leaked out of the OCME?"

"I suppose," Aria repeated yet again. She'd gotten the message that NYU was concerned about publicity and wondered why Carl was beating a dead horse. It wasn't rocket science.

"What is it about this case that has caught your interest? I mean, I'm glad you're suddenly taking advantage of the fabulous experience the NYC OCME affords our residents, but why has it been this case particularly? Vernon Pierce asked me to ask you. He's even more afraid this unfortunate overdose of one of our own will turn into a publicity nightmare than I."

She started to respond, but he interrupted her by saying: "I should warn you that Mr. Pierce might be contacting you directly, so you should be prepared. Have you ever met him?"

"No, I haven't," Aria said. Nor did she want to, but it certainly begged the question of why the hospital president would be so concerned about the passing of one social worker out of the thousands of people who worked in the medical center.

"Well, he might call. He even went so far as to ask me for your number. As you can imagine, he's also taken an interest in this social worker's death for obvious reasons,"

Carl said. "Sorry to interrupt earlier! What were you about to say?"

"Regardless of possible publicity implications, I think the father has to be found," Aria said with rising anger. "The goal of forensics is to determine the manner and cause of death. Because of the opioid crisis, it's natural to think that the cause of Kera's death was a drug overdose, particularly an overdose of fentanyl. And fentanyl was already found on a rapid test of the drugs found at the scene. Yet there was little or no pulmonary edema at autopsy, which is, as I understand it, always found with a fentanyl overdose. There was also no scarring on Kera's arms that would indicate a long-term drug problem. In fact, before we stumbled onto the fetus, I was thinking of a channelopathy as the cause of death, even if it wasn't related to fentanyl. I mean, is there an association with fentanyl and exacerbation of a channelopathy?"

"I have no idea," he said. "I'm not sure if anyone would know the answer to that."

"So, the cause of death in my mind is up in the air," she said. "And now let's think about the manner of death. Obviously, there's a knee-jerk reaction to calling an opioid death accidental. Most drug users don't want to kill themselves, which is why overdoses are labeled accidental. But with Kera I'm not so sure I'm willing to jump on the accidental bandwagon. Here was an unmarried, educated woman having a covert love affair. Why the need for the big secrecy? In all likelihood it was the father who insisted on keeping the relationship hushed up. It just stands to reason. If that is the case, and I believe it is, why wasn't Kera's body found earlier than it was? To me, that's not a rhetorical question. Why didn't the boyfriend find the body instead of letting it rot for two or three days?"

"Are you asking me?" Carl questioned. He was clearly impressed with her line of reasoning. After being at the OCME for just over a week she was sounding like an experienced forensic pathologist.

"What I'm doing is asking myself," Aria said. "How was this unknown boyfriend involved in this drug overdose? Did he supply the drugs? Did he participate in some way? I think these are reasonable questions because maybe Kera's death wasn't accidental. Hell, it could have been homicide."

"You've convinced me," Carl said without hesitation. "Wow! It sounds to me that you are getting a lot more out of your forensic rotation than most pathology residents, myself included. Now you have me personally engrossed in the case, whereas before I just wanted it to go away. However, it also makes it even more imperative for you to keep it all close to your chest and tell no one of your suspicions and progress except, of course, Dr. Montgomery. She told me on the phone that she asked you to keep her informed of what you're up to. I'd like you to do the same for me since I'll need to keep Vernon Pierce up to speed. If your worst fears are realized, this case could be a true publicity nightmare for the medical center, and I'd like to be able to brief the head of our publicity department as well as the president before the press gets wind of it. If it turns out this overdose wasn't accidental, there is no way to keep the press from becoming involved."

"That's probably true," Aria said.

"So, your current goal is to try to find the father."

"Yes," she said.

"How are you going to do that?"

"I'm going to start by talking to the coworker who found the body."

"Who was that?" he asked.

"A social worker named Madison Bryant. The medical-legal investigator on the case said that she and Kera Jacobsen were close friends. My hope is that she'll know something that could be key."

"When do you intend to talk to her?"

"Whenever works," she said. "I'll see if she's available tomorrow. If not, then the next day." She shrugged.

"I'm glad you are involved in this case, Dr. Nichols," Carl said. "Good luck!"

"Okay," Aria said. She stood. "I'll be happy to keep you and Dr. Montgomery informed of any progress. And I understand the publicity issue."

"And I'll try to find out if anything is known about any association between cardiac channelopathies and fentanyl," Carl said. He got to his feet as well. "If I do, I'll let you know right away."

"Whatever," she said. "I'll be in touch."

"And I'll be looking forward to hearing from you," Carl said.

She hustled down the center of the empty office. The janitors had departed and most of the lights had been switched off. As she waited at the elevators appreciating the silence, she thought back over the short meeting with Dr. Henderson and tried to get past her reflexive dislike of male authority figures. Although a tad weird, the tête-à-tête hadn't been all that unpleasant. To her the most unusual bit of information was the surprising interest of the medical center's CEO, Vernon Pierce. Then she remembered telling Dr. Henderson that she wanted to start trying to find Kera's lover by talking with Madison Bryant tomorrow, yet the more she thought about that idea, the less possible she thought it might be. As a hospital social worker, Madison Bryant most likely would be booked the whole day. Although it was late, Aria suddenly thought it reasonable to give the woman a try and see if she might be available that evening. After fumbling in both side pockets of her white coat, she got out the index card from David Goldberg. Then she took out her phone and punched in Madison Bryant's number, hoping the woman would be available.

CHAPTER 11

When Laurie slid out of the back of the Uber in front of their house on 106th Street, she felt more tired mentally and physically than she could ever remember. So far it had been a fourteen-hour day without a lunch break. The only time she had slowed down was during the MRI, when she had to lie still for an hour. And the day wasn't over yet. She still had to talk with Jack about two things in particular, as decisions had to be made. The most troubling from her perspective was the disastrous positive breast-cancer screening result. She had been tempted to at least broach the issue with him when he'd popped into her office while she'd been on the phone with the chief of Pathology, but she didn't, thinking there wasn't enough time to do it justice. Besides, her mind was in total turmoil, with lots of denial about the situation. The other issue she had to bring up before passing out from exhaustion was the need to get the whole story of his apparently disastrous visit to the Brooks School that morning. In retrospect, she wondered what she had been thinking by asking him to go in her stead. Jack had a lot of good qualities, but discretion and impulse control weren't among them when it came to a medical issue he cared about. She knew full well that the current indiscriminate prescribing of Adderall was a hot-button issue for him, right up there with vaccination conspiracists. He'd done multiple autopsies on kids who had died because of both problems.

Pausing on the top step of the granite stoop, Laurie turned around to look across the street. From that vantage point she had a good view of the outdoor basketball court that was part of the small neighborhood park that also had a few swing sets, sandboxes, and wrought iron park benches. At that hour the sun, which had yet to set, had disappeared behind the buildings to cause dark shadows, and the LED lighting that Jack had paid to have installed over the court was on. From where she was standing, she could see a game was in progress with the shirts and skins alternately sweeping up and down the court, running from one basket to the other. Although she couldn't be certain from that distance, she thought she could pick out Jack, who was one of the players not wearing a shirt despite the temperature being somewhere in the fifties.

Laurie shrugged. Jack's continued playing of street basketball was a passion of his that she didn't share. She just hoped to heaven that he'd eventually see the light and recognize it wasn't worth the risk of serious physical injury, which he'd already experienced, requiring knee surgery. With a sigh, she pushed through the front door of their building and began the three flights up to their apartment. The higher she went, the heavier her legs and her soft-sided briefcase felt. It almost seemed as if the stairs were longer and steeper than usual. She hadn't expected to get home so late, but such was the burden of being the chief of the NYC OCME. That evening, just when she thought she'd wrapped up the calls she had to return after doing the autopsy with Aria Nichols, she'd been informed that one of the new Sprinter Medical Examiner Transport Team vans had been in a serious accident while bringing a corpse back to the morgue. Immediately she'd had to coordinate with Mortuary/Transportation, Legal, Human Resources, and the NYPD. Luckily the OCME drivers were wearing their seat belts, and although hospitalized, were doing well. The same could not be said about the vehicle, and it was lucky that the sole passenger was already dead.

After hanging up her spring jacket in the front hall closet and putting on her slippers, Laurie climbed the flight of stairs leading to the fifth floor. Progressively the family room and the kitchen came into view. It was a peaceful scene with JJ at the table in front of his laptop and Caitlin, their nanny, busy in the kitchen. Every single day Laurie thanked her lucky stars that they had stumbled across Caitlin O'Connell. Without her, life wouldn't have been the same, particularly after Emma's autism diagnosis. There was no way that Laurie could have continued her role as chief medical examiner if it hadn't been for the multitalented Irishwoman.

As Laurie reached the top of the stairs, she could now see and hear that the TV was tuned with low volume to the local PBS station, most likely for Caitlin's benefit. She now could also appreciate that the couch was empty. Laurie's eyes swept the rest of the room. Emma was no-where to be seen and most likely already in bed, pulling on Laurie's heartstrings. Instantly her self-critical mind questioned what kind of mother she was, leaving in the morning before her child was awake and returning when she was already in bed. Laurie knew other women, even those with neurotypical children, struggled with this same issue as it was one of the female burdens in modern society. That recognition didn't make it any easier.

"Hello, everyone," she said with more cheer than she felt. She couldn't help but again find fault with Jack out on the playground, putting himself at risk rather than spending time with his children.

"Hello, Laurie," Caitlin called out in her sweet-sounding Irish brogue. "How was your day?"

"It was interesting," Laurie said in an attempt to be truthful. "Is Emma already in bed?"

"She is indeed," Caitlin said. "Poor thing was exhausted after having to deal with three therapists and Dorothy."

"How did things go today?" Laurie asked. Her mother, Dorothy, in conjunction with the pediatrician and a psychiatrist with a particular interest in the autism spectrum, had employed a board-certified behavior analyst organization that was handling Emma's case.

"I think it went very well," Caitlin said. "Emma happened to have short sessions of behavioral therapy, speech therapy, and physical therapy all in the same day, and she handled it like a champ. Everyone agreed she's definitely making progress."

"Terrific," Laurie said. She was relieved that Emma was responding to the therapies but couldn't help but feel a little guilty that her progress came about because they as a family had the resources to deal with such an issue. The fact that the United States, supposedly the richest country in the world, made money the deciding factor in health care was a moral and ethical travesty from Laurie's perspective.

"Want some dinner?" Caitlin called out as Laurie put her briefcase on the dining room table. JJ hadn't even looked up from his laptop.

"I'll make some pasta and a salad in a little while," Laurie said. Such was the usual weekday routine. Whenever Laurie got home, after interacting with the children, she would make some food for Jack and herself. Sometimes Jack helped, but not all the time, and even less when the weather was good like it was now.

Laurie took the seat next to JJ. She could see he was playing *Minecraft*, his favorite pastime. She watched for a while and, as usual, was impressed with his concentration and his hand-eye coordination. He was building a virtual castle-like structure with blistering speed.

"Aren't you going to say hello to your mother?" Laurie said at length.

"Hi, Mom," he said without taking his eyes off the screen or his hands from the keyboard.

"I assume you already did your homework?"

"Yeah, it was easy," JJ said.

"Maybe you could stop for a minute," Laurie said. "I want to ask you a question."

He rolled his eyes, but he did turn away from his computer to look at her. It was obvious he didn't care for the interruption.

"Your dad stopped into your school this morning," Laurie said. "Did you know that?"

"Yeah, I saw him."

"Before or after he spoke with Miss Rossi?"

"Both."

"Did you talk to him on either occasion?"

"No, we were playing kickball. Besides, he looked mad after he talked to Miss Rossi. His face was all red when he came out and got on his bike. Still, he waved at me, and I waved back."

Uh-oh, Laurie thought. For JJ to notice Jack was angry was saying something serious. Instead she asked: "How did you do today in school?"

"Fine," JJ said.

"Any fights out on the playground?" she asked. Aggression was the main complaint the school had communicated, although they were also concerned about JJ's talking in class, his not following directions, his lack of impulse control, and other symptoms typical of hyperactivity.

"No, no fights," he said.

"You do know that Miss Rossi is concerned about your behavior."

"Yeah, I know," JJ said. "She said if I didn't get better, I might have to go to another school."

Good Lord. That was the first she'd heard of a possible expulsion, which raised the stakes. With everything else going on, she couldn't imagine having to look for a new school for JJ. Instead of responding directly, she asked him if he had any idea why he was fighting and why he was talking so much during class.

"It's Barry Levers's fault," JJ said with conviction. "And people talk to me first."

"Okay, okay," Laurie said. The little she knew about child psychology told her that it was almost a certainty that a boy JJ's age would externalize responsibility as a matter of course. Instead of continuing what would have been a pointless conversation, she asked him if he might show her what he had been building that evening.

"Yeah, sure!" JJ said with great alacrity.

After about a half hour of watching him and *Minecraft* to the point of feeling a little dizzy on top of her exhaustion, she thanked her son, told him she was really impressed with what he had built, and got up from the dining room table. Climbing the stairs up to the top floor, she went into Emma's room to look in at her daughter. She appeared just as angelic as she had that morning.

Returning to the kitchen, Laurie set out to clean and prepare salad makings and throw together a simple pasta dish. JJ was still at his computer. Caitlin had retired to her own room down on the fourth floor, as was her habit once Emma was asleep. Laurie was about to put the pasta into the boiling water when she heard the apartment door close. Jack bounded up the stairs a moment later. He was in his shorts and T-shirt and his light-brown hair, tinged with a touch of gray over his ears, was plastered to his forehead. There were circles of sweat under both arms. He was in a great mood.

"Greetings to all," he said gaily. He tousled JJ's hair, causing him to duck out of his reach without interrupting his play. Jack approached Laurie, but she held up the spoon she was using to stir the pasta to keep him at arm's length.

"You need to shower," Laurie pretended to scold. She didn't have to pretend too hard, given that she was still irked about the time he spent on the court.

"I believe you're right," he responded good-naturedly. "It was a great game tonight. My shots were falling like there was no tomorrow. I couldn't miss."

"I'm happy for you," she said without trying to keep the irony from her voice. "I'll have dinner on the table in fifteen, so make tracks."

It was more like twenty minutes later that the food was ready. Jack had shown up dressed in his normal evening apparel, which consisted of a clean T-shirt and sweatpants. JJ had fled upstairs to his own room to avoid being bothered.

"So, let's hear about Chet's girlfriend resident," Jack said as he helped himself to the pasta.

"I have a couple of things to talk about that take precedent," Laurie said. "First we have to decide what to do about JJ. I feel strongly that we should go ahead and have him professionally evaluated. Not only is it a reasonable idea, but I don't think we have a lot of choice." She went on to tell him what JJ had told her the teacher had said to him after Jack's visit about possibly having to go to another school.

"So, my mini-tantrum supposedly gave Miss Rossi an understanding of why JJ gets into fights on the playground: a chip off the old block."

"I can't imagine that JJ would make something like that up," Laurie said. "You must have really mouthed off."

"I suppose I did," he said. "The whole issue irks me to death. He's just being a normal boy. Hell, I was probably worse if I remember correctly. Boys are competitive with each other. Little scuffles are the norm. I tell you, our child is not going to take Adderall or anything similar. No way."

"But the school is not insisting he take meds," Laurie said. "They just want us to agree to have him professionally evaluated, which I don't have any problem with. Times have changed since you were a kid. Same with me. And having him evaluated is not necessarily going to mean meds are prescribed. We're the parents. It's up to us if drugs are to be used."

"It's the first step in the process," Jack said, but with somewhat less emotion. "The pharmaceutical industry has cleverly hoodwinked an entire generation of people to believe boys need medication so that they can sit still like girls. Just having him evaluated means that we're admitting we think something is wrong with him."

"I disagree," she said. "I'm sorry, but you are being ridiculous. You're starting to sound like one of those conspiracists that you're always railing against. The better we understand him, the better able we'll be to make informed decisions. JJ's school handles conflict very differently than when you and I were in elementary school. And your experience isn't as relevant as you might think. I'm concerned about his impulse control, and I'd like to learn more about it if we can."

"So, you really think I'm off base here?" he said.

"Yes, I do," Laurie said. "We will be having him evaluated to see if a professionally trained person thinks he has an issue that can be addressed in any one of a number of ways. We are not agreeing to drugs. Not by a long shot. I don't think we have much choice. I'm afraid if we refuse, which I don't want to do, JJ might be asked to leave the school, and unless you want to find another school for him on your own, we have to respect their concerns."

"Okay," Jack said, throwing his hands into the air in surrender. "You win. But I have one stipulation. I want the psychiatrist or psychologist who does the evaluating to be a male."

"That's rather sexist," she said.

"Maybe yes, maybe no," he said. "It will just make me feel a bit better that the analyst can understand my point of view. Humor me!"

"All right, fine," Laurie said. She was certain that there were plenty of equally qualified men and women in the field, but if a male therapist made Jaek feel better, she was for it.

"Okay, now let's hear about this resident. What's her name? Nichols?"

"Yes, that's her family name," Laurie said. "Her whole name is Dr. Aria Nichols. But first there's something else we have to discuss. You never asked me about my breast screening today."

"You're right," Jack said. His face fell, and he guiltily put down his fork, giving his full attention to Laurie. "I'm sorry. The visit to the Brooks School this morning got me all out of whack right out of the gate. I've been struggling to get back to some kind of equilibrium all day. Lou's case of the scalded child added to my general muddle. So, what happened at your screening? Or shouldn't I ask?"

"The news wasn't good," Laurie said. She could feel her anxiety ratchet up as the denial she'd been nurturing all day began to crumble. She was able to appreciate Jack's feeling out of sorts, since she'd been struggling to maintain her own equilibrium since she'd had the MRI. Even now, it took her a moment to pull herself together. "Initially the mammogram was fine, but then something was found on the MRI. When they repeated the mammogram and did a diagnostic study in contrast to a screening test, they could see the questionable mass on the X-ray as well. It's a little more than a centimeter, but it is a definite abnormality that has to be evaluated. It's especially important to be looked into because of my status with the BRCA1 gene and since both my mother and grandmother have had breast cancer."

"I'm so sorry," Jack said with obvious alarm. "Oh my gosh! That's awful and frightening news for you to have to bear. And I sincerely apologize again for forgetting you were having your screening today. There is no excuse, although maybe I'm guilty of a bit of denial."

"It's okay," Laurie said. "I had to process the news myself, so I probably wouldn't have wanted to talk about it much. At least we're home now and can think about it relatively rationally. At least I hope so. One of the problems is that it seems so very inconvenient with everything else that is going on with Emma and now this issue with JJ."

"This is super-important no matter what else is happening," he said. "Are there any plans in place for the next step?"

"It's the benefit of being a medical VIP," she said. "The studies have already been looked at by a coterie of radiological higher-ups who all concur the lump is suspicious even though the fact that I have dense breast tissue makes the interpretation more difficult."

"So, it will need to be biopsied," Jack said. "Have you spoken to anyone about it?"

"Absolutely," Laurie said. "They wouldn't let me leave until I had spoken with both a surgeon and an oncologist, both of whom specialize in breast cancer."

"Oh, good Lord," Jack said. For a moment he stared off with unseeing eyes. Ever since his first family had died in a small plane crash after visiting him in Chicago when he was retraining in forensic pathology, he worried that he was somehow a jinx for anyone he loved. The horrid notion had been underscored by JJ's being diagnosed with neuroblastoma as an infant. Then the superstitious fear had come roaring back when Emma started to retrogress and was diagnosed to have autism. Now, it was again returning big-time with the threat of Laurie's having breast cancer.

"Jack, did you hear what I said?" Laurie had reached out to grasp his forearm and give it a squeeze.

"No, sorry," he replied. He refocused his eyes on her, realizing he hadn't heard what she had just added.

"I said that both the surgeon and the oncologist want to schedule a biopsy."

"Yes, of course," Jack said. He shook his head and breathed out through puffed cheeks, sounding like a tire deflating.

"I didn't want to schedule anything until I spoke with you," Laurie continued. "What has to be decided in advance is what should be done if surgical pathology determines it is cancer. At that point it can't be a discussion because I'll be under anesthesia. Of course, if it is cancer, the cell type has to be considered to some degree, as does whether there is any spread to the lymph nodes. But complicating all that is that I have the mutation in my BRCA1 gene. Should I just schedule a mastectomy rather than a biopsy?"

"God," Jack murmured while he cradled his head in his hands for a moment, massaging his temples. When he looked up at Laurie, he added: "I'm sorry, but I'm having trouble processing all this."

"The oncologist and the surgeon both suggested I just have the mastectomy," Laurie went on, ignoring Jack's admission. "But I just don't know how I feel. I know what Angelina Jolie would say: Go for it. But it seems so drastic to me. And then there's the issue about my ovaries. Should I have them removed at the same time because of the danger of ovarian cancer from the same mutation?"

"Honestly, these are questions that only you can answer," he said as he began to get hold of himself. "We had all these discussions back when we first learned you carried the mutation. You were pretty adamant then about avoiding disfiguring surgery."

"That was then, and this is now," she said. "I'm a bit older and we have two children, which we didn't have then. I'm certainly more amenable to the idea now, not that I like it. But do you have a feeling one way or the other?"

"You are a lot more important to me and to our children than your God-given breasts and ovaries," Jack said. "Obviously I'll be ruminating about all this, but if you asked for my opinion right this minute, I'd say go for it. Have the mastectomy and the oophorectomy, and if surgical pathology says there's no cancer in your breast lump then the reconstruction is easier. If it is positive, then the reconstruction is a little more difficult."

"You think I should go ahead and have both breasts removed?" The idea was still an anathema to Laurie.

"I do," Jack said. "That's if you forced me to give my opinion right now. Maybe tomorrow I'll feel differently, but I don't think so."

"As the person in the center of all this, I can tell you one thing that I am absolutely sure of . . ." she said, fighting back tears, "and that is that I don't want to put this off. If I have a cancer smoldering in my breast, I want it out today, not tomorrow."

"I can appreciate that," he said. "I'm sure I would feel the same. I think everybody would feel the same. It's like walking around thinking you have a time bomb ticking away inside your body, ready to explode at any moment."

"Exactly," Laurie said. She closed her eyes tightly and breathed deeply. After getting reasonable control of herself, she added: "Well, I'm glad I brought it up, as hard as it was. Yet just talking about it is helpful. It's been in the back of my mind since the MRI."

"I can only imagine," Jack said. "I can't believe you managed to work all afternoon with that on your mind. How could you concentrate on anything? And how the hell were you able to do that overdose autopsy with Miss Congeniality?"

"Your sarcasm is on the money," she said, managing a mirthless laugh. "It wasn't easy. Dr. Aria Nichols might be the most unappealing resident who has ever rotated through the OCME. At least in my experience."

"I'm amazed," he said, latching on to the change of subject. "That means her behavior, at least to Chet, wasn't just predicated on his making a pass at her."

"I don't think so," Laurie said. "But there is still

room for doubt. According to her, Chet floated the idea that they have a drink sometime when he first met her in his capacity as the director of education at the OCME."

"There you go," Jack said. "So, I wasn't totally off base."

"Maybe not," Laurie said. "And I'm afraid I will have to say something to Chet about making sure his off-hours persona isn't brought in-house. But getting back to Miss Congeniality, she's a strange bird who might even be sociopathic to some degree. She doesn't seem to have much empathy or care what other people think of her. She said her father was sociopathic. Do you recall if that has a hereditary aspect?"

"Not offhand," Jack said. "So, she's that bad?"

"I believe she is," Laurie said. "Knowing your sensitivities, you'd be appalled at her vulgar language. In her defense, according to her, she had a difficult childhood and was abused physically by her true father, who committed suicide when she was a young teen, and then abused sexually by her new stepfather."

"My word," he said. "You learned all this doing an autopsy with her?"

"She's remarkably up front," she said. "But who's to know where the truth is. According to Chet she openly lied to him."

"She certainly wasn't very gracious to me when I introduced myself down in the pit."

"I wouldn't take it personally," Laurie said. "She doesn't like men in general and said as much."

"Good grief," Jack remarked. "She'd better stay clear of me and my openness."

Laurie laughed in spite of herself. "You are so right. You and she would get along like oil and water. But to give her some credit, she is smart, and Dr. Henderson mentioned she has a gift for surgical pathology. She's only been here at the OCME a little more than a week and has picked up a rather amazing amount of forensic knowledge from just observing a handful of autopsies. On top of that, she's a talented prosecutor. I was impressed with her professional capabilities."

"What about you? Did you enjoy doing the autopsy even if you found working with Dr. Nichols trying? I know how much you've been missing the nuts and bolts of forensics."

"Very much so," she said.

"When I was in your office and asked you why you were doing an autopsy when you had made the general decision not to do them, you said you were doing it to evaluate Dr. Nichols but also for political reasons. What did you mean by that?"

"I was doing the autopsy to evaluate the resident," Laurie said. "But the particular case I was doing as a compromise for NYU."

"What do you mean?" He picked up his fork and tried a bite of the pasta.

She explained as briefly as possible the circumstances surrounding Kera Jacobsen's overdose and Dr. Henderson's and the medical center's CEO's subsequent concerns about the media getting wind of the autopsy. Jack whistled.

"Well, I hope you don't get inundated with requests

to do autopsies because you agreed to do this one," Jack said.

"I hope so, too," Laurie said. "Not too many people here in the OCME know I did it. With most everyone upstairs in the afternoon conference, I thought I could sneak it in. I told Marvin and Vinnie to keep it to themselves."

"Good try, but something like this is not going to remain a secret," he said. "But, be that as it may, was the case successful in accomplishing what you wanted?"

"Very much so," she said. "First of all, I enjoyed it. Just getting away from all the headaches of being chief of the OCME for an hour was a professional delight. Second of all, it turned out to be a much better case than I expected for changing Miss Congeniality's appreciation of forensics. It wasn't such a garden-variety overdose case. Although there was a positive rapid test for fentanyl on the fluid in the syringe, there was little pulmonary edema and no cerebral edema. And there was a surprise finding: the patient was pregnant. About ten weeks, from the looks of it."

"Why would a pregnancy have that kind of an effect on our sociopath?"

"It has to do with her mistrust of men," Laurie said. "Since the patient wasn't found for several days and wasn't discovered by the father of the child, she's convinced the father had something to do with the drugs."

"That's quite an assumption," Jack said.

"I felt the same," she said. "But I could tell she was truly interested in investigating the case further to make sure of the manner of death. Before the autopsy, she told me that she thought forensics was a waste of her time. Now she's truly motivated. Who knows, maybe I've been responsible for a new convert to forensic pathology."

"God forbid with her personality," Jack said. "Would you have her here as a fellow?"

"Not on your life," Laurie said with a laugh. "She told me she hates patients, which was the reason she went into pathology: to avoid them. Little does she know how often we have to deal with bereaved families. They are our patients, not the corpses. She'd make a terrible forensic pathologist."

"How is she going to investigate the case?" Jack asked.

"I'm assuming she would do it just the same as you or I," Laurie said. "She'll talk to all the people involved, like the woman who found the body, probably the patrolmen who answered the nine-one-one call, maybe the neighbors, and maybe other friends she can find. It will be interesting if she finds the father to get his side of the story. Then when toxicology is back, we'll know a bit more about the cause of death and that can be added in to the equation. My hunch is that the fentanyl level is going to be really high to explain the lack of pulmonary edema. Kera Jacobsen didn't suffer with a progressive suppression of her breathing like usual. She died very rapidly."

"That's enough about this sociopathic resident," he said. He pushed away his bowl of pasta. "I'm sorry, but I'm not hungry after hearing about what happened today at your screening. I think you should seriously consider the definitive solution. I feel even stronger than I did ten minutes ago."

"I appreciate your thoughts," Laurie said. "I'll sleep on it." Although she was generally a night person who normally got a second wind sometime during the evening, tonight was different. Just mentioning the word *sleep* made her feel like she might have trouble getting up to the bedroom. She pushed back from the table and stood up on mildly wobbly legs. "I'm not even sure I'll be able to stay awake to take a bath."

"You go ahead," Jack said as he, too, stood. "I'll clean up here and see you upstairs. But first I need a hug."

She welcomed him wrapping his arms around her. After giving her a gentle kiss, he leaned back, still holding her tight. "You are the most important thing in my life. I want you to know that."

"Thank you," Laurie said. "This isn't easy for me, but I'm glad we have each other."

CHAPTER 12

May 8th
8:32 P.M.

ere you go, miss," the Lyft driver said, pointing off to
the right. "Have a great meal."

Aria opened the door and got out of the black
Toyota, which whisked away before she even got to the
curb. For a moment she stood looking at the restaurant.
She'd heard about Cipriani Downtown, located in SoHo,
but had never been there. It wasn't a big place, maybe
twenty-five or so feet wide, with a bright yellow awning.
How deep it was, she couldn't tell. Despite the chill in
the air, there were a half dozen or so round tables outside
on the sidewalk, but all were pulled back and under the
awning. Some sliding glass doors had been opened so
that there wasn't much separation between the outside
tables and the inside ones. There were several gas-fired
heat lamps among the outside tables, whose warmth Aria

could feel on her face from where she was standing at the curb.

Having heard the restaurant was popular among the in-crowd, which was reason enough for her to avoid it, Aria wasn't surprised it was jam-packed. Every seat at every table that could be seen was occupied, and there were a lot of tables mashed together. The bar to the left was almost completely concealed by standees. There was even a rather large group of people standing on the sidewalk near the entrance that was positioned half under a retractable metal stairway that rose up to the apparent darkness of the second floor. Most intimidating was the bright light and noise of the hundred or so competing conversations that burst out from the interior like a tsunami, especially compared with the immediate neighboring commercial establishments, which were all closed for the night and dark. To add to the confusion, waiters in white coats and bow ties were darting around carrying trays of food despite the mob of customers milling about. Busboys in less impressive white jackets without ties were collecting soiled dishes and rolling out clean tablecloths. The scene was frantic. For Aria it wasn't promising for an interview.

After leaving Dr. Henderson's office, she had managed to get Madison Bryant on the phone right away, which was initially encouraging. Unfortunately for Aria, the woman wasn't at home stressed out from the Kera episode like Aria had hoped. Instead Madison had been in a taxi when the call had gone through, heading downtown to eat with someone she described as a friend. To make it less auspicious, she sounded tipsy. Even though Aria knew she was overstepping her bounds, when she declared herself to be a medical examiner who needed to talk with her as soon as possible, Madison was unintimidated. Instead of immediately agreeing, she had invited Aria to come to the restaurant if it was so important. When Aria suggested they meet after her dinner, Madison said that she hoped she wouldn't be available after dinner, meaning that if Aria wanted to talk with her that evening, it had to be at the restaurant. With serious misgivings, she had acquiesced to the plan.

Skirting the people standing outside, some of whom were smoking, she approached the entrance. A dark-haired man in a dark jacket stood by the door, watching people go in and out. He obviously was employed by the restaurant, but in what capacity, Aria had no idea. He smiled at her as she passed. She ignored him.

Inside the restaurant was as chaotic as it looked from the outside. Although most of the tables were round, those to the far right against the wall were rectangular and had bench seats. On the walls were framed photographs. One large one was of a young woman who looked like a model wearing seriously distressed jeans not too dissimilar from Aria's. Since she'd not been home, Aria was still dressed as she had been all day, in a white cotton designer blouse, jeans, pink leather sneakers, and her resident white medical coat. To avoid any hecklers who might catch her name, she'd removed her DR. ARIA NICHOLS NYU Medical Center name tag.

She was looking for the host, but it wasn't an easy

task. Madison had said she would leave her name with the host and say she was expecting her to join them. Pushing through the standees crowded around the bar, Aria continued deeper into the restaurant.

"Hey, baby," a man said, holding a drink as was everyone else standing or sitting at the bar. "Are you a real doctor or one on TV?" He laughed uproariously, as did his friends. Aria ignored him just as she had the man at the door.

Once she had managed to push her way ten or fifteen feet into the restaurant, she could see that the dining room extended back farther than the room was wide. In the depths of the dining area things seemed to be a bit calmer. The party scene and the noise were all up front, mostly around the bar and the more closely grouped tables. To Aria's chagrin there didn't seem to be any host stand. Just when she was thinking of giving up and retreating, she spotted a man in a dark business suit, white shirt, and dark tie who was about her height and who seemed to be giving orders to the serving staff. Aria approached and caught his eye. Although he had hair almost as dark as that of the man standing at the entrance, he looked more Hispanic than Italian. She gave her name, practically shouting to be heard, and said that a Madison Bryant was expecting her.

After a moment of thought the man said: "Yes!" Then he raised an index finger and motioned for her to follow him. Aria did just that but continued to find making progress difficult. Ahead, the man, who still had his index finger raised for her benefit, seemed to effortlessly slide between standees. A moment later they broke free of the crowd and entered the back area of the dining room. Not only was it less crowded, but the noise level dropped considerably.

Like a slalom skier on a packed hillside, the host rapidly worked his way through the dining room to approach a two-top table against the back wall. He then gestured toward it and moved aside. Aria stepped up to the table and took stock of its occupants. Both Madison and her male dinner partner were African American, with Madison having a considerably lighter complexion than her muscular, bearded male companion. She was dressed casually, while he was in a white shirt open at the collar with a loosened tie. A business suit jacket hung over the back of his chair. The table was chock-full of plates, breadbasket, olive oil, and wine and water glasses. Taking up most of the space was a platter of pasta in red sauce.

"I'm Dr. Aria Nichols," she said to the woman. "Are you Madison Bryant?"

"None other," she said with a broad smile. "And this is Richard Abrams." She nodded to her companion.

The host who'd momentarily disappeared produced a chair for Aria, posing a mystery from where he had found it in the crowded environment. With flair he positioned it closer to Richard than to Madison. He didn't put it in the middle to avoid blocking the aisle for the waiters' benefit. Without a second's hesitation she moved it over next to Madison and sat down. Richard's self-satisfied expression changed. He'd taken offense from being slighted.

"I want to make this as short as possible," Aria said to Madison, totally ignoring her dining partner.

"Would you like something to drink?" the host said. "How about a Bellini?"

"They're terrific," Madison said excitedly. "I had two." Then, talking directly to the host, she added: "She'll have one!"

"You got it," the host said and quickly disappeared.

"I need to talk to you about Kera Jacobsen," Aria said.

"Why?" Madison demanded. Her happy mood disappeared in the blink of an eye. "Listen, I had the worst day of my life today. My friend is dead. I'm trying to recover. I talked to a medical legal investigator at the scene. After that I was dragged over there to the medical-examiner's office, and I identified her body. I cooperated fully. Why are you bothering me now? I mean, I said everything I know. The whole situation has me bummed out. And Richard says I don't have to talk to you if I don't want to. And he's a lawyer."

Aria briefly glanced over at Richard and had to suppress a surge of anger at his interfering. She was tempted to say something along the lines that his legal advice was not necessarily true if she were a real medical examiner. But then she sensed whatever she said would only serve to get them into an argument about subpoena power and complicate the situation. She turned back to Madison.

"Something has changed," Aria said. "I did the autopsy this afternoon, and something unexpected was found."

"What?" Madison challenged. "What could change? She's dead. That's not going to change."

"No, but . . ." She paused. She found herself about to regurgitate the shit that Dr. Montgomery had spewed out that afternoon about the role of the forensic pathologist listening to the dead tell their stories. Feeling embarrassed about the urge, she changed tactics. "You are a social worker who I am sure understands the issues about HIPAA and the constraints it puts on us medical professionals to honor patient privacy. Correct?"

"I suppose," Madison said. Her voice had lost a good bit of its stormy intensity.

"Because of HIPAA I cannot out-and-out tell you what was found, but in New York the autopsy record can be requested by the family or even a personal representative, and what was found will certainly be in the autopsy report that I will be dictating. So this is medical information that falls somewhere in between being part of the public record and not being part."

Aria looked at Richard. "As a lawyer, even you must understand what I mean."

Richard pretended to laugh. He started to say something, but she ignored him.

"So," Aria said, redirecting her attention to Madison. "I'm going to ask you some questions that will enable you to figure out what it is that I can't tell you. I know that sounds ridiculously indirect, but here goes . . . David

Goldberg, the MLI, said that you had told one of the responding patrolmen that Kera did not have any current boyfriends. Do you remember saying that?"

"Yes, I did," Madison said.

"And you considered yourself a good friend of Kera's, so if she had had a boyfriend you would have probably known. Correct?"

"I know she absolutely didn't have a boyfriend during the fall," Madison said. "No question. But after the holidays, we didn't see as much of each other socially. I mean, at work we saw each other pretty much every day. She could have had a boyfriend then. In fact, there were times that I thought that might have been the case, but she denied it when I asked her."

"Did she ever talk about her old boyfriend from LA, Robert Barlow?"

"Back in the fall she did, but not recently."

"Do you know if he ever came to NYC to visit her?"

"Not to my knowledge. She was over him. I'm certain."

"Do you know if she had any other particularly good friends like yourself who she might have confided in?"

"Not that I know of. But I suppose it is possible after the holidays, like I mentioned."

"I gather from what you have said, there is a chance she had developed some relationship with someone, possibly male, after the holidays that she kept secret from you."

"That's what I thought on occasion, but I didn't know for sure and I didn't press her on it. I mean, she was entitled to her life, so I moved on."

"Okay," Aria said. "I suppose by now it's apparent

enough that what was found at autopsy needs a male participant."

Madison exchanged a glance with Richard and then returned her attention to Aria. Before anyone could respond, a waiter in a spotless white coat appeared at Aria's side with the Bellini. He placed it in front of her, positioning the champagne glass dangerously close to the edge of the crowded table. It was the only spot available.

"Are you planning on eating something?" the waiter asked Aria. "Would you care to hear our specials for tonight?"

"No, I'm not going to eat," Aria said.

The waiter nodded and retreated.

Aria dug into one of her side pockets and pulled out a small pad of paper. Taking one of her pens from a breast pocket, she wrote down her number. "The reality is that after the autopsy and its surprise discovery, the cause of death is not as definitive as it seemed when the autopsy began. Nor is the manner of death, if you get my drift. Unfortunately, the NYPD is not concerned about yet another overdose, and as far as I know are not investigating at all and won't be investigating. Of course, that is entirely understandable with four overdose deaths a day in the city. I think your friend Kera Jacobsen deserves for this mysterious boyfriend/lover to be found so he can explain why it had to be you, Madison, who had the burden of finding Kera's putrefying corpse and not he. He also needs to explain exactly what role he had in the overdose. Locating this missing male is something that I'm committed to doing."

Aria picked up the Bellini and tossed it back. She wiped off her lips with the back of her hand as she set the empty glass back on the table. "Here's my number in case you think of anything that might help me find this bastard." She reached out and handed the slip of paper to Madison. She then stood up, purposefully avoided looking at Richard, and walked away without another word.

CHAPTER 13

May 8th
9:05 P.M.

With some difficulty Aria managed to squeeze her way through the throng of people, mostly men, standing around the bar at the front of the restaurant hoping to get a table. Inevitably her presence garnered a few very unclever, snide remarks about her white coat, but as was the case on her way in, she ignored them. Such behavior only served to cement her general feelings toward the male gender. Once on the street, she pulled her phone from her pocket with the intention of using one of the ride apps. But at that very moment, a yellow cab pulled up. Suddenly, convenience outweighed Aria's preferences. Stepping into the street, she climbed in and gave her home address on West 70th Street as she sat back and fastened her seat belt.

As the car sped north, Aria had some time to think about the conversation she'd just had with Madison Bryant. It had been much more productive motivation-wise than she would have imagined when she'd been first confronted with how busy and noisy the restaurant had been. She was glad she'd made the effort. Now she was even more sure than she'd been before talking to the social worker that Kera Jacobsen was telling her loud and clear that the mysterious boyfriend had to be found.

Suddenly, after checking the time on her phone, she undid the seat belt and slid forward so she could talk more easily to the driver through the Plexiglas divider. She knew the divider was there to protect the driver, but she disliked them, and they were one of the many reasons she preferred to use Uber, Lyft, or Juno over regular taxis. "I want to change my destination," Aria said. She fumbled in her pocket for the piece of paper David Goldberg had given her. When she found it, she held it up to the light coming in through the front windshield.

"Twenty-Third and Second," she said.

"*D'accord*," the driver said agreeably.

She sat back and redid her seat belt. The reason she had suddenly changed her destination was that she felt she was on a roll from having spoken with Madison. Even though it was rather late, a little after nine, she thought it wasn't too late to see if she could also talk with Kera Jacobsen's possibly nosy neighbor, Evelyn Mabry. Short of Kera having another close friend with whom she might have shared information about a secret lover, which Madison said she didn't have, the neighbor might be the only person who could confirm the possibility. Despite the hour, Aria thought it was worth the chance.

After paying the fare in cash since she'd been burned before using a credit card in a taxi, Aria climbed out and looked up at the building. It was a nondescript six-story brick structure almost identical to its immediate neighbors on both sides. The only difference was a bit of architectural detail framing the double front door. To Aria's encouragement the four windows on the right side of the fourth floor were illuminated, suggesting that Evelyn Mabry was home and hopefully not in bed.

Wasting no time since it was now almost 9:30, Aria entered through the building's outer door into the foyer to confront the clustered mailboxes. It took her a moment to find the box for 4A. When she did, she immediately pressed the buzzer. Hoping for the best, she waited. After several minutes of silence, she was about to press it again when the speaker crackled to life.

"Who is it?" a disembodied voice said in a less-than-friendly tone. "It's almost ten o'clock at night!"

"My name is Dr. Aria Nichols," she said, going up on her tiptoes to get closer to the speaker in hopes of being heard. "I'm a medical examiner from the Office of the Chief Medical Examiner here in New York. I'm sorry for the late hour, but I need to speak with you right away about the death of Kera Jacobsen."

Silence reigned for what seemed like a discouraging length of time. Finally, Aria said: "Evelyn Mabry. Do I have to call the police to become involved here? This needn't take but fifteen minutes of your time."

"What kind of name is Aria?" Evelyn questioned.

"I'm not sure what you mean," Aria said. She slapped a hand to her forehead in frustration. It never failed that dealing with the public was such a damn pain in the ass. It was the reason she couldn't stand patients.

"Are you a man or a woman?" Evelyn said.

"A woman, last time I checked," Aria said with annoyance.

"Why do you need to talk to me again? I already talked to the investigator and the police."

"An autopsy was done today, which raised additional questions that we feel only you may be able to answer."

A raucous buzz suddenly filled the foyer to announce that the inner door had been unlocked electronically. Aria lunged for the door lest she miss being able to pass through. With a sense of relief, she was inside and able to summon the elevator. As she rose up, she was reminded of not being fond of old elevators, especially small ones like the one she was in. It repeatedly clunked against the walls of the shaft as if it was just freely dangling on its cable. She was relieved when she was able to exit on the fourth floor.

As she walked down to ring the bell for 4A she tried to breathe shallowly. The corridor smelled like a century's worth of grilled onions. After ringing the doorbell, she again had to wait longer than she would have expected.

"Who is it?" a muffled female voice demanded through the door. Without the electronic interference of the PA system downstairs, Aria could hear a strong Brooklyn accent. Although Aria was tempted to say something sarcastic, she controlled herself and merely repeated her name. Looking at the peephole at eye level, she detected a subtle movement, suggesting Evelyn was giving her the once-over. Aria was tempted to wave or make an impatient gesture, but she restrained herself and did nothing. Being this close to speaking with the woman in person, she didn't want to ruin her chances. Nor did she want the woman to ask her to provide some official identification, which was a worry that had suddenly popped into her mind as the seconds ticked by.

Finally, it was apparent that Aria had passed muster as there was the sound of multiple locks and chains being undone. The door opened three or four inches but with a remaining chain in place. There was also a bloodshot eye and part of a nose visible. Aria didn't move or say anything, allowing Evelyn to inspect her further. Twenty or so seconds later, the door closed again, the final chain was removed, and the door reopened significantly wider. Aria got a partial view inside and it was apparent the woman was a hoarder as David Goldberg had described. She could see the room beyond was completely filled with all sorts of junk, including a vast number of cardboard boxes of varying sizes, dozens of old suitcases, and stacks upon stacks of newspapers and magazines. There was even a grocery cart that was overflowing with old clothes among the mounds of clutter. There was so much stuff that no normal furniture could be seen, and only a narrow path passed through it all.

"What do you want to ask me?" Evelyn said. She was

wearing an aged housecoat. Her hair was in curlers covered by a clear plastic shower cap, and some kind of light-colored cream covered her face save around her eyes, giving her a raccoon look. She made no move to invite Aria to come inside, which didn't bother her in the slightest. The smell wafting out of the apartment was worse than what was in the hallway.

"We need to know more about the late-night visitors to Miss Jacobsen's apartment," Aria said. "You told the medical-legal investigator, Mr. Goldberg, that you heard people arrive and leave, usually during weeknights. Is that fair to say?"

"That's what I told him," Evelyn agreed. "But over the last month or so it had stopped. Thank God."

"Was this one person or a group that showed up?"

"I think it was one person," Evelyn said.

"You also said that you didn't know if it was a man or a woman."

"That's right."

"Well, that troubles me," Aria said. "I notice that your peephole here in your door looks out into the hall directly toward Miss Jacobsen's door. Are you trying to tell me you never looked out when you heard this late-night visitor arrive or leave? That's a little hard to believe."

"I might have looked out once or twice," Evelyn said defensively. "But only when the visitor arrived. I'm in bed by ten sharp every night."

"And when you did look out on these rare occasions when the visitor arrived, was it a man or woman you saw?"

"It was usually a man."

"Usually or always? Remember, I don't want to have to get the police involved, but I will if I think you are not cooperating."

"It was a man."

"Would you guess it was the same man each time? The light here in the hall is bright enough for you to have an idea."

"I think it was the same man. It always looked like the same hat and coat. It was a camel coat. My husband, God rest his soul, had one like it."

"That's very helpful, Evelyn," Aria said. "How about the hat? How would you describe it?"

"It was just a hat, a man's hat."

"Was it like a baseball hat or a dress hat?"

"A dress hat, I guess. My husband never wore a hat."

"One last question, Evelyn, and I would like you to think before you answer. Would you recognize this man if you saw him on the street? Did you ever see his face or at least his profile?"

Evelyn blinked a few times, giving Aria the feeling that she was thinking or trying to think. Aria didn't interrupt whatever process was going on.

"No, I wouldn't be able to recognize him," Evelyn said finally. "I never saw his face."

"Okay, Evelyn. That's it. If I have any more questions, I'll come back."

Aria walked away, back toward the elevator although she contemplated taking the stairs. Behind her she heard Evelyn's door close with a resounding thud. Even though talking with the woman had brought back unpleasant memories of patients she had been forced to deal with as a medical student, she was glad she had made the effort. It had been a rewarding labor. Aria was now convinced of what she had already suspected, namely that Kera Jacobsen was having an affair, presumably with someone she met over the holidays, and for some reason, it was a clandestine affair, making Aria question why. Having watched her share of soap operas as a tween in the Greenwich mansion, she guessed it was because lover boy was married. And if Aria had learned anything from those hours of schmaltzy story lines, lover boy had probably told Kera he was getting divorced but needed to wait for some questionably plausible reason to drop the bomb on wifey. Then came the inconvenient pregnancy, forcing the issue and resulting in Kera Jacobsen's untimely death.

"The fucking bastard," she said through clenched teeth as she pounded the elevator doors with the palm of her hand. "I'm going to find out who you are, come what may!"

Seemingly in response to her mini-tantrum, the elevator arrived. Aria pulled open the door and boarded. As the inner door closed and she remembered how the damn thing sounded earlier, she hoped to hell the antique wasn't going to suddenly break loose and plunge down the four stories with her trapped inside. She'd had nightmares of that scenario ever since her nanny, Fabiola, had told her that it happened in small elevators. Until Aria had heard that fact, she'd liked to ride the elevator they had in the Greenwich house for the sheer pleasure of going up and down to thwart Fabiola's control over her.

CHAPTER 14

May 8th
9:48 P.M.

Soon Aria was back heading north. This time it was on Eighth Avenue and the traffic was light, and they were moving faster. Partially mesmerized by the phantasmagoria of the city lights as they passed by in a blur, Aria let her mind wander. Just as she had felt pleased with having made the effort to meet with Madison Bryant at the chaotic restaurant scene, she was glad she'd made the equivalent effort to talk with weird Evelyn Mabry at her depressing tenement. Both conversations had contributed to giving Aria a contented sense of purpose. She'd been bored silly with her month's rotation at the OCME up until that afternoon and the surprise discovery of the gravid uterus. Now she was excited and turned on with the possibility of achieving a modicum of gender retribution. There was zero doubt in her mind that somewhere out there in the pulsating city was an overly entitled man, like all males she'd known, who had the mistaken idea that he could have his fun with Kera Jacobsen, could mislead her to accept the need for secrecy, could irresponsibly help to create a pregnancy, and then possibly contribute to snuffing out a young woman so that he could go on with his sham life. Aria was intent on proving him wrong, but there was a big problem. She didn't have any idea about how to do it. The boyfriend's apparent emphasis on secrecy was going to make finding him difficult, if not impossible. Of course, she could interview more of the residents of the 23rd Street building, but realistically she thought that Evelyn Mabry was the best lead she'd find. The only other course of action would be to talk the police into starting a real, professional investigation. Yet from what David Goldberg had said that seemed highly unlikely.

Although prior to meeting with Dr. Henderson she had turned off the ringer on her phone to avoid any interruptions, she could feel it vibrate against her buttock, indicating she was getting a call. Its normal resting place was in the back pocket of her jeans. Leaning to the side and with a bit of a struggle, Aria managed to get it out. Knowing it was almost ten P.M., she fully expected it to be a robocall. Except for when she was on call at the hospital, she rarely got calls at night. Yet with the uniqueness of the circumstances, and especially after getting the text from Dr. Henderson earlier, she wanted to check. She was surprised to see it was Madison Bryant.

"Is this a butt-dial from putting my number in your

contacts or a real call?" Aria said in lieu of a hello. She could hear Madison briefly laugh. It was a nervous laugh.

"It's a real call," Madison said. "I hope I'm not bothering you, but I wanted to apologize for being short with you at Cipriani."

"You didn't seem short to me," Aria said.

"Well, I was," Madison insisted. "It's been the worst day of my life. Something like this has never happened to me. I'd never even seen a dead person, much less someone I'd grown to care for. I was trying to recover, and you showed up wanting to talk about it. It freaked me out. I'm sorry."

"One of life's burdens," Aria said. There was no way she was going to apologize, if that's what Madison wanted.

"And then when you essentially told me she was pregnant it totally freaked me out. It made me feel terrible, like I let her down by not having been a better friend. I really got upset."

"Well, I'm sure your current companion, Richard the lawyer, will come up with a way of cheering you up."

"I'm not with Richard any longer. I got up and walked out of the restaurant. When I tried to talk to him about my feelings and started crying, he was less than empathetic in what I interpreted as an irritatingly misogynistic way, and I saw red."

"I'm not surprised," Aria said. "He struck me as a dick, and a conceited one at that. From my perspective, you're better off recovering without him."

"Actually, I think you burst his bubble by ignoring

him. He started acting weird when you left. But I don't want to talk about him. Where are you right now?" Madison asked.

Surprised by the question, she looked out of the car's window and saw the sign for 43rd Street flash by. "I'm in an Uber heading home."

"Me, too," Madison said. "Where's home?"

"Upper West Side," Aria said. She was surprised Madison asked and equally surprised she'd answered.

"That's a coincidence," Madison said. "Same with me. Listen, I'd like to talk to you about locating this unknown boyfriend and finding out his role in Kera's death. The more I think about it, the more I agree with you. I mean, Kera never took drugs. Never! She hated drugs, especially because, as a social worker, she'd seen firsthand what they can do to people."

"It's late," Aria said. "Maybe tomorrow we can get together. I haven't eaten yet tonight, and at the moment that takes precedence."

"I've got patients all day tomorrow," Madison said. "And I was gone for half a day today. Getting together tomorrow is not going to work. Where exactly are you right now?"

Aria looked out the window to catch the next cross street sign. "I'm just passing through Forty-Fifth Street and Eighth Avenue."

"I'm on Eighth as well," Madison said. "Just a few blocks behind you. That's convenient, and it gives me an idea. How about we meet somewhere where you can get a bite, I can get another drink, and we can talk. The reason I'm excited to talk with you right away is that I think I have a great idea of how to find this unknown boyfriend."

"Come again?" Aria said. Madison's words seemed like pennies from heaven after Aria's recent lament that she might have been at an early dead-end.

"I truly believe that if I didn't know Kera was seeing someone, no one did. Finding him is not going to be easy, but I think I know how to do it. Are you interested?"

"Very," Aria said. "Where do you suggest we meet?"

"Have you ever been to Nobu Fifty Seven? It's more or less on our way at Forty West Fifty-Seventh, and it's got a good bar and great bar food if you like sushi. Are you game?"

"I'm game," Aria said. "See you there." She ended the call with a smile before leaning forward in her seat. "Driver, I want to change my destination." Settling back in her seat, she found herself wondering exactly what this great idea could be that Madison had in mind.

CHAPTER 15

Aria's first impression of Nobu Fifty Seven was that it was the antithesis of Cipriani Downtown. Instead of noisy, crowded, claustrophobic, and brightly illuminated chaos, she was presently standing in an expansive and subdued, subtly lit barroom with a soaring ceiling some thirty feet above. Over the bar was a huge display of thirty large sake barrels. Although Aria imagined the bar had been busy earlier, it was now a calm refuge from the day with only a bit more than a half dozen customers. Behind the bar were two attentive bartenders dressed in black. It seemed unreal to her that on the same night she was visiting two trendy establishments that she never imagined she might patronize. She'd been in New York City for almost four years and had never had the urge to set foot in either one.

Finding a section of the bar with five empty seats, she took the middle one. The bar itself was an enormous slab of wood, three or four inches thick, and finished with glossy epoxy making the surface absolutely smooth. As soon as she was seated, one of the bartenders came over and placed a cocktail napkin in front of her. He then stuck out his hand and said, "Welcome to Nobu. My name is Alex. And yours?"

Aria looked at the proffered hand and then back up at the bartender's smiling face. He was a man of medium height with a dark complexion, dark hair and eyes, and a short half-beard, giving him a mild but interesting Mephistophelian aura. Despite finding him intellectually attractive, she had no intention of shaking the hand of a stranger with whom she had no common interest other than being in the same place at the same time. "I want to eat something," she said. "What do you recommend?"

Without a moment's hesitation or evidence of chagrin, Alex retracted his hand and reeled off a bewildering number of possibilities. He ended his spiel with the question of whether Aria had any food allergies or strong dislikes.

"I like pretty much everything except entrails," she said.

"Then I recommend the salmon and avocado roll and white fish with dried miso, provided you're okay with sushi and sashimi."

"Fine," Aria said.

"Something to drink? Wine? Cocktail?"

"I'll have a glass of prosecco," Aria said. "What time do you close?"

"Midnight," Alex said.

While she waited, she looked to either side. Everyone else at the bar was a couple. She looked back up at the ceiling. It seemed impossibly high since the room was higher than it was wide.

Her drink came first, and she took a sip. It was a good prosecco. She knew because she'd had bad prosecco. Glancing back at the entrance, Aria wondered how long she would have to wait for Madison's arrival. She wasn't happy being there, but she was still intrigued by Madison's offer of providing a way to find Kera's missing lover. She was the first to admit that she had absolutely no idea of what Madison was going to suggest. The only thing that had come to her mind was perhaps there was something significant that Madison had failed to tell her at Cipriani.

Madison arrived before the food. Aria saw her the moment she came into the restaurant. Their eyes met, and Madison came quickly over to where she was sitting.

"I appreciate your willingness to meet with me," Madison said right off the bat. "Thank you for taking the time."

Aria stayed silent as Madison took off a light jean jacket, draped it over a neighboring empty barstool, and sat down. Attentive as ever, Alex came over immediately to place a cocktail napkin in front of Madison. He repeated the introduction he'd given Aria, including extending his hand. In contrast to Aria, Madison shook the hand and gave her name in return. After a brief conversation, it was decided Madison was not hungry but would have a drink.

"I'll have the same as she," Madison said, nodding toward Aria's glass.

"It's prosecco," Aria said, surprised someone would order something when she didn't know what it was. She wondered if it meant Madison had already had enough to drink during the evening.

"Whatever," Madison said. "I like prosecco well enough."

"What is your suggestion about finding Kera Jacobsen's secret lover?" Aria asked, eager to turn the conversation to business. It was at that moment when Alex brought Aria's food. With it he provided chopsticks, a cloth napkin, several small dishes, and a small kettle-like container of teriyaki sauce. Although Madison said she wasn't going to eat, he brought chopsticks and a napkin for her, too.

Aria tried a piece of the sushi and a piece of the sashimi, then pushed both dishes closer to Madison. "Not bad," Aria said. "I'm starved. Try it! The sashimi is particularly good."

Madison followed Aria's lead. "Yum," she said, then got down to business. "To explain what I have in mind, I have to ask you a question. Do you remember the arrest of the Golden State Killer in 2018?"

"I think so."

"Do you remember how he was found?"

"As I recall, he was found by someone matching his DNA through one of the ancestry websites?"

"Exactly," Madison said, becoming excited about the subject.

"Is this what you have in mind for finding Kera's boy-friend?" Aria asked. She was immediately disappointed. She had expected at a minimum to get names of people who might have known Kera's secrets.

"That's exactly what I have in mind," Madison said.

"Well, I can tell you right off, it's not going to work," Aria said, not trying to camouflage her disappointment. "Finding the Golden State Killer was a completely differ-ent set of circumstances. They had the man's DNA from his semen. We don't have our perpetrator's semen or his DNA." Aria put down her chopsticks. She was so disap-pointed that she was tempted to just leave.

"That's true, but there is a good chance we can con-struct his DNA."

"Oh, please," Aria scoffed. "What the hell do you mean, construct his DNA?"

"About a year ago my mother gave me a present of having my DNA analyzed by one of the major DNA ge-nealogical companies. At this point I can't even remem-ber which one it was. I think it was Ancestry dot com, which has the largest database. But it doesn't matter be-cause I've gotten into a genealogical obsession, and I've had just about all the commercial DNA companies ana-lyze me. I tell you, once you start, it becomes addictive. And it works. I've found ancestors going back to the eighteen hundreds who were slaves."

"I'm happy for you," Aria said. She checked the time on her phone. It was nearing eleven, which explained why she was suddenly feeling like she wanted to be in bed. Normally she was in bed by ten or ten thirty to read.

"The point I'm trying to make is that I have become reasonably knowledgeable about the ins and outs of genealogical DNA. It's complicated stuff, but if you are persistent, like I am, you can figure most of it out."

"I'm afraid I'm going to have to cut this short," Aria said. She glanced down the bar and raised her hand with the idea of getting Alex's attention.

"I think finding this boyfriend will be rather easy because we will have both the child's DNA and the mother's. That means we already have half the father's DNA."

Aria lowered her hand and looked back at Madison. "That might be correct," Aria said. "But that still leaves one and a half billion base pairs that are unknown."

"Yes, but there are some clever tricks to fill that in by using tools developed by the commercial DNA companies and aided by websites that are called open databases. Let me explain: When you send in your saliva sample to a company like Ancestry dot com, what you get back is called a kit. It is not your DNA completely sequenced, although maybe in the future it will be. But for now, it's your particular collection of varying nucleotides at various precise locations spread through your entire genome. These precise locations are called SNPs, standing for single-nucleotide polymorphisms. It is sort of like a fingerprint in chemistry."

"I understand all this," Aria said with a bit more interest. Madison seemed to know what she was talking about. Aria had never thought about the idea of finding someone by figuring out what their DNA was from close relatives. She'd always thought that such a process was unidirectional, the way the Golden State Killer had been found, by having his DNA to start with.

"Of course, you know most of this stuff about DNA since you are a doctor," Madison said. "I'm sure you know more about the nuts and bolts than I. At the same time, I can tell you're not up on the latest about what genealogical DNA is capable of doing. These days there are some wild tricks that have been developed, particularly by companies like GEDmatch dot com. One's called phasing, which separates the child's DNA into DNA obtained only from the mother and DNA only from the father into new kits. There is even a really cool one that involves making a manufactured kit for the 'evil twin,' meaning an artificial kit of the DNA the real child didn't get from the parents.

"But that's getting ahead of ourselves. All you have to understand at the moment is that these new manufactured 'phased' kits can also be used to find ancestral matches. In Kera's case we will only be interested in matches from the paternal side, which is why the phased kits are helpful. And if paternal matches are found that are closer than third cousins, chances are we will be lucky, especially if these matches have made the effort to construct family trees. If we end up getting even closer matches, such as siblings, half-siblings, parents, or aunts or uncles, even first cousins, it would make finding him a piece of cake."

"Really?" Aria said, her mind in a swirl. For several beats she stared at Madison. What she was hearing was opening up a whole new possibility that had not occurred to her, and she struggled to put it into context. "This means we'll have to have kits made for both Kera and her child by any one of the commercial DNA companies."

"Right on," Madison said with building enthusiasm. "And the more companies we use, the greater the chances for matches to be found. I'm going to turn you into a convert, I'm sure of it." She let out a little laugh of satisfaction at Aria's response. "What I've learned studying all this stuff is that on average a person has about 850 relations who are third cousins or closer. Just to remind you, third cousins share great-great-grandparents. Now, don't be discouraged by thinking we'll have to be sorting through 850 people. No way. By guessing the mysterious boyfriend's age, we can probably halve that number. Then by excluding female matches, we can halve it again. And finally, restricting the matches to the New York City area, we'll be halving it again."

"So, you think we'd end up with a hundred people or so?" Aria questioned with renewed discouragement. Trying to narrow down a group of a hundred people in a city like New York would be a monumental task even for a team of professional investigators.

"No, no," Madison said. "Probably less than twenty. Restricting the matches by age narrows it more than fifty percent, a lot more. And if there's a close match like a sibling, a parent, or an aunt and uncle, then we'd be looking at a lot less than five or six people. It might only be one person. Bingo! We got the bastard." She smiled. "All this excites me because it will hopefully provide some redemptive value. I'll feel like I'm doing something for Kera by finding this dude, even if it's too late to save her."

"When do you think we can start?" Aria said. Some of Madison's excitement was beginning to rub off on her.

"Tomorrow," Madison said. "Why not? I'll find out what the commercial DNA companies would like for samples since we won't be able to send saliva, which is what they usually use."

"I'm sure I can get body fluid or tissue samples from both the mother and the fetus. You'll have to let me know what they want."

"That reminds me," Madison said. "What was the sex of the fetus?"

"It wasn't yet definitive," Aria said. "We estimated the age to be around ten weeks. At that stage it's not easy to tell, since the forming penis and clitoris are around the same size until about fourteen weeks. If I had to guess, I'd say male."

"It would be a big help if it were a male," Madison said.

"Why is that?"

"Because the Y DNA is inherited only from the paternal side."

"Even I know that, because it is the Y chromosome that determines the male gender. Why is that any better than the autosomal DNA for genealogy?"

"It's not better, it's just different and additive," Madison said. "But mainly because it can provide a surname. If we can determine the proper family name, the field of significant matches narrows decidedly, provided there wasn't anything to mess things up like an adoption."

"Why would an adoption mess things up?" Aria asked.

"The surname changes but the Y chromosome doesn't. It can really cause a problem when trying to construct family trees, and it is family trees that we'll need to use if we don't get a really close match right away, which we probably won't. There's too much chance involved."

"Okay," Aria said. It was progressively apparent to her that she needed to read up on genetic genealogy. She'd not known it was as complicated as it seemed to be, although as a doctor she should have. Having studied biology she knew about chromosomal recombination, which was one of the main sources for heritable diversity. "What about mitochondrial DNA?"

"If we had the father's DNA and were trying to reconstruct the mother's, then mitochondrial DNA would be helpful. As you know, it is only inherited along the maternal line because the sperm doesn't contribute mitochondria. All the mitochondria come from the ovum."

"Of course," Aria said. She felt a twinge of embarrassment for asking her question and appreciated Madison for not calling her on it. "Obviously I need to get myself up to speed on all this genetic genealogy. Are there any particular books that you'd recommend?"

"Oh, yes," Madison said. "There are two, actually. The one that's more general is called *The Family Tree Guide to DNA Testing and Genetic Genealogy* by Blaine Bettinger. The other one, which will be more helpful for our search, is *The Adoptee's Guide to DNA Testing* by

Tamar Weinberg. Adoptees have been using genetic DNA to search for their natural parents from the very beginning of DNA genealogy with improving success. The other group of people who have surely benefited from genetic genealogy's developing power are those who have been conceived with donor sperm. What this group in particular has learned over recent years will help us a lot since that is essentially what we're doing, and there are a number of websites that might be willing to help us."

"How are you ladies doing?" Alex asked. He'd approached and waited for an opportunity to speak. The women had been locked in conversation. "Can I get you any more food or drinks?"

"I've had enough," Aria said.

"Me, too," Madison said, although she quickly polished off the dregs of prosecco.

"How do you guys want to handle this?" Alex questioned, pointing to the glasses and the dishes in front of the women.

"I'll take the check," Madison said. Then, to Aria, she said, "I talked you into stopping here, so my treat."

Aria stayed silent. If Madison wanted to pay, who was she to complain?

"What's the quickest and easiest way to get those books you mentioned," Aria asked while Madison was finger-signing the reader that had her credit card poked into its base.

"The quickest way is to come back with me to my apartment," Madison said. "You can borrow mine, provided you don't mind if they're underlined and a bit dog-eared. I've read both several times." She finished signing and handed the device back to Alex, who immediately produced a receipt.

"Thank you, ladies," Alex said. "Come back and see us again."

"Where do you live exactly?" Aria said to Madison.

"West Seventy-Third between Columbus and Amsterdam."

"That's close to me," Aria said. "I live on Seventieth between Columbus and Central Park West."

"That's certainly convenient enough. Do you want to come and get the books? If you want to get a jump on genetic genealogy, I'd recommend it for sure."

"Okay," Aria said. "We can take a rideshare to your apartment, and I can walk home from there."

"Sounds like a plan to me," Madison said as she pulled on her denim jacket.

———

When they climbed out of the car in front of Madison's apartment building, Aria said: "I'll wait out here." Although it was on the cool side, it was still a pleasant mid-spring night and it was still early enough for significant vehicular and pedestrian traffic particularly on the bounding avenues.

"Suit yourself," Madison said. Not having to be hospitable was preferable as she wanted to get to bed as soon as she could. Earlier in the evening she'd worried about what sleep that night was going to be like after the disturbing day, but following the conversation with Aria in Nobu and the prospect of doing something positive for Kera, her natural exhaustion had caught up with her.

Up in her one-bedroom rear apartment, Madison had to scan her sizable bookcase for the two books she'd described to Aria. Once she had both books, she returned outside to the front of her building. Aria was sitting on one of the granite blocks that lined the three steps up into the building. A man with a dog had stopped and was trying to engage her in a conversation. Madison felt sorry for the man as it was apparent things were not going well. Madison wondered if Aria ever let her guard down with anyone. She was a mystery to Madison, who'd never met anyone quite like her. *Unpredictable* was the word that came to mind. One minute she seemed tolerable enough, the next minute disagreeable. Madison wondered if Aria was typical of all forensic pathologists. Considering the experience she'd had that day, she wondered if they all might be a bit weird. Dealing with death on an everyday basis had to have a consequence. She couldn't imagine doing it herself.

Aria stood, ignoring the man with the dog, and took the books from Madison. "These do look used," she said as she quickly flipped through them.

Holding her tongue from what she initially thought to say in response, Madison said instead, "I think you'll find them useful. And let's talk tomorrow. I've got patients all day, but I'll be able to talk in between them if that works for you. Then we can decide how we're going to proceed."

"Sounds good," Aria said. "I'll be able to have these books back to you quickly. I'm a fast reader."

"Whatever," Madison said with a wave of her hand. "Keep them as long as you like. As I said, I've read them several times."

"Okay," Aria said with a nod before striking off toward Columbus Avenue.

———————————

Aria walked quickly. Now that she had the books about genetic genealogy, she wanted to get home and start reading. Although she'd been initially disappointed in Madison's suggestion about using genetic genealogy to locate the missing man, she now felt encouraged. Sensing that Kera had been an intelligent, culturally endowed, educated woman despite her appearance that day prior to the autopsy, it seemed to make sense that she would have been involved with a man with similar traits and interests. If so, it stood to reason that his relatives would be similar, and Aria surmised such people would have the means and interest to indulge in genetic genealogy. All that meant was finding him by this process would be that much easier.

As it was dog-walking time before bed, she encountered several other men who tried to engage her in conversation, using her white coat and their dog as a convenient entrée. Aria either ignored them completely or told them that she couldn't stand dogs, which was a convenient turnoff. In less than ten minutes she was mounting the steps up the front stoop of her building.

When Aria first came to New York for her residency, she thought it best to buy herself a condominium rather than have to deal with a landlord. She'd always liked New York because the sheer number of people made it easy to ignore everyone. In medical school at Yale, she'd not had that luxury, as New Haven in comparison seemed like a small town. She'd wanted to live on the Upper West Side because of its proximity to Central Park and because it was a real neighborhood. Within a short walking distance, she had everything she needed. She didn't own a car and didn't want one.

The apartment she ended up buying was on a street lined with brownstones. Although they were originally single-family dwellings, many were now converted into condominiums. She was particularly drawn to 70th Street because some of the buildings were still single family, significantly reducing the congestion. Her building, strangely enough, had been painted white to cover up the many repairs that had been done on the brownstone. Her unit was on what was called the ground floor even though it was elevated from the street by the ten steps of the stoop. Beneath her was another unit whose windows were partly below ground level.

Originally Aria's two-bedroom apartment had been the building's parlor and formal dining room when it had been a single-family home. During the building's conversion, the floor plan had been altered. Now as she came through the apartment's door from the common hallway, she was in the living room/kitchen/dining area with a wood-burning fireplace. To the left was a corridor to her bedroom and the apartment's only bathroom. Such a setup was a little unfortunate since it meant that the bedroom was exposed to street noise like ambulance sirens and drunk neighbors on summer Saturday nights. To the right from where she was standing there was a doorway in the corner that led to a final small room. When Aria had originally been shown the apartment by the Realtor, this last room had been marketed as a bedroom without a bath. Instead Aria had turned it into a study, and it was in this room that she spent most of her awake time. All in all, the apartment was a pleasant environment, particularly with its twelve-foot ceilings that magnified the sense of space.

After draping her white coat over the back of the sofa, Aria went directly into the study with the two borrowed books. One of her fortes was the ability to concentrate regardless of what was going on around her, and despite being tired from a full day's activities, she intended to become significantly more knowledgeable about genetic genealogy.

CHAPTER 16

May 9th
5:15 A.M.

I t was a déjà vu for Laurie as her eyes blinked open far
earlier than was her norm for the second day in a row.
The problem was that as soon as her eyes opened, she
instinctively knew that more sleep was an impossibility.
Her mind was already in gear, processing everything that
was going on, but mostly relating to her breast situation.
That was how she referred to it in her mind: a "breast
situation." She didn't like the word *cancer*. It had too
many emotive and irrevocable connotations, even if it
was just one of several possible outcomes.

As she had done the morning before, she turned her
head to the side to see the time and was dismayed it was
still so early. Although it was light outside, the sun had
yet to rise. Having slept poorly most of the night, she

knew she was going to be tired during a day with obvious challenges.

Using her hand, she gingerly palpated the involved breast. She hadn't done it yet since the positive screening, despite having been sorely tempted. She was very careful as she did so, wondering if touching could possibly dislodge a few wayward cells if it indeed was cancer. As a doctor, she knew all too well how significant it was whether the possible cancer had spread to distant sites with what were called metastases. A cancer in situ where it had originated was a far different story than a cancer that had already metastasized.

As per usual, she could feel multiple tiny lumps in her breast. None stood out. Was that reassuring? Partially, but she didn't know which of the various irregularities she could always feel was the lump that had the radiologists alarmed. It made her feel betrayed that her own body could turn against her.

Throwing back the covers, Laurie sat up and wriggled her feet into her slippers, which were exactly where she had left them. She'd been up in the middle of the night after having essentially passed out from sheer mental and physical exhaustion soon after she and Jack had had their supper. For a while she'd wandered around in the dark apartment, going room to room while mulling over the difficult question of what to do about dealing with her worrisome breast lump. Unable to come to any conclusion with such an existential question, she'd eventually gone into the study, turned on the light, and got out the

architectural plans for the new OCME Forensic Pathology building. Despite her personal concerns about her
health and mortality, she knew that the plans had to be
finalized in the near future before getting a final cost
estimate and then presenting them to the City Council.
To her surprise, she actually was able to concentrate
enough to make some progress, or so she thought. It
wasn't until she'd felt sleepy enough that she'd turned
out the desk light, returned to the bedroom, and climbed
back into bed.

After donning her robe, she glanced at Jack. He
looked as peaceful as he had yesterday morning, lying on
his back with his hands clasped on his chest. He wasn't
actually snoring, just breathing particularly deeply. Laurie assumed he was dreaming as his lidded eyes were
clearly darting about. As close as she felt to him, it was
moments like this that emphasized they were in reality
two very separate people who thought of themselves as
the center of the universe. It was a fleeting thought that
made her figuratively smile since it was proof that she had
no way of knowing what was going on in his mind.

Just as she did the previous morning, Laurie silently
left their bedroom, walked down the hall, and entered
Emma's room. Again, peering down at the angelic four-
year-old girl, she had an abrupt epiphany. Her children,
particularly Emma, needed her, which answered the
difficult question of how she should handle the breast
lump. Since she was positive for the BRCA1 mutation,
which raised her chances for both breast cancer and ovarian cancer, she had to take the most conservative choice

even if doing so challenged her self-image as a woman. She had to follow Angelina Jolie's lead and have the mastectomy and the oophorectomy. The choice was suddenly completely clear.

"Thank you, my child," Laurie whispered under her breath. Emma and her autism had shown her the way to deal with the current problem. Feeling suddenly relieved of an oppressive weight, she walked out of her daughter's room, and the moment she did so, she could see that the sun had cleared the horizon, again bathing that water tower on the neighboring building in golden light. To Laurie it seemed symbolic of having come to a decision.

When she entered the bathroom for a shower following a quick visit to JJ's room, she wished she could pick up her phone that very instant and call the surgeon and the oncologist to get the whole issue of the breast situation out of the way now that she had made up her mind. She felt that as soon as she'd made the call, she could relegate the problem to the back of her mind, thereby allowing herself to concentrate on all the other things that needed her attention, like writing up the death certificate for Kera Jacobsen. Laurie again smiled to herself as she turned on the water from outside the shower and adjusted the temperature. With all the other, bigger-picture things on her mind involved with running the OCME, it seemed pathetic that she would single out a particular case. Yet she understood. The personality of the pathology resident aside, she had enjoyed doing the autopsy, which again underlined how much she missed the mental rigor of forensic pathology. Was she really cut out to be an administrator at the expense of having to give up doing her own cases? She didn't know. The pregnancy discovered during the autopsy had been a surprise, and she wondered if it might have the significance in regard to the manner of death, as Dr. Nichols had suggested. Laurie doubted it purely from a statistical basis, but she wasn't going to restrict Dr. Nichols from pursuing it as Laurie probably would have done the same if their roles were reversed. One thing that was clear: The hour or so doing the autopsy had been the only time that the breast situation hadn't been at the forefront of her consciousness since the moment she'd gotten the bad news from the radiologist reading her MRI.

As she climbed into the shower and allowed the water to cascade down onto her head and from there onto all the curves and creases of her body, she remembered one other important thing she had to do prior to eight o'clock. She had to call the Brooks School and tell Miss Rossi that they had decided to have JJ evaluated. Hopefully the school psychologist could recommend someone to do the evaluation, particularly a male psychiatrist or psychologist. The more Laurie had thought about the issue, the stronger she felt that receiving a professional opinion would only help her and Jack make effective parenting decisions.

CHAPTER 17

May 9th
6:45 A.M.

It was hard for Madison to remember how cold it had been during the winter on her three-minute walk from her apartment on 73rd Street to the subway entrance in Verdi Square. Now that spring had truly sprung, it was a pleasure to be outside to smell the fresh morning air, even in the middle of the city, and hear the birds sing, especially in the tiny park's trees. Only a month and a half previously it had been so cold and raw one morning, with a mixture of snow and rain, that she had been willing to call a rideshare. She only did that on average of once a month during January and February.

Her normal route, which she had been doing twice a day since September, was to take the number 2 or 3 express train down to 42nd Street, transfer to the number 7 that took her to Grand Central, and then hop on the

Lexington Avenue 6 line down to 33rd Street and Park Avenue. From there it was a pleasant twelve-minute walk in decent weather to the hospital. Despite having to take three trains, the whole trip was usually a bit less than a half hour door-to-door provided there were no train delays.

When she had first arrived in the city from St. Louis, she'd been intimidated by the subway. It seemed like such a scary netherworld, often filled with unpleasant smells, occasional random ear-splitting screeches of metal against metal, and strange-looking people that ran the gamut from the well-dressed to the apparent homeless. But over the months she'd become immune, and now she hardly batted an eye at the varying cavalcade of people she encountered. And like so many travelers, she could read one of her professional journals on her phone if she felt motivated to better herself, or the *Daily News* if she didn't. That morning she'd brought a spiral notebook she'd filled with her genealogy notes over the previous two years. Madison's method of studying was to write things down. Once she did, it was generally committed to memory. If she wanted to review, like in her present circumstance, the notes served as a superb way of doing so.

When she reached the subway entrance, an architecturally interesting head house in Verdi Square, she girded herself for the general subway smell. It wasn't particularly unpleasant, just unique. As usual, she had plenty of company as millions of New Yorkers relied on the subway to commute to their places of work. It gave Madison a sense of belonging to a grand, common enterprise.

With her monthly pass, going through the turnstile was a breeze, and she was soon on the relatively narrow southbound platform with a sizable crowd of other people all waiting for the arrival of the next train. The tracks for the local were on the right, the express on the left. When she'd first started using the subway, she'd stayed far away from the edge of the platform, which to her was like the edge of a dangerous precipice. She didn't like looking down at the dark tracks, frequently covered with litter and other filth, and what was called the third rail, which was electrified to run the train. It was even scarier being close to the edge when the subway burst out of the tunnel and came thundering in with a crescendo of deep-bass rumbling, like a mini-earthquake. The trains' arrivals were even accompanied by a sudden blast of wind and an uptick of the trademark subway smell. Now inured to the whole experience, she flipped open her notebook to review the first few chapters of Bettinger's book. She was concentrating enough that she didn't look up as the first train came barreling into the station. It wasn't until she heard the doors open that she raised her eyes. She could take either the 2 or the 3 express. This was the 2, so she boarded.

As was invariably the case, the train was crowded and there were no seats available. But it wasn't unexpected. Instead of sitting she stood, like she usually did, finding a convenient pole to grasp. Soon the doors slid closed and with several repetitive lurches the train pulled out of the station and picked up speed. Like so many mornings, she was on her way.

As she headed south at what seemed like a breakneck speed, she again tried to read her notebook, but the shaking and lurching made it so difficult she quickly gave up. Instead she closed her eyes and once again thought about how terrible a day yesterday had been until it had been partially salvaged by the nightcap in Nobu with the unusual Aria Nichols.

Ever since Madison had awakened an hour earlier, she'd marveled at the personality of the medical examiner. Although Madison had been initially put off by her bluntness, self-centeredness, and apparent lack of social graces, she'd learned to think of her as a unique and interesting individual. She'd also come to realize how remarkably committed Aria was to finding the man with whom Kera had been having an affair, a quest that Madison had come to share. The more Madison had thought about it, the greater the redemptive power such a discovery would have for her. It had become progressively clear to Madison that she had taken Kera's unavailability much too personally and, as a result, hadn't been the friend she should have been. If she had, maybe Kera would be alive today.

The moment the train stopped at the 42nd Street station, which was the busiest in the entire NYC subway system, Madison and a good portion of the train's occupants rushed to get off. She was then part of a surge of people who power walked, almost raced, to catch their various connections. For Madison her goal was the platform for the 7 train heading east out to Main Street, Queens. It was two levels below, taking her deeper into the earth. When she arrived, she was slightly out of breath. It was a type of herd mentality that made everybody rush.

Madison moved down the platform by weaving among the people waiting. From having done the commute so many times, she knew which car of the 7 train would deposit her in the most convenient position for getting to the next platform for the final leg on the 6 train. At one point as she headed east, she managed to get close enough to the platform's edge to look back into the subway tunnel to see if she could see the distant light of an approaching train. But the tunnel was dark, so she continued on. When she got to the proper spot, she stopped and went back to reading her notebook. Most other people were fussing with their phones. Those who weren't just stared off with blank faces. Only a few people talked. Riding the NYC subway was not a social exercise.

For the eastbound 7 train, the 42nd Street station was the first stop, so the train was often not full, and on this particular morning, Madison got a seat. So, on this second segment, which was only two stops, she was able to do a bit more reading. It was becoming clearer to her exactly how she and Aria were going to go about finding Kera's lover. First, she would get kits for both the fetus and Kera from a number of the commercial DNA companies, maybe even all four of the main ones. To do that she needed samples from Aria. Her plan was to contact the companies to find out what kind of samples would be best. Getting those kits from mother and child was step one in whatever path ultimately was to be taken to find ancestral matches. While waiting for the kits, Madison planned on contacting the many websites set up to help adoptees find their natural parents, and even more apropos, she would reach out to those websites set up to help people who were conceived with donor sperm. In a very real sense, finding the identity of a sperm donor was the same situation she and Aria faced with Kera's lover. After all, most sperm donors expected anonymity, just as Kera's lover apparently did.

Madison got off at Grand Central 42nd Street station and once more joined the crowded race to make the next connection. Part of the reason for rushing was to try to avoid the situation where the connecting train would be just leaving the station. It had happened to Madison all too often, sometimes as much as once a week. For Madison the worst part of the journey was waiting for the train to arrive here at the Lexington Avenue subway line, as it could become unpleasantly crowded.

As she quickly ascended the final flight of stairs to reach the proper platform, she was relieved to see that there was no train with its doors about to close in her face. In response she slowed her ascent to a more normal pace. Other people around her did the same. Gaining the platform, she moved to the left. Over the months she'd found that the rear of the train always seemed slightly less crowded. Like on the first train, on this leg of her journey she rarely got to sit down.

Reaching what she considered to be an appropriate spot to wait, she opened her notebook yet again. She

wanted to reread what she had written about GED-
match's latest tools for maximizing matches yet still keeping false positives to a minimum. From sore experience
Madison knew that false positives were a bane to genealogists. They used up time and effort and had no redeeming qualities whatsoever. She'd been down that
road far too many times.

With such interesting reading, Madison's sense of the
passage of time was suppressed, but after a while, it suddenly occurred to her that she was still standing on the
platform, waiting for the local 6 train. Glancing up from
her notebook, she could tell that the crowd had significantly swelled on the platform from when she had arrived. That was what always happened when trains were
running late.

Pulling out her phone, she checked the time. It was
already almost twenty past seven, the time she usually
was walking into the Hassenfeld Children's Hospital,
meaning she'd been standing there reading for fifteen to
twenty minutes. Repocketing her phone, she could see
that the commuters standing near her were all becoming
restless like herself.

Madison did not want to be late after missing half of
the previous day, some of whose patients had been re-
scheduled to be squeezed into that morning. With no
countdown clock in view from where she was standing,
she cocked her head and tried to listen for an oncoming
train. She couldn't hear one. Instead she moved forward,
between other standees, and approached the edge of the

platform. Still keeping back from the yellow line painted on the very edge, she leaned forward out over the tracks and looked to the right into the subway tunnel that was relatively close to her. She could see that the tracks made a curve to the right, limiting how far she could see into the darkness. There were only a few distant, tiny points of light at intervals along the wall. It was at that very moment that she did see the headlights of an approaching train. A second later she could hear and feel the distant earthshaking rumble followed by a sudden gust of wind being pushed out of the tunnel. Mesmerized for a moment by the thunderous approach as the black silhouette of the train grew in size, Madison continued to watch. As the 360-ton behemoth rapidly neared the tunnel opening, Madison leaned away and was about to step back when something suddenly pushed her violently forward. Completely off balance, she frantically flailed her arms, sending her notebook flying, but there was no way she could keep her footing as she was catapulted out over the tracks. An instant later, to the collective gasp of the crowd, the huge train shot into the station with a tremendous screech as the emergency brakes were applied but far too late. It took almost a minute for the train to come to an abrupt halt half-in and half-out of the tunnel. Madison Bryant was nowhere to be seen. A few of the people waiting on the platform screamed. Several others who had witnessed the shameless event yelled at a heavyset, dark-haired, and bearded man in a shabby overcoat whom they had seen push Madison in front of the oncoming train. They shouted for him to stop, but the homeless-appearing man ran up the stairs and quickly disappeared in the packed concourse. Others frantically dialed 911 even though the traumatized train's engineer had already reported the incident and Emergency Services were being dispatched. The trick now was to get the body out from under the middle of the train.

CHAPTER 18

May 9th
7:40 A.M.

During most of her rotations as a pathology resident, Aria was already at the hospital complex by 7:30 in the morning. It was routine and expected. While on her forensic rotation, however, she was arriving progressively later, aware that things generally didn't get under way at the OCME until 8:00 or even 8:30. This more relaxed schedule didn't bother her in the slightest. In fact, it seemed to make more sense. She'd always wondered why American medicine felt obligated to start the day so early, particularly surgery, where scalpels were expected to make the first cut at 7:30 sharp, meaning all the other preparations had to be done by then. She also knew that in Europe things were different, particularly in the United Kingdom, where the gentlemanly time of 9:00 A.M. seemed appropriate. So, it wasn't out of the question for Aria to be just climbing into a rideshare at twenty minutes to 8:00.

In keeping with her late start, she had gotten significantly less sleep than she was accustomed to having. The night before she'd stayed up until the wee hours engrossed in genetic genealogy. With her ability to concentrate, Aria was a fast and effective reader, a skill that had made getting through medical school significantly easier for her than for most other students. She had now read, or at least skimmed, which for her was just about the equivalent of reading, both books that Madison Bryant had loaned her. The highlighting and underlining that Madison had done had not hindered Aria in the slightest and had actually helped to a degree. The benefit of having digested the two books was that now she shared Madison's belief that genetic genealogy might very well work in finding the unknown male whom Aria was now calling "Lover Boy." The more she had thought about the affair combined with what she had been able to learn from Madison Bryant and Evelyn Mabry, the more convinced she'd become that Lover Boy had had some significant role in Kera's death. Whether it was a homicide, even if inadvertent, she wasn't prepared to contend, but she certainly intended to find out. What she hoped was that Madison would prove to be as helpful a resource as she had suggested she'd be when they had met at Nobu.

As per usual, the morning rush-hour traffic was horrendous, particularly along Central Park South, the road that bordered the park at its southern end. A bit nervously, she checked the time with her phone. Although she'd not been at all concerned about her time of arrival since she'd started the forensic rotation, now that she had found something that truly interested her, namely finding Lover Boy, she didn't want to annoy anyone, particularly the chief, Laurie Montgomery. At least until she'd solved this current quest, Aria preferred to stay in the chief's good graces.

Instead of fretting over what she couldn't alter, she put her phone away and went back to her musing about Lover Boy. Her first thought had been that Lover Boy was probably married, and now that she had had time to think about it, she was convinced that had to be the case. It might also explain why the sudden conception was most likely not thought of as a blessing. Instead it could have made serious waves. It seemed to make sense, and as such further lowered Aria's opinion of the male gender.

With a sudden feeling of restlessness and the need to do something, Aria struggled to get her phone back out from the pocket of her jeans. Thinking about Lover Boy prompted her to put in an early call to Madison, hoping to catch her before her first client. With the phone pressed against her ear, she listened to the simulated ringing. After the fourth ring, she sensed that Madison wasn't going to answer, and she guessed why: It was a bit after eight, and Madison most likely was meeting with her first family of the day.

Aria was planning on leaving a voice message to request a call back as soon as it was convenient, but voice mail never picked up. With a shrug, she disconnected.

Instead she typed a text message, asking for Madison to contact her as soon as possible. As a teaser, she added: I read both books and I'm psyched.

Once Aria managed to get to Second Avenue, the trip picked up speed. Although she had made the same trip in just over fifteen minutes without traffic, on this particular morning it ended up taking almost an hour. She was dropped off at 8:35, and despite reasonable expectations of being close to being on time, she was more than a half hour late.

Normally Aria first went to the so-called residents' room on the second floor to leave her personal belongings like a coat and any books she'd brought. It was located just beyond the space euphemistically called the lunch room, thanks to its assortment of vending machines. Both were subpar in most every respect, although the lunch room at least had some high windows that let in a bit of outside light. Of course, there was no view as the neighboring building was a scant fifteen or twenty feet away. The residents' room was more like a closet with two aged metal desks pressed up against each other and no windows. The redeeming part was that both desks supported monitors with Internet access and first-class microscopes.

Being late and having no coat other than her white resident's jacket, she went directly to the ID, or identification, unit, where she had been told all the medical examiners gathered in the morning. She'd learned that one of the medical examiners on a weekly rotating basis made a final decision about which of the bodies that had come in during the night should be autopsied and dispersed them among his or her colleagues. By the time Aria walked in there were only two medical examiners still there, Dr. Chet McGovern and a woman of Indian extraction named Dr. Riva Mehta. Both were seated at what was generally called the scheduling desk. A small number of case charts littered the desktop. Everyone had already gotten their assignments and had left to descend to the pit.

"Well, well!" Chet said. "It's so nice of you to grace us with your presence."

Aria ignored his sarcasm and went to the communal coffeepot, which she had been pressured to contribute to monetarily. She poured herself a cup and mentally prepared to deal with McGovern, who had rubbed her the wrong way from the first moments she'd met him. It was the way he had looked at her that keyed off her sixth sense even before he'd said anything. Dr. Mehta she had also met and had observed doing a trauma victim. It had been a pedestrian hit and run over by a yellow cab and dragged a hundred yards or so. Aria had found the case mildly interesting although she'd not learned anything that wasn't obvious. To her, so much of forensics was just common sense.

"There was more traffic than usual," Aria said after walking back to the scheduling desk.

"How come your colleague, Dr. Muller, manages to get here on time every day?" Chet said more as a statement than a question. He had an accusatory smirk on his face that irked Aria to no end.

"I wouldn't know," she said with disinterest. And then, not being able to control herself, added, "Maybe he mistakenly thinks he is learning something valuable." The reality was that she had little respect for Tad Muller. The ass-kisser was still acting like he was trying to get into medical school rather than someone who was almost within a year of finishing his residency. Aria was almost embarrassed to be on the rotation with him.

"Well, let me tell you something, young lady," Chet said. "I went out of my way to talk Dr. Stapleton into allowing you to work with him on an interesting gunshot case this morning. The problem is that Dr. Stapleton is a dynamo and has been down in the pit since seven thirty. For all I know he could be nearly finished. My advice is to get your butt down there ASAP. When you're done, find me, and I'll assign you another case. We've got a full schedule today."

Irritated anew by the patronizing "young lady" appellation and without bothering to respond, Aria broke off staring at Chet and walked out of the ID area. She was carrying her coffee mug even though on her first day McGovern had told her to avoid doing it. She considered it was one of those pointless hazing rules that only residents were supposed to honor. Once at the rear elevator, she had to wait for it to arrive. She could have used the stairs as it would have been quicker, but she felt a passive-aggressive urge not to make any effort. Once downstairs, she passed the mortuary office and went into the women's locker room to get into scrubs. Five minutes later she was pushing into the autopsy room. The odor immedi-

ately reminded her of yesterday's autopsy of Kera Jacobsen, making her wish she could just skip the autopsy
room altogether and work on the case she was actually
interested in.

As she expected, Dr. Jack Stapleton and his favorite
technician, Vinnie Amendola, were using table #1 at the
far end. She had learned that since he started before
everyone else, he got to choose which table he wanted.
With her apron, gloves, and face shield already in place,
she was prepared to participate. How much she did
depended on the whim of the individual medical examiner, and it ranged from her essentially doing the case as
with Dr. Montgomery the previous afternoon, to doing
next to nothing as had happened with the deputy chief,
Dr. George Fontworth, two days before that. Since she
had yet to be slotted to work with Dr. Stapleton, she had
no idea of what to expect. Word had it that he was fast as
Dr. McGovern had just suggested, which under the circumstances Aria appreciated. What she really wanted to
do was get back to Kera's case. Before she left the locker
room, she'd checked her messages in hopes of having
some response from Madison, but there wasn't any.

All the tables were in operation, making it necessary for
Aria to walk the length of the room. The corpses on each
table were in varying stages of dissection, with some intact
and others gutted. Dr. Stapleton's was one of the ones that
appeared to be near the end of the autopsy. The corpse
was that of a mildly overweight Caucasian male, who Aria
guessed was in his twenties or early thirties. The right side
of his scalp had been shaved to expose a grazing bullet

wound. A second entrance wound was on the right thigh. She couldn't tell if there were any wounds to the chest or abdomen because the body was flayed open with the margins folded back.

"Speak of the devil," Dr. Stapleton said loud enough for Aria to hear, when he caught sight of her approaching. "Vinnie, check this out! Our prayers have been answered. It seems that Dr. Nichols has deigned to join us after all." He was holding a wooden dowel about three feet long. One of the OCME photographers was standing nearby, obviously taking pictures as Dr. Stapleton would position the dowel. It was Aria's immediate impression they were most likely documenting the tracks of bullets.

"Good afternoon, Dr. Nichols," Dr. Stapleton added when she reached the table. "Did you have a nice lunch?"

Tad Muller had already warned Aria several days earlier that Dr. Stapleton thought of himself as being sarcastically humorous and clever at double entendre. She wondered if anyone had warned Stapleton that she was immune to such barbs.

"Traffic was heavier than usual," Aria said simply.

For a minute Jack stared at this resident as he recalled most everything that Laurie had said about her, including her having an unappealing, possibly sociopathic personality and a negative appreciation of the male gender. Although blaming traffic for being that late seemed almost comical to him, he held back from calling her on what he imagined was a passive-aggressive stunt. What was the point, especially since Laurie was making a considerable effort on her behalf? It was Laurie who he was worried about, not this apparently damaged individual. Besides, she was supposedly smart, particularly with surgical pathology, and could contribute without having to deal directly with patients. Uncharacteristically, Jack forwent the grand opportunity to do verbal battle with someone he guessed might be a reasonably worthy opponent. With those thoughts in mind, he cleared his throat and said: "Sorry about the traffic, and now that you are here, let us fill you in on this rather interesting case."

Vinnie's head popped up and he stared at Jack with disbelief. Although he personally had not had any interaction with Aria, he'd heard the rumors about her uppity and privileged attitude from the mortuary techs who'd had to deal with her. When Jack had told him that morning that she would be joining them on the gunshot case, Vinnie had been secretly pleased. He'd fully expected to witness the woman's deserved comeuppance, which Jack would surely supply.

"How many forensic gunshot cases have you observed?" Jack asked in a normal tone of voice.

"This is my first," Aria admitted, almost afraid of what might be coming. She didn't want a lecture. All she wanted was to get an idea of the forensic approach to a victim of gun violence and then get the hell out of the autopsy room. She had far better things to do that were going to be far more intellectually stimulating and emotionally rewarding. With her reading speed and retention ability, she could read an entire forensic textbook chapter on gunshot wounds in thirty minutes without having to put up with the autopsy room odor or the need to stand around on a concrete floor for several hours with people she couldn't have cared less about.

Unfortunately, from her perspective Jack did launch into lecture mode. He started by giving the background on the case they were doing. The victim was a reputed burglary suspect who had resisted arrest by drawing a gun and shooting at the arresting officers. The officers returned fire and killed the individual, striking him six times. What the police were looking for was "justifiable homicide."

"After the full-body X-ray to see all the retained projectiles," Jack said, "it is important to examine the body with all the clothes on. The reason is to see if there is any powder residue on the clothes since one of the main objectives of the forensic autopsy is to determine the range of fire, or how far away the gun was from the victim."

Aria nodded. She wanted to tell Jack that he needn't bother telling her stuff that was intuitive, but she didn't. She felt she had to grin and bear it as Jack droned on, talking about the need to try to determine the sequence of injuries when there were multiple gunshot wounds, as was the situation with the current case. Next Jack began to talk about differentiating entrance wounds from exit wounds and why such a determination was key. "On this case, two of the entrance wounds were in the back, which doesn't bode well for what the police are hoping we will be reporting, especially when you take into consideration the angle of entrance. Let me show you what I mean."

Jack picked up one of the cadaver's arms and reached it across to Vinnie. "Give me a hand. Let's show her the back."

With Vinnie pulling on the arm and Jack lifting the edge of the torso, the cadaver was rotated onto its left side. "Here you can see two entrance wounds. The one on the upper back is circular and defined. See it?"

"Obviously," Aria said. After looking at the wound, her eyes rose up to take in the institutional clock on the wall. It had been only a little more than a half hour since she'd checked for messages from Madison Bryant, and she wondered if there was one now waiting for her when she was able to break free from her current bondage with this would-be professor. To her it was amazing how he could carry on with so little feedback. For the last five minutes or so Aria had been back to mulling over the ins and outs of genetic genealogy.

"So, what do you think?" Jack suddenly said, interrupting her chain of thought.

"About what?" Aria asked.

"About this type of linear entrance wound," Jack said. He was pointing toward the victim's lower back, which bore a splayed-out wound that resembled a leafless tree a child might draw. The base pointed caudally, the branches pointing toward the victim's head.

"I'd say the bullet had to strike at an acute angle," Aria answered.

"Give the lady a prize," Jack said. Despite what he knew about her, he was impressed. He had planned on mounting an extensive explanation of the shearing forces of the bullet creating the tiny skin tags that pointed toward the point of initial contact, but he scrapped it. Jumping ahead, he said: "Since you were able to figure that out so quickly, what does it say to you that might be important in the forensic report?"

"I'd say that the victim had to be either falling or already prone on the ground when the bullet struck him."

Jack straightened up and gently clapped with his gloved hands. "You are a quick study when it comes to forensics," he said. "And I suppose you have a sense of how this information might be received by the police and the district attorney."

"It would throw a cloud over the justifiable-homicide claim, especially when added to any bodycam footage, if it exists."

"Okay," Jack said to Vinnie. "Let Mr. Karpas roll back so we can continue our photographic documentation of the pathways of all the bullets." He picked up the dowel he had been holding when Aria had first arrived and turned to her and said: "Let's show you the tracks of all the bullets, including this last apparent coup de grâce."

It was another half hour before the case was over. Jack was finishing his elaborate diagram of all the gunshot markings while Vinnie went to get a gurney. Vinnie had already finished labeling all the envelopes with the bullet fragments that had been painstakingly found, their locations described and documented. For a moment no one was paying the slightest attention to Aria, so she merely turned around and made her way back to the entrance.

She hoped that the director of education, Dr. McGovern, wasn't involved in any of the autopsies she passed for fear he would try to assign her yet another case. As if it might help, she kept her vision concentrated on the exit, looking neither to the right nor the left. A moment later, with a sense of relief, she pushed through the autopsy room doors and emerged into the deserted main hallway.

Inside the locker room, the first thing she did was get out her phone. She fully expected by this time to have a text from Madison, hopefully saying where and when they could get together. To her utter dismay after what she'd had to endure in the autopsy room, there was no message from Madison. Nothing. No emails, texts, or voice mail. Cursing under her breath, she changed into her clothes.

When she was almost finished, she heard her phone indicate she was getting a text. With a sense of excitement and expectation, she struggled to get the phone out of her back pocket. When she finally managed to do so, she was disappointed. The text wasn't from Madison. It was from Dr. Montgomery, and it was terse. It merely said: I need to talk with you. Please come to my office.

CHAPTER 19

So that's the long and short of it," Laurie said to Dr. George Fontworth, who had been appointed two years ago to serve as the deputy chief medical examiner under Laurie, replacing Paul Plodget. At first she had been disappointed with the selection because she and Jack had never believed George lived up to his potential. He had stellar credentials, perhaps the best of the OCME, having been trained by some of the forensic greats, but he had been content seemingly to do mediocre work over the years as one of the staff MEs. But to Laurie's pleasant surprise, the appointment as deputy chief had lit a fire under the man to the point that she had to give the Selection Committee credit for seeing his potential. Particularly over the past year, he turned out to be a huge asset to her on multiple fronts. Jack had labeled the transition *astounding*.

"Any questions, George?" she asked. They were in Laurie's office, she behind her huge desk and George seated across from her. The desk was a partner's desk, so for meetings such as this one, the seating arrangement was natural. For meetings involving more people, Laurie preferred to use the large library table she had at the other end of her office that had adequate space for up to ten people. For meetings of that size, they had to raid other offices for chairs.

"I can only think of one question," George said. His expression was appropriately serious in respect to what Laurie had just told him. "How long do you think you will be hospitalized?"

"That's hard to say," she said. "Of course, I'd like it to be the minimum possible, but it all depends on what is found."

"I understand," George said solemnly.

Laurie had just finished telling George that she had made plans within the hour to undergo semi-emergency surgery. As soon as she'd got to the OCME that morning, she'd put in a call to Dr. Claudine Cartier, one of the NYU Langone Medical Center's busiest surgeons, who specialized in breast surgery. She had been highly recommended by the oncologist Dr. Wayne Herbert, who had in turn been recommended several years ago by Dr. Sue Passero, Laurie's internist and old college chum. She had already briefly spoken with Claudine Cartier the previous day after getting the bad news from the screening and had been told she had to make the decision as to how to approach the biopsy dilemma. When Dr. Cartier had returned the call that morning, Laurie had told her she had decided to deal with the suspicious lump with the "Angelina Jolie approach," namely with bilateral mastectomies and an oophorectomy. Laurie had already had one ovary and one fallopian tube removed years earlier when she'd had an ectopic pregnancy. Her only other wish was to do the procedure as soon as possible. Dr. Cartier said she understood, would check her schedule, and get back to Laurie, probably that afternoon, about when it could be done. Optimistically she'd added that the chances of scheduling the operation within the next few days were very good because she'd had several cancellations due to patients having influenza.

"I'll be letting everyone know as soon as the operation is scheduled," Laurie said. "I wanted to tell you first since you'll be the one shouldering most of the burden. There is nothing key scheduled except for the need to finalize the plans for the new Forensic Pathology center so it can be sent out to bid. But even that can wait. Thank goodness I got the City Council Health Committee meeting out of the way yesterday. I wouldn't have wanted you to suffer through that."

"I still might have to, after what happened last night," George said.

"I certainly hope not," she said, although she knew there was a slight chance. That morning when Laurie got to the OCME, intending to call the surgeon immediately, she had to deal with another mild calamity first by having a lengthy and unpleasant meeting with the director of the Mortuary/Transportation Department. Even though at the City Council Health Committee meeting the day before she'd testified that the problem of bodies being misdirected had been solved with the changes that she'd instigated to the case management system, it had happened again, just last night. Similar to the previous episode, the deceased shared the same family name. This time it was Cooper. However, they did not share the first name as had been the case with the two Nortons, so the incident highlighted pure, unadulterated mismanagement on the part of the responsible mortuary technician. On this occasion it was an Arlene Cooper and an Alan Cooper, meaning they didn't even share the same gender. Luckily the mix-up was immediately discovered by the first funeral home, so the involved families remained in the dark about their loved ones taking one extra final ride before their funerals.

George pushed back from the desk and stood; Laurie did the same.

"I want to thank you in advance for what you'll be doing," Laurie said. She was genuinely grateful, and it was going to be one thing less to worry about with George at the helm while she was in the hospital and convalescing at home if that was necessary.

"I'm here to help you, Laurie. We will all want you to be back as soon as you can. I hope all goes smoothly."

"I appreciate your thoughts and well-wishes," she said as she accompanied George to the door. "I'll keep you up to speed as things develop. Until I make an announcement, I would prefer that you keep what I've said to yourself."

"It goes without saying," George said. "Will you be at this afternoon's conference?"

"I certainly plan to," Laurie said.

After George walked across the outer office and into his own, Laurie called out to Cheryl that she was expecting Dr. Nichols and to send her right in. In anticipation, she left her door ajar.

Returning behind her desk, she sat down. She needed a little breathing time as it had been nonstop activity since she'd arrived. But it wasn't to be. Almost the moment she sank into her desk chair Aria walked through the open door. Curious whether their time together the day before doing the autopsy would influence Aria's haughty, almost aggressively hostile attitude, Laurie watched her from the moment she appeared. Most people were mildly intimidated by the size of the office in conjunction with Laurie's lofty title. But not Aria. She didn't so much as glance at her, nor did she seem to survey the scene. Instead she just marched in and plopped herself down into the seat that George had just vacated as if it were her office, not Laurie's. Only then did she look across the desk at Laurie with an expression of contemptuous boredom. With some effort Laurie controlled her irritation.

The two women eyed each other for a moment, each expecting the other to break the silence. Laurie was the first to respond. "After working together yesterday, don't I deserve at least a 'Hello, Dr. Montgomery'?"

"You're the one who asked me to come here, not the other way around."

"I suppose you're right," Laurie said, inwardly smiling at her own behavior. It wasn't like her to have such petty thoughts. She reminded herself she was dealing with an individual with obvious psychological problems, which was one of the reasons she had requested to see her. That morning, like almost every morning, Laurie made what she called *autopsy chief rounds*. Just after nine she'd gone down to the pit despite how busy she was and went from table to table to hear extemporaneous presentations by each medical examiner of the case they were doing. The overt justification for the exercise was the idea of her possibly adding some bit of knowledge or experience to the case. For the newer MEs and the Forensic Pathology fellows, this often was helpful and educational, less so for the more experienced. But for Laurie, it was a pleasure as well as an acknowledgment of how much she missed participating in the nitty-gritty of forensic pathology these days. Around 9:15 as she was nearing table #1, the table that Jack invariably used, she became aware of Aria's presence. Although it sounded as if things were going okay with Jack lecturing and Aria seemingly listening, which surprised her, she didn't want to be the spark that might set off a major conflagration between two potentially flammable personalities. So she deliberately avoided table #1 or even advertising her presence by saying hello. Yet her curiosity had been aroused. When she got back to her office a few minutes later, she sent Aria a text that she wanted to see her. Finding out why she and Jack had not been at each other's throats was just one of the reasons why.

"How is your day going?" Laurie asked.

"That's what you needed to talk to me about?" Aria asked with obvious disbelief. Small talk to her was clearly a total waste of time.

"I understand you were assigned a gunshot case this morning," Laurie said. "Did you find it interesting?"

"No! It was a bore," Aria said. "Dr. Stapleton likes to lecture too much, overly explaining even super-simple stuff."

"Most people don't find working with Dr. Stapleton boring," Laurie said. She couldn't help but feel a little defensive. She wondered who had been acting out of character. When she had first realized they were together, she'd regretted not telling Chet to avoid pairing them. Yet her concern obviously had been without basis. Her curiosity ratcheted upward.

"Most people are probably reluctant to tell the truth about Jack Stapleton because he is married to the chief," Aria said.

"Maybe so," Laurie said to humor her but also thinking there might be some truth to what she had just said. It was an issue she'd not given too much thought. None-theless, she couldn't wait to hear Jack's side of this strange episode, recognizing that he had to have been on remarkably good behavior for some unknown reason. With that decided, she moved on to the real reason she wanted to see Aria. "Have you made any progress with the Kera Jacobsen case?"

"Some, but not a lot," Aria said. "Enough to realize I've hit somewhat of a brick wall." Although *brick wall* was a common term, Aria had found in her reading about genetic genealogy that the field had commandeered the term for problems some people faced while filling out their family trees. Curiously enough, it applied already to Kera's case even though the genealogy part hadn't begun.

"You'll have to explain," Laurie said.

"I spoke with the MLI on the case as you insisted," Aria said. "He was helpful in that he put me onto the only two people who might have been able to help me locate Lover Boy: Kera's close friend and coworker, Madison Bryant, and a nosy, paranoid, misfit neighbor, Evelyn Mabry. I already spoke at length with both of them. By far Madison Bryant was the most helpful. Evelyn Mabry was a dud. She saw Lover Boy on multiple occasions by looking through her peephole but claims she never saw his face. All in all, Lover Boy managed to keep his identity unknown from either one, which has just magnified my suspicions about the guy."

"So 'Lover Boy' is what you've decided to call the missing father?" Laurie said.

"Yeah," Aria said. "Seems appropriate. My sense is that they didn't do a lot of socializing. I think they just met at her place for sex, which was most likely his decision, not hers, which makes me guess he is married."

"It seems to me that you are making a lot of assumptions."

"You wouldn't think so if you'd been forced by your nanny to watch as many soap operas when you were a kid as I did," Aria said.

"Perhaps," Laurie said, feeling sorry for Aria and the kind of childhood she must have had. "But I think I should point out that calling the missing father 'Lover Boy' sounds distinctly pejorative. I need to remind you that as the forensic pathologist on the case, you should try to stay neutral and unemotional. Our job is to get at the truth of the manner and cause of death, and let other people cast blame if it's warranted."

"To me that's just a lot of bullshit," Aria said. "Please, no lectures! I got enough lecturing this morning watching the gunshot autopsy. Maybe maintaining neutrality is the goal you people strive for, but it isn't realistic. Not for me, and not for your hubby yesterday afternoon. I could hear him and that cop carrying on about how they felt about the shithead that dunked that poor child into a bathtub of scalding water. I feel the same about Lover Boy. I want to find him."

"On some cases it's hard to remain emotionally neutral. I give you that. Regardless, the more unemotional you force yourself to remain, the better job you'll do. Trust me. Forensic pathology is a fantastic resource for a ton of reasons, including helping law enforcement. But it has its limitations, and this Jacobsen tragedy might be one of those cases where it can't answer all the questions. Unless we learn something unusual from Toxicology or get a surprise about someone else's fingerprints or DNA on the syringe, I believe we're going to have to sign it out as an accidental overdose. Tell me, did you do the dictation of the autopsy as you said you would do?"

"No, I didn't," Aria said. "I'll do it this morning. I've been busy since we finished yesterday."

"It's best to do the dictation immediately after the case to keep from forgetting important details," Laurie said, hearing the mild accusatory tone in her voice.

"Relax," Aria said. "I'm not going to forget any details. Trust me."

"I'll trust you only after I read the autopsy report, and it is complete," Laurie told her.

"I spent most of the night studying some new stuff," Aria said. "I think forensic pathology has a lot more to add to this case. Despite the brick wall, I think it can find Lover Boy."

"And how do you imagine that might happen?"

"By taking advantage of the fact that the NYU OCME possibly has the biggest and best DNA lab in the world." Aria moved forward in the chair as evidence of her excitement. "What needs to happen is that the Molecular Genetics Department has to team up with ancestral DNA or genetic genealogy companies. Genetic genealogy has overnight become a powerful tool now that fifteen million people plus have been encouraged by the companies to have their DNA added to the ancestral database."

For a few beats, Laurie stared at the pathology resident sitting in front of her while she struggled to figure out how to respond. Laurie could immediately sense the woman's enthusiasm and commitment, which she appreciated and didn't want to suppress. After all, one of her goals for having done the Kera Jacobsen autopsy with her was to get a struggling resident interested enough in forensics to perform adequately to avoid a potential brouhaha between the NYU Department of Pathology and the NYU Department of Forensic Pathology. Yet the idea of the OCME using ancestral DNA as part of the forensic investigation was inherently flawed, and from an administrative point of view a nonstarter.

"I can sense your disbelief," Aria said in response to Laurie's silence. "I have to admit, that was my initial reaction as well. Ironically enough, it was Kera's friend and coworker who brought up the notion by reminding me of the relatively recent apprehension of the Golden State Killer in California. Do you remember that? It was all over the news."

"Of course I remember that case," Laurie said.

"Did you know that they went back to find common great-great-great-grandparents who lived in the early 1800s in order to find the guy? Then they had to construct some twenty-five family trees with thousands of relatives, but they still found him. It's pretty remarkable when you think about it."

"I agree," Laurie said. "But finding the Golden State Killer was different from what we're facing with Kera Jacobsen. They had the killer's DNA. It was just a matter of law enforcement matching the DNA with a specific individual."

"That was exactly my response when Madison Bryant

suggested the idea to me," Aria said. "But I had no idea how this genetic genealogical field has progressed scientifically over just the last few years, and how popular it has become. Overnight it's practically created a virtual army of homegrown genealogists who are truly dedicated. At first these people were interested in uncovering their personal family tree, but then they seemed to get hooked and now are eager to help other people solve their issues. I think we could get a virtual army working on Kera's case."

"Well, that's all very interesting," Laurie said. "But there's a reality here that I must bring to your attention above and beyond the problem of us not having the father's DNA."

"We might not have the father's complete DNA, but with the fetus's DNA we have fifty percent of it right off the bat. We also have the mother's DNA, so we don't have to guess which half of the fetus's DNA comes from the father. Interestingly enough, this situation turns out to be exactly the same as an individual who was conceived with donor sperm. Many of these people are very interested in finding their genetic fathers if for no other reason than to feel genetically connected. Entire websites and organizations have popped up just to help these people, along with fascinating statistical tools to help them find genetic matches in the vast DNA database, which is expanding on a day-to-day basis. I'm sure that it will work."

Laurie cleared her throat, not sure how to begin explaining to Aria that her suggestion wasn't about to happen. With her elbows on the desk, Laurie tented her hands and looked her straight in the eyes. Aria stared back with even more intensity, absolutely confident in what she had just said.

"It sounds to me that you've given this idea some serious thought," Laurie said, wanting not to sound too negative in light of Aria's zeal.

"You bet your ass," Aria said. "I stayed up most of the night reading about genetic genealogy. It's surprisingly complicated stuff, which I am amazed has been absorbed and understood by so many people trained in neither biology nor statistics."

"I hate to break this to you, Aria, but unfortunately, there is a legal restriction here that is insurmountable."

"Oh, come on," Aria snapped. Her mouth dropped open in shock. "What the fuck are you talking about?"

Laurie gritted her teeth at Aria's choice of words. "I know you like to speak your mind," she said. "But in my presence, I ask you to refrain from vulgarity."

Aria rolled her eyes.

"I see you don't agree," Laurie said. "Well, be that as it may, I need to tell you that here in New York State we have a Commission of Forensic Science established by law. One of the commission's major roles is accreditation of DNA laboratories, which is necessary if DNA results are to be accepted in the court of law. The OCME Molecular Genetics laboratory is accredited, as I'm sure you are aware, and we must maintain that accreditation, which requires constant effort. Commercial genealogy companies are not accredited DNA laboratories, and if our lab has anything to do with them, we would instantly lose our accreditation. Do you understand?"

It was now Aria's turn to stare with disbelief at Laurie.

"Your silence tells me you don't understand," Laurie said. "Let me give you an example. In the court of law, evidence must have a clear chain of custody that cannot be challenged. Commercial DNA laboratories accept saliva DNA samples with absolutely no chain of custody. All they have is the consumer's word of the origin of any given sample. Same with how the sample is treated in their laboratories. Obviously, we here at the OCME have to do it in a completely different fashion. Also, our laboratory has to adhere to specific rules about training and mechanisms to uncover negligence or misconduct. The commercial labs have none of that. We're two different worlds that cannot work together or interact."

"I think this sucks," Aria said. "It's bureaucratic bullshit. Here's an opportunity for a major witness to be discovered, and it has to be abandoned. That doesn't make sense to me. No way!"

"You are entitled to your opinion," Laurie said. "But that's the way it has to be. Perhaps we can find another forensic case for you to become interested in pursuing."

Aria stood up. "I'm not going to give up on this one even if I can't get the Molecular Genetics lab involved. As you said yesterday, I'm still listening to Kera Jacobsen."

"Suit yourself," Laurie said. "But I'd like you to keep me informed of what progress you make and don't make, and you cannot involve our Molecular Genetics Department. In the meantime, I'd like you to dictate the autopsy report."

"Okay," Aria said simply. She stood and walked out without saying goodbye or looking back.

For a few minutes Laurie stared at the open door, replaying some parts of the conversation and marveling anew at Aria's personality. For a moment, she entertained the idea of giving Jack a call to find out what had transpired during the autopsy he'd done with the woman. She still couldn't believe there had been no fireworks, knowing what she did about both people. But she didn't have time for such a personal indulgence, when she was imminently expecting a call from the architects about the new Pathology building.

CHAPTER 20

May 9th
11:25 A.M.

Disconnecting from the dictation service after finishing Kera's autopsy report, Aria removed her feet from the corner of the beat-up metal desk that she'd been assigned and let them fall to the floor. That way she was able to tilt forward enough to get her phone out of her back pocket. She'd not felt any buzz of incoming messages, but she was still hopeful. But there were no emails, texts, or voice mail, which confused and aggravated her. She'd left Madison a text to contact her almost four hours ago. As an added inducement she'd added that she was psyched to connect with her. Yet there had been no communication whatsoever. It never failed to amaze her how people were generally unreliable.

With sudden resolve, Aria decided to pay Social Services at the Hassenfeld Children's Hospital a visit. After

Madison's apparent enthusiasm last night at Nobu for finding Lover Boy, Aria was shocked she'd not gotten in touch that morning even if she was ridiculously busy, which was probably the case. Although Aria knew she could call the Hassenfeld Social Services line, she decided that wasn't all that different from leaving a message on Madison's mobile, which had gotten no response. The solution, simply enough, was to walk over there, barge in on whatever she was doing, and talk to her directly. It was only the equivalent of four city blocks away, and having been an NYU pathology resident for almost four years, she knew exactly where the Social Services Department was in the pediatric outpatient clinic.

The weather was again stellar, with a transparent blue sky and bright sunshine that seemed a world away from the windowless OCME autopsy room. Walking north up First Avenue, Aria passed the busy front of the NYU Langone Medical Center with taxis and a few ambulances lined up in the turnout. She continued on, passing the Emergency Services entrance until she arrived at the driveway for the Kimmel Pavilion. Turning right again on 34th Street, she passed the huge, whimsical sculpture of the Dalmatian balancing a full-size yellow cab on its nose and entered the Hassenfeld Children's Hospital. With her resident white coat and ID card, she wasn't challenged by the security personnel.

The clinic was packed with children of all ages and their parents. She skirted the reception desk and went directly to the tiny Social Services scheduling office. Inside were two secretaries manning two desks pushed together to face each other. They wore headsets, as they were almost constantly on the phone scheduling visits. Aria had to wait until one of the women looked up and beckoned to her to indicate she was momentarily free. "Can I help you, Doctor?" she asked.

"I'm looking for Madison Bryant," Aria said. "Can you direct me to her office?"

Instead of answering directly, the secretary looked over at her colleague as if she needed help. The other secretary had heard Aria's request and in what was clearly a nonverbal exchange between the coworkers, merely shrugged her shoulders.

"Her office is the third door heading down the main hall," the secretary said. "But she's not there. She's in intensive care in Bellevue Hospital."

"What?" Aria was sure she'd misheard. "Why? What happened?"

"An awful accident from what we have heard," the woman said. "The poor woman was hit by a train."

Taken by surprise and without verbally responding, Aria abruptly turned around and walked out into the busy clinic. She knew that subway accidents were not unheard of in New York City. In point of fact they were relatively common, on average of two or three a month with people jumping in front of trains or even being pushed.

Just beyond earshot, she stopped and cursed under her breath: "Damn, fucking, shit!" She had become progressively irritated when Madison hadn't contacted her all morning. Now she was even more pissed because she had been counting on this woman's help. Madison had talked her into the idea of using genetic genealogy to find the missing father, and now she'd gone and gotten herself hit by a train. Aria couldn't believe how inconvenient this was, putting the burden of dealing with these commercial ancestral DNA companies on her shoulders. But then she had another thought, remembering instances when people who'd ended up on the subway tracks managed to hunker down between the rails to allow the train to pass over them with minimal damage, maybe just a broken leg or a few broken ribs. The reality was that Madison wasn't at the OCME waiting to be autopsied but rather was in critical care in Bellevue, a familiar hospital to Aria because NYU residents were part of the staff just as they were in the NYU hospitals that made up the NYU Langone Medical Center. All that meant that Madison had to be alive. How alive, was the question.

Quickly getting her phone out of her pocket, Aria checked for news of a subway accident by looking at the websites for the *Daily News* and the *New York Post*, which loved such stories. As expected, there was reference to a woman having been pushed in front of a Lexington Avenue train at Grand Central, but it was a bare-bones piece with no word about the woman's condition other than that she'd been taken to Bellevue Hospital. With that meager information, Aria decided to do a bit of her own reporting. If Madison wasn't hurt too badly and could talk, there was still a chance she could contribute to the Lover Boy effort since her experience of dealing with the commercial DNA companies could be critical. After all, there was a mild time restraint for her as she was only scheduled to be on her forensic rotation for another couple of weeks. Once she transitioned back to being a regular pathology resident, she knew she wouldn't have the time to pursue a paternity investigation regardless of her current emotional motivation.

But before setting out, Aria called the main switchboard operator at Bellevue to find out where Madison was since the hospital had a number of intensive-care units. Aria assumed that she'd be in the Shock-Trauma ICU connected to the Emergency Department, but it turned out she was wrong. Madison was in the unit on the second floor of the west wing that had private rooms. In a way that was good news as it suggested that not only was Madison still alive, but she must be in reasonably stable condition and therefore could probably talk. It was all the more reason for her to make the effort to visit.

Leaving Hassenfeld, Aria retraced her steps, now heading south on First Avenue. Moving quickly, she again passed the four-block expanse of the Langone Medical Center and then even OCME as well. Now she was walking along several of the aged brick buildings that had been part of the old Bellevue Hospital and were still standing. As she'd done many times walking between the hospitals, she wondered what kind of horror stories they could tell if they could talk. The new Bellevue was just beyond, and she entered through the front door.

Once again, her NYU Medical Center identification

card that hung around her neck on a lanyard was the ticket for uninterrupted access to various portions of the hospital. Pushing her way through the crowds, Aria used an elevator to get to the second-floor west wing, where the ICU was located.

As a pathology resident Aria had had little reason to visit Bellevue ICU except when she'd rotated through the hospital as an anatomical pathology resident. On several occasions she attended teaching rounds, so she was acquainted with how it was set up. The fact that it had private rooms made being an ICU patient a bit more tolerable from the patient's perspective and was intended to keep them from getting PTSD. It afforded the opportunity to be shielded to a degree from calamities happening to other patients. Until recently, the mental trauma of being an ICU patient had not been given the thought it deserved. The 24/7 full illumination and activity combined with the sounds of the respirators and cardiac monitors were enough to drive someone mad.

From her experience as a sub-intern while she was in her fourth year of medical school, she knew whom to speak with first. The ICU charge nurse essentially ran the unit during her shift even if critical care residents were present, which was usually the case, or even intensivist attendings. As Aria entered the unit, she was surprised to see a number of NYPD personnel standing off to the side and chatting among themselves, both uniformed and some in plainclothes who she guessed were detectives. Aria found the charge nurse at the central desk, which was the equivalent of the brain of the ICU with a bank of monitors showing each of the patients' vital signs as well as their cardiac function. Each patient had their own intensive-care nurse who spent seventy-five to eighty percent of the time at the bedside. On this particular shift, the charge nurse was Maureen D'Silva, and she was running the show as if she were a conductor of a symphony orchestra. Aria had to wait to get a word in edgewise.

"I'm here to see Madison Bryant," she said the moment she had an opportunity.

"You and everyone else," Maureen said. But then her attention was demanded elsewhere, and she had to yell across the room about blood work that needed to be done. A moment later she redirected her attention to Aria. "Who was it you were inquiring about?"

"Madison Bryant," Aria said.

"Right, the subway victim," Maureen said. "She's in room eight."

"Is she conscious?" Aria asked. "Is she able to talk?"

Maureen held up her hand horizontally and wobbled it in midair. "She's in and out of consciousness, but reasonably oriented to time, place, and person when she's with us. Considering what happened to her, she's one lucky unlucky woman. Medically she is surprisingly stable, which is why they moved her up here."

"Were you joking about other people coming to see her?" Aria said.

"Not at all," Maureen said. "All these policemen are here because of her, as well as a bunch of bigwigs, who are in her room right at the moment."

"Why the fuss?" Aria asked.

"Apparently she was pushed by some homeless guy," Maureen said. "At least that's the word."

"What do you mean by 'bigwigs'?"

"Try the president and CEO of Langone Health and Hospitals," Maureen said. She was obviously impressed. "It's the first time I've seen the man in the flesh. Plus, there are some NYU Medical School department heads and the head of Bellevue Emergency Department in there, too."

"You mean Vernon Pierce is here?" Aria asked. From where she was standing at the central desk, she could see into room 8. The room looked full, and as she watched, people started coming out into the hallway. She even saw someone she recognized: Dr. Carl Henderson.

"That's Vernon Pierce," Maureen said, pointing at the first man who had emerged from room 8. He was of a bit more than average height and heavyset, with moderately long black hair slicked back and parted on the left. His face was full but not flabby, with a dark complexion and a five-o'clock shadow. It occurred to Aria that if he weren't a hospital president, he could have passed for a mob boss.

"What is the extent of Madison Bryant's injuries?" Aria asked, still wondering about the chances of her helping with Lover Boy's identity.

"A broken leg, a few broken ribs, a fractured skull, and a broken arm. The worst part is that she lost a foot from just above the ankle. Luckily, she landed between the rails except for the foot."

Holy shit, Aria thought. Fractured skull meant con-
cussion or worse, which argued against her being in any
condition to help, at least on this particular day. Before
even trying to talk with her, Aria was now feeling progressively negative about making the effort. Although
getting run over by a train was a damn good excuse for
not returning a text, Aria couldn't help but feel irritated
that Madison had allowed herself to be victimized. She
must have been standing too damn close to the yellow
line painted on all subway platforms that people were
told to stay well behind. It reminded Aria of New York
City pedestrians who always crowded out into the street
waiting for the traffic light to change, practically daring
the taxis to run them over, which happened on a fairly
frequent basis.

"Dr. Nichols!" a voice called out, catching Aria off
guard as she was debating whether to attempt to talk
with Madison or just leave. Turning in the direction of
the voice, Aria saw Dr. Henderson coming in her direction, dragging the mob boss with him. If she could have
fled, she would have, but there wasn't time.

"What a coincidence," Carl said, crowding close
enough to Aria so that she could smell his coffee breath.
"I was just talking about you to our president five minutes
ago. Vernon, this is Dr. Aria Nichols, who was involved
with the autopsy on Kera Jacobsen. Remember, you asked
me for her number?"

"Of course I remember," Vernon said with the mild
irritation of a man under stress. He stuck out his hand,
which Aria shook against her better judgment. She had

an instantaneous dislike for Vernon and his dark beady eyes. To her he seemed inappropriately cast as a hospital president.

"The administration wants to thank you for your understanding of the sensitivity of the Jacobsen tragedy," Vernon said. Aria nodded. At least the man had a commanding voice. "We hope you will not draw any more attention to it since we're still concerned it could adversely affect our medical center, especially now with this new, supposedly newsworthy event that is indirectly associated. As you are well aware, we much prefer to stay out of the tabloids."

Aria chose not to answer, which created an uncomfortable moment.

"Well, that's it, then," Vernon said. "I'm glad to meet you, Dr. Nichols, and thanks again. Now, if you'll excuse me, I have to deal with these detectives here and hopefully keep the fallout of this latest unfortunate episode to a minimum." With a kind of bow, Vernon moved on. Carl stayed where he was.

"Well, this was an unexpected surprise seeing you," Carl said. "What brought you here?"

"I wanted to try to talk with Madison," Aria said. "Is she capable?"

"Oh, that's right," he said. "No, she's not. At least not now. Maybe tomorrow or the next day. She's been severely traumatized. But on a more positive note, I was going to get in touch with you this afternoon. I checked the literature and there is no information about channelopathies and fentanyl."

"I've kind of lost interest in looking into channelopathies on this case," Aria told him.

"That's probably appropriate," Carl said. "And how is the forensic investigation going about finding the father?"

"I've hit the proverbial brick wall," she said, again borrowing the term from her night's reading. "But I have a new idea, and that is to see if genetic genealogy can help at all."

"Now, that is an interesting concept." Carl nodded several times, obviously giving the idea some thought. "Very creative! That would mean essentially trying to construct the father's DNA, or at least part of it from the fetus, and then use that like they did with the Golden State Killer."

"That's more or less the idea," Aria said. She was duly impressed that he saw the concept had at least some possible merit, although how much, she really didn't know herself.

"I can't imagine it will be easy," Carl said. "But good luck. As I said yesterday, I think you're getting more out of your forensic rotation than most pathology residents. I commend you."

"Let's see where it leads before offering any kudos."

"Please, keep me informed of your progress," Carl said. "I find it fascinating."

"Yeah, sure," Aria said. "But I have a sense that Vernon Pierce wouldn't find it so fascinating."

"Why do you say that?"

"If the father is located, it could draw general attention to the case," she said. "Especially if it turns out the father was involved with the drugs Kera Jacobsen was using."

"I see your point," he said. "That's true, but Vernon isn't trained as a doctor but rather as an administrator. He's not as aware as he should be of how DNA science is changing medicine and law enforcement. But let's not worry about his attitude at the moment."

"Believe me, I'm not," Aria said.

Carl reached out and gave her shoulder a quick, reassuring squeeze. It happened so fast that she didn't have time to duck away. She didn't like to be touched like that.

"Keep up the good work!" Carl said, totally unaware of Aria's reflex reaction. "Are you going to stay here and try to talk with Madison? I really don't recommend it."

"No, I think I'll come back tomorrow," Aria said.

"Probably best," he said. "Anyway, stay in touch."

With that, he returned to where Vernon was talking with several men. In contrast to Vernon, these men looked perfectly cast as NYPD detectives according to their dress and seen-it-all attitudes. For a beat she watched Carl as he joined the conversation. She briefly wondered if she had been too hasty in her judgment of the man. Perhaps he was acting more like the father figure she'd always wanted but never had.

CHAPTER 21

May 9th
12:45 P.M.

As Aria approached the front entrance to the old, ramshackle OCME Forensic Pathology building, she had to pass under scaffolding, the presence of which was odd since there didn't appear to be any construction going on. To Aria it was a curious New York phenomenon that she had noted since becoming a Manhattan resident. There was scaffolding spread all around most NYC neighborhoods, and it stayed up for years without any apparent rationale. Nobody seemed to question it. There was even semi-permanent scaffolding with electric lighting around the Plaza Hotel building with no apparent construction that she passed most mornings on her way to the Langone Medical Center.

Once inside she flashed her ID card to the receptionist, Marlene Wilson, who manned a high-topped counter and guarded entrance both into the identification area, where most visitors were directed to identify the dead, and into the building proper where the chief and deputy chief had their offices. Except for all the medical examiners and the Department of Toxicology, most other OCME functions had been moved to the much more palatial high-rise building at 421 East 26th Street. Hoping to avoid running into Dr. McGovern, Aria used the stairs rather than the elevator to get up to the second floor.

As she passed through the area charitably labeled lunchroom with its sad Formica-topped card tables and molded plastic chairs, she tried to be as unobtrusive as possible since Dr. McGovern was a frequent visitor, particularly at lunchtime. Although the room was reasonably crowded, Dr. McGovern wasn't one of the patrons, but Dr. Tad Muller, Aria's resident colleague, was. Despite her efforts, he caught sight of her and called her over to his table. He was lunching with several of the mortuary techs. Reluctantly, she veered in his direction.

"Hey, Aria," Tad said, leaning in her direction and speaking under his breath. "I'm glad I saw you. I wanted to warn you that Dr. McGovern is looking for you, and he's not all that happy. He said you weren't answering any texts or voice mail."

"If you run into him, don't tell him that you saw me," Aria said. She briefly looked at the mortuary techs sitting with Tad, daring them to say anything as they had undoubtedly heard the exchange.

"He seemed pretty uptight," Tad said in a more normal tone. "I'd recommend you call him. I know there are some interesting cases that came in during the morning that he wants us to observe."

"I'm sure there are," she said. "But I'm flat-out busy on the one that I actually did yesterday, rather than merely observe, and that promises to teach me more about forensics than standing around holding the dick I don't have, watching a couple more autopsies."

"I think you're making a mistake," he said, clearly offended.

"You're entitled to your opinion." She was tempted to add *and you're a hopeless ass-kisser*, but she restrained herself. She glanced briefly again at the mortuary techs, whose bored expressions had changed to smirks. They at least seemed to have a sense of humor.

Once inside the residents' office, which was again a charitable designation considering its size and décor, Aria took off her white coat, hung it over the back of the aged desk chair, and sat down in front of the monitor. A moment later she was on the internet. Her goal was to try to figure out which of the major ancestral DNA companies might be the best for finding Lover Boy now that Madison Bryant had made herself incapable of lending a hand. Deciding on which DNA company to use was going to be up to Madison, at least in the beginning.

From Aria's reading she knew that Ancestry.com had the largest database, which might turn out to be a benefit since matches—people who shared segments of DNA of varying length with the dead fetus—were going to be what she needed. As she scrolled through the website, she saw that it was essentially divided into two parts. One part would help build a family tree through various and sundry records. Almost immediately Aria recognized that this service might provide information about Kera's family but wouldn't help with the father's, so Aria avoided that selection and clicked on TAKE A DNA TEST AND UNCOVER YOUR ORIGINS. That got her to a page where she could click on WHAT YOUR RESULTS WILL INCLUDE. Clicking on this allowed her to scroll through ETHNICITY ESTIMATE, which she wasn't particularly interested in, until she got to DNA MATCHES. This was what she needed, and the screen looked like the result some previous individual had obtained from Ancestry .com. It showed seventy-two matches with people who were either first or second cousins.

Already Aria was encouraged. If she could manage getting something like that, even one first or second cousin, she would be optimistic that the whole idea of finding Lover Boy would work. With a sense of building excitement, Aria scrolled down farther. All this was only going to cost a modest amount of money, which considering the implications, seemed to be quite a deal. Down near the bottom the screen read GET STARTED IN A FEW SIMPLE STEPS. The first thing she needed to do was to order a kit. The second thing was to activate the kit, whatever that meant, followed by providing a saliva sample. This was an issue that she had already considered since under the circumstances she would be unable to provide saliva for either Kera or the fetus. What Aria intended to do was contact the company and make sure that she could supply blood instead. Her research had suggested the blood would actually be better, anyway.

Aria's eyes then shifted to the final step on the current screen she was looking at. It was then that her building excitement took a sudden nosedive. She read that in roughly six to eight weeks the results would be available.

"Six to eight weeks!" she said with utter disdain, slapping a hand to her forehead. "That's a disaster." She tipped back in her chair. She couldn't believe it. She assumed that such DNA testing was all automated and done with microarray chips. Why would it take six to eight weeks? She was only going to be on her forensic rotation for another two to three weeks. Tipping forward again, she searched for a phone number to call the company. Although the website was generally rather well designed, finding a phone number to call was not easy and took persistence. When she finally got a customer service representative on the line, the woman wasn't able to provide an explanation for the six- to eight-week wait other than suggesting it had to do with sheer volume. More to the point, the woman seemed to have no conception of the actual process, nor did she have the ability to connect Aria with anyone who might. Out of frustration, Aria ended up just disconnecting while the woman was in midsentence trying to extol her company's level of service once the results had been obtained.

With rising frustration, she quickly checked the rest of the main ancestral DNA companies that she had read about the night before, namely Family Tree DNA, 23andMe, and

MyHeritage. Although all three had slightly shorter estimated sample turnaround times than Ancestry, they were in the same ballpark, with the shortest being 23andMe, which estimated their results would be available online between three and five weeks. Still, that was much too long as far as Aria was concerned. She also tried calling these other companies, but the result was similar to her experience with Ancestry, namely that she only got to speak with a customer service representative who had little comprehension of the actual technological way the results were obtained. At the same time, all the representatives seemed to be reasonably conversant with the basic concepts of DNA science, including knowledge that their respective companies were relying on SNPs, or single-nucleotide polymorphisms, as the way that people's DNA or genome were unique and relatives were varyingly similar, depending how close the relative was.

Aria rocked back again in her chair, wondering if she would have to give up this mini-crusade practically before she started it. As a soon-to-be senior, fourth-year pathology resident, she had too many other claims on her time than trying to figure out Kera Jacobsen's fetus's paternal family tree. Once she left the OCME rotation, which she considered almost a vacation, she would be back to working ten- to eleven-hour days with real responsibility. But the pause gave her an idea. Realizing that the ancestry DNA or genetic genealogy was a growing business as reflected in the long wait for samples to be analyzed, she reflected that there must be a lot of companies that were comparative start-ups, eager to get their firms in a competitive status with the big four, which were getting a lion's share of the business.

Tipping forward yet again, Aria googled "ancestry DNA companies," and as usual, Google came through. One website jumped out at her. It was a list of some thirty to forty testing companies. As quickly as she could, she started looking at all the websites, trying to find companies that were new to the game. After she found a handful of newbies, she started to locate them with the hopes of finding a relatively new company in the New York metropolitan area. After only fifteen minutes she hit gold. GenealogyDNA was fresh on the ancestral DNA scene and its home office was right there in Manhattan's touristically trendy Meatpacking District on West 13th Street, which was a cab ride away. When Aria used Google Maps to locate the address, she was moderately taken aback from glancing at the photo. It was a six-story brick building devoid of any decorative elements but with a stylish boutique and a contemporary restaurant on the ground floor. The upper five floors were apparently recycled commercial space, which she assumed could be rented by a start-up for a decent rate in the near term, at least decent for Manhattan.

Going on the company's website, which wasn't as polished as those of the big four, she found another difference. The number to call for information was much easier to find, suggesting GenealogyDNA encouraged potential customers to call. And even more important from Aria's point of view, there was a number to call for investment opportunities, meaning they were surely new to the game.

For a few minutes she stared at this second number while remembering how unproductive her calls to the other companies' customer service personnel had been. She felt she needed to talk to someone a bit higher in the company's hierarchy if she was going to have any luck circumventing this sample-processing delay. If she could manage to talk with one of the principals, she might have the best chance. But if that were to work, she needed a much more compelling story than trying to find the lover of a person who overdosed on opioids, as that was just too common and uninspiring. Aria knew enough about human foibles to know you had to offer something to get something.

Hoisting her feet onto the corner of her desk and crossing her legs in the process, which was Aria's posture for serious thinking, she tried to put herself in the shoes of the people who had started GenealogyDNA. Although fully accepting she was laboring under stereotypes, she envisioned they were probably a group of relatively young, male, Silicon Valley–type computer techies, all of whom had been nerds in high school. Thinking along those terms, she tried to come up with something sexy, which she thought shouldn't be too hard since the Kera story did involve consummated sex as evidenced by the existence of the fetus. But nothing came to mind that wasn't overshadowed by the drug issue. That was when she had to abandon the overdose situation totally. In fact, she suddenly realized that what-

ever story she was going to come up with, it had to involve life, not death, meaning the father needed to be
found to save the kid's life. That was the kind of story
that people could sink their teeth into, especially a young
genetic genealogy company trying to make a go of it
among giants.

All at once it came to her in a sudden burst of creative
conceptualizing. It had to involve a child because kids
always pulled on everyone's heartstrings. By closing her
eyes, she could envision a cherubic toddler with a rare
disease, the kind of disease that spelled doom in most
people's minds. As a pathologist she thought immediately of an aggressive childhood leukemia, which hereto-
fore was synonymous with death, yet against which great
strides had been made of late.

"Perfect," Aria said as she let her feet fall to the floor.
Once again, she pulled herself up to the desk. All at once
the whole story came to her. It involved a three-year-old
boy conceived with donor sperm who was in a terminal
state with advanced leukemia and who desperately needed
a bone marrow transplant if he was to survive. Complicating the situation was the recent death of the mother days
ago from a broken heart. Aria had to smile at herself for
that last part, knowing she'd have to come up with something better, like an auto accident, while racing to the
hospital. "Who could resist such a story?" she asked herself. And best of all, she imagined that the powers that
be at GenealogyDNA would see the whole thing as a
potential publicity gold mine even though Aria would
have to remind them that because of HIPAA rules, they

couldn't be told the name of the stricken infant or the dead mother.

With significantly more confidence, Aria dialed the number on the GenealogyDNA website for those people interested in investment opportunities. When the phone was answered after the second ring, she was even more hopeful. When she'd called the other genetic DNA companies, the phone had had to ring ten or more times before being answered.

"GenealogyDNA," a male voice said. "How can I be of service today?"

"My name is Dr. Aria Nichols, and I'm a senior resident in Pathology at New York University," she said. As someone who wasn't always glued to the truth starting in childhood, she knew from experience that if she was going to lie, it was best to at least start with the facts.

"And I am Vijay Srinivasan. How can I help you?"

"I'm calling about a major problem here at the Hassenfeld Children's Hospital," she said, quickly improvising. "I was hoping that GenealogyDNA might be able to help because genetic genealogy helped find the Golden State Killer. I assume you remember that story?"

"Most definitely," Vijay said. "That was good PR for our business."

"I can understand why," Aria said. "We, too, need to find a missing man. What I'd like to do is speak with someone in your company's hierarchy and not a customer service representative."

"I am one of the founding partners," he said.

"Well, that's perfect," Aria said. She hadn't expected

to hit pay dirt so quickly. "Before I start, I need to be certain you are aware of HIPAA rules that protect the confidentiality of patient information."

"I understand about patient confidentiality," Vijay said, "but I don't know anything about HIPAA, per se. Is that an acronym?"

"It is indeed," she said. "To tell you the truth, I always have to look up the actual name, but the long and short of it is that I will not be able to tell you any of the names of the people involved in our situation even though one is deceased. Nor will you be able to use the name of our institution if and when you wish to tout this endeavor for the benefit of your company. Is that understood?"

"I believe I understand," Vijay said.

"Then let me tell you the gist of the problem," Aria said. "We have a very sick toddler who was conceived with donor sperm and whose mother just passed away a few days ago. To make a long story short, we desperately would like to find the father to obtain some donor bone marrow. Has GenealogyDNA had any experience helping people who have been conceived with donor sperm find their genetic fathers?"

"Yes, we have," he said. "And we are proud of our record in that regard. I don't know how much you know about ancestral DNA and how matches are found, but it is in this arena where our company excels. DNA matches are found by algorithms, and it is our belief that our algorithms are probably the best in the business. Did you know that the algorithms are proprietary in that each of the commercial DNA companies have their own?"

"I wasn't aware of that," Aria said.

"We not only get the most matches with a customer's kit, but we get the least false-positive matches. We may be the new kids on the block, but we believe we have the best software, which is the reason we've been willing to challenge the established companies and have been able to find financing to do so."

"How long has GenealogyDNA been in business?" she asked.

"Next month will be our first anniversary," Vijay said. "If you are interested in investing, this might be the perfect time."

"I'm more interested in solving this current problem," Aria said. "But there is one other issue that I'd like to ask you about."

"Please," Vijay said. "This sounds like a situation that can be mutually beneficial."

Such a comment was music to Aria's ears. She needed GenealogyDNA to be selfishly interested on top of the Good Samaritan aspect, and it seemed that they were.

"To be entirely up front," she said, "we already approached several of the more established ancestral DNA companies. I have to say that with none of them did I have the pleasure of talking with someone of your stature."

"Thank you. You are too kind," Vijay said.

"The other problem I encountered was an unacceptable delay in producing results," Aria said. "With all of the companies it was weeks just to analyze the DNA samples whereas in our situation we are looking at days if we want to save the toddler's life."

"I'm not surprised," Vijay said. "Processing time is another issue where GenealogyDNA has made a point to be competitive. Many of the established ancestral DNA companies outsource their analyses. We here at Genealogy-DNA do not. We have our own lab to provide vertical integration, and we rent our high-density SNP microarrays so they can be upgraded as soon as newer arrays or chips are available. We intend to stay ahead of the curve."

"You have a lab here in the city?" Aria asked. This was sounding better and better.

"No, not in the city," he said. "Our lab is on Long Island, about an hour's drive away."

"So, you could get results faster than the weeks it takes in the other companies?"

"Absolutely," Vijay said proudly. "If the DNA amplification goes smoothly, we could do it overnight in this type of emergency circumstance."

"That's fantastic," she said, and meant it. "Now, there is one other issue. With the mother recently deceased, we obviously cannot use saliva as the other companies use. Would blood suffice?"

"Of course," Vijay said. "Saliva has been used purely because of its ease for the customer, even though it creates an added problem of having to deal with the DNA of aural bacteria and fungi. It creates an extra step of isolating the human DNA. Using blood is far superior and will make the amplification process profoundly simpler."

"This all sounds very encouraging," Aria said. "Let me tell you a bit more of the circumstance that we are in. The child has an aggressive form of myelogenous leukemia, which has been resistant to any of the newer forms of treatment. A bone marrow transplant is the only hope and the father would be the best possible source. It is a crisis situation and only a matter of days or a week or two at most. Do you think you could help?"

"Most definitely," he said. "There is no guarantee, of course, since it depends on at least some of the relatives of the father having contributed their DNA to the ancestral DNA pool and created family trees. But from purely an organizational standpoint, we can certainly produce the kits for the mother and the child on a timely basis. On top of that, for such a cause, I could have our in-house software people, including me, do the matching and try to construct a family tree for the ailing toddler. As an aside, do you have reason to believe the unknown father is from the NYC metropolitan area?"

"Yes," Aria said. "I'm quite sure that he is."

"That could possibly help," Vijay said. "Sometimes talking people into sharing their genealogical information can be difficult and a face-to-face meeting can make the difference."

"That's good news," she said. "When can we start?"

"When can you get us the blood samples?" Vijay said.

"How about this afternoon?" Aria said. "I can bring them to your office."

"Fine," he said. "I will be here all afternoon. When you come in, just ask the receptionist for me."

"I'll be there shortly," Aria said, and disconnected. Before she pocketed her phone, she noticed she'd gotten three texts as well as two voice messages from Dr. Chet McGovern. She ignored them all.

CHAPTER 22

May 9th
2:05 P.M.

A ria was duly impressed upon stepping off the elevators into the sixth-floor toxicology lab, her first visit there since she'd arrived at the OCME at the beginning of the month. Although the entire building was slated for demolition sometime in the not-too-distant future, the lab looked as if it had recently been renovated with banks of spanking-new, obviously high-tech equipment, and lots of counter space. The only thing that looked old and outdated were the windows. Two technicians in laboratory garb were monitoring the mostly automated machines. Aria went up to the nearest individual, a tall black woman whose hair was completely contained in a hood.

"I'm Dr. Nichols," she said. "I need some samples of blood that was sent up yesterday. How can that be arranged?"

"You'll have to speak with the department head, Dr. DeVries," the woman said, pointing to an open office door.

Aria walked over and into the office. A slim, older Caucasian man with thinning white hair was seated at a desk, signing a stack of reports. Aria repeated her request but was shunted to the neighboring office to find the assistant supervisor, Peter Letterman. Yet again she asked for the samples, this time from a youthful-looking, diminutive tow-haired man.

"What was the name?" Peter asked with a pleasant smile after Aria introduced herself and repeated her request.

"Kera Jacobsen," Aria said. "There was also a fetus associated, obviously with no name but perhaps with a different accession number. I don't know how that is handled."

"I remember the case," Peter said. "It was an overdose."

"That's right," she said.

"What do you need blood samples for?" Peter asked.

"DNA test," Aria said.

"Blood had already been sent over to the Molecular Genetics lab at 421 for DNA analysis," Peter said.

"This is for a different DNA test," Aria said irritably. She didn't want to have trouble with this nerd after making so much potential progress on the phone with Vijay Srinivasan.

"How much blood will you need?" Peter said. "There

wasn't a lot obtained from the fetus, considering the age and size."

"Whatever you can give me," she said, shifting her weight from one foot to the other. She was about to say something abusive when Peter got to his feet.

"I'll be right back," he said. He smiled. Aria did the same but hers wasn't as sincere.

As she waited, Aria glanced around the windowless office. Although it looked newly redecorated, the desk was as old and pitiful as the one she'd just been sitting at in the residents' room. There were pictures of two kids thumbtacked to a cork bulletin board, and one framed photo of an overweight, smiling woman on the desk.

Just when she was about to go out and search for Peter he returned. He handed her two tiny, capped test tubes with labels. One obviously contained about a cc of blood, the other a quarter of that amount.

"That's all we can spare of the fetal blood," Peter said. "Sorry, but we might have to redo our drug screen for the fetus if a problem develops with the first sample."

Aria merely nodded and walked back into the lab proper. Without wasting any time, she continued out into the hall and summoned an elevator. As she waited, she checked the time on her phone and inwardly groaned as it was already after two. As she boarded the elevator, she acknowledged it wasn't a good time to be wandering around on the first floor since the afternoon conference that Dr. McGovern ran would soon be starting. Yet she had little choice. With the blood samples in hand, she was intending to head directly over to the Meatpacking District, which required going out the front door. The problem was that she preferred not to run into McGovern even though it wouldn't be the end of the world.

As it turned out she needn't have worried about running into him on the first floor because the elevator stopped on the fourth floor, and he boarded, to her exasperation.

"My goodness gracious!" he marveled, making an exaggerated expression of total surprise. "The Phantom herself! I'm so lucky! Such a nice coincidence. Here I thought you might not grace us with your presence until morning."

Aria took a deep breath to gird herself against this Don Juan who obviously took himself way too seriously, coming up with such a stupid nickname.

"Where have you been?" Chet snapped with a 180-degree change in his demeanor. "I've texted you and tried to call. This is getting absurd, young lady."

She gritted her teeth. There was that offensively condescending "young lady" again.

"I really don't understand your attitude," Chet said. "Dr. Stapleton was reasonably complimentary this morning, but he said you just disappeared at the end while he was finishing his bullet-tracking diagram. And you were supposed to find me after the case so I could assign you another. Where on earth did you go?"

"I'm still working on the case I did yesterday," Aria said. "There's a big difference between observing and doing. I've done enough observing."

"What do you mean 'the case you did'?" Chet asked. "Are you talking about Dr. Montgomery's autopsy yesterday?"

"Dr. Montgomery let me do the case," Aria said. "I was the prosector, and she the observer, which is a lot more appropriate considering I'm a senior pathology resident. And now I'm doing some follow-up investigating on the case to try to determine the manner of death. Most important, I'm learning something, which you should applaud as the supposed director of education."

"Let's not be sarcastic," Chet said.

"You can be patronizing, and I can't be sarcastic?" she questioned with exaggerated uptalk. "How is that fair?"

"How am I being patronizing?" Chet asked.

"The fact that you have to ask is pathetic," Aria said as the elevator bumped to a stop on the first floor and the doors opened. Aria didn't wait. In a blink of an eye she was out and heading toward the front of the building.

"Hold up!" Chet called after her. "Aren't you coming to the conference?"

She didn't even bother turning around. Instead she flipped him the bird over her shoulder as she pushed through the door leading out to the building's public foyer.

CHAPTER 23

Climbing from the taxi she'd hailed in a hurry in case she'd been pursued by McGovern, Aria gazed up at the building that housed GenealogyDNA. It didn't look any more interesting in person than it did in the Google photo, although now she could tell it had been recently renovated. A plaque attached to the wall by the entrance to the upper commercial spaces described it as the Ferrara Canning Building circa 1880. Inside she could tell that most of the building except the ground floor was vacant. GenealogyDNA was the only tenant on the sixth floor.

"Can I help you?" said a youthful, extraordinarily casually dressed lavender-haired woman sitting at a reception desk in the small, nondescript outer office. She also had a collection of piercings in her ears and a nose ring.

"I'm here to see Vijay Srinivasan," Aria said.

"Are you Dr. Nichols?" the woman asked, eyeing her white resident jacket, which Aria had left on in the hopes that it would give more legitimacy to her leukemia story.

"I am," Aria said.

"You can go right in," the woman said. "I'll let him know you're here."

The second she stepped into the office proper, she could tell that her initial stereotypical assumptions about GenealogyDNA's character were correct. What she found herself surveying was far from the typical office. It was a large loft-like space with exposed, hand-hewn roofing beams and no floor dividers or window treatments of any kind. Without a dropped ceiling, the various piping and ducting was in full view, all of which was painted white. The two biggest pieces of furniture were a Ping-Pong table and an elaborate computer game station. Both were in use. Although there were a few desks, most of the furniture was composed of couches and beanbag chairs, popular in an era before Aria had been born. A few of the workstations were mere slabs of plywood set up on sawhorses. What was most apparent were dozens of computer screens and keyboards being used by casually or even sloppily attired, nerdy-looking youthful males. At least that was Aria's initial assessment until one of them stood up and came toward her. In contrast to the others, he was tastefully dressed in a clean, pressed white shirt and designer jeans. His hair was thick and dark, and his skin tone was a deep brown that made his teeth seem whiter than white. He exuded a Bollywood attractiveness.

"Dr. Nichols, I presume?" Vijay said with a smile. His accent was distinctly Indian as she remembered from the phone conversation.

Wary of men in general, Aria felt an immediate unease as he approached, his hand outstretched in greeting. Instead of shaking his hand, she reached into the side pocket of her doctor's jacket and pulled out the two capped test tubes. She handed them to Vijay.

Without the slightest hesitation or acknowledgment of Aria's apparent rebuff, he took the samples. "Ah, yes! The blood samples," he said. "Thank you. We'll send these directly out to our lab in Garden City. I've already alerted them, and we'll get right on it."

"Thank you," Aria said. "We're appreciative of your help."

"Do you have a few extra minutes?" Vijay asked.

"I guess so," she said, not sure what was coming. She felt a little like a fish out of water.

"I've let the whole team know about your dilemma," Vijay said, "and we've discussed it. We are all going to pitch in. But would you mind if I introduced you?"

"I suppose not," Aria said. She wasn't wild about the idea, but if it could help, she was willing.

He gestured ahead toward an open area among the various furniture, most of which looked like it came from yard sales. Aria walked in the direction he indicated. As she moved, she noticed that the dozen or so people in the room had all stopped what they were doing and were watching her, including the Ping-Pong players. She also felt Vijay's hand touch her arm and then grasp it to pull her to a stop. Just when she was going to yank her arm away, he let go of her. She and Vijay were now standing in the middle of the room. Directly in front of them was a particularly large, old leather couch. The two men sitting on it looked to Aria like the computer techies she'd imagined, who'd never dated in high school and could play *League of Legends* with the best of them. To Aria they appeared totally bored. Both were dressed in sweats and high-top sneakers with their laces untied.

"Okay, listen up!" he called out to quiet the background chatter. "This is Dr. Nichols. Here's your chance to ask any questions about this leukemia project. She just handed me the blood samples from the mother and the child, so we'll be getting the respective kits probably sometime tonight or at the latest tomorrow."

Vijay pivoted around to look at everyone. A hand popped up. It belonged to a skinny fellow with facial hair that had not yet turned to whiskers. He also had a sprinkling of acne. "How long do we have before the toddler dies?"

Vijay turned to her and raised his eyebrows.

"That's hard to say," Aria said. "It could be days or it could be weeks."

He again looked around. No one had any more questions. He turned back to Aria. "Do you have any questions?"

"So, your whole team here is going to work on our toddler's problem?" she asked him, just to be sure. It sounded almost too good to be true.

"That's right," Vijay said. "We think a project like this

could put us on the map where we deserve to be. I told you that our algorithms are the best in the business with the least false positives."

"Will you be using phasing and triangulation?" Aria asked. She remembered Madison saying that was how the process worked, and Aria's reading had confirmed it, particularly the triangulation, which was the best way to determine if matches were real, meaning matches by descent from common ancestors. She had to remember that the process was matching pinpoint variations along a chromosome, the so-called SNPs, or single-nucleotide polymorphisms, not the actual full chromosome sequences. She knew that in the future when full sequencing was faster and cheaper, which was undoubtedly coming sooner than most people realized, it would all be infinitely easier and much more accurate, striking a mortal blow to the concept of individual privacy.

"Of course," Vijay said. "That's how this genealogy system works. It's relatively easy to find matches but finding the real IBD, or identical-by-descent, matches is the tricky part and that requires triangulation."

"Then I guess I don't have any questions," Aria said. She couldn't be more pleased. With just a few white lies, she'd managed to get a whole team of genealogical software experts working on the problem of finding Lover Boy.

"Before you go, let me show you the type of family tree we'll be constructing for this child. Do you have the time?"

"I'll make the time," Aria said.

CHAPTER 24

Knock, knock," Jack said as he rapped on the jamb of Laurie's open office door. She looked up from the architectural plans for the new Forensic Pathology building that would be housing the autopsy room and offices for all the medical examiners. She'd worked on them in the middle of the night and thought they were nearly done, but now had different ideas in the light of day. Although the Toxicology Department had stayed in the old building by moving up to floors five and six, the Histology Department had been moved down to the new OCME high-rise. The problem was that there was a particularly strong connection with both departments and the autopsy work that the medical examiners did. Laurie could remember the many times she'd visited both departments while trying to complete her investigations to sign out the death certificates. Having them at different locations logistically didn't make a lot of sense, so she'd gone back to the plans to see what she could do.

"Is this a good time to chat?" Jack asked. He looked and sounded intense.

"It is," Laurie said. "Whenever the door is open, I'm available. I've been looking forward to seeing you all day. Come on in!" In contrast to Jack she tried to sound casual, almost carefree.

He came in, closed the door behind him, and went directly to the couch, which was his usual destination on visits to her office. He was still dressed in scrubs, as he'd been in the pit most of the day. "So, what did you learn about your projected surgery?" he asked. He was sitting but leaning forward with his elbows on his knees. He didn't blink. He was obviously stressed.

"Where is my quick-witted, wisecracking, double-entendre Jack?" Laurie asked, trying to make light of the situation. She stayed seated behind her desk.

"He's on vacation until all this is put to bed," Jack said, not minding he was mixing his metaphors. "Stop torturing me! What's the story?"

"I spoke twice today with Dr. Claudine Cartier," Laurie told him. "The last time was just a few minutes ago. She's being wonderfully accommodating. She understands perfectly my interest in getting this handled as soon as possible. If my questionable one-centimeter lump is cancer, I can't help but feel that I'm taking a risk with every minute that goes by. All that's needed to change my prognosis is one cell out of billions to detach itself and set up shop in a distant location."

"I understand," he said. "I'd feel the same way. So, what did she say?"

"She's had several cancellations of her scheduled surgeries due to the patients coming down with influenza, and she's willing to fit me in on a semi-emergency basis. She wants me to be in the Kimmel Pavilion because of the accommodations. Now it's up to the OR and their scheduling. I guess I'm essentially on call, which is fine by me. Now that I have decided to go through with it, I want it done."

"So that means it could happen at any time?" Jack asked.

"No, not at any time," she said. "I'll have at least eight to twelve hours' notice. I'll be having general anesthesia, so I'll have to be prepared."

"Does our deputy chief know he's about to be the captain of the ship for a period of time?"

"He does," Laurie said. "I had a meeting with him this morning to tell him, and he's fine with it. I did tell him not to spread it around until it was actually scheduled."

"I wish I was the one having the surgery and not you," Jack said. "I could handle that a hell of a lot easier."

"It's all going to be fine," Laurie said as much to bolster her own courage as his. "Let's talk about something else. I've been dying to ask you about our favorite NYU pathology resident. When I was making my autopsy rounds this morning, I saw she was at your table. How did that go? From afar, it seemed to be going fine. I was actually afraid to make my presence known for fear of upsetting the apple cart and causing trouble."

"It wasn't a problem," Jack said.

"I'm shocked, knowing what I do about her," she said. "And what I know about you, too, for that matter." She laughed as a way of lightening the mood.

"To be completely honest, for your benefit I was on good behavior."

"What do you mean, 'for my benefit'?"

"You're making a big effort on her behalf," Jack said. "You did a case with her, and that's the first one you've done since I don't know when. And I agree with your motivation: It's not worth getting into a slugfest with NYU Department of Pathology over a possibly sociopathic resident. She obviously is not enamored of forensic pathology. She didn't even appear in the pit until eight thirty or thereabouts."

"Did she use any profanity? She did with me, and I know that's one of your buttons."

"No vulgar language at all. My only complaint, if I had to come up with one, is that at the end of the case she just disappeared. One minute she was there and the next minute gone. Not a word of thank-you or goodbye or can I help finish up. She's clearly not a team player."

"That's exactly how Dr. Henderson described her," Laurie added. "He also said she wasn't popular with the other residents. She doesn't seem to have any social sense. Whether it's ingrained or learned, I haven't the foggiest."

"On the plus side, she is smart," he said.

"I agree," Laurie said. "And so does Dr. Henderson. And to her credit, she has really immersed herself in the case I did with her yesterday. So much so, it reminds me of you and I when we were new hires."

"In what way is she immersed?" Jack asked.

"She's convinced that it's imperative to find the father of the unexpected fetus we found. She thinks the father might well have had something to do with the drugs the patient used to overdose. And as a millennial, she has come up with a novel way of possibly tracking him down that I don't think you or I would have thought of, namely using genetic genealogy." Laurie briefly filled him in on the logistics of Aria's plan.

"Really?" Jack questioned. "Now, that is a uniquely cool idea. You're right, I wouldn't have thought of it."

"I wouldn't have, either," she said. "I'm afraid it just shows how quickly we can fall behind the times, given how fast technology is changing. Anyway, I find it all fascinating, and I've encouraged her to look into it. At the same time, I made it absolutely clear that our Molecular Genetics Department can have nothing to do with it or we would lose our accreditation."

"That's for sure," Jack said.

"I've encouraged her to keep doing what she's doing, provided she stays away from our DNA lab, keeps me informed of what kind of progress, if any, she is making, and respects HIPAA rules. For someone who's obviously not going to go into forensics, and whether or not she's ultimately successful in finding the father, she's probably learning more about forensic pathology's capabilities than by observing a disjointed bunch of autopsies."

"Could be," he said.

The intercom light on her desk phone illuminated. She picked up the receiver. It was Cheryl, saying that Dr. McGovern was there to see her.

"Send him in." Laurie said, after getting a nod from Jack that he was okay with Chet's joining them.

A minute later, an aggravated Chet McGovern swept into her office. "I give up! I cannot handle this woman, and she's driving me crazy," he barked as he strode in, heading for her desk. Halfway there he caught sight of Jack sitting on the couch and stopped. "Oh, sorry," he added, redirecting his attention to Laurie. "Am I interrupting something? I didn't know you were busy."

"No problem. She's all yours," Jack said. He got to his feet. "I'm on my way out."

"No, stay!" Chet said. To reorganize his thoughts, he smoothed back his receding hair and stroked his goatee. "Where was I? Oh, yeah! You have to hear this. I just had another crazy run-in with my bête noire resident, Aria Nichols. I'd been more or less looking for her since she disappeared after Jack's gunshot case, and then *bingo*, I ran into her in the elevator. When I tried to ask her where she'd been, she accused me of being patronizing. Can you believe it?"

"Were you?" Laurie asked. She remembered what Aria had said about Chet asking her to have a drink soon after their initial meeting and how she felt about his following her over to the Langone Medical Center. She was tempted to bring both issues up but decided against it.

"Hell, no," Chet said. "Unless calling her 'young lady' could be considered patronizing. I actually wanted to call her something else entirely but resisted."

"Calling a senior pathology resident 'young lady' certainly qualifies as being out-and-out patronizing," Laurie said. Then she turned to Jack. "Do you agree?"

Jack raised his hands as if surrendering. "This is an issue for the chief medical examiner to adjudicate. I'll take the Fifth."

"Coward," she said with a smile.

"Hey!" Chet said. "Whose side are you guys on? I'm the aggrieved party here, not this sassy pathology resident." Then he smiled himself, realizing how he was sounding. "All right, I get the message. Maybe I'm taking this a bit too personally."

"I can actually commiserate with you to a degree," Laurie admitted. "I find her provocative also. It's as if she has no empathy."

"I'd call her outright hostile," Chet said. "As we were getting off the elevator, I asked her if she was coming to the afternoon conference. And you want to know how she responded?"

"I can't imagine, knowing how she's responded to you on previous occasions," Laurie added with her smile returning.

"She flipped me off," Chet said with great indignation. "She didn't even answer. She just gave me the finger."

"In a way she did the same to me," Laurie said. "When we finished the case yesterday, I asked her to help Marvin clean up. She told me she didn't have the time and walked out. She might as well have given me the finger."

"I don't know what's wrong with you guys," Jack interjected. "I got along with her fine this morning. She couldn't have been nicer."

"Really?" Chet questioned, but then he saw Jack's smile and knew Jack was merely teasing.

"Don't let Jack get your goat," Laurie said. "He was on artificially good behavior with Dr. Nichols for my benefit. Ironically enough, we had been talking about her just before you arrived."

"That reminds me," Chet said. "She justified her absence by saying she was still working on the case that you let her do yesterday, trying to investigate the manner of death. Is all that true?"

"Yes and yes," Laurie said. "I did let her act as the prosector, which is a point I think we should discuss at some time in the near future. Perhaps we should routinely let the NYU pathology residents do the cases rather than just observe them even though the medical examiner is responsible for the death certificate. From a teaching standpoint it makes a lot of sense, considering where they are in their training. And yes, she is still following up on the case, under my supervision."

"Fine by me," Chet said. "But it is an issue that we should discuss with all the medical examiners to see if they are comfortable with it. I can bring it up at our next meeting."

"Sounds like a plan," she said. "I'll also bring it up with Carl Henderson and get his take."

"Meanwhile, what can I do in the short run?" he asked with an audible exhale. "I've got to face her again in the morning and try to control my irritation."

"Assign her to me for my first case," Jack suggested. "Laurie says she's a good prosector, and she is smart. I don't mind letting her do a case as long as she doesn't drag it out. Strangely enough, she and I might get along. One way or the other, I'll see if I can straighten her out a bit."

"Are you sure that's a good idea?" Laurie asked. She didn't want to make a bad situation worse if Jack and Aria Nichols got into a real tiff.

"It will be fine," Jack said. "I promise to continue to be on good behavior with this woman. Hearing you two talk has raised my curiosity."

"She's taxing," she warned. "Maybe even exasperating."

"I'll take it as a challenge to try to help the situation," Jack said. "I won't take anything she says personally, I'll avoid being patronizing, and I'll gird myself against possible profanity. Trust me."

"I'll trust you," Chet said with alacrity. "You're on!"

CHAPTER 25

May 9th
5:05 P.M.

Aria's phone buzzed fifteen minutes after leaving the GenealogyDNA building. She'd decided to power walk the two miles or so back to the OCME rather than hail a cab or rideshare. Not only could she enjoy the early spring weather, she could use the exercise. She also thought that going by foot, at least from the west side of Manhattan to the east side, might even be faster since she'd be avoiding rush-hour crosstown NYC traffic, which had become appalling.

The display on her phone said the call was from David Goldberg. She answered.

"I'm glad I got you," David said. "Kera Jacobsen's mother just arrived from LA. She's in the OCME ID area up at 520 and will be confirming the identification.

I'm on my way over there to talk with her about my investigation. Are you there now?"

"No, but I'm on my way," Aria said. "I should be there soon, certainly before six."

"Are you interested in talking with her?" David asked.

"Maybe." At this point she didn't think the mother could add much, but then again, it couldn't hurt. "Actually, yes. I think I would like to ask her a few questions."

"Okay, that should work. We'll probably be in one of the ID rooms. Come and join us if you'd like."

Aria disconnected and seriously picked up her pace. Once she got across town, she took a cab up First Avenue, where the traffic was heavy but not stop-and-go. By the time she arrived at the OCME, the trip had taken just over a half hour, which wasn't bad considering the time of day. As David Goldberg suggested, she found him in one of the cubicles used by the ID team to show family members or other people pictures of the deceased for identification purposes. Digital images were used now instead of Polaroids although family members could see the body itself if they demanded to do so. Few did. The blank room had a Formica desk supporting a computer monitor and a box of tissues. There were also a half dozen molded plastic chairs.

As soon as David saw Aria in the doorway, he stood up. "Dr. Nichols, I'd like you to meet Shirley Jacobsen." Shirley extended a limp hand in her direction but didn't stand. Aria ignored the gesture. She didn't want to make this meeting last any longer than necessary. She leaned her backside against the edge of the desk and folded her arms. To her Shirley looked like a lot of middle-aged Scandinavians she'd met: small features, high cheekbones, and a slightly sallow complexion that suggested she lived in Minnesota, not Los Angeles. Her watery, cornflower-blue eyes reminded Aria of Kera's, at least in terms of color. The same was true with the hair that probably had been blond but was now a light brown with dark roots. Unlike Kera, Shirley had a few gray hairs mixed in. It was obvious the woman had been crying.

"I only have a few questions," Aria said. "I understand that your daughter, Kera, had broken up with a long-term boyfriend before coming to NYC this past fall, and his name, I believe, is Robert Barlow. Is that correct?"

"Yes," Shirley said, taking a deep breath. "But Kera was okay with it, and actually used the breakup as the motivation to come here, which had always been her dream. As far as I know she wasn't upset about the relationship ending, certainly not to the extent of starting to use drugs."

"Did she use drugs in high school?" Aria asked.

"Not at all," Shirley said. "I mean, like all teenagers, she tried pot but didn't particularly like it, as far as I know. She was always very open with me about what was going on in her life. Same with my younger daughter. Neither of them were ever into drugs. That's why this shocks me so."

"As far as you are aware, did Robert Barlow ever visit your daughter here in New York, particularly a couple of months ago?"

"No. I'm sure not," Shirley said. "Kera would have told me. Besides, he's a medical student and never goes anywhere. That had always been a bone of contention between Kera and him and might have been one of the reasons they went their separate ways."

"Mr. Goldberg told me yesterday that you had mentioned on the phone that Kera had recently seemed a bit depressed when you spoke to her. Is that correct?"

"Yes, it is," Shirley said. "But just over the last few weeks. It was vague at first. My younger daughter and I attributed it to her having trouble dealing with the weather or just homesickness, and we thought it was just a temporary thing and would pass with spring coming. But then she surprised both of us the last time we spoke, just a few days ago, by suggesting she was thinking of coming back to Southern California. That was a huge change. Up until then, we both thought she loved the city and would become a real New Yorker."

"Did Kera talk about any of the people she was meeting here?" Aria asked.

"Absolutely," Shirley said. "She spoke frequently about Madison Bryant, one of her fellow social workers, particularly through the fall. My understanding was that they were very close."

Aria wondered what Shirley Jacobsen would say if she told her that at that very moment Madison Bryant was down the street in an intensive-care unit at Bellevue after being run over by a subway train. New York hadn't been so good to either woman. "What about romantic relationships?" she questioned, struggling with exactly how she was going to bring up the issue of the pregnancy without actually violating HIPAA rules. At first, she thought about ignoring HIPAA, but with David Goldberg sitting right there, she knew she'd be taking a serious risk.

"She didn't say anything about meeting any men," Shirley said.

"Did you find that a little strange?" Aria asked. "Supposedly, there are a lot of available and desirable men here." Aria had to bite her tongue, knowing that she didn't believe what she had just said. She hadn't found any, but then again, she hadn't been looking.

"I guess it did cross my mind," Shirley said. "But I assumed it was just a matter of time. In the meantime, it seemed to me that Kera was too wrapped up doing all the cultural things New York has to offer."

"Although the final toxicology report hasn't come back yet, the rapid test of the drug your daughter was using was an opioid-fentanyl mix," Aria said. "We believe that she was not a habitual user but rather had just started. We'd like to find out, if we can, where she obtained the drugs she was using."

Shirley nodded to indicate she was following Aria's line of reasoning. She also dabbed the corners of her eyes with a tissue she was holding.

"We also believe that she was involved in an intimate relationship with someone who has yet to step forward. We'd like to find him and question him about the drugs. Do you have any idea whatsoever who this individual might be?"

"I don't," Shirley said. "Like I said, Kera didn't say anything about being in a relationship. She would have told me."

"It seems that there was some secrecy involved, so I'm not surprised she didn't say anything to you. But to be clear, we're sure she was involved with someone."

For another few beats Aria stared at Shirley, racking her brain about whether there was anything else this woman might be able to provide. When she couldn't think of anything, she looked over at David's doughy face to see if he had anything at all to add, but it was clear that he didn't. She then pushed away from the desk and left.

Aria's intent was to go out to the public lobby and order a rideshare to get home. She was exhausted from getting so little sleep the night before and practically running across Manhattan. But when she got out there, she had another thought. Dr. Montgomery had told her on several occasions to keep her up to speed on her progress. Believing the coup of procuring the services of at least a dozen computer geeks schooled in ancestral DNA to work on finding Lover Boy was an accomplishment in and of itself, Aria felt an irresistible urge to see if Dr. Montgomery was still on the premises. She had had the impression the chief didn't think she was going to be successful finding the identity of the fetus's father; getting an entire team of experts involved suggested otherwise. Although Aria rarely sought affirmation of her efforts, she thought this instance deserved it, even though she had no intention of explaining how she had managed to pull it off.

Although it was only about a quarter to six, Aria

found the front office completely deserted. All the secretaries had departed for the day, leaving just their hypnotic screen savers running in constant loops. The only other artificial light was spilling out of the chief's office, suggesting she alone was still at work.

Aria advanced to the open door and looked in. Laurie was at her desk, hands supporting her head with elbows on the surface, poring over massive blueprint pages. Without knocking or announcing herself, Aria walked in and went to the same chair facing the desk she'd sat in that morning. Although she knew she'd been quiet, thanks to the carpeted floor and her sneakers, Aria was amazed Laurie hadn't seen her out of the corner of her eye or even sensed her presence. It was obviously a tribute to Laurie's ability to concentrate.

Once she was seated, she watched Laurie for a few beats before pretending to clear her throat. Reacting to the sudden noise and with an obvious sense of surprise, Laurie's head popped up. Seeing Aria, she let her hands drop to the desk's surface. The two women stared at each other for another couple of beats before Laurie spoke: "Such a surprise! I didn't expect to see you tonight."

"You told me to keep you informed of my progress locating Lover Boy," Aria said with a self-satisfied smile. "I've had a stroke of luck that I thought you might find interesting. Although I'm not prepared to reveal how I managed it, I've arranged to have ancestral DNA analysis for Kera Jacobsen and her fetus in record-breaking time, meaning overnight, whereas under normal circumstances it takes weeks if not more than a month to produce what they call 'kits.' On top of that feat, there's going to be an entire team of ancestral DNA computer geeks from a company called GenealogyDNA here in New York City who will be analyzing the results so that burden is not going to fall on a novice like me. If ancestral DNA can find Lover Boy, it's going to happen sooner rather than later."

———————

Laurie stared at Aria, trying to understand the person she was looking at. It wasn't easy, and Laurie knew she was no psychiatrist. Nor did she really have the mental energy to deal with yet another conundrum considering what she was up against, facing imminent major surgery and the other problems of running a busy organization with more than a thousand employees. The problem of Dr. Aria Nichols had to be relegated to a lower status from her perspective and handled by the director of education, even if Chet was struggling with his own issues. There was always the chance that Jack could actually help as he offered, provided he didn't make things worse.

"That's terrific," Laurie said at length, and not knowing what else to say. In actuality, she was impressed. As both she and Jack had said, the promise of ancestral DNA contributing to forensics was intriguing.

"I just thought I should let you know since you asked," Aria said. She stood up. She still had the same complacent smirk on her face, as if enjoying Laurie's bewilderment. "I'll let you know as soon as I learn more."

"Yes, please do," Laurie said. She then watched as Aria headed for the door without a goodbye, just as she'd done that morning. Laurie called out to her, bringing her to a stop: "Excuse me, Dr. Nichols. Thanks for keeping me up to date on your progress. It sounds encouraging, but I want to mention something else. It was brought to my attention that you haven't been arriving here at seven thirty as you were told to at the start of your rotation. I'd like you to be on time for the rest of the month. And in the future, I would prefer that you announce yourself when you come to my office."

Aria didn't respond, though the smile disappeared. A moment later she was gone.

CHAPTER 26

May 10th
3:05 A.M.

I t was time and timing was critical. Through the day he'd given the problem a lot of thought and ultimately decided the best time to do what had to be done was between three and four A.M. That was the hour when the night shift had their respective lunches, so that at any given time within that interval there would be half the usual complement of hospitalists, nurses, nurses' aides, and orderlies lurking in the area.

Getting up from the reading chair where he'd been sitting for several hours while trying to read and failing and instead watching mindless YouTube videos on his tablet, he went to the mirror he had hanging on the inside of his office door. The moment he'd gotten to his feet, he'd felt a surge of adrenaline course through his system such that as he tried to don the dark wig while looking into the mirror, his hands were shaking.

"Pull yourself together," he commanded. For a moment he let his arms fall to his sides, closed his eyes, and he took a series of deep breaths. Within just a few seconds he felt better. If he was going to pull this off, and there was really no choice in the matter, it was important to control his anxieties and remember that he had planned everything to the T. It was going to work and work extremely well. He remembered his mother telling him when he'd been a boy that you shouldn't lie because lies tended to propagate more lies. No one had told him that it was the same when you murdered someone, but then again, he should have known. Every contingency had to be accounted for, even the most unexpected. He'd been relatively certain that Kera had not told Madison his identity, but he couldn't take the chance, especially now that the woman had somehow lived through getting run over by a train, which he'd never expected.

With his tremor under control, he went back to pulling on the wig, which was made of real hair, dyed black. The style was medium length with a central part so that the sides covered his own sideburns completely. Once the wig was in proper place, he used a wide-toothed comb to tame it a degree. As he regarded himself in the mirror when he was finished, he was pleased. Although it was only hair, the overall effect was quite a transition. He truly looked like someone else. But he wasn't finished. The next part of his disguise was a pair of heavy-framed black glasses that reminded him of Woody Allen. With those in place, he was amazed. He hardly recognized himself.

The last part of the costume was the long white doctor's coat. His idea was to look like a surgeon, and he was confident that he did once he pulled on the coat and put some hemostats and bandage scissors in the breast pocket, along with a few pens and a pencil flashlight. The final touch was the stethoscope, which he hung casually around his neck. With that in place, he stepped back a few paces and checked himself. It was perfect.

Walking over to the desk, he picked up the syringe that he'd prepared earlier. It was a ten-cc syringe that was already full. He'd gotten it that evening, which had been easy since there were hundreds of places he could have chosen. What had been a bit harder was the contents, an injectable form of potassium chloride, or KCl, which was the perfect drug for murder as it was fast, certain, and essentially undetectable. Obtaining it on short notice had been a bit more difficult but not impossible. He'd found a stash in the supply room for the Emergency Department with its main store of saline and other intravenous fluids. It wasn't under lock and key like all the other drugs.

Now fully prepared, he left the office, taking the stairs to avoid the unlikely situation of running into anyone in the elevator even though he was certain no one would recognize him. Once outside, he made his way over to First Avenue and headed south, walking briskly as the temperature had fallen into the upper fifties.

At that time in the early-morning hours, the front

entrance of Bellevue Hospital was almost deserted. He pushed through the revolving door and then crossed the expanse of the lobby where there was only a handful of people. The information desk was manned by several uniformed security people who were carrying on an animated conversation, which he guessed was most likely about the Yankees or the Mets as the complaints about the Knicks had finally fallen off.

Again, he avoided the elevator. Fortunately, he was only going up two floors. Exiting from the stairwell, he headed toward the ICU, which was in the west wing on the second floor. As he got closer, he began to see progressively more people, mostly nurses and nurses' aides or assistants. No matter what time of day or night, there was always lots of activity in the various intensive-care units, as the name implied.

Without any hesitation, he headed to the central desk where there were a number of people sitting around chatting. Some were obviously nurses, but others in scrubs could have been hospitalist physicians or residents. Walking up to the counter, he stopped. From there he could see into the various rooms, including room 8, where Madison Bryant was located. He was encouraged. There seemed to be only one nurse or nurse's aide in the room at the moment. He wasn't surprised, as he had checked on Madison's status a few hours ago. He'd learned that she was stable, although still critical, and was scheduled to be moved to a regular room the following day. Looking into other ICU rooms, he could see much more activity, some more than others. In one of the semi-private rooms there was a lot of action, suggesting a patient was in dire straits.

As he expected, dressed as he was, no one paid him any heed, which was good. He was just another one of the cavalcade of people necessary to run one of the busiest parts of the hospital. People came and went, especially doctors.

"Excuse me," he said to one of the nurses behind the counter. "Who is the charge nurse tonight?" He knew he was taking a chance by asking for her, but he hoped he'd arrived when she was at lunch. It was a fifty-fifty risk, but even if he was wrong, he already had a plan of how to deal with her or him.

"That's Barbara Strassman," the nurse said.

"Is she here?"

"She's at lunch but should be back any minute."

"Okay, thanks," he said. He was pleased. He knew that the ICU was significantly more efficient when the charge nurse was present, as it was her job to keep things under control with all the patients, a kind of watchful gatekeeper who knew what was happening at any given moment to everyone under her responsibility. That was important as far as he was concerned because he was planning on causing a scene and the less anyone anticipated it, the better. With what he had in mind, he needed only about ten seconds.

Leaving the central desk, he walked over to the open door leading into room 8. The bed was against the back wall. There were no windows. Above Madison's head were several monitors displaying her vital signs, EEG, and cardiac rhythm. The nurse or nurse's aide was busy hanging up a fresh container of intravenous fluid and then adjusting the drip rate. Madison herself seemed to be either sleeping or resting. Her eyes were closed. All that was perfect, almost more than he could have hoped for.

When he entered the room and got a look at the attendant's name tag, he could tell that she was a nurse's assistant trained with intensive care skills. He thought that was also helpful as fully trained nurses tended to be more questioning, particularly those trained in critical care.

"How is she doing?" he asked in a whisper as he approached the bed on the patient's right side. He wanted to be on the right because he was right-handed.

"She's doing very well," the aide whispered back. "She's asleep now, but she's been talking a lot and has been taking fluids by mouth."

"Does she know what happened to her?" he asked.

"She does but only because she's been told," the aide said. "She still can't remember the details. All she remembers is ascending onto the Lexington Avenue subway platform."

"Where's the assigned nurse?"

"She's at lunch."

He inwardly smiled. Things seemed to be falling into place almost too perfectly. "Could you bring me some gauze and tape? I'd like to take a look at her stump and see how much bleeding there's been."

"Of course, Doctor," the aide said. "I'll be right back."

"Thank you," he said. He watched her until she disappeared out the open door. He could see over to the main desk. No one was looking in his direction. Quickly he pulled out the syringe from his jacket pocket, took off the protective plastic cap from the needle end, and inserted the needle into the intravenous port just above the catheter that disappeared into Madison's right arm. In the next second, he injected the entire contents into her IV line in one rapid push, causing the fluid level in the drip chamber to suddenly rise. This was the critical stage because he knew from his reading that the pain would be considerable as the potassium chloride rushed up Madison's arm vein.

Madison's eyes shot open, her lips drew back, and a scream started in her throat. But it never got out. With all his might he tightly slapped his right hand over her mouth, forcing her lips closed so that the scream was transformed into a mumble that was easily drowned out by the metronomic beeping of the cardiac monitor. She tried desperately to wrest his hand off her face with the hand of her unbroken arm, but he leaned the entire weight of his upper body onto her while his eyes shot up to the cardiac monitor. Already he could see the telltale signs of imminent cardiac failure as the potassium chloride bolus reached the heart and instantly interrupted its electrical conduction. A moment later the heart essentially stopped beating and became a quivering mass of uncoordinated muscle known as ventricular fibrillation. Instantly the raucous sound of the cardiac alarm reverberated off the walls.

Knowing that in a few seconds the room would be full of doctors and nurses and a cardiac resuscitation team, he quickly let go of Madison's face, pocketed the syringe, and then put down the side rail of the bed. As the first people came charging in, he was already climbing up on the bed to start cardiac massage.

"She's in fibrillation," someone said, rushing up to the bedside.

"I know," he said frantically, starting the massage by alternately pressing down on her chest. Other people crowded around the bed, including the cardiac resuscitation team, which quickly took over. One of them climbed up onto the bed to replace him. Others yanked the bed away from the wall so someone else could intubate and then ventilate her with one hundred percent oxygen.

He backed up, giving the team space to do their thing. There were now ten to twenty people in the room, which gave him the opportunity to get out of the way and move toward the exit.

"Let me have the defibrillator paddles," he heard the team leader call out. A moment later there was the characteristic thud of the defibrillator being discharged, followed by a short silent pause while everyone stared at the ECG screen in hopes that the heart would have returned to a normal rhythm. He knew it wouldn't, and he knew that by now there was probably no way possible to save Madison. With a potassium chloride overdose, the corrective measures would have had to have been started immediately, and even then, they wouldn't necessarily be successful, and there was no way the resuscitation team could even determine that the problem was hyperkalemia, or too much circulating potassium.

He heard the team leader yell out to defibrillate again, and while everyone was occupied and totally absorbed in the resuscitation attempt, he walked out into the hallway. At that moment there was no one at the central desk, which was convenient. Pleased with what he'd been able to accomplish, he headed in the direction of the elevators. After the anxiety he'd suffered for most of the day, his relief was palpable. He was also exhausted both mentally and physically and in dire need of a stiff drink.

CHAPTER 27

May 10th
6:45 A.M.

The weather was perfect and at least for a few minutes Jack wasn't thinking and wasn't worrying, he was just enjoying himself as the wind whistled through his bicycle helmet. He was on the West Drive in Central Park heading south, perched on top of his relatively new Trek road bike, and pedaling to beat the band. When he'd just joined the roadway up near 106th Street, he'd happened upon a group of serious, significantly younger bikers all decked out in expensive biking finery and riding custommade bikes from Italy or France. He loved to ride with these guys because they took themselves inordinately seriously and looked down on his wearing a corduroy jacket, jeans, a chambray shirt, and a knit tie. He got a kick out of not only keeping up with them, but challenging them, particularly on the uphill sections. Because of his pickup basketball, Jack was in superb cardiovascular shape.

He had not slept that well, which seemed mildly ironic because Laurie had. Now that she'd made up her mind about her surgery, she could relax, while the immediacy of it had the opposite effect on Jack. This morning had been his turn to wake up early and wander around the apartment, stealing long looks at his sleeping children. As he had said to Laurie the previous day, he wished it was he who was having the surgery. If that had been the case, there was no doubt in his mind that he would have been fast asleep at that point, waiting for the alarm and not being tortured by dark thoughts concerning Laurie's well-being.

At the southeast corner of the park, Jack bid farewell to his fellow riders with a nod of his head as he peeled off, going south on East Drive while they went north. When he got to the Grand Army Plaza, he headed south on Fifth Avenue. It was his normal route, which he followed without giving it much thought. At that time in the morning the traffic was light. Although not that many years ago he used to challenge taxis on his morning commute, he didn't do that anymore. In that regard he'd become relatively conservative now that he had family obligations.

Eventually he traveled east over to Second Avenue. This was the only portion of the bike ride that he varied on a whim from day to day. On this particular morning he took 54th Street. As per usual, he looked forward to getting to the OCME. Work was one of the ways that

Jack dealt with his submerged anxieties, and whenever something was bothering him, he invariably worked harder. Yesterday he'd done four autopsies and the day before, five, such that cases were piling up on his desk, crying out to be completed. In contrast to most of the other medical examiners, he preferred to be in the pit actually doing the autopsies rather than the more sedentary aspect of sitting at his desk collating all the material to complete the death certificate. At least that was his preference unless there was a particularly challenging conundrum. Jack loved to do field work even though he was supposed to leave that aspect up to the medical-legal investigators. The problem was that Jack was trained at a forensic program that encouraged the medical examiners to go out in the field when it would be helpful, and from day one at the NYC OCME he'd strained at the limitations.

On reaching Second Avenue, he turned south. Here the traffic was significantly lighter than usual, which gave him a chance to think. After his run out on the neighborhood basketball court last night, where he didn't play up to his expectations with everything on his mind, he'd had another talk with Laurie about Dr. Nichols. Laurie had told him that although she didn't mind continuing to collaborate with her regarding the autopsy she'd done with her, she didn't have the time or energy to deal with the problem her general performance created. She said she was going to tell Chet that it was up to him but wanted to encourage Jack to lend a hand without making the situation worse. Jack had promised he'd do so, which was going to require him to be more accommodating than usual.

As was his customary habit, he rode his bike down 30th Street alongside the OCME building and entered at the loading dock. Hefting his bike onto his shoulder, he brought it inside and locked it in its usual location not far from the autopsy room. From there he went up to the ID area on the ground floor, where the day started for all the medical examiners. Since it was only 7:15 there were only two people in the room, Dr. Jennifer Hernandez and Vinnie Amendola. Jennifer was there because it was her week as a junior ME to be the on-call ME, one of whose jobs was to go over the cases that had come in overnight, decide which of them should be autopsied, and to divvy them up to the various MEs. Vinnie, one of the more senior mortuary technicians, was there to make sure the transition from the night shift to the day shift proceeded without a hitch and, maybe more important for the OCME community, to make the coffee in the communal coffeepot.

As Jack passed Vinnie, he swatted the newspaper Vinnie was holding up in front of his face, totally engrossed in the sports pages. Vinnie didn't respond overtly because Jack did it every day. When he first started doing it years ago, Vinnie used to visibly jump and complain. But after so many repeats, he took the harassment in stride in the vain hope Jack would tire of it.

Approaching the desk where Jennifer was sitting, Jack said, "What kind of night was it? Are people still dying to get in here?"

"Very funny," Jennifer said. "It was a relatively busy night." Jack was known for his black humor, which some people thought was clever, others less so.

"Any intriguing cases?" Jack asked. It was his modus operandi to cherry-pick cases according to his interests, which was why he made it a point to arrive before anyone else other than the ME on call. Most of the other medical examiners tolerated this behavior because everyone knew that he did more cases than anyone else, a lot more.

"Quite a number of interesting cases," Jennifer said. "Especially if you find getting run over by a subway train interesting."

"Was it accidental or suicide?" Jack questioned. In general, he didn't find such cases particularly interesting since the OCME saw about thirty of them a year. When a person got hit by a train there wasn't a lot of question what killed the individual. Jack liked mysteries and challenges.

"Neither," Jennifer said. "It's possibly a little complicated, or so the MLI thought, and the MLI was Bart Arnold."

"Complicated how?" he asked, immediately becoming interested.

"The subway part wasn't accidental or suicide," Jennifer said.

"You mean, someone pushed the victim in front of the train?" Jack asked. Unfortunately, that was becoming more common of late.

"Yes. According to Bart it was a homeless-appearing man who fled the scene," Jennifer said. "The police are still going over the video feeds, and as of yet there are no suspects in custody. There's also several eyewitnesses. But here's the catch: There were almost twenty-four hours between the event and the death, with the patient having spent the time in the Bellevue ICU, where she had been conscious and oriented. She had survived getting run over by the train. The terminal event was a heart attack."

"Hmm, the plot thickens," Jack said. "I get your point. If a good defense attorney could convince a jury that the death was due to something that was done in the hospital to cause a heart attack, a suspect could potentially get off with a slap on the wrist."

"That's the fear," Jennifer said.

"Let me take a look," he said. He took the folder from her and quickly read through Bart Arnold's investigative report of Madison Bryant. As the head of the MLI unit, combined with his years of experience, Bart's work was always top-notch. Besides describing the victim as an NYU hospital social worker, he had laid out the problem just as Jennifer had described. Prior to the final heart attack or ventricular fibrillation, there had been no history of heart disease, and there had been no symptoms or signs of impending heart trouble during the time she was in the emergency room or in the ICU.

"It's got me hooked," Jack said. "Mind if I take this one to start?"

"Be my guest," Jennifer said. "How many more do you want? There are plenty to go around today."

"As many as you need to give me," Jack said with a

smile. Normally he would go through the rest of the stack to see what else caught his eye, but he was adequately intrigued with the Madison Bryant case. For him it was a good way to start the day and get his mind off Laurie's upcoming surgery and JJ's imminent psychological evaluation, the two things that were weighing him down.

"There's a case of a high school baseball player that looks interesting," Jennifer said. "He got hit in the chest with a baseball."

"That sounds good, too," he said. "Put my name on it. I'd also like to ask you to do me a favor."

"Of course," she said.

"If and when the NYU pathology resident Dr. Nichols decides to show up, would you tell her she has been assigned to work with me once again?"

"Does Dr. McGovern know about this?" Jennifer asked.

"He does indeed," Jack said. "We discussed it yesterday late afternoon."

"I'll be happy to tell her," Jennifer said.

Jack walked over to the overstuffed easy chair where Vinnie was sprawled and this time snatched away the newspaper. Vinnie clawed after it but without bothering to sit up. This paper grab was also a daily pantomime. He and Vinnie had been working together for so long that teasing each other had become ritualized.

"We have work to do," Jack said, keeping the paper just out of Vinnie's reach for a few beats before giving it back.

"Why can't you act like every other civilized medical examiner and start at eight or even nine?" Vinnie griped as usual.

"The early bird gets the worm," Jack repeated for the thousandth time.

"I haven't finished my coffee," Vinnie said, pretending to go back to reading his sports page.

"Actually, I have a surprise for you," Jack said, catching Vinnie off guard. This statement was not part of the usual script.

Vinnie lowered the paper and regarded him quizzically. "What kind of a surprise?"

"Remember the gracious debutante we had assist us yesterday on our first case?"

"You mean Dr. Nichols?"

"None other," Jack said. "I've invited her for an encore."

"Why?" Vinnie complained.

"It's too long a story for your pea brain," he said. "But I want you to be on good behavior for a change." He then dropped Madison Bryant's folder in Vinnie's lap. "Let's go, big guy." He extended his hand and hoisted Vinnie to his feet.

In the elevator on the way down, Vinnie reiterated his question about why Jack was willing to work with Aria Nichols. "It doesn't make sense after the way you carried on yesterday when she disappeared at the end of the gunshot case."

"As I said, it's a long story, but a condensed version is that she's giving Dr. McGovern a hard time, and I offered to help." Jack didn't say anything about Laurie and her specifically asking him to lend a hand with Aria so that it was one problem she didn't have to think about. He knew that Laurie had yet to announce that she would be having surgery except to the deputy chief, so the rest of the OCME was in the dark.

Working in tandem, which was the way they always handled the first case of the day, Jack helped Vinnie get Madison Bryant's body put out on table #1 and the X-ray up on the screen. The endotracheal tube that had been inserted during the resuscitation attempt was still in place, which was standard procedure with such a case. Jack removed it after making sure it had been positioned properly.

"She looks pretty damn good for having been run over by a train," Jack commented as he continued his external exam. He and Vinnie had noted the broken left humerus, the three broken ribs, and the linear skull fracture on the X-ray, as well as the missing left foot.

"We've seen worse with people falling off their front stoop," Vinnie agreed.

"My sense is that she fell headfirst between the rails," Jack said, examining the scalp laceration that had been sutured in the emergency room after the area had been shaved. "Had it not been for the foot getting caught, she might have been able to walk away."

"I don't know," Vinnie questioned. "I kind of doubt it, considering that skull fracture."

"You're right," Jack said. "I wasn't being literal because she was probably knocked out cold. But she looks a hell of a lot better than my last subway victim, who appeared as if he'd been practically skinned alive."

Using one of the digital cameras, Jack took photos of all the injuries. He also drew them on a schematic diagram and indicated their size and location by referencing various anatomical landmarks. As he was finishing taking urine and vitreal samples, he caught sight of Dr. Nichols pushing in through the swinging entrance doors. Jack was surprised. It was only 7:38, an hour earlier than yesterday. He watched her as she approached, noticing even from a distance that she had an aura of confidence, almost arrogance, as if she owned the place. Jack girded himself, sensing that the morning might be more difficult than he'd anticipated.

Without acknowledging either Jack or Vinnie, Aria marched up to the autopsy table, gloved hands and arms akimbo. She stared down at the cadaver. Jack and Vinnie exchanged a glance, during which Vinnie rolled his eyes.

"Holy fuck," Aria said to no one in particular. Vinnie winced as if he'd been slapped, knowing what Jack's response was going to be to her choice of words.

"Excuse me?" Jack blurted. He'd heard but wanted to pretend otherwise. He thought he'd prepared himself for this woman, but it was obvious he hadn't. With great effort he controlled himself and merely said: "Dr. Nichols, such language offends me, and I have to ask you not to use it. I'm old-school, and I find it disrespectful to me, to this patient, and to the institution."

"I know this woman," she said, ignoring Jack's comment. She was still staring at the body on the autopsy table and acting as if she were angry.

"Did you hear what I said?" Jack pressed.

"This is fucking unbelievable," Aria said, seemingly hypnotized and angered by the sight of Madison Bryant's body. "I know this woman. She was supposed to help me with the Jacobsen case I did two days ago, since she worked with her and was her goddamn best friend. I don't believe this! First, she goes and gets herself hit by a train and now she fucking dies. What is this, a conspiracy?"

Jack felt his face suffuse with color as his blood pressure headed north. Not only was Aria's language threatening to drive him up the wall, so was her total lack of empathy for this victim of a horrible crime and possibly a therapeutic complication. He was at a definite crossroads: Either he was going to bodily toss this antisocial woman out of the autopsy room, or he was going to have to accept that some of his old beliefs needed to be updated and modified with the times. In his mind he counted to ten as he reminded himself of his promise to Laurie not to make the Aria Nichols situation worse. Throwing her out of the autopsy room would definitely cross that line.

"Somebody must have screwed up over there in the Bellevue ICU big-time," she continued. For the first time since she'd marched into the room, she looked Jack in the eyes. "I was over there yesterday and was told she was stable and doing well. How the fuck could she die? She was a healthy young woman as far as I know."

"How she died is what we need to find out," Jack managed. He had to restrain himself from dashing out of the autopsy room to find something to vent his anger on just to get himself under control.

"Where's the goddamn folder?" Aria demanded, as if she were in charge, and seemingly totally oblivious of the effect she was having on Jack.

"It's over on the countertop," Vinnie said, pointing.

Aria strode over, flipped it open, and rummaged through the contents until she found Bart Arnold's investigative report. She pulled it out and started reading. Meanwhile Jack and Vinnie exchanged another glance but didn't speak. Vinnie could tell just by looking at Jack that he was struggling with his self-control, and Vinnie didn't want to become the spark that ignited a conflagration.

"Ventricular fibrillation!" she called out when she finished reading. She replaced the investigative report in the file and came back to the table. Neither Jack nor Vinnie had moved.

"In my book, ventricular fibrillation is a diagnostic sign, not a diagnosis," she added. For the first time her voice was calm and reflective, as if her anger had somehow evaporated after reading the MLI report.

"You're right," Jack managed to say. Somehow, he was finding the strength to avoid an explosive confrontation with this insensitive, self-centered woman. What helped was her sudden change of tone along with her avoidance of any further vulgarities, making him optimistically wonder if perhaps they had reached a secret bargain.

Hoping to start a reasonable conversation, he said, "What are your thoughts about the causes of ventricular fibrillation?"

"Are you gearing up to provide me with another lecture?" Aria asked in a supercilious tone. "If you are, I'd prefer you don't, if you don't mind."

"I'm just trying to understand your thinking before you begin doing the autopsy," Jack said.

Aria eyed Jack with obvious surprise. "Are you suggesting that you want me to do the autopsy?" she asked hesitantly.

"That's what I have in mind." It had been a sudden decision when he remembered Laurie's comment about the pathology resident's rotation not being challenging enough. He also recalled Laurie's compliments about Aria's prosecting ability. Combining the two by giving her more responsibility had suddenly suggested itself as a way to deal with her aggravating antisocial eccentricities.

"Well, that's a step in the right direction," she said. "Okay, here's what I think. In general, the causes of ventricular fibrillation are usually related to preexisting heart disease of some sort, like a previous heart attack or a congenital heart defect or the history of a channelopathy. Of course, cardiomyopathy could cause VF, too, as well as some drugs like cocaine or methamphetamine. The only other things I'd keep in mind are the possibility of electric shock from some malfunctioning hardware or electrolyte abnormalities with potassium, magnesium, or calcium."

"Very well said," he remarked with surprise. He was

actually impressed and for a beat stared at her, thinking she was a piece of work yet clearly medically knowledgeable despite her behavioral issues. "With all that in mind, what might you be expecting to find on this case?"

"Statistically I'd put money on previous heart disease either acquired or congenital," Aria said. "Probably the most important part of the forensic autopsy will involve the careful examination of the heart. But knowing she was on intravenous fluid in an ICU unit for almost twenty-four hours, I'd want to get electrolyte levels and a toxicology screen. And there is always the possibility of deep vein thrombosis and embolism, especially after the trauma she suffered."

"Vinnie! Would you mind handing the lady a scalpel?" Jack said. "Time's a-wastin'. Let's get this show on the road!"

CHAPTER 28

May 10th
7:52 A.M.

Similar to Laurie's assessment, Jack found Aria to be a talented prosector. She handled the scalpel with confidence and precision. Although he was prepared to offer criticism or suggestions about her technique, he didn't feel it was necessary. Best of all from his perspective, she became totally engrossed and worked silently, so his ears had a break from the vulgar language. In short order she had the body open with the breastbone, ribs, and intestines in view. Taking bone shears from Vinnie, she quickly cut through the ribs, exactly as Jack would have done, and reflected the breastbone cephalad. Jack generally removed the breastbone, but it wasn't necessary, and he didn't interfere. Next Aria reflected the thymic fat pad to expose the pericardium of the heart.

"It all looks normal to me," she said to no one in particular as she proceeded to run the balls of her fingers over the heart still covered by its pericardium. Without looking up at Jack, she asked him if he wanted to feel it as well.

"It's not necessary," Jack said. "I trust your judgment, and it looks normal to me, too."

Wasting no time, Aria took a couple of clamps and dissecting scissors from Vinnie and opened the pericardium to expose the heart itself. Using her right hand, she palpated the softball-size organ and commented that it, too, seemed entirely normal. After she pulled her hand away, Jack reached in and did the same, with the same conclusion. Taking a large syringe outfitted with a fourteen-gauge needle, Aria lifted the base of the heart high enough to get a look at the posterior aspect of the left atrium. After inserting the needle through the atrial wall, she took a sizable blood sample for Toxicology.

With that job out of the way, she double-clamped all the major cardiac veins and arteries and cut them, freeing up the heart. While she did this, she used the opportunity to look for any large clots, particularly in the veins. "So far no emboli," she announced. She then lifted the heart out of its bed, where it had been nestled between the two lungs. She weighed it and then put it on a cutting board that Vinnie had brought over along with a standard butcher knife. During the next fifteen minutes Aria carefully opened the heart to peer at the various heart valves. Then using fine dissecting scissors, she began painstakingly tracing out each coronary artery.

Around 8:15 other medical examiners and mortuary

techs started to appear in the autopsy room to begin their cases. A number of them detoured to take a peek at the subway case because of its morbid appeal. Those who did asked a few questions, and some even indulged in a bit of dark humor. But each interaction was short-lived as Jack made it plain that he was intent on watching Aria. That was the case until Chet showed up when she was busy with the coronary arteries. Sensing it was an opportune moment, Jack pulled Chet to the side, out of her earshot.

"My God," Jack said under his breath. "She is a trip!"

"I told you so," Chet said with apparent satisfaction.

"I almost lost it when we first started," Jack said. "In retrospect, I'm embarrassed my reaction was so over the top. I came close to literally throwing her out of the pit. Her language would make the proverbial sailor blush."

"Tell me about it." Chet chuckled behind his hand.

"You won't believe this, but she knew the patient personally," Jack said. "That was what keyed off her orgy of profanity. She was mad the person got hit by a train and died because she was supposed to help her. I don't think I've ever witnessed a worse case of self-centered lack of empathy in my life."

"I can tell you that she's not been concerned about my feelings," Chet said. "I've been victimized by her profanity, too. I mean, I'm not as bothered by profanity as you are, but in my case it was specifically directed at me."

"Did you really ask her to have a drink sometime?" Jack said. "You should have your head examined. Especially in this day and age and you essentially being her boss. What were you thinking?"

"Hey, I wasn't thinking," Chet confessed. "I'd just met her, she said she was single, and there was something vaguely appealing about her before she opened her foul mouth."

"You must be more desperate than I realized," Jack said. "She's the last person you should have a drink with, so in some ways maybe she did you a favor. Anyway, Laurie asked me to help you with her, God knows why, with my short fuse. So how can I help?"

"You're already helping, bro," Chet said. "You've kept her entertained two days in a row. I owe you." Chet glanced around Jack and watched Aria for a beat as she was examining the heart. "Are you letting her do the case like Laurie did?"

"I am," Jack said. "I hadn't necessarily planned it, but after what Laurie said yesterday, I thought it might be best for everyone. She's got good hands, and she's definitely savvy."

"I'm running out of people to ask to let her assist," Chet said. "She pretty much turns everybody off."

"I've got another case that I know of after this one," Jack said. "Why don't you let her stay with me. I'll offer her that case, too. At least that will let you get through today. And who knows, if she continues to act like she has during this case, I can tolerate her."

"You got her," Chet said. "Have fun!"

"Yeah, sure," Jack said. He turned away and walked back to where she was working on the heart. He could tell she was nearly finished.

"I'm surprised, but this is a normal heart," Aria said

when she became aware of Jack's presence. She stepped to the side so Jack could take a look at the opened organ. "There are absolutely no signs of any heart disease or congenital abnormalities like I expected. Of course, we can't rule out a channelopathy, but if she had a channelopathy, chances are there would have been a history of cardiac rhythm problems. The MLI report says there was none, so we're back to square one."

"I'm surprised, too," Jack said as he picked up the heart and quickly glanced at its interior and at the coronary vessels. A moment later he put the organ back on the cutting board. "I agree. The heart's clean. I would have put money on some anatomical cardiac abnormality. I guess we'll have to wait for Toxicology to provide us with some answers, or Molecular Biology concerning the possibility of a channelopathy. We are certainly going to need to get her entire hospital record for this latest Bellevue admission and any other hospitalization she's had while growing up in Missouri. Meanwhile, why don't you go ahead and finish this case?"

The rest of the autopsy proceeded rapidly as there was no pathology to speak of except for the skull portion, where it was important to expose the fracture lines. As soon as Aria was finished, she stripped off her double-layered gloves, tossed them onto the cadaver, and started for the door. Jack, who was finishing a diagram of Madison's external injuries, had been planning on making sure that she didn't do a repeat of her disappearing act like she'd done the previous day, but she again took him by surprise.

"Hey!" Jack called out. "Dr. Nichols! Hold up."

Still holding the diagram and the pencil he was using, Jack caught up with Aria, who had gotten halfway to the exit. "This is not how we MEs end autopsies here at the OCME," he said. "It's customary to help get the body off the table as well as organize the specimen jars, decontaminate them, and make sure they are all labeled properly."

She went up on her tiptoes to see over Jack's shoulder. She could see that Vinnie was guiding one of the gurneys next to the autopsy table. She looked at Jack. They were both still wearing plastic facial shields, and neither could really see the other's expression. "I'm not an ME nor am I a mortuary technician," Aria declared as if the issue wasn't up for discussion. "And I've got something more important to do. I have to check my phone about getting information on the case I did with Dr. Montgomery."

"You're scheduled to be with me for the next autopsy," Jack said. "I'm going to suggest you do that one, too, but I expect you to carry your own weight, which means helping out."

"I'll be back," Aria said. "I appreciate you letting me actually do the case rather than having me just standing around sucking my thumb. And it is damn appropriate, considering in a month I'll be in my last year as a pathology resident. But I'm not a mortuary technician, nor a janitor."

"This isn't an argument," Jack said. "Vinnie needs some help because all the other mortuary technicians are busy, which you could see if you just looked around. And

I have to go upstairs to see the chief in between cases."
Jack was dying to find out if Laurie had heard from her
surgeon about when her surgery was to take place. He
was afraid it was going to be as soon as tomorrow.

"That's their problem, not mine," Aria said dismis-
sively. "I became a doctor so I didn't have to do that kind
of shit." She turned around and recommenced heading
for the door.

Once again Jack was dumbfounded, and before he
gave any thought to the propriety of what he was about
to do, he quickly caught up to her and grabbed her left
arm just above the elbow, yanking her to a stop. Aria
reacted with even more speed by twirling around and
using a karate-like blow to free her arm. "Don't you dare
touch me," she snarled, loud enough for most people in
the pit to hear.

The background conversation and activity in the autopsy room suddenly stopped, and for the briefest moment there was a pregnant silence as people either turned
their heads or raised their eyes to stare at the two people
glaring at each other. But then Aria broke off and continued to the door, which she shoved open with an outstretched hand, like a football player stiff-arming an
opponent.

In the next instant all the conversations and activities
in the room resumed as if nothing had happened. Jack
took a deep breath, realizing that he had his fists balled
despite still holding the pencil and the now crumpled
trauma diagram. With a twinge of embarrassment, he
glanced around to see if anyone was still looking at him,

but no one seemed to until he locked eyes with Chet, who immediately came over.

"What on earth was that about?" he asked in a forced whisper.

"I almost lost it again," Jack said with a shake of his head. "She certainly knows how to push buttons. I was just trying to get her to help clean up and prepare for the next case."

"Did she tell you to fuck off like she told me?" Chet questioned with a smirk.

Jack shot his former roommate a sharp glance. They had shared an office at the OCME for several years, back when they'd been first employed. "Don't you start," Jack warned, but then added a laugh. He knew that Chet was teasing him, and he knew he deserved it.

"Do you want to renege on having to put up with her for another case?" Chet asked. "I'm sure I could find someone. Maybe you deserve a rest."

"No, I'll do it," Jack said. "I told Laurie I'd help with her, and I'll see it through. It's my cross to bear."

"What about tomorrow, if I'm not being too bold to ask?"

"Sure, why not?" Jack said. "By then I should be immune."

———

Aria couldn't quite believe it. The moment she had started to think that her rotation through Forensic Pathology wasn't that bad and wasn't a total waste of time,

someone tried to shame her into acting like a maidser-
vant. She'd found the mortuary technicians hard to bear,
as they all had gigantic chips on their shoulders. There
was no way she was about to let them shame her into doing their job.

Pushing into the locker room, Aria first used the toi-
let. Then she went to get her phone. As soon as she
opened it, she was encouraged. Vijay Srinivasan had sent
her a text a little after eight. It wasn't a newsy message
because all it said was for her to call him. Although the
phone signal wasn't all that great in the locker room, she
placed the call. It went through okay, but then she had
to wait for Vijay to be found. Since the office was essentially one big room, she wondered why it took so long.

"Sorry to keep you waiting," Vijay said when he finally came on the line and before even saying hello. "I
was on the other phone, but I was working on your leukemia project, so I deserve a bit of leeway."

"Are you making any headway?" Aria asked, eschew-
ing small talk as usual.

"We are indeed," Vijay said. "That was the reason I
asked you to call. The kits were completed for the mother
and the child overnight by keeping our lab open instead
of closing by five, which is our usual time. By the way, we
have given them the names Hansel and Gretel with the
child being Hansel, of course, and the mother being
Gretel, and the witch being leukemia. Don't ask me how
the names came about because it should be mother and
son and not brother and sister, but I wasn't consulted. It
was a team decision. If I had to guess, I'd say it was the

product of one of our best programmers having been a literature major."

"I'd much rather hear about your progress," Aria said impatiently.

"As soon as the kits were available the team went to work," Vijay said. "We created phased kits, including an evil twin, and uploaded all of it into our system. Our software automatically created a Lazarus kit for the missing father by phasing the child and the evil twin against the mother, but that's probably more detailed than you want to hear. The long and short of it is that we got a match right off the bat that has proven to be one better in terms of a generation than what the people got with the first match associated with the Golden State Killer's DNA. We have been able to find a paternal great-great-grandfather of Hansel with a family name of Thompson using Y-DNA testing, which, as you know, is inherited through the paternal line. And of particular significance it has already been confirmed as IBD, or identical-by-descent. Next we are going to upload the kits into GEDmatch, as well as check and see if Family Tree DNA has a Thompson surname project."

"That's encouraging," she said. "At this stage do you have any guesstimate how long it might take to find the father?"

"No, and I don't want to mislead you into the trap of that kind of thinking," Vijay said. "Just because we've made significant progress, there is no guarantee of ultimate success. It all depends on how many of Hansel's paternal relatives have joined the genetic genealogical craze, sent in the DNA sample, and constructed a genetic family tree."

"But you are optimistic?" Aria questioned.

"Of course I'm optimistic," Vijay said. "I wouldn't be pushing my team as hard as I am if I wasn't optimistic. We will be actively searching for more matches by using the databases of other genealogical companies through GEDmatch. And if we can find a close relative, I'll start getting progressively more optimistic."

"How close is close?" Aria asked.

"Anything closer than a third cousin of Hansel would be great," Vijay said. "And if we come across first cousins or aunts and uncles then it is almost a given that we'll be successful, provided there are some family trees available. Even if we get that close and there are no family trees, we can start constructing one for Hansel, but that would take time. Let's hope there are some trees already in existence that Hansel can be added to."

She remembered what Madison had told her in Nobu, and it was pretty close to what Vijay was saying now. "What if you find half-siblings of Hansel?" Aria asked. She thought that the existence of half-siblings was a definite possibility because of her belief that Lover Boy was married. If that was true, and children were involved, they would all be Hansel's half-siblings.

"If half-siblings were found, the case would be solved as their father would be the person we are seeking. But I personally think the chances of that happening are statistically negligible. But let's not get ahead of ourselves.

Presently I'm hoping that GEDmatch will give us a number of new matches that we can use for triangulation."

"I'll be waiting for any news," she said.

"I'm sure we'll have information in the next few hours," Vijay said. "Perhaps it would be best if you came by and we can show you what we have been able to do."

"Why not?" Aria said. She was beginning to share Vijay's optimism.

———————

With Jack helping, Vinnie was able to get Madison Bryant's cadaver back in the walk-in freezer, the table cleaned, specimens taken care of, and Jonathan Jefferson on the table. He also got all new specimen jars and clean instruments, while Jack quickly read the investigative report done by one of the evening shift's MLIs, Steve Mariott. It was the story of a sixteen-year-old who'd been in Central Park playing baseball and hit in the chest by a pitch. CPR had been administered immediately by the coaches. When paramedics had arrived, ventricular fibrillation had been determined and defibrillation attempted without success. CPR was continued during the ambulance ride to the hospital, where defibrillation was attempted another eight times along with the administration of standard cardiac resuscitation drugs, all to no avail.

Taking a deep breath, Jack put the investigative report back in the autopsy folder. As a medical examiner he was accustomed to death to the point that for him it had become just another part of the cycle of life. But there were exceptions, and this case was one of them. Of course, it had a lot to do with the age of the victim. Jack always found dealing with children emotionally stressful, and the younger the child, the harder it was, like with the scalded infant two days ago. But this current victim, a mere teenager, likewise pulled hard on his heartstrings. It seemed so unreasonably cruel and senseless that such a child's life could be so easily extinguished while in apparent good health, playing athletics. Thinking about the unfairness of it all made him feel embarrassed about his reaction earlier with Aria. In such a context it seemed so trivial that he cared about her use of vulgar language, lack of empathy, or refusal to lend a hand cleaning up after an autopsy. Certainly, it was his responsibility to act as the adult and control himself, especially since he had told Chet and Laurie he'd help out. After all, the only actual negative was that he hadn't had the opportunity to go upstairs and find out about Laurie's surgery.

"The X-ray is up on the view box," Vinnie called out, interrupting Jack's mild epiphany.

Jack walked over to it. As he imagined, the X-ray was completely normal, including the sternum, where he assumed the boy had been hit by the baseball. Sudden death, mostly involving completely healthy young boys playing sports, was not unheard of. It mostly involved baseball, although softball, hockey, karate, and lacrosse were adding to the toll of about ten kids a year in the US alone. It came from being struck in the chest at a very specific, short interval of time during the normal heart-beat to throw the entire cardiac conduction system out of whack, resulting in ventricular fibrillation.

As Jack was still struggling with his emotions, he became aware of a presence next to him, and when he turned to look, he was surprised that Aria had joined him in looking at the child's X-ray. While he stared at her profile, she continued to study the film.

"What happened to the kid?" Aria asked. "I don't see any broken bones."

"My guess is that it is a case of commotio cordis," Jack said. "He was hit with a baseball and went into ventricular fibrillation. Is commotio cordis something you are familiar with?"

"Only through reading," Aria said. "And you?"

"Likewise," Jack said. "Luckily, I've never personally had a case, but I know Dr. Montgomery had one her first year here. Emotionally she found it difficult to handle." Jack felt a little silly calling his wife Dr. Montgomery, yet he thought it was appropriate under the circumstances.

"Will I find anything at autopsy?" she asked, finally breaking off looking at the X-ray to glance at Jack.

"Probably not," Jack said. "But it is a diagnosis of exclusion. In that sense it will be like Madison Bryant."

"Well, let's get it over with," Aria said. "I've got things to do. Am I still going to be the prosector?"

Jack continued to stare at Aria for a beat while she stared back with a slight smirk. Even though he'd promised himself he'd be the adult, she had already ruffled his feathers by suggesting she had more important things to do than the autopsy on a child who'd died before his life could really begin. It was she who broke off and walked back to the table with a spring to her step. There wasn't the slightest hint she found the case emotionally upsetting.

Although Aria looked closely at the child's chest and even palpated the boy's breastbone, she could not find any evidence of the child's being hit by a baseball. There was no bruising or abrasion whatsoever. Nor did she find anything on the rest of the external exam. Like with Madison Bryant, Aria was standing on the patient's right side while Jack and Vinnie were on the opposite side.

"Scalpel," she said, extending her hand toward Vinnie. Vinnie had the instrument tray next to him.

"What about examining the inside of the mouth just in case the boy choked on something?" Jack said, making an effort to make it sound like a suggestion and not a criticism.

Without responding verbally, Aria did search the mouth and palpate the throat. When she was finished, she then took the knife to start the case with the usual Y incision.

Like with Madison Bryant, Aria worked rapidly but skillfully. Jack helped when he could, especially when she was using the bone shears. When the heart was fully exposed yet still covered by the pericardium, Aria bent down to look closely.

"I don't see any signs of trauma whatsoever," she said as she straightened up.

"Nor do I," Jack said, responding to the first words

Aria had said since the case began. He had learned his lesson to stay quiet and not lecture.

"Okay," she said more to herself than to Jack or Vinnie. Just as she'd done with Madison, she carefully opened the pericardium and then finally removed the heart entirely. Jack watched intently and was convinced that the heart was entirely normal, at least from the outside. Specifically, there were no signs of bruising. As Aria began opening the heart, Jack caught sight of Laurie coming into the autopsy room for her morning autopsy rounds. Jack was eager to talk with her but was hesitant to leave Aria with the most important part of the autopsy under way. Laurie started at table #8, which was closest to the door to the hallway.

"The interior of the heart is normal," Aria announced to no one in particular. Jack had been watching over her shoulder. "That leaves coronary vascular abnormalities as the only other possibility."

"I agree," Jack said. "The coronary arteries have to be exposed."

Aria put down the butcher knife she'd been using and picked up more delicate dissecting instruments and began tracing out the coronary system. Jack watched for ten minutes or so to make sure there wasn't obvious pathology, which there wasn't, and to make sure she was following the normal protocol. When he was sure things were copacetic, he elected to leave her under Vinnie's capable supervision and have a few words with Laurie. A moment later he caught up with her as she was moving from table #4 to #3.

"I was on my way down to check in on you two," Laurie said, practically bumping into him. They stepped back to be out of everyone's way. "I couldn't help but notice that things seemed to be going well between you and Dr. Nichols."

"That's a bit deceptive. It's more like the calm after the storm," Jack said, trying to make light of the situation.

"Was there a problem?" she asked with concern.

"I had to struggle to keep myself under control," Jack said. "In retrospect, I'm a little embarrassed at my behavior since I was fully warned by you what she was like, and I promised you not to make things worse."

"What happened?" Laurie asked anxiously. She looked around him to see Aria calmly working at a cutting board.

"Nothing happened," Jack assured her. "Ultimately, I was able to restrain myself, but it required about as much self-control as I can muster. What was it that Carl Henderson said about her, that she's not a team player? Well, I can assure you he was correct. And she is definitely antisocial. Whether she has an antisocial personality disorder, I seriously doubt, as she wouldn't have gotten into or through medical school, but she certainly has zero empathy. To give you a glowing example, it turns out that she knew the first case on a personal basis. Instead of being concerned about the person and the tragedy she suffered, she was irritated the woman had gone and allowed herself to get run over by a train and then die in the Bellevue ICU."

"She actually was friends with the person you guys autopsied?" Laurie asked with astonishment.

"Well, I don't know if they were friends," Jack said. "I'm not sure she's capable of having what we call friends. I'd say they were acquaintances. She was mad because the victim was supposed to help her with the case that you and she did together the other day."

"You mean the Kera Jacobsen case?"

"Yes!"

"Then it is a double coincidence," she said. "What's the name of the patient?"

"Madison Bryant," he said.

"That is extraordinary. I remember Dr. Nichols talking about her. She was supposedly Kera's best friend. Regardless, the point that you're trying to make is that Dr. Nichols didn't express any appropriate grief or sadness at all?"

"None, zero, nada. Just irritation, and the language she used to express it was certainly colorful."

"I experienced a bit of her bad language as well," Laurie said. "And I know it irks you even more than it does me. I'm proud of you for keeping yourself calm. And thank you."

"Thank you for thanking me," Jack said. "Part of the reason I was able to hold myself in check was because I'd promised you I wouldn't make things worse, even though I almost did."

"I'm glad she's a pathology resident and not a forensic fellow," Laurie said. "In a matter of weeks we're going to be able to kick the can down the road and send her back to the Pathology Department. She's really their problem, not ours."

"Amen to that," Jack said. "One of the reasons I wanted her to help Vinnie in between cases was so I could pop up to your office."

"Oh," she said. "And why was that?"

"Oh, please!" he commented with a short, forced laugh. "As if you couldn't guess. I wanted to ask if you'd heard from Dr. Cartier about your surgery."

"Oh, yes! My surgery," Laurie said. "I'm sorry, I should have told you right away. You know, I find it mildly interesting that now that I've made up my mind about what to do, and it has been scheduled, I can put it aside and deal with the other things that need my attention. Before those decisions were made, I could hardly think of anything else."

"It's just the opposite for me," Jack complained. "I liked it better when things were up in the air. Anyway, are you going to continue torturing me or are you going to tell me the schedule?"

"Dr. Cartier has made arrangements for the operation to be tomorrow afternoon. She has a couple of cases in the morning, and I'll be a 'to follow.' I'm supposed to show up at Admitting at noon and not have had anything to drink or eat besides water."

"Okay," Jack said, trying to adjust to the finality of this news. "As I said yesterday, I wish it were me having the surgery, not you."

"I'm glad it's me," Laurie said.

"Did she give you any idea as to how long it's going to take?"

"We talked about that, but she said it all depends on

what ends up being done. If the suspicious lump is positive for cancer, she'll be doing more surgery. How much will depend on a number of variables, including whether any cancer is found in any lymph nodes. You know the process. I don't have to tell you."

"And if the lump is benign, you'll have simple mastectomies and reconstruction," he said.

"And the oophorectomy," she said. Then she bent over to look up into Jack's face as he had tilted his head down. "Hey, let's not make this more than it is. Everything is going to be fine."

"All right, I'm sorry," Jack said. "Of course everything is going to be fine. I just worry . . ."

"Worry about what?" Laurie said when he didn't finish his sentence.

"You know. It's my old worry that I am a risk to everyone I love," he said.

"Stop it!" Laurie said with finality bordering on anger. "I don't want to hear any more of that kind of nonsense. We've had this conversation before, and we talked it out. You were not responsible for the tragedy of your first family or our kids' medical issues. You know that, and I know that. So, buck up!"

"Okay, okay," Jack said. "Let's change the subject! What about your responsibilities here at the OCME? How is that going to be handled now that your surgery is scheduled?"

"There will be a formal announcement this afternoon that George Fontworth will be taking over the helm while I have a minor surgical procedure."

"God! I hope it is minor," Jack said.

"More important, I've been on the phone with Caitlin and my parents," she said. "They will be helping with the kids. That is really my main concern. I trust that you will also step up to the plate as far as the kids are concerned."

"Absolutely," he said. "That's a given."

"It means no basketball," Laurie said. "That would be all we'd need if you got injured at the same time I'm in the hospital. Promise me you'll forgo the basketball while I deal with my problem."

"Scout's honor," Jack said as he held up three fingers.

"I'm serious," Laurie said.

"I am, too," Jack said. "In my state I'd be a detriment to any team. What I need to do is get busy. I've got a stack of cases on my desk upstairs that need to be finished. I'll jump into that. Meanwhile, I better get back to my challenging charge, and the current case. By the way, what probably saved the day is I've let her do both cases, which kept her busy and interested. I think you were right yesterday when you said that the NYU residents should be given more autopsy responsibility to get them to be more involved."

"She definitely needs more involvement, so I think it was great for you to let her do the cases," she said.

"So, you are okay?" he said, staring directly into her eyes.

"I'm okay," Laurie said. "I think I am calmer than you are about all this."

"Maybe so," Jack said. "Listen, I better get back to

Miss Congeniality before she and Vinnie come to blows. It could be an understatement to say that she's not all that popular with the mortuary techs."

"As high and mighty as she acts, it's no wonder," Laurie said. "But there's one thing that I can say about her: She's honest about her emotions. She says what she thinks and doesn't care what others think. In that way she reminds me of someone else that I know and have grown to love."

"Touché," Jack said. "At the same time, I'm not antisocial, just choosy, and I don't lack empathy. And I've never lied to Chet. LOL."

"Go! I'll see you later. But to give you a heads-up, tonight we have to talk some more about JJ because I got some recommendations of potential psychological evaluators from the Brooks School this morning."

"Oh, great," he moaned. "Okay." He turned away and headed back toward table #1 thinking that if it wasn't one thing, it was another. But he recognized he couldn't think about JJ. At the moment Laurie's surgery was totally dominating his mind.

CHAPTER 29

May 10th
10:20 A.M.

Aria straight-armed the door into the locker room with such force that its inside handle smashed hard enough against the wall to crack one of the tiles. She didn't care but rather derived a bit of pleasure from the damage. Although she'd enjoyed doing the two autopsies, it irked her to death that at the end of each, she had to get in the same damn argument about being asked, or, worse still, commanded, to play mortuary tech or, worse, janitor. She had rebelled about that kind of hazing when she'd been a medical student and a first-year pathology resident, and she certainly wasn't going to stand for it now.

Throwing open the door to her locker with similar force, she got out her phone to check for messages. She had a sense that she might hear from Vijay again, and she was right. It wasn't much of a text message but still en-

couraging. It read: Another good match. Onward and upward. We look forward to seeing you later and hope to have
even more positive news.

With a definite sense of excitement, Aria got her
clothes out of the locker and dressed rapidly. Her intuition was telling her that her efforts were soon to be consummated, which was going to give her an almost
orgasmic high when it happened. As the search for Lover
Boy had continued, she'd become progressively interested in its successful conclusion as a kind of payback for
the harassment and the concealment she'd suffered from
the male gender from as early as she could remember. In
her mind, whether Lover Boy played any role in Kera
Jacobsen's overdose by supplying the drugs, or, worse,
didn't make any difference. What vexed her the most was
his ostensible desire for secrecy, which she considered an
affront to Kera. Aria was fixated on blowing this bastard's veil of secrecy to smithereens.

Before she was even finished dressing, Aria ordered a
rideshare so that it would be waiting for her when she
emerged from the OCME. The last of her clothing was
her resident's white coat. Once again when she arrived at
GenealogyDNA, she wanted to look the part of a physician. In some respects, it had surprised her that Vijay had
not asked her what kind of doctor she was, although she
had been prepared to say she was a hematologist in keeping with the mythical toddler having leukemia.

Like the day before, the ride was quick. In less than
twenty minutes she was climbing out of the car and
heading into the building's commercial entrance. When

she entered the GenealogyDNA office, the lavender-haired receptionist recognized her and told her that she was to go right in.

Just inside the inner office door, she paused. The atmosphere of the large barnlike room was different. No one was playing Ping-Pong, and no one was at the game station. Although it appeared as if there were the same number of people present or even a few more, a heavy silence reigned. Everybody seemed to be working with their respective laptops, whether at a desk or sprawled in a beanbag. As she was scanning the room, Vijay stood up from the large leather couch close to the center of the space. Like Aria, he was dressed the same as he'd been the day before but with a freshly pressed white shirt.

"Welcome, Dr. Nichols," he said as he approached with a welcoming grin. On this occasion he held back extending his hand, waiting for Aria to make the gesture. When she didn't, he merely pointed back where he'd come from. "How about joining me on the couch, or would a table be more to your liking?"

She shrugged. "Whatever," she said.

"Then the couch it is," Vijay said.

Aria made her way in that direction, walking ahead of Vijay and weaving among the varied furniture. A few of the people briefly looked up in her direction but then went back to their screens. As had been the case the day before, the people in the room were overwhelmingly geeky males, although Aria did see several equally geeky females with spiky hair. Although she thought of herself as a young millennial, she felt light-years older than this group.

Gesturing for Aria to sit at one end of the couch, he sat at the other. In between was a stack of papers. "I want to show you some of what we have accomplished," he said. He picked up the top paper that was a diagram of a family tree and handed it to her.

"Here is the very first match we got that we can map to Hansel: Arnold Thompson, through the great-great-grandfather and then the great-grandfather. To do that is a tribute to our proprietary software, since he is, at best, a third cousin of Hansel's, meaning they share very little DNA. You do understand what a third cousin represents, don't you?"

"I'm not sure," Aria said, not wishing to reveal her general ignorance. She'd read about it two nights ago, but some aspects of her reading were a blur.

"Third cousins share a common ancestor that is a great-great-grandparent," Vijay explained, "which means they generally share very little DNA, in fact on average

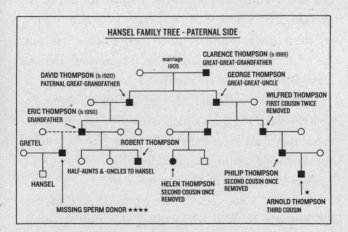

HANSEL FAMILY TREE - PATERNAL SIDE

less than one percent. With some of the genetic genealogy companies, that is too small to even come up as a
match for fear it would be a false positive. But our software automatically combined the Y-DNA results with the
autosomal results. By the way, you didn't mention that
the toddler was a boy."

"I didn't?" Aria questioned, trying to sound as if it
were an oversight whereas in actuality, she didn't know
the fetus's sex and had been afraid to guess. She thought
if she had been wrong, then it would have blown her
whole story.

"We were pleased when we determined it was a boy
for the very reason that I am explaining. The Y chromosome doesn't recombine like the autosomal chromosomes nor mutate at the same rate, which is why it's more
helpful in ethnicity estimates than genealogy studies.
But in this case, it was key. What we did was contact this
potential third cousin. You can see from the diagram.
His name is Arnold Thompson. Luckily for us, he is a
genealogical enthusiast and was eager to help by supplying the results that he'd obtained for one of his first cousins once removed, named Helen Thompson. Do you
know what *once removed* means?"

"I think so," Aria said. "It's a generational thing. For
an individual, a first cousin once removed means the ancestor they share is the individual's great-grandparent but
the cousin's grandparent, meaning they are genetically
connected but separated by a generation."

"Exactly," Vijay said. "When we matched Hansel to
this new kit, we were happy to see that the match was

significantly better: up to almost six percent. That meant that the potential third cousin was indeed a third cousin by descent, so we had a legitimate great-great-grandparent. His name was Clarence Thompson."

"Does that mean that Hansel's father's name is Thompson?" Aria said with awe. It had been only a matter of hours that GenealogyDNA had been working on this.

"That was our initial thought," he said. "But we believe we have hit a brick wall."

"That's unfortunate," she said. She remembered from her reading that the term's genealogical meaning referred specifically to situations where there was an apparent break in a family tree that couldn't be solved by following the paper trail of birth certificates and marriage licenses. Donor conception, as she was claiming with her leukemia scam, was one issue that could create such a brick wall. So was adoption, misattributed parentage, or even hospital baby switches that caused a sudden change in the genetic family tree defined by DNA inheritance.

"Yes, it is unfortunate," Vijay said. "And it is discouraging. Using a lot of tricks and taking advantage of the huge ancestral DNA database that now exists, we've traced down the appropriate Thompson family tree to where we should have found our target, but frustratingly enough, we haven't. An hour or so ago we even found what we believe to be half-siblings of Hansel's father using the Lazarus kit we developed for the missing sperm donor. And one of the half-siblings, named Robert Thompson, even created a very complete family tree, all the way back to Clarence Thompson, that he was willing to share with us. That gave us Hansel's paternal grandfather and several half-aunts and half-uncles. That should have been more than enough, but we are still empty-handed. Unfortunately, the paternal grandfather, Eric Thompson, wasn't helpful like his son. When we tried to explain the situation to him, he told us we had to be mistaken and that he only had the three kids, two girls and Robert, all of whom we already had on the Thompson family tree. He also denied ever being a sperm donor. Of course, that flies in the face of what genetic genealogy is trying to tell us, meaning in all likelihood a son of Eric Thompson had to have been the sperm donor for Hansel's creation. When there's this kind of problem, it's really frustrating. What we are beginning to believe is there was an adoption involved."

"So, what does all this mean?" Aria said with irritation. It seemed that after all the effort she was going to be deprived of success. It wasn't fair. "Does this mean the search is over?" The way everyone was working suggested otherwise, but how was she to know?

"No, not yet. We haven't totally given up," Vijay said. "What we are concentrating on now is the maternal side of the missing sperm donor's family, or Hansel's paternal grandmother, who would be the mother of the missing individual. If we can find her, and if she is cooperative, and if it was an adoption as we now suspect, and if it was an open adoption, we'll have the father. Otherwise, all bets are off as adoption records here in New York State are sealed."

"Would they be sealed in a situation of life or death

like we're facing?" Aria asked. She looked down at the family tree diagram she was holding, lamenting that all this work might be in vain.

"My understanding is that New York State has some of the most restrictive laws guarding confidentiality in adoption, even for medical reasons. Unsealing a record can happen if all parties agree, but it is a time-consuming process that would take months, if not a year. At the same time, if criminality is involved, I believe a district attorney can subpoena them, but that is the exception, not the rule."

"Shit," she said, feeling progressively depressed.

"Hallelujah!" someone cried out suddenly, causing Aria's head to pop up. Simultaneously a round of applause broke out along with accompanying cheers from many of the people in the room. Aria could see the youthful, skinny boy with mild acne who had asked her the sole question the previous day pumping his hands in the air like a professional bicyclist having just won a race. He had apparently jumped up from the desk where he'd been sitting at his laptop. "I've come across another first cousin, but this time on the father's maternal side," he cried. "And it's a good match, with over eight hundred centimorgans."

From her reading, she knew that centimorgans were a complicated method of measuring distance on a chromosome. The more centimorgans involved, the better the match. Thanks to the applause and excitement, she was encouraged. "Are we back in business?" she asked.

"Let's hope," Vijay said. "This should give us the grandmother we are looking for. Excuse me, I'll be right back."

CHAPTER 30

Hesitating at the curb for a moment, Aria looked up at the building she was about to enter. She knew enough about New York to know that the Fifth Avenue structure was considered a prewar building, meaning it had been built sometime in the early twentieth century. She knew such buildings contained coveted apartments but had no idea why as she had never been in one. The building itself was a nondescript fifteen- to twenty-story structure with a few penthouses perched wedding-cake-style on the top. It also had the de rigueur blue canvas awning ringed with lappets that stretched from the front door to the curb. Inside the door and peeking out through glass was a doorman in a blue uniform that was mildly worse for wear.

She was on her way to talk to a woman named Diane

Hanna, whom Vijay and his team had successfully located with their genetic genealogical magic. An hour or so after the skinny geek had come through with a new match, one of the few woman techies stumbled across a brand-new results kit from AncestryDNA, the company with the largest database: a thirty-two-year-old unmarried woman named Patricia Hanna, who shared a whopping twenty-five percent of DNA with the Lazarus kit of the missing sperm donor. At that point Aria had learned from Vijay that this newly found woman had to be either an aunt or a half-sibling of the target individual because of the amount of DNA they shared. From the woman's age alone, Vijay explained that Patricia had to be a half-sibling, which meant that her mother, named Diane Hanna née Carlson, was most likely the missing man's mother. From Patricia they had learned that Diane was currently a vigorous, healthy sixty-five-year-old socialite married to a highly placed New York lawyer. At no time during Vijay's phone conversation with Patricia, who considered herself to be an only child, was she told of the motive for the sudden interest in her mother.

The reason Aria was dawdling was that she still had no idea what she was going to say to Diane Hanna. If she was Lover Boy's mother, which Vijay and his team were convinced of, Aria had multiple major problems. First off, if Diane was the mother it had most likely been a premarital teenage pregnancy that had been relegated to the distant past, meaning the chance of its having been an open adoption was minimal at best. Even though Aria wasn't all that concerned about other people's feelings, she couldn't imagine Diane was going to be excited about an unpleasant and potentially socially jarring issue being suddenly dredged up and brought to the light of day. As if that wasn't bad enough, the story she had concocted to get GenealogyDNA interested in pursuing the case certainly could not be used with Diane. The woman would instantly see the mythical leukemia toddler as a grandson, which would evoke an emotional connection and rapid exposure of the story as a hoax. Nor did she think she could tell the truth, namely that she believed the adopted son had played a role in the overdose death of a young woman, as that would certainly reflect badly.

"Can I help you?" the doorman said. After eyeing Aria for a few minutes, he had stepped outside.

"In a minute," Aria said. She glanced away so she didn't have to look at the man's expectant face. She hated it when people, particularly men, intruded in her space. Gazing with unseeing eyes across the street into the newly leafed trees in Central Park, she went back to her musing about what she was going to say to Diane Hanna that might not turn her into a persona non grata and get her immediately kicked out of the apartment. She again wished that Vijay had been willing to talk to her, but he had absolutely refused. He said the role of GenealogyDNA was to supply what information customers wanted or needed, and then let them deal with it. He reminded Aria that adoption situations were fraught with emotional difficulties, as if Aria couldn't guess.

Suddenly she had an idea. Maybe she could pull on Diane's heartstrings. Aria could claim she was the result of Lover Boy's sperm donation, meaning she and Diane were genetically related, and that Aria's interest was to uncover her genetic past. A slight smile found its way to the corners of her mouth. It was by far the best idea she'd come up with and might work.

Armed with a new approach, she turned around and walked up to the doorman, who was now positioned just outside the front door. "I'm here to see Mrs. Diane Hanna," she said.

"And your name?" the doorman asked.

Aria told the man her name, and his response was cordial. "Yes, she is expecting you. The apartment is 7A."

Aria nodded and walked into the building's foyer. One of the two elevators was waiting. As she rode up, she went over the basics of the story she was going to present. The more she thought about it, the better it seemed. In many respects, she was amazed she had already gotten as far as she had. Before she'd called Diane from GenealogyDNA using the number that Patricia had supplied, she questioned if Diane would see her at all, but that had been when she thought she'd have to tell the woman why she wanted to speak with her. As it turned out, it hadn't been necessary. She had started the phone conversation by saying that she was a doctor at NYU Langone Medical Center and asked to speak with her person to person. Somehow that had been enough because Diane said she had time around five P.M. if Aria wanted to come over. Pleased, Aria had quickly accepted the invitation.

The elevator bumped to a stop, and she exited onto the seventh floor. She again questioned why prewar buildings were considered desirable as the hallway was claustrophobically narrow. The walls were painted a sickly pale yellow. She rang the bell for 7A, and the door was immediately opened by an Asian woman in a black uniform-type dress with a bit of lace around the collar. When Aria stepped over the threshold she suddenly understood the prewar appeal. In sharp contrast to the hallway, even the apartment's foyer had a sense of grand space with a high ceiling, crown moldings, baseboards, and high-gloss hardwood floor. And then when she was shown into what was obviously the library since one entire wall was bookcases floor to ceiling, the sense of space was even more dramatic, especially with the large window looking out over the expanse of Central Park.

A woman whom she assumed was Diane Hanna stood from the couch where she had been sitting. She appeared well kept for a sixty-five-year-old. She had a relatively slim body and a face that had seen some plastic surgery. Instead of any wrinkles or creases, the skin was pulled tight over the cheekbones and her lips were a bit too full. Although she hadn't taken a step forward, she had extended her hand in a kind of greeting.

Advancing into the room, Aria took the hand even though it was a gesture she usually avoided. On this occasion she wanted to make the best impression possible. After a brief handshake, Diane gestured to a chair facing the couch and sat back down herself. Aria noticed that the woman's sculpted hair didn't move one iota, as if it were glued in place.

"What kind of doctor are you?" Diane asked. Her voice was slightly nasal and seemed artificially restrained.

"I'm a resident in Pathology," Aria said. Again, she thought it best to start out with the truth. She was still wearing her white coat, so she knew she looked the part.

"Pathology?" Diane questioned. "That's a unique choice."

"It seems to fit me very well," Aria said. "It's a very intellectual specialty, especially surgical pathology."

"I suppose," Diane said, but she didn't sound convinced.

"Let me tell you something about myself," Aria began. On the spot she made up an elaborate story of being the child of a married lesbian couple who used sperm donation for her conception and for the conception of her brother. She then said that she and her brother shared a mild medical problem that made them want to find out about their genetic heritage. At that point, she paused to see if Diane was following the narrative and whether she had any questions.

"This is all very interesting," Diane said. "But why are you telling this to me?"

"I'm glad you asked," Aria said. "My brother and I hired a genetic genealogy company to see if we could find out about our ancestors, particularly our father. As I'm sure you know, twenty to thirty years ago men who donated sperm were assured that their generosity would remain anonymous. Things have changed today, for the reason I'm talking about. Anyway, after a lot of work, the genealogy company has determined that our father was adopted, so we've hit a brick wall in trying to figure out his identity."

Aria paused at this key moment in her narrative and watched Diane for the slightest sign of comprehension of where the conversation was going. Unfortunately, there was none. Diane stared back as if she was totally in the dark. If anything, she looked as if she was becoming progressively bored.

"Let me ask you this," Aria said, trying to decide exactly how to drop the bomb. "Do you have any idea whatsoever why I might be telling you my story?"

"No," Diane said with a shake of her head. "When you called earlier and said you were a doctor at the NYU Langone Medical Center, I thought it had something to do with my husband and I being rather generous donors. Is that why you're here?"

"Hell, no!" Aria said. The comment so surprised her that she'd not had the opportunity to filter her response. Aria was aware her choice of language often affected older people negatively and generally didn't care.

"Then perhaps you had better tell me," Diane said. "My husband and I are going to the opera tonight, and he'll be home imminently."

"The genetic genealogy company that my brother and I hired has determined with a high degree of certainty that our father is your son."

For a few beats it seemed to Aria as if the earth stopped its rotation. Even the birds in Central Park, which had been making a comparative racket, seemed to go silent. For a brief moment there seemed to be no horns blowing or sirens sounding, which were otherwise part of the constant background noise of New York City.

The only change that she could detect involved Diane's face. Simultaneously her overly pouty lips became compressed to practically disappear, the nostrils of her artificially small nose spread, and her powdered face flushed. By reflex Aria leaned back in her chair to avoid whatever was coming.

"I do not have a son!" Diane snapped while she stood up and glared at Aria, daring her to suggest otherwise.

Although Aria distinctly remembered reading in the Bettinger book in a section discussing adoption that "navigating this minefield of potential ethical issues can be difficult," she thought Diane was carrying it to the extreme with her response. In contrast, Aria kept her seat and tried to project a sense of calm.

"Did you hear me?" Diane practically yelled.

"Yes, I heard you," she said. "But I have several family trees that the genetic genealogy company has constructed to show how they have come to the conclusion they have. By any chance, back when you were Diane Carlson, did the name Eric Thompson mean anything to you?"

"Get out of here before I call the police!" Diane raged at this new information. As if Aria needed any help in finding her way, Diane used her extended index finger to point multiple times in the direction of the door leading out to the hall.

"I'd prefer to discuss this situation further," Aria said, with diminishing hopes Diane might reconsider and be encouraged to sit back down. "I'm only trying to find my father."

"I want you out of here, and I never want to see you again," Diane shouted.

"All right." Aria stood. "Whatever you say, you plastic-surgerized, fake piece of shit. You probably couldn't have helped me anyway."

With a strong feeling of disgust, Aria headed for the door.

CHAPTER 31

May 10th
5:35 P.M.

Emerging from the Hanna apartment building onto a Fifth Avenue clogged with rush-hour traffic, Aria stopped at the curb just under the very end of the blue awning. She needed a moment to take a few deep breaths and allow herself to calm down. Diane's intransigence to even speak about her adoption experience seemed like the final nail in the coffin of Aria's commitment to expose Kera Jacobsen's homicidal-at-worst, inconsiderate-at-best lover. It was particularly frustrating after having spent all afternoon closeted at GenealogyDNA with a bunch of arrested-development nerds.

Gazing at the beckoning park greenery over and through a rising haze of exhaust coming from the slowly passing cars, taxis, and buses, Aria thought she should walk home rather than trying to languish in traffic. Not only would it be more pleasant, walking across town would undoubtedly again be faster.

Just when she was about to cross the street, Vijay's comment about the district attorney having the power to unseal adoption records popped back into her consciousness. What brought the thought to mind was having learned during her first week at the OCME how close a working relationship the OCME had with the district attorney's office. On many cases of homicide, of which there was almost one a day in New York, both organizations had to collaborate closely for justice to prevail. What that said loud and clear to Aria was that Dr. Montgomery, as the OCME chief, would undoubtedly know some of the DAs personally and thereby could have significant clout. Maybe there was a way to get around the problem of sealed adoption records. One way or the other, it suddenly seemed to Aria to be worth trying.

Quickly Aria got her phone out and checked the time. By coincidence it was almost the same time as yesterday when she found Laurie Montgomery alone in her office. Gambling that might be a regular occurrence for the chief, Aria opened the Uber app. Just as she was about to order a vehicle, a taxi pulled up directly in front of her and disgorged a resident of 812. After checking with the driver to ascertain that he was free, Aria jumped in.

A little after six Aria paid the fare and got out in front of the OCME at 520 First Avenue. After being buzzed in by a uniformed security man, she headed directly into the front office. To her encouragement, the scene was almost an exact visual repeat of what she had encountered a bit more than twenty-four hours previous. Once again, the only artificial light was spilling out of Dr. Laurie Montgomery's office, suggesting that all the secretaries had departed and the chief was still toiling away. Advancing to the open inner office door, Aria saw that even Dr. Montgomery was in the same position, elbows on the desk, hands supporting her head, studying what might have been the same architectural plans.

"Hello, hello!" Aria called out as she walked in, which Laurie had specifically asked her to do rather than sneak in and surprise her like she'd done the night before. Since she was going to be essentially asking Laurie for a favor, Aria felt compelled to be more considerate, despite the fact that to her an open door was both literal and figurative.

"Come in and have a seat, Dr. Nichols!" Laurie said, even though by then Aria was already nearing the desk. "Seems that you and I are on the same schedule."

"It does appear that way," Aria said, choosing initially to remain standing rather than sitting down. "I wanted again to bring you up to date with my progress or, sadly enough, the lack of it. A lot has been accomplished, but I'm afraid we've hit up against that brick wall we spoke about earlier."

———————

I'm sorry to hear," Laurie said. She took her hands away from supporting her head and sat back, studying Aria. To her there seemed to be a subtle change in the wom-

an's projected persona, with less of the in-your-face defi-
ance than she'd exhibited on previous occasions. "What's
the latest?"

"First let me show you some family trees," Aria said.
She reached across the desk with the two that she'd
brought and positioned them in front of Laurie. "The
first one, as you can see, is of the Thompson family,
which is the genetic family of the fetus we found at Kera
Jacobsen's autopsy, going all the way back to a great-
great-grandfather. That takes it back to the late eighteen
hundreds. And just so you know, the fetus was male."

"Interesting!" Laurie said while studying the Thompson family tree, as Aria took a seat in the desk chair facing her. "So, you believe the surname of the individual
you are calling Lover Boy is Thompson."

"That was what was thought initially," Aria said.
"Unfortunately, that's where the genealogical brick wall
plays an unwelcome role. As you can see from the
Thompson family tree, Eric Thompson is the father of
Lover Boy. But today, when Eric Thompson was called,
he wasn't all that cooperative, but he was cooperative
enough to deny absolutely that he had any other children
other than the three you see on the family tree with his
wife, Clara."

"I hope you weren't the one who spoke with him,"
Laurie said.

"No, I wasn't," Aria said. "It was one of the principals
of GenealogyDNA. But what difference would it have
made if it had been me?"

"Early in my career as a medical examiner I learned

the hard way that doing my own investigating can be dangerous if there's strong emotion or potential criminality involved."

"Oh, for shit sake," Aria said. "That's the last thing on my mind."

"I thought the same way until I managed to almost get killed by some organized-crime people," Laurie said. "It's just a word to the wise. You can take it or leave it."

"Whatever," Aria said with a wave of her hand. "The brick wall is that it seems that Lover Boy was adopted, ergo has a different surname than that which his Y chromosome would suggest."

"Okay," Laurie said. "I understand. Adoption can cause a break in a family tree, and in this instance it means that it's the end of using genetic genealogy to find the father of the fetus. I'm still impressed. There's no doubt genetic genealogy will be useful to forensics."

"It was my fear it was the end, too," Aria said. "But GenealogyDNA had more to offer, and that was to create a family tree of the fetus's paternal grandmother. That's this one. You understand who the fetus's paternal grandmother would be?"

"I think so," Laurie said. "She would be Lover Boy's mother."

"Exactly," Aria said. "The thought was that maybe Eric Thompson wasn't lying when he said he only had three children. There's a definite possibility he could have sired a son as a young teenager and never knew about it. Although that is not the rule, we all know it happens."

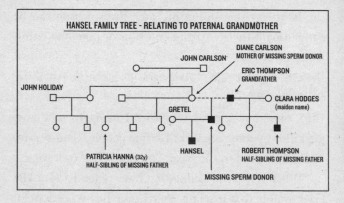

HANSEL FAMILY TREE - RELATING TO PATERNAL GRANDMOTHER

JOHN CARLSON

DIANE CARLSON
MOTHER OF MISSING SPERM DONOR

ERIC THOMPSON
GRANDFATHER

JOHN HOLIDAY

GRETEL

CLARA HODGES
(maiden name)

PATRICIA HANNA (32y)
HALF-SIBLING OF MISSING FATHER

HANSEL

ROBERT THOMPSON
HALF-SIBLING OF MISSING FATHER

MISSING SPERM DONOR

"True," Laurie said.

"So GenealogyDNA put their entire team into seeing what they could find out about the paternal grandmother's side of the family. With a bit of luck, they did find a distant match, but while trying to follow up on that, they struck gold, as they called it. Like pennies from heaven, they came across a thirtysomething woman named Patricia Hanna, who'd just uploaded her genealogical kit and who turned out to be a half-sibling with Lover Boy. That meant that her mother, Diane Hanna née Carlson, was Lover Boy's mother and the fetus's paternal grandmother."

"I see that," Laurie said, studying the second family tree. She then looked up at Aria. "So, did someone try to call her?"

"I called her," Aria said. "But I didn't try to talk to her over the phone. I wanted to do it in person, which I did. In fact, I just came from her posh Fifth Avenue apartment overlooking the park."

"Good grief," Laurie said. "I hope you weren't misrepresenting yourself as a medical examiner." The idea of Aria out in the field, visiting well-connected people and perhaps posing as a representative of the NYC OCME, could have disastrous legal ramifications besides being possibly risky. Issues surrounding out-of-wedlock pregnancy and adoption were potentially emotionally explosive even with today's mores.

"Absolutely not," Aria said. "I was representing myself as a resident in Pathology at NYU."

"What happened?" Laurie asked, with rising concern. "Were you well received, I hope?"

Aria laughed hard enough to need a minute to regain control even though her laughter wasn't completely mirthful. "Sorry," she said. "No, I was not well received. Well, that's not entirely correct. Initially, I was well received, but that changed one-hundred-and-eighty degrees when I got around to bringing up the issue that I was there to talk about, namely that she had had a son with a man named Eric Thompson some fifty years ago."

"I can imagine how that went over," Laurie said with a sense of dread, suddenly regretting that she'd encouraged Aria to follow up on the Kera Jacobsen case. Knowing what she did about city politics, she started to worry whether she was going to hear about this episode from the mayor's office. There was little doubt in her mind that if there was a formal complaint followed by an investigation, the incident would be traced back to the OCME.

"She went ballistic," Aria said. "She practically threw me out into the street."

"I'm not surprised," Laurie said with a sense of alarm. "Will I be hearing any fallout from this? Did you mention the OCME or anything about Kera Jacobsen's death?"

"No! Don't worry," Aria said. "I didn't involve the OCME or Kera Jacobsen in any way. If you want to know, I concocted a story about me being the product of a sperm donation with the source of the sperm being her unacknowledged son, and I was just trying to find out something about my heritage. I made an effort for the news to be as benign as possible, maybe even a little complimentary because if it were true, she'd be my grandmother. But it didn't work. The bitch of a woman who apparently thinks of herself as a socialite is a total fake who's had enough plastic surgery to make her lips look like a fish."

"Okay," Laurie said, trying to calm herself. With the concern of having her surgery the next day, she was having trouble dealing with this new, potential problem and Aria in general. "Perhaps we should try to think of how we might mitigate any fallout. How angry would you guess Mrs. Hanna was? Do you think there's any chance she'll be vindictive enough to possibly have you investigated or censured?"

"Certainly not," Aria said with a wave of her hand. "And her overreacting guarantees it. She knows that if she were to make any kind of stink, like complaining to someone about my visit, the truth would come out. She doesn't want that. She wants the whole issue just to go away so it doesn't mar her fake life. There's no doubt in my mind, and there shouldn't be in yours, either."

"Maybe you're right," Laurie said. The idea did make sense, and it did provide a modicum of relief. "Can I assume now that since neither the mother nor the father are willing to acknowledge the son, you won't be harassing them anymore?"

"I'm done with them," Aria said. "Actually, I never had much hope either one would be able to help, particularly not the father. The only way they might have been useful was if the adoption had been an open adoption, at least from the mother's side. In retrospect, the chances of that were extraordinarily slim, but I had to try."

"What exactly did you intend to do if you had discovered Lover Boy's identity?" Laurie suddenly asked. "I hope you weren't entertaining any thoughts of confronting him."

"What would I have done personally?" Aria questioned. She pondered the question for a moment and then shrugged. "I hadn't thought that far ahead, but I'd have to say no, I wouldn't have confronted him. I just want the guy exposed. It irks me to death that he is free and clear without having to face any questions about Kera Jacobsen's death. In my experience, it happens too often. Too many men get away with fucking up women's lives and walking away. I still feel that way, which is why I came over here to see you tonight."

"What do you mean?"

"The only thing that stands between my finding out Lover Boy's identity is the strict adoption laws here in New York State," Aria said. "The records are sealed, but I was told that a district attorney can unseal them. What

I'm hoping is that you might persuade the Manhattan district attorney to do it. I know you and the DA's office have to work together closely so it occurred to me . . ." Aria let her voice trail off.

For a moment Laurie averted her gaze to give herself the opportunity to let the idea percolate. She wasn't completely averse to mentioning the problem to one of her frequent contacts in the DA's office to get a sense of their interest, yet with her impending surgery the timing was hardly opportune. Redirecting her attention back to Aria, she said, "All right. I'll talk to someone at the DA's office. But to be completely open, there are two problems that immediately jump out. First is that our relationship with the DA is dependent on facts, not conjecture. What I'm saying is that the idea that Lover Boy had something to do with Kera's overdose is conjecture, not fact. Second is that there is a specific reason adoption records are sealed, and that is to protect people's lives from information that can sometimes be disruptive. On top of these two issues, there is a timing circumstance that I will share with you. Tomorrow I'm scheduled to have major surgery here at NYU, which is certainly going to keep me mentally occupied at least through the weekend. Physically a bit longer. Be that as it may, let's plan on talking again by phone on Monday or Tuesday. That will give me a chance to think about everything you've told me. Does all this sound acceptable to you?"

"I suppose," Aria said without a lot of emotion. Although what Laurie was saying did sound reasonable, Aria wasn't convinced of Laurie's sincerity, thinking that maybe she was merely putting her off. "What kind of surgery are you going to have?"

"I don't think that's relevant," Laurie said calmly and without rancor. "I'm already sharing privileged information with you. Let me add that my surgery plans are for your ears only and that you don't say anything to anyone, although there will be a general announcement. And I have another request: I'd like you to give the Jacobsen case a rest until we talk." Laurie handed Aria the family trees across the desk. "Is that a deal?"

Aria took them back, nodded several times, and then started for the exit.

"Wait!" Laurie suddenly called out, halting Aria halfway to the door. "I wanted to ask you how the autopsies went this morning. When I was in the pit doing my rounds, you were totally absorbed in dissecting a heart."

"They went fine," Aria said. "A subway accident and a commotio cordis."

"I heard the subway accident victim was Madison Bryant, Kera's friend. That's quite a coincidence, and a tragedy."

"I guess," Aria said. And then she was gone.

For a time Laurie continued to stare at the open doorway, marveling at how strange and complicated a person Aria was and how smart yet disruptive she could be. For a moment she felt sorry for Carl Henderson, because Aria was his problem, not hers, provided she could be shepherded through the rest of her time at the OCME. Laurie also realized that Jack was right; although Aria had a lot of antisocial symptoms, including her obvious disrespect for others, her manipulative behavior, and her lack of empathy, to name a few, all of which made her difficult to deal with, she certainly didn't have an antisocial personality disorder. She was much too high-functioning. It seemed to Laurie that a good psychiatrist or psychologist could have a ball trying to get behind her insufferable shell.

CHAPTER 32

May 10th
6:25 P.M.

More discouraged than when she arrived, Aria wandered out of the OCME front office and into the public lobby. A large group of people, half of whom were crying, were mostly congregating at the far end of the room. They were also occupying most of the ample seating. Aria stopped and observed them for a moment, feeling some kinship with their distress, although she was more irritably depressed than sad. Coming as close as she had to Lover Boy's identity and yet still being denied success didn't seem at all fair to her. Yet what could she do? Coming to the OCME in an attempt to snare Laurie's help with the DA's office had been the last gasp of her search for the missing father. Short of walking into the DA's office herself come morning, which she was convinced would be a total waste of time, she had no more ideas except possibly going to the police. Unfortunately, David Goldberg had nixed that idea by explaining that the police didn't like to make paperwork for themselves except when it was reasonably clear homicide was involved, which certainly didn't include overdose cases.

All of the sudden one of the grief-stricken mourners let out a particularly loud wail that grated on Aria's nerves. She glanced at the uniformed security guard, whose expression didn't change, suggesting that he'd seen it all over the years and was immune. Aria felt otherwise, and quickly pushed out through the front door onto First Avenue. The scene in the lobby was making her feel more depressed.

Just being outside helped, despite the roar and exhaust of the rush-hour traffic. What made it somewhat pleasant was that the weather continued to be almost perfect, with the late-afternoon sun again bathing the tops of the buildings in a golden glow. Intending to summon a rideshare to get her over to the Upper West Side, Aria pulled out her phone. Once she did, she hesitated before opening the Uber app. Something about merely holding the phone keyed off the memory of having gotten the surprising text from Dr. Henderson while she was talking with David Goldberg two days ago. It had been just about the same time of day. Out of curiosity, she pulled up the message and reread it, which brought to mind the rather strange meeting she had with the head of Pathology that the text had initiated. What particularly popped into her mind was his being supportive of her search for Lover Boy and his interest in being kept up to date on her progress. He'd also expressed immediate fascination with her idea of using genetic genealogy when she'd mentioned it.

For a few moments she stared blindly into the chaotic traffic scene playing out in front of her while she thought about Dr. Carl Henderson. As the chief of the Department of Pathology at a major academic medical center, he was, by definition alone, a connected individual who might be not only willing to help but also possibly highly capable. As soon as the idea occurred to her, Aria wondered why she hadn't thought of it before. Suddenly it seemed so obvious.

Without a second's hesitation, Aria used the text from Carl to call him. It certainly wasn't too late to be calling, especially since it had been slightly later when she'd called him two nights ago. With each ring, her optimism lessened, but then on the fourth, he picked up.

"Aria?"

"I hope I'm not calling at a bad time," she said, even though she didn't care if she was.

"Not at all," Carl said. "What's up?"

"I'm wondering if you might be free. I've made some significant progress in finding the missing lover, but I've hit up against a problem. I need to ask for your help, but I'd rather explain it to you in person. To explain it, I would·like to show you something I think you will find fascinating."

"This sounds intriguing. By all means, I can meet you. Are you in the neighborhood?"

"Yes, I'm at the OCME. Are you in your office?"

"No, but I could be in a matter of minutes," Carl said. "I'm nearby in my lab. Coincidentally, your question about channelopathies and fentanyl keyed off my interest. Since there was nothing in the literature when I looked, I'm putting in for a grant to investigate the association."

"I can be at your office in ten minutes," Aria said, ignoring the channelopathy and fentanyl issue.

"Fine! See you there!" he said sprightly.

After pocketing her phone, Aria set out at a good pace, walking north. Once again, her mood had changed and was now on the upswing. Even so, she couldn't help question why she hadn't considered Dr. Henderson's help before she had. It now seemed so intuitive.

With her newly regained motivation, she was on the floor where Carl had his office in just over five minutes. The scene was an exact repeat of when she'd visited last, including the same janitors vacuuming the carpet in the otherwise deserted office area. Even Dr. Henderson's corner office door was ajar, and, also like that visit, Aria walked directly in without any hesitation. On this occasion Dr. Henderson saw her the moment she appeared and stood up and began to come around from behind his desk.

"Why don't you stay at your desk, Dr. Henderson," Aria half suggested, half commanded. She didn't want a repeat of the couch scene. Besides, she wanted to be able to put the family tree diagrams she'd brought on the desk surface so Dr. Henderson could check them out to his satisfaction. She was certain he would find them captivating.

"Okay, fine by me," Carl said with a shrug. "But I thought we had established that we're on a first-name basis."

"Whatever," she said, even though she wasn't happy about the familiarity it implied. Without asking permission, she grabbed one of the two straight-backed chairs from the office's sitting area and brought it over in front of his desk. As she did so, she avoided looking at any of the various displayed memorabilia that reminded her of her father's study back when she was a preteen. The moment she sat down, Carl did the same.

"This is a nice surprise," Carl said. He leaned back in his ergonomic tiltable desk chair and briefly put his hands behind his head to stretch. Then he tipped forward again. "You've certainly stoked my curiosity. What have you brought to show me?"

Aria pulled out of her jacket pocket the two family trees, unfolded them, and smoothed them out. As she did so, the sound of the vacuum cleaners in the outer office reached a crescendo, meaning the janitors had reached the area just outside of his office. With an irritated shake of his head, Carl got up and closed his office door.

"Sorry about that," he said as he retook his seat.

"Not a problem," Aria said. She reached across the desk and placed the two diagrams side by side, directly in front of Carl. She then repeated almost word for word what she had told Laurie about what they represented.

After she finished her explanation, she fell silent and let him study the sheets. He was obviously totally absorbed. Finally, he looked up. "This is unbelievable," he said in awe. "I'm shocked that you were able to find all this out so quickly. When you said you were going to use genetic genealogy in your search for the father of the fetus, I thought it might take months."

"The credit goes to the computer geeks at a company called GenealogyDNA," Aria said, "particularly with the help of one of the company's founders, Vijay Srinivasan. I wouldn't have been able to do it even if I had months."

"To make sure I'm understanding," Carl said, "these two family trees are really the family trees of the missing father, isn't that correct?"

"Obviously," she said. She restrained herself from adding something derogatory.

"Why is the embryo called Hansel?"

"Just disregard that," Aria said. "It's immaterial. It was just a label some computer techies came up with since there was no name attached to the fetus. The important thing to note is that Diane Hanna née Carlson is the missing father's mother, and Eric Thompson is the father. That's the long and short of it. Case closed!"

"That means the father's name must be Thompson," he said. "Why isn't that written on these trees?" He raised his eyes to hers.

"I'm glad you asked," Aria said. "On the phone I said I need your help. The last piece of this puzzle is the name of the fetus's father. It has been determined that it is not Thompson because there was an adoption that has broken the genetic family tree away from the genealogical family tree. It seems that the father was an out-of-wedlock love child of Diane Carlson and Eric Thompson, neither of whom are willing even to acknowledge the blessed event."

"You spoke to these people?" Carl asked, his awe of Aria's investigative work magnifying dramatically. He went back and studied the family trees, which had him totally engrossed.

"I didn't speak with Eric Thompson," Aria admitted. "That was done by Vijay Srinivasan. But I did speak with Diane, whose surname is now Hanna. In fact, I was speaking with her just a little more than an hour ago."

"Does she live here in the city?" Carl asked.

"On Fifth Avenue, overlooking the park," she said. "I was just there."

"Is she married to the well-known attorney Michael Hanna?" he questioned in wonderment.

"I have no idea," Aria said. "Diane lives in decent splendor and acts and looks the part of a socialite, so I imagine her husband has some reasonably responsible position."

Carl tipped back again in his chair and raised his eyes once again to look directly at her.

"Did you confront Diane Hanna with these family trees?" Carl asked.

"I never got to show them to her," Aria said. "As soon as I told her that GenealogyDNA had determined she had a son that had been put up for adoption, it was the end of the conversation. She all but threw me out of her apartment."

"Sounds like she has been trying to forget her wanton

ways when she was young," he said with an off-color chuckle.

"Something like that," Aria said. "When I first walked in and got a look at her I didn't have high hopes."

"When you called you said you needed my help," Carl said. "Are you thinking there might be a way for me to aid you with this final step of getting the surname of the father?"

"Exactly," she said. "I wanted to ask you if by any chance you know someone who is acquainted with a New York district attorney." She knew she could have said what she said in a less roundabout fashion, but she was hoping for any connection with the DA's office, no matter how tenuous.

"That's easy because I know someone particularly well," Carl said with a broad smile. "Me! I've been friends with the Manhattan District Attorney Paul Sommers since we were in boarding school together. Why do you ask? How can the district attorney help?"

"New York State has strict rules governing adoption records, for obvious reasons," Aria said. "But I've been told a district attorney can unseal the records. All we need is the adoptive family surname."

"That shouldn't be that difficult," he said. "Actually, arranging it will provide me with a good excuse to get together with Paul. We've been trying for weeks, and this could be the reason to make it happen. Or better yet, I could stop in on my way home tonight. He's been eager to show me the condo he bought recently at Fifteen Central Park West. It's that gorgeous Robert Stern building on the corner of Sixty-First Street. Do you know which building I'm talking about?"

"I do," Aria said. "It's in my neighborhood. I live on Seventieth Street between Central Park West and Columbus Avenue."

"You and two other of our residents live on the Upper West Side," Carl said. "I remember when my wife and I were going over the resident list. I believe you are at Forty-five West Seventieth, if my memory serves me."

"That's right," she said. She was impressed. "It's a good neighborhood with restaurants and services a half block away on Columbus Avenue and the park close by in the other direction."

"I really have to compliment you on your forensic work," Carl said. He placed the flat of his hand on the Thompson family tree. "I can't get over these genealogical family trees you've managed to come up with. It's really been a terrific job. Tell me, have you changed your mind about forensics? Do you possibly see it in your future?"

"Hell, no!" Aria said. "Personally, I can't stand it. The patients might be dead but dealing with the families is a pain. No, it's probably the last pathology subspecialty I'd consider. But I have to say that this investigation has been captivating, even if it's also been frustrating."

"Has Dr. Montgomery been kept up to speed with your work on this case?" he asked.

"She has," Aria said. "In fact, I was just in talking with her before calling you."

"Has she seen these family trees?" Carl asked. "And is she as impressed as I am?"

"Yes, she's seen the diagrams," Aria said. "And she seemed impressed, but not as much as you. She's more worried about possible fallout from my having gone over and talking to Diane Hanna. But I truly don't think that there's going to be any fallout. I can't imagine Diane is going to complain to anyone because it risks exposing herself."

"Has anyone else outside of the genealogy company seen these family tree diagrams?" Carl asked.

"Nope," Aria said. "Just Dr. Montgomery a few minutes ago."

"Did you ask her about interceding for you with the district attorney's office?"

"I did, but she said she wanted to think about it over the weekend and let me know on Monday or Tuesday. She's preoccupied because she is scheduled to have major surgery tomorrow." Aria remembered that Laurie had told her not to say anything to anyone about her surgery, but what did it matter and how was she to know?

"I'm sorry to hear that," he said. "Is she having her surgery here at NYU?"

"Yes," she said.

"I hope the surgery goes smoothly," Carl said. "But this way, with me picking up the slack, I can assure you the records will get unsealed. I'm certain that my contact with Paul Sommers will be far superior to anything that Dr. Montgomery might be able to provide, regardless of her decision."

"No doubt," Aria said.

"Do you mind if I keep these family trees?" Carl

asked. He held them up in the air. "I'd like to show them to Paul so that he can see exactly why the adoption records must be unsealed."

"No problem," Aria said. "You can even give them to him, if you'd like. And if he'd like to talk to me, I can make myself available." She had to make an effort to restrain her excitement. This was suddenly turning out so much better than she could have imagined.

"I have a request," he said. "This case is turning out so interesting, I think I'd like to have you present it at one of our Thursday Grand Rounds. I think the whole department would be interested. What do you say? We could even project the family tree diagrams on the big screen so you could explain exactly how they were constructed."

"I'll think about it," she said. She believed the idea had merit, but she never liked the extra work involved in preparing for Grand Rounds. "Thank you for being willing to help in this final stage. I wasn't sure you would since from the start of the Kera Jacobsen case, you've been afraid of the tabloids getting hold of the story. If it turns out that the father of the fetus did play any role in Kera's overdose, the tabloids certainly will be back in the picture."

"Frankly, we're not as concerned about that as we were," Carl said. "Mainly because Vernon Pierce is less concerned, which is the reason I was concerned in the first place. It seems that the second death, the subway tragedy, has made the media sympathetic to our cause. It's as if by our loss, we're getting the credit for underlining the need for our subway system to be upgraded and made safer."

Aria stood up. "Thank you for helping, Dr. Henderson," she said. "You've saved the day."

"My name is Carl. I think it's you, Aria, who has saved the day by coming to me."

"Whatever," she said. "Needless to say, I'd like to hear the moment the DA agrees to unseal the records."

"Absolutely," he said, while he jokingly held up his index and middle fingers to form a *V*. "I promise, you'll be the first to know."

CHAPTER 33

May 10th
7:30 P.M.

Following the highly auspicious meeting with Dr. Henderson, Aria's mood had completely changed. For the first time since she'd started her quest to find Lover Boy, she felt confident she was going to be successful and had even begun imagining what her next step might be. The easiest would be to involve David Goldberg but that would hardly be satisfying as the MLI would undoubtedly merely dump the information into the laps of his police contacts, which were surely extensive. Instead Aria began to fantasize about learning something about the individual, even possibly somehow arranging to meet him and talk with him with the knowledge that she had the power to throw a good bit of sand into the workings of his life, especially if he was married with children as she had imagined. At the same time, Laurie's admonishment about possible danger if he had played a role in Kera's overdose came to mind, so it wasn't an easy decision. Yet the mere fact that she was going to have a choice was a source of great satisfaction.

As soon as she got home after the meeting with the Pathology chief, she took a shower and got into clean jeans and a sweatshirt. Armed with one of the genealogy books Madison had loaned her, she walked two blocks west to one of her favorite neighborhood eateries, Cafe Luxembourg, for some grilled *loup de mer* and quinoa salad.

After her meal, Aria returned to her apartment to watch *PBS NewsHour*, which she recorded nightly. By 10:30 she decided to have a bit more to eat prior to getting into bed to read. All in all, it was a typical night until her door buzzer sounded.

"What the hell?" Aria mumbled. It was rare for her to have visitors, especially after eight in the evening unless she had called for takeout food. Her first thought was to ignore it as it was probably someone pressing the wrong button. Her building had a total of six units, and since the light on the address panel was notoriously unreliable, she'd had her share of mistaken calls. But then her curiosity got the best of her so she went to the intercom and answered by merely saying *yes*.

"Is this Aria?" a crackly voice asked.

"Who wants to know?" she said.

"It's me, Carl. I know it's late, but I just came from Paul Sommers's. Since I was in the neighborhood, and since I promised to tell you the moment I had any information about the possibility of unsealing the Carlson adoption case, I thought I'd take a chance you'd still be up."

A smile broke out on her face. She'd had a positive inkling of success leaving his office, and suddenly it seemed entirely justified. Quickly she pressed the buzzer, allowing him into the building's common hallway. Now she was glad she'd not gotten into her jammies and robe as she'd been tempted to do when she'd returned from dinner. Crossing her living room area, she went to the door to the hall and opened it. Carl, carrying a shopping bag and dressed in a dark overcoat and a fedora despite the balmy temperatures, stood just beyond her threshold.

"Success!" he said with a broad, self-congratulatory smile. "It's a done deal."

"He'll get us the names of the adoptive parents?" Aria asked, just to be a hundred percent certain.

"Yup, no problem," Carl said. "Can I come in and tell you the details?"

"Sure," Aria said. She stepped out of the way and he entered. After only a few steps he stopped and gazed around. "Nice pad."

"It's not bad," she said as she closed the door. She had the sense Carl was trying to sound hip. Inwardly she smiled. It sounded pathetic. "Can I take your coat?"

"No need," Carl said. "I can't stay but a minute. But I would like to sit down."

"Why not?" Aria said. She gestured toward the couch, and after he sat down, she sat in an easy chair facing it. A

coffee table separated them. The two dog-eared genetic
genealogy books were on the table.

Carl put down his shopping bag and looked across at
Aria. "Paul and I ended up having dinner together, so
thank you for being the instigator. And I have to say his
apartment is to die for."

"How did you bring up the issue about the sealed
adoption case?" Aria asked. She had zero interest in his
evening other than how it related to getting the information she needed.

"It was easy," Carl said. "I showed him the family trees
you had created and told the story. It's gripping. Truly!
And he was immediately enthralled. I did leave the family
trees with him. I hope that was all right. Which leads me
to question if we can get additional copies."

"I don't see why not," she said. "GenealogyDNA
surely has it in their database."

"Paul did have a question about GenealogyDNA,"
Carl said. "He wants to know if they are aware of Kera
Jacobsen's death."

"They do not know the name," Aria said. "Right
from the outset I told them the name was protected by
HIPAA rules."

"That's good," he said. "It was one of Paul's concerns."

"They don't even know that the subject of the family
trees is a dead fetus," Aria said. "To spark their interest
and get them involved I concocted a completely different
scenario."

"That was clever," Carl said. "Do you mind telling me
the story you used?"

"I felt it had to be more compelling with a time constraint," Aria said. "Instead of a dead fetus coming from a woman who had overdosed, the subject was a toddler conceived by sperm donation with aggressive myeloblastic leukemia that had been unresponsive to treatment. The only hope was a bone marrow transplant. Since the mother had died and there were no siblings, the sperm-donating father had to be found as soon as possible to save the child."

When she finished her story, a silence hung over the room for almost a full minute. Aria and Carl stared at each other, with Aria wondering if she'd told too much, thereby dumbfounding him by the sheer creativity of the scenario and the impressive manipulative ability of its author.

"Wow!" Carl commented at length.

"It normally takes weeks for commercial genetic DNA companies to process samples," she explained. "I had to make it an emergency situation."

"I understand," Carl said. "And it certainly worked, considering what was accomplished in so little time."

"There was luck involved," Aria said. "It all depended on relatives having joined the genetic DNA bandwagon on both sides of the missing father's ancestry."

"I understand," he said. "Paul will be interested to hear that GenealogyDNA is not aware of the real-life story involved here, which was his only concern. What that means is that he will get us in short order the name of the adoptive parents."

"Good," Aria said.

"I think it's more than good," Carl said. "In fact, I think it calls for a celebration. And to that end I've come prepared." He moved the shopping bag he'd brought closer and proceeded to extract two cut-crystal, fluted champagne glasses, which he placed on the table, one directly in front of her and the other in front of himself. Next, he pulled out a wine bottle nestled in an insulated sleeve.

"Do you like prosecco?" he asked.

"I like it okay," Aria said as she watched these unexpected preparations. Normally she didn't like people doing her favors, particularly men, because she always thought they wanted something in return. But on this occasion, she was comfortable with it as there was reason to celebrate.

With a flourish as if he were a sommelier, Carl pulled the chilled bottle from its insulated covering and presented it for Aria's appreciation. "It's called Bortolomiol Filanda Rosé. I don't have any idea why it's called Filanda, which sounds like Finland, because the vintner is from the Veneto region of Italy. What I do know is that it is terrific prosecco." He untwisted the wire cap and then removed the lead covering. He carefully dropped both back into the shopping bag. He then loosened the cork and allowed some of the contained gas to escape before a final explosive pop.

"Okay," he said. He leaned forward and filled her glass first with the effervescent wine and then his. Putting down the bottle, he lifted Aria's glass and extended it to her, then picked up his own. "Cheers, and once again, great job!"

Aria took the glass, clinked it with his that he had outstretched, and took a sip.

Carl hesitated, watching her. "What do you think?" he said. "How is it?"

"It's all right," she said. Actually, it was tasty, and it was a pleasant shade of pink, to boot.

"To me it is the best one I have ever had," Carl said. "And I've had a lot of prosecco because I'm not a champagne fan. Even the best champagne doesn't do much for me, whereas a nice prosecco is like a bit of summer in a bottle."

Aria took another drink, with more volume. After the marked ups and downs of the day, it was a pleasure to feel the wine's effervescence in her mouth along with its subtle taste. Whether it was more suggestion or reality, it did seem to have more flavor than the prosecco she'd had at Nobu, making her wonder if it was because it was rosé or because she was in a different frame of mind. When she'd been at the bar in Nobu, she'd just had two disheartening conversations, first with Madison Bryant and then with Evelyn Mabry. Both of those talks had made her feel that she'd already hit up against a dead end of finding the fetus's father. In contrast, she was now enjoying the high of success.

"Don't hold back," he said. "We have a whole bottle." He was already pouring himself more. He then gestured toward Aria with it, and she allowed him to top off her glass.

"How did you come up with the clever idea of using genetic genealogy to find the father?" Carl asked.

"It was Madison Bryant's idea," she admitted. "It wouldn't have occurred to me because I thought you had to have an individual's DNA if the process was going to help find someone."

"That was my understanding, too," Carl said. "That's interesting you got to talk with Madison Bryant. Was that after you and I spoke when she was in the Bellevue ICU?"

"No, it was the night before," Aria said. She took yet another healthy drink while settling back comfortably into the club chair as if it were enveloping her. The wine was providing her with a wonderfully relaxing sensation, as if there was a sudden increase in the force of gravity. All at once the idea of going to bed sounded immensely appealing.

"That means you saw Madison Bryant after you and I talked in my office," he said. "My, my, you were motivated, which begs the question . . ."

Once again Aria took an ample drink of her pleasantly bubbly wine, and as she swallowed, she felt a new sensation. Suddenly a dizziness spread through her that wasn't so pleasant. At the same time Carl's words seemed to have no meaning. She could see he was still speaking, and she heard the words, but they made no sense. Then her vision blurred. Blinking repeatedly in an effort to clear her vision, she put her glass down on the coffee table and in a mounting panic, tried to stand.

"What's the matter?" he questioned. He moved to the edge of the couch and reached toward her with his hand.

He was afraid she was about to pitch forward and fall out of the chair.

"I need . . ." she mumbled, but she didn't finish her sentence. In slow motion, she sagged to the side and would have tumbled from the chair had Carl not stood up and eased her back against the rear cushion. Then he got out a pair of surgical gloves and put them on.

CHAPTER 34

May 11th
5:45 A.M.

Jack had been awake for almost an hour but hadn't moved while he worried about the coming day. The moment it was apparent that the sun had risen, he slipped out of the bed, being careful to avoid allowing the mattress to spring back suddenly into position after being relieved of his muscular 168 pounds. He'd made that mistake before, almost causing Laurie to be catapulted out on her side. On this particular morning, Jack certainly did not want to wake her in hopes that she could sleep as long as possible. With the anticipation of general anesthesia sometime after noon, she wouldn't be able to eat or drink anything but water.

For a few moments he merely looked at her. She was on her side, facing him with her head framed by her rich auburn hair. He knew she'd taken a zolpidem sleeping pill the night before, and on the rare occasions she did, she was able to sleep a surprisingly long time. He hoped the biopsy would prove to be negative and her operation would go smoothly. He still wished it was he who was having the surgery because worrying about Laurie was going to make it hard to get through the day. Knowing himself, he knew that the best way was to bury himself in work.

Going into the bathroom, he shaved quickly and then showered even more quickly. Because of the way they had designed the master suite, he could go from the bathroom into what they called the dressing room without going back into the bedroom.

Once he was dressed, he first looked in on Emma. She was fast asleep and appeared as adorable as ever. He wasn't worried about her for today because for her it was going to be like any other day, with no comprehension her mother's life would be in jeopardy. Unfortunately, the same could not be said about JJ, with whom he and Laurie had had a talk the night before. There was no doubt JJ understood the situation. It was also clear that the boy chose to put on a face that said that he wasn't concerned and didn't care. But Jack knew differently as he was sensitive enough about his son to recognize the discrepancy between his outward behavior and his inner persona.

Leaving Emma's room, Jack went into JJ's. He had to smile when he saw how twisted up JJ was in his bedsheets even though his face at the moment was the picture of total repose. Jack could clearly remember himself in the fourth grade and how rambunctious he'd been. It made him wonder if he were in JJ's school and acted as he had in his grammar school, would they also be asking to have him psychologically evaluated. Of course, there was no answer to such a question, yet Jack couldn't help but ponder it. He had acclimated to the idea of having JJ evaluated, going along with Laurie's idea that the more they knew about him, the better parents they could be. At the same time, Jack felt as strongly as he did before about the current rampant overdiagnosis of ADHD and the folly of putting so many children, particularly young boys, on stimulants. From his perspective, if there was going to be such a recommendation for JJ, there would have to be one hell of a good argument, and it would have to come from multiple sources.

Although JJ's alarm wasn't due to wake him up for another fifteen minutes or so, Jack put his hand on the boy's shoulder and gave it a gentle jostle. He had to do it again several times with increasing force before the boy's eyes opened. When he saw Jack, he sat up.

"What time is it?" he asked nervously, apparently thinking he'd overslept.

"It's still early," Jack said, speaking quietly. "Everyone is still asleep. I just wanted to talk with you before I go off to work."

"What about?"

"About Mom's surgery today," he said. "Have you thought about it since you, Mom, and I discussed it last night?"

"Yeah, a little."

"How do you feel about it?"

"What do you mean?" JJ said.

"Does it scare you? Are you worried that she will be in the hospital for a few days? Anything like that?"

"I don't know, maybe a little. Can I stay home from school today?"

Jack regarded his son. He tried to tell from JJ's expression his motivation for asking if he could stay home from school. Knowing his son's penchant for computer games, it was natural for Jack to be suspicious that electronic gaming was more the driving force than emotional turmoil, but how could he be sure?

"Is that what you'd like to do?"

"Maybe," JJ said.

Jack smiled inwardly, sensing he'd already got his answer from his son's equivocation. To test his suspicions, he said, "If you stay home, there will be very limited computer gaming."

"Aw, why?"

"We'd have to get your school to send us the work you would be doing in class so you could do it here," Jack said. "But let me tell you something. If you're worried about Mom going into the hospital, going to school might be better to keep your mind occupied. That's why I'm going to work, and I'm going to work particularly hard. What do you think?"

"I think I should go to school," JJ said.

"I'll call you as soon as I know her surgery is over," Jack said. "How's that?"

"That's good," JJ said.

"And you can call me whenever you want for whatever reason."

"Yeah, I know," JJ said.

"Do you want to come downstairs and have some breakfast with me?" he asked.

"Okay," JJ said, as he struggled to untangle himself from his sheets.

Breakfast was a simple affair consisting of orange juice and cold cereal. Conversation involved the coming weekend with the promise of bike riding and using the lacrosse sticks in the park. When they were finished eating, JJ went back upstairs to dress for school while Jack wrote a note to Laurie. Although he had offered to stay home for the morning and drive her to the hospital, she had insisted otherwise. She'd said that she wanted him at the OCME to help George Fontworth if there was a need, which she doubted. She'd insisted that Jack not make a production of her having her *minor procedure*, as she called it, and that she preferred to get herself to the hospital. He hadn't argued.

The last thing that Jack did was have a brief chat with Caitlin for final instructions and to make sure she had his mobile number front and center in case there was any need to get hold of him even though neither she nor Jack could see that happening. Then after a final goodbye to JJ, he got on his Trek, and headed south.

For the next thirty-one minutes Jack was able to enjoy himself. A combination of the weather and the required physical exertion cleared his mind. Even the traffic seemed slightly lighter than usual, and Jack had more tolerance than he often did for the yellow cabbies and the new bane of rideshare drivers. It was exactly 7:15 when he walked into the ID room to swat Vinnie's newspaper and ask Jennifer if any interesting cases had come in overnight.

"It was kind of a slow night," Jennifer said as he helped himself to a mug of the communal coffee. "But there is one here that might catch your interest. It's a death by hanging that has the police confused as to whether it's a homicide or a suicide."

"Was there a suicide note?" Jack asked.

"I don't know," Jennifer said. "I didn't read the MLI report. Especially with the police expressing that kind of confusion, I knew it was a case that needed to be autopsied, so I just put it in the to-do stack."

"Let me see it," Jack said. He took the folder from her, leafed through the contents until he came across the MLI sheet, and pulled it free. He enjoyed doing cases that involved any type of controversy. The first thing he noticed was that the assigned MLI was Janice Jaeger, someone with whom he had worked on innumerable cases over the years and whose experience and acumen he truly admired. Often, she would anticipate the need for additional information or records and went ahead and ordered them before Jack even made a request.

Speed-reading through the investigative report, Jack learned that the victim was a twenty-eight-year-old Caucasian male who had been found hanged from a five-foot-high garden gate. He had been out drinking with friends but had gotten into a bar fight with someone who had been heard threatening that he was going to kill him. Later the victim had been escorted home by friends who'd described him as depressed and intoxicated. They said they had left him at the gate to the garden fronting his apartment. Hours later he'd been found by a passerby who'd called the police. At the very end of the report there was a final sentence that Janice had added as a postscript. It read, "See diagram and photos."

Surprised by this suggestion, he went back to the case folder, which was more like a paper pocket for all the autopsy forms and labels it had to contain, and quickly found the diagram that Janice had hastily sketched with a stick figure. Stapled to the diagram were several pictures taken with a digital camera. They showed the victim in a sitting position with his back to the gate, his legs splayed out in front of him, and with his collar caught on the gate latch.

Jack slipped the investigative report back into the case folder. "I'll take it," he said to Jennifer. "And, just so you know, I want to stay busy today. Translated, that means I want you to keep me in mind for more cases."

"I always do," Jennifer said. She was telling the truth. Whenever she was the on-call ME and was presented with a case that she didn't quite know what to do with, she knew she could call Jack, and usually did.

"One other thing," he said. "When Dr. Nichols deigns to show up, send her down."

"Don't tell me we have to work with her again," Vinnie whined from behind his newspaper.

"I'm afraid so," Jack called over to him. "I promised both my wife and Dr. McGovern."

When Vinnie didn't bother to respond, Jack walked over and snatched away his newspaper. Instead of causing Vinnie to flinch, which was what he hoped and expected, Vinnie merely rolled his eyes. "You don't need me if you have that miserable bitch's capable hands."

"Let's not be nasty, and watch your language," Jack said, feeling mildly frustrated by Vinnie's total lack of response to having his paper taken. "Come on, big guy!" With his free hand he offered to pull Vinnie to his feet. "Let's get a move on. I'm hoping for a big day ahead of us." How big, Jack had no idea.

———————

Juliana Santos and her younger brother Luiz had managed to immigrate to the US from Belém, Brazil, six years ago. Initially it had been a struggle to get by in Miami, where they first arrived. But thanks to some help from a couple of distant relatives as well as the Miami Brazilian community in general, they'd succeeded. Following an economic opportunity offered by an uncle, they moved on to New York, where they'd started a domestic housecleaning service called Very Clean. Known by word of mouth as being thorough and reliable, they had relatively prospered, hiring five young women and buying a used Subaru station wagon and three vacuum cleaners. Luiz would drive the women to their respective sites, where they would work in groups of two. The entire day would find Luiz keeping in touch by phone and ferrying each team from one apartment to another.

The first stop on May 11 was 45 West 70th Street, where Juliana and her current partner, Antônia, climbed out from the Subaru bursting with women, cleaning products, and vacuums. *"Adeus, vejo você mais tarde,"* Juliana said with a wave. She was carrying a vacuum cleaner with the hose over one shoulder, a plastic bag of rags, and a roll of paper towels. Antônia had the buckets, mops, and cleaning products. With some difficulty and a lot of clanking sounds they climbed the granite steps.

Pausing at the building's front door, Juliana put down everything she was carrying to get out her sizable key ring. After finding the appropriate key, she opened the front door only to discover it hadn't been completely closed and latched and she would have been able to use her hip to push right in. *"Merda!"* she mumbled as she gathered up her belongings and stumbled into the building. It was the struggle with the vacuum cleaner that made it difficult. Once inside, she held open the door for Antônia. After walking down a short, narrow hallway by bypassing the contrasting rather grand staircase that swooped up and curved out of sight to her right, Juliana again put down everything to repeat the key process. With the door for the first-floor apartment, she knew she needed the key. In contrast with the door to the street, which was frequently not shut all the way, the apartment door was always latched.

Juliana had met this client on only one occasion several years earlier. She knew the woman was a doctor and hadn't been all that friendly. On the positive side, she paid on time and never complained. Juliana marveled at the differences in the way various clients treated her and whomever she happened to be working with. Some people were openly condescending, others remarkably friendly, and others indifferent. Luckily the nature of the clientele was such that she didn't have to interact all that often.

Once she got the door unlocked, she opened it and then gave it a shove out of the way. Picking up the vacuum cleaner once again, she stepped into the room. The moment she did, she noticed a stale odor that she couldn't place. As Antônia followed her into the room, Juliana put her head back and sniffed the air. As someone perceptive to the ins and outs of cleaning, she sensed that there had to be something that needed attention but had no idea what it was. She was about to ask Antônia if she smelled an odd odor, when she realized that the client was home, seated in the chair directly in front of her but facing away so that she couldn't see the woman's face.

"Hello!" Juliana called out. She immediately regretted she'd not rung the bell or even knocked on the apartment door. Never before had this client been home. "Hello!" she called out again, only slightly louder. When there still was no response, she put down the vacuum cleaner and stepped around the chair. The second she caught sight of the woman's face, she screamed, causing Antônia to do the same by reflex. A moment later Juliana had recovered enough to get out her phone and call 911.

———————

Okay," Jack said to Vinnie. "Armed with all the information we have from this masterfully done autopsy and the superb MLI investigative report, what do you think the OCME can tell the police about this case?"

It was now well after nine and the autopsy room was full, meaning all eight tables were in operation. Chet had appeared a little after eight and had come over to Jack's table to ask if Aria Nichols had shown up as she was scheduled. When Jack had said no, he'd merely rolled his eyes before moving off to do his own case.

"I assume you're asking about the manner of death," Vinnie said in response to Jack's question. He straightened up to stretch his back. He and Jack had been involved in a rather lengthy and tedious dissection of the victim's neck, which was only done on cases like the present one, where neck trauma was expected. The main part of the autopsy, including the contents of the chest and the abdomen, had shown the victim to be free of disease, congenital malformations, or signs of trauma. The only abnormal finding had been some partially dissolved capsules in the stomach, suggesting the victim had taken some kind of medication or drugs along with his reputed alcohol. What the capsules were would have to wait for Toxicology, same with the ethanol content in his bloodstream.

"Well, it's definitely not homicide," Vinnie said.

"How can you be so sure?"

"With all the hemorrhage in the neck muscles, he

wasn't dead before he was suspended by his shirt collar," Vinnie said. Vinnie enjoyed these sessions he had with Jack and felt that he'd learned an enormous amount about forensics over the years. "And I've never heard of a homicide done with a shirt collar."

What he and Jack had found with their careful neck dissection was that the hyoid bone and the thyroid cartilage were both intact, both of which were often damaged in hanging situations. Besides the hemorrhage in the neck muscles, the only other pathology they found was the occlusion of the left carotid artery and left jugular vein, which coincided with a deep furrow or groove on the left exterior aspect of the victim's neck that angled upward toward his right ear.

"I agree with you that the chances of this being a homicide are negligible," Jack said. "So, what are we going to tell the police?"

"I don't know," Vinnie said. "The investigative report mentioned that his friend thought he was depressed. I suppose it could be suicide."

"With no note?" he asked.

"That doesn't influence me," Vinnie said.

"I'm glad to hear that, because you're right," Jack said. "It's estimated that two thirds of those who commit suicide don't leave a note. If this guy was drunk and depressed, he certainly wouldn't have searched around for pen and paper. But after doing this autopsy and rereading Janice's investigative report, do you want to hear what I think happened here?"

"Lay it on me," Vinnie said.

"I think this poor guy was so inebriated that when he tried to open the garden gate, he just sank relatively straight down, not falling over backward, but just collapsing like his legs became rubbery, and in the process the collar of his shirt caught on the gate latch. It didn't completely suspend him, but it provided enough pressure to occlude the left carotid and the left jugular. End of story."

"That means the manner of death was accidental," Vinnie said.

"That's going to be my interpretation," Jack said.

"Dr. Stapleton," a voice called.

Jack turned to face Sal D'Ambrosio, another mortuary tech.

"Excuse me, Dr. Stapleton," Sal said. "Sorry to bother you, but I've been asked to let you know that Bart Arnold is here and needs to speak with you right away." He pointed back toward the doors to the hallway. Through the wire-mesh-embedded windows, Jack could just make out Bart's face, and that he was waving at Jack to come out.

"Why the hell doesn't he throw on an apron and come in?" Jack questioned. As head of the MLI Department, Bart was a long-term employee who'd been in the autopsy room on multiple occasions.

"I wouldn't know, Doctor," Sal said. "But he's pretty upset about something."

"Oh, for Chrissake," Jack muttered. One of his pet peeves was to be disturbed in the middle of an autopsy. At the same time, he knew he'd taken longer doing the current case than usual, trying to draw it out in case there wasn't going to be another assigned to him. In many ways the autopsy room was Jack's sanctuary.

He put down the blunt-nosed scissors he'd been using for the neck dissection, told Vinnie to go ahead and remove the skull cap, and headed for the exit door.

"What's up?" Jack asked when he confronted Bart. Bart was a heavyset man with a mostly bald pate and just a tad of grayish straggly hair that ran around the back of his head from temple to temple. Although normally remarkably calm since he'd seen just about everything in his career as a death investigator for the OCME, he was noticeably agitated.

"Something unexpected and distressing has happened," Bart said. "One of the NYU residents assigned this month to the OCME is either in the cooler already or on the way in."

"My God!" Jack murmured. "Which one?"

"The woman," Bart said in a forced whisper, even though no one else was in earshot.

"Are you talking about Dr. Nichols?" he said with disbelief.

"That's exactly who I'm talking about," Bart said with a nod of his head. "The call came in about an hour ago that the victim had overdosed. I mean, talk about this fentanyl-opioid epidemic getting close to home; I'm blown away. This is like one of our own. Anyway, knowing the potential repercussions and all, I handled it myself rather than assigning it to one of my team. I visited the scene and found it a typical overdose with drug paraphernalia out on the coffee table, including the syringe she'd used. My estimate is that she'd been dead eight to ten hours with her algor mortis and her full rigor mortis."

Jack's mind switched into overdrive, trying to think of the best way to handle the situation.

"I've already called Dr. Montgomery," Bart added, stumbling over his words.

"That's unfortunate," Jack said, immediately thinking that Laurie didn't need this kind of stress hours before she was scheduled to be admitted for her surgery.

"I didn't quite know what to do," Bart confessed. "I know your wife is scheduled for surgery this afternoon but . . ."

"You could have called George Fontworth," he said. "He's the acting chief at the moment."

"I tried," Bart said. "He wasn't immediately available, so I left my name and number. When he didn't call right back, I thought I should let Laurie know. It seemed like an emergency."

"Okay, what's done is done," Jack said. "What did she say? Should I call her?"

"She told me to speak directly with you, which is why I'm here," Bart said. "She said you should be the point person and do the autopsy. She also asked me to ask you to call Dr. Henderson, to make sure he knows what's happened. And she wants you to give Mrs. Donnatello a heads-up so Public Relations can deal with the press."

"Did she say anything about me getting in touch with her?" Jack asked. For him, that was the key question. If

Laurie was distressed or worried about the situation, he needed to call her. If not, he didn't want to bother her. She surely had enough on her mind.

"I don't think she expects a call about this," Bart said. "That was my sense."

"All right, good," Jack said. "Is your investigative report already done?"

"I'll make sure it's in the case file," Bart said. "But I can assure you that there will be no surprises. As I said, it was a very typical overdose scene."

"Thanks for letting me know," Jack said. "I appreciate you coming all the way up here to 520." Ensconced in relative luxury in the new high-rise digs, the MLIs rarely ventured back to their old haunt.

"You're welcome," Bart said. "Apparently the mother is coming in from Greenwich, Connecticut. If I learn anything pertinent, I'll let you know."

"On your way upstairs, would you do me a favor?" he asked. "Let Dr. Hernandez know I'll be doing the Nichols autopsy."

"I certainly will," Bart said. "And let me know if you find anything unusual."

With a sudden burst of energy, Jack pushed back into the autopsy room. What he'd just heard from Bart was certainly terrible news as Jack didn't wish death on anyone, even someone he found personally trying, yet the awfulness of the news provided a modicum of secondary gain. He was in desperate need of something to take his mind off Laurie's surgery, and the shocking death of Aria Nichols was certainly going to qualify as a major distraction. As unliked as she was by the mortuary techs, he vaguely wondered if anyone at the OCME was going to miss her.

"Okay, let's get this case done," he said when he returned to table #1. In his usual efficient manner, Vinnie had already made a saw cut around the victim's skull, allowing Jack to lift off the top of the cranium, exposing the brain.

As he was freeing up the brain in anticipation of lifting it out of the skull, Vinnie waved his hand in front of Jack's face to get his attention. Having worked together on so many cases, they knew each other intimately. "What's up, boss? You seem mighty stressed."

Jack straightened up. "You'll never guess what Bart Arnold wanted to see me about."

"Sensing your reaction, I wouldn't even want to try," Vinnie said.

"I'm afraid the reason Dr. Nichols hadn't shown up to help us on this case is because she is going to *be* our next case."

"Come again?" Vinnie said. He froze. He was holding a pan in anticipation of Jack putting in the brain he'd just removed.

"Dr. Nichols is our next patient," Jack said. He went back to the business at hand.

"Holy shit," Vinnie murmured. It was his turn to stare off into the distance.

"Could you hold the pan a little closer?" By this time Jack was juggling the brain in his hands, and because of its texture and consistency, it couldn't have been more slippery. The last thing he wanted to do was drop it on the floor.

"Sorry," Vinnie said as he extended the pan for Jack to slosh in the brain. "How the hell did she die?"

"Another apparent overdose," Jack said. "Can you believe it?"

"God, no!" Vinnie said. "It doesn't seem possible. We just did two cases with her yesterday. I had no idea she was a drug user. Good riddance."

"Let's not be nasty," he said. "Besides, I'm supposed to be the sarcastic one, not you, and let's not forget that Aria had her good points. Personally, I think she was going to be one hell of a good pathologist."

"I can tell you that none of us techs are going to miss her."

"As expected, the brain looks a little edematous and congested," Jack said, trying to return his and Vinnie's attention to the case at hand. He'd put the brain on the cutting board and had made a few slices with a butcher knife. He then put it all into a jar of fixative. Vinnie meanwhile started sewing up the body to close the main Y incision, the incision made in the neck, and the skull cap.

A few minutes later the autopsy was complete. Wordlessly the two men organized the specimen jars and did basic cleaning. Finally, Jack helped Vinnie move the body from the table to a gurney.

"Thank you for helping make this case go so smoothly as usual," Jack said. "While you take the body into the cooler and finish preparations for the next case, meaning

Dr. Nichols, I have to make a call. It won't take me long, so go ahead and set up. It's going to be one hell of a strange situation. Are you up for it?"

"I suppose," Vinnie said. "And you?"

"I guess," Jack said, although he wasn't completely certain. It was emotionally uncharted territory.

CHAPTER 35

On his way to his office, Jack used the back elevator to get up to the fourth floor. The short ride gave him a moment to try to anticipate what the conversation was going to be like with the head of the NYU Pathology Department. It was not going to be pleasant. Although Jack had only met the man on one occasion, he felt like he knew him from Laurie's description of her recent talks with him. From his own meeting he recalled that he at least had a sense of humor, which he thought he was going to need when Jack filled him in about Aria Nichols.

Not wanting to keep Vinnie waiting, he ran from the elevator down the hall toward his office, but he did a double take as he breezed by Chet McGovern's door.

Retreating a few steps, he poked his head in. Chet was at his microscope.

"Have you heard the news about your favorite resident?" Jack said.

Chet looked up. "Only that she didn't show up for your case."

"Meaning you haven't heard why she didn't show up?" Jack questioned. He was surprised, since news of this sort normally spread around the OCME at the speed of light. He assumed that his being in the pit meant that he was the last to know.

"Are you going to tell me, or do I have to guess?" Chet asked.

"She died," Jack said.

"Come on!" Chet complained. He sat back in his seat and stared at Jack.

"I'm serious. She's in the cooler. Vinnie and I are about to do her."

"Are you joking with me?" Chet asked with incredulity.

"No, I'm not," Jack said. "Believe it or not, she's yet another victim of the opioid crisis. She overdosed."

"Awww," Chet moaned insincerely. "What a tragedy. She was such a sweet person."

"I just thought you'd like to know," Jack said. "At least it will make the rest of the month a hell of a lot easier for the director of education."

"Amen to that," Chet said. "There's some good in every disaster as long as you look hard enough. But what a waste, considering all that education."

"Are you still being sarcastic?"

"No. I got the feeling she knew pathology cold."

Jack gave Chet a quick nod of agreement before continuing down to his office. Throwing himself into his desk chair, he pulled out the NYU Medical School catalogue and looked up the phone number for the Pathology Department. Using his landline, he put in the call. As he waited for it to go through, he recalled Laurie telling him that Carl had called her when Kera Jacobsen had overdosed, asking if his department could do the autopsy. Jack wondered if there would be the same request, which he'd certainly have to deny.

The call was answered by one of the departmental secretaries, and Jack asked to be put through to Dr. Henderson. Without being asked, he gave his name and that he was calling from the Office of the Chief Medical Examiner. While he waited on hold, he was treated to some elevator music, something that he thought had gone out of style.

"Dr. Henderson," Carl said with a resounding baritone voice.

Jack explained again who he was and was about to break the news when Carl said: "I apologize for interrupting, but I imagine you're calling about Dr. Aria Nichols. I should let you know that we have already been informed by the police of her demise."

"Okay, good," Jack said. He felt he could hear the travail in the man's voice. "That's exactly why I'm calling. My wife, Dr. Laurie Montgomery, specifically asked me to give you a call to make sure you were aware. Were you told it was an apparent overdose?"

"Yes, we were told it was yet another overdose," Carl said. "As you probably know, this is the second member of our healthcare community who has taken this deplorable path in a single week. I suppose it's a reflection of our times that so many of our young people are resorting to drugs. Something drastic needs to be done."

"I couldn't agree more," Jack said. What he thought but didn't say was that maybe so many elementary school boys shouldn't be put on drugs for supposed ADHD.

"Earlier this week when the social worker, Kera Jacobsen, passed away, I called your wife to offer that we do the autopsy ourselves to keep it in-house, but she turned us down. We'd like to extend the same offer for Dr. Nichols. Our president, Vernon Pierce, is understandably even more concerned with this second overdose. The last thing we want is for our institution to be associated with drug abuse."

"We have to do the autopsy here at the OCME by law," Jack said. Having anticipated this request, he knew what to say.

"That's what your wife explained," Carl said. "But I trust there's no harm in our offering. We do hope you again limit the access the media has to this unfortunate episode, particularly the tabloid media."

"We try to be very careful about what information the media gets," Jack said.

"And we are appreciative of that," Carl said. "Changing the subject, I have to say I'm not terribly surprised by Dr. Nichols's having a drug problem. I can see how drugs would have an appeal to her. Although gifted in some respects, she was a troubled, strong-willed young woman. I can tell you as chief of the department, her tenure here as a resident has been rocky over the years, which I heard from your wife was the same initially at the OCME."

"Dr. Nichols and our director of education didn't see eye to eye," Jack said without being specific.

"When I spoke with your wife by phone, her impression was that Dr. Nichols wasn't taking her OCME rotation seriously. That prompted me to have a talk with her. During that conversation she fully admitted that in the beginning of the rotation, she was totally bored with forensic pathology and thought it should be an elective, not a required course. But then she said that things changed."

"Things probably changed when my wife allowed her to do the autopsy on Kera Jacobsen rather than just observe," Jack said. "The decision wasn't a spur-of-the-moment idea. My wife feels that NYU pathology resident rotation here at the OCME hasn't been given the attention it deserves over the years and that the residents need to be given more responsibility."

"Whatever the reason, it worked wonders," Carl said. "I got the impression that finding the unexpected fetus caught Dr. Nichols's attention and motivated her to find the child's father by using genetic genealogy. That marked a significant transition from apathy to zealous investigator. Were you personally aware of that change in her attitude?"

"I was more or less aware," Jack admitted. "My wife mentioned Dr. Nichols's interest in investigating the case. I have to admit, I found the idea of using genetic genealogy as a forensic aid an intriguing notion, especially with the remarkable geometric ballooning of the ancestral DNA databases. My sense is that for some homicide cases, it could have significant merit."

"Dr. Nichols certainly thought it did," Carl said. "She showed me some impressive family trees she'd helped to create for the Kera Jacobsen case to find the father of the fetus. Did you see them, by chance?"

"No, I didn't see them," Jack said. "Dr. Nichols was working under the supervision of my wife on that case, and I wasn't involved. But I did do several cases with her yesterday. I was impressed with her as a prosector, but I found her not to be the easiest person to work with."

"That's a kind way to put it," Carl said. "As I told your wife, Dr. Nichols was not a team player and was often antisocial. That said, she apparently related well with your wife, well enough that your wife confided she was having surgery soon. Is she having her surgery here in our medical center?"

"She is," Jack said. After a quick glance at his desk clock, he added: "In fact, she's probably on her way to Admitting as we speak, which is the reason she asked me to call you in her stead."

"I thought that might be the case," Carl said. "I hope it all goes well although I'm sure it will. And thank you for calling." Then he abruptly hung up before Jack had a chance to respond.

Jack pulled the handset away from his face to look at it as if it would explain the sudden termination of the call. As he replayed the conversation in his mind, he had the odd feeling that he had been interrogated but couldn't figure out why or about what. He shrugged, then slowly lowered the handset toward its base, letting it drop for the last fraction of an inch, causing a finalizing kerplunk.

Taking out his mobile phone, Jack placed a call to Laurie. She had told him not to bother, to concentrate on holding down the fort at the OCME, and that she would be perfectly fine, but he couldn't resist. She picked up quickly, as if she already had the phone in her hand. "Are you on your way to the hospital or still at home?" Jack asked after mutual hellos were exchanged.

"I'm in an Uber at the moment," Laurie said. Her voice was upbeat. He wondered if it was a true reflection of her feelings or if it was for his benefit. "I should be there in a half hour, traffic permitting."

"I wanted to give you a follow-up on the Nichols situation," Jack said.

"Thank you," she said. "What a shock! What a tragedy."

"I couldn't agree more," Jack said. "When Bart Arnold first told me about it, I was flabbergasted. But I wanted to let you know I have everything under control. I'll be doing the autopsy, and I've already called Dr. Henderson like you requested."

"Thank you, dear," Laurie said. "I'm sorry to dump this on you, but Bart wasn't able to get George Fontworth right away, which was the reason he called me. Anyway, I think you're better suited to deal with this than George for a number of reasons. I suppose Dr. Henderson was shocked as well."

"He already knew about it," he said. "The police had contacted him or Vernon Pierce. Anyway, he already knew."

"Good," Laurie said. "That made it easier for you. They must be at wit's end over at the medical center. This is two overdoses within a week. That's not good PR, to say the very least."

"He again offered to do the autopsy over there," Jack said. "I told him it had to be done here at the OCME by law."

"I think that's just pressure coming from the top," Laurie said. "I'm glad you again set them straight on that issue."

"More important, how are you holding up?" Jack said. "I know we talked about it last night, but I felt guilty leaving you on your own this morning."

"I'm perfectly fine," she said. "Trust me! I've adjusted to this need for surgery. I knew it was coming at some point, so I'll be glad to get it out of the way. Obviously, the whole situation is more difficult for you than it is for me. I'm absolutely convinced it is better for you and for the OCME that you are there and working. I'm going to be fine."

"I could meet you at Admitting if you'd like," he suggested.

"It's not necessary, Jack," Laurie said with a hint of exasperation in her voice. "How many times do I have to tell you, I'll be fine? As I understand it, I'll be going directly from Admitting to Pre-op. I won't be sent to a room until I'm released from the post-anesthesia unit after the surgery is over. You concentrate on handling this situation with poor Dr. Nichols."

"Okay, okay," Jack said. The last thing he wanted to do was make things more difficult for Laurie. "I will take care of the autopsy, and then I'll see you in your room after your surgery. Any idea of what room you'll be in?"

"I've been assigned to 838 in the Kimmel Pavilion unless something unforeseen happens," she said. "I'll see you there. I love you."

"I love you, too," Jack said.

For a few minutes he sat in his office. Both calls left him feeling mildly uneasy without knowing exactly why. Slapping the surface of his desk with both palms, he stood, stretched, and walked out into the hallway. On his way down to the elevator his mind switched from musing about his phone calls to the task at hand: doing the autopsy on Aria Nichols. He couldn't help but wonder what it was going to be like dissecting someone with whom he had worked just the day before. There was no doubt it would be unsettling on some level and made more complicated by the negative feelings he'd had about the woman's personality.

CHAPTER 36

May 11th
11:15 A.M.

After the phone conversation with Dr. Jack Stapleton, Carl felt better than he had for almost a month. Figuratively speaking, it seemed as if the clouds were beginning to part to allow at least a tiny ray of sunshine to penetrate through what had been a dark, threatening, overcast sky. The nightmare had started less than a month ago, when Kera turned what he'd hoped to be a pleasant evening into a disaster by informing him that she was pregnant. And not only was she pregnant, but she was happy about being so.

Initially Carl couldn't believe it and thought Kera was joking. Although she had expressed a distaste for condoms, it had been his understanding that she was very careful about her cycle, which she insisted was as regular as clockwork. On several occasions she'd informed him when it might not be a good time to get together, and he'd understood and respected her judgment by rescheduling their trysts. The fact that there hadn't been a warning on the evening in question he had to believe wasn't totally a mistake on her part but rather something she'd half planned.

The affair had started the night of the medical center Christmas party, and from his rendition of the story, it involved Kera's actively pursuing him. One way or another they had found themselves enjoying each other's company, exchanging entertaining and self-deprecating stories of their respective childhoods, his in Massachusetts and hers in Los Angeles. They also found that they were both avid skiers in winter and enthusiastic surfers in summer. When the evening had drawn to a close, they had exchanged numbers with the idea that they would have a drink together at some unspecified date.

When they did get together for a drink that had been instigated by Carl a week later, he didn't hide that he was married, had been for just shy of twenty years, with three children, one in college and two in high school. He also felt he had been up front and entirely honest in explaining that his wife had gone back to her successful career as an advertising executive when their youngest child had entered middle school and that their intimacy had suffered to the point of being almost nonexistent, all of which was true. What he didn't tell her was that he'd had a series of affairs over the previous ten years. He also didn't tell her that his wife's income trumped his and he had no intention of getting divorced as he was literally and figuratively wedded to his lifestyle.

As soon as Carl had been told by Kera that she was pregnant, he offered to arrange and pay for an abortion. Having already had the experience with a previous lover, he expected Kera would eventually see the light and agree and that would be the end of it. But instead of coming around to his way of thinking, Kera became progressively committed to having the child. At the same time, she became progressively committed to the idea that she and Carl had to arrange a meeting with his wife and put it all out in the open despite his having said over and over that he had no intention of leaving his family. It was when Kera threatened to call his wife that Carl had decided he had little choice and that it was either his life or Kera's life.

Having been successful in keeping the relationship with Kera a secret and out of the medical center's potent gossip mill, he was certain he could accomplish what needed to be accomplished with the help of the lethal power of fentanyl and with the opioid crisis as a cover. What he hadn't expected was to be thwarted by Aria Nichols and her unexpected and dogged interest in finding the father of the fetus. That was the beginning of the dark clouds, especially when he realized he had no idea how much Madison Bryant knew about his affair with Kera.

Solving the potential Madison Bryant threat had not been easy, especially when she somehow managed to live through getting run over by a train, which he had managed to make happen. Yet persistence paid off, thanks to potassium chloride, and once again Carl had thought he was in the clear. But instead of the storm clouds dispersing, they re-formed with the unexpected arrival of genealogical family trees that would have fingered him if he hadn't come up with the story that he was friends with Paul Sommers, the Manhattan district attorney. Carl had known he had been adopted since he was a child and had never had any interest whatsoever in his genetic past until now. At some point in the near future he'd get the family trees Aria Nichols had made from the safe-deposit box, where he had stashed them, and find out about his genetic family. It was heady stuff. The idea his birth mother was living over on Fifth Avenue was intriguing although after Aria's description, he had little interest in meeting her.

Taking care of the direct threat that Aria Nichols presented had been easy, since she lived alone like Kera. It had also been helpful that she'd used a background story with the genealogical company she'd worked with that couldn't possibly incriminate him. But the most worrisome part of Aria's involvement, and the one that frightened him the most, was that she'd shown the family trees to Dr. Laurie Montgomery. When Carl had heard that, the clouds truly thickened and threatened a catastrophic storm. But then, as if manna from heaven, he learned that Dr. Montgomery was to have surgery that very day, meaning she'd be in the hospital and undoubtedly have an intravenous line in place, and it all had just been confirmed by her husband. It was this information that had parted the clouds, allowed a bit of sun to shine through, and made him feel like celebrating.

Glancing at the antique wall clock, Carl thought this was an opportune time to pay a quick visit to the Emergency Department. He stood up and got his long white doctor's coat. He then checked himself in the mirror mounted on the back of his door. Although he had plenty of syringes, he needed more potassium chloride. Like with Madison Bryant, he planned to visit Laurie Montgomery's hospital room during that same early-morning time interval when the night shift took their lunch breaks. With Laurie, the task would be considerably easier than what he'd had to face with Madison. As a VIP Laurie would undoubtedly be in a private room, especially if she was in the Kimmel Pavilion, which Carl expected she would be. With Madison, he had to worry about nurses and nurses' assistants in constant attendance. That was not going to be the case with Laurie. And 3:00 to 4:00 was when most hospital deaths occur.

Confident he looked very much the part of a clinical professional, Carl walked out of his office. He informed his private secretary that he had a short meeting he needed to attend but would be back in about a half hour. She said that she would hold all his calls.

CHAPTER 37

May 11th
12:40 P.M.

This is big-time weird," Vinnie said. He and Jack had paused just after they finished removing the clothes from Aria Nichols's corpse, which was lying on table #1 in the autopsy room. Since there was only one other case going on at that moment all the way down on table #8, they felt like they were by themselves, facing the unique situation of autopsying the body of a person they had interacted with on a personal level just the day before. "I've always wondered what it would be like to autopsy someone I knew, and now I know I don't like it."

"Me, neither," Jack said. "It's a jolting reminder of the fragility of life. And it's not just emotionally disturbing. From a professional point of view, it's going to make it more difficult to maintain the objectivity that is required.

It also makes me embarrassed that I'd found her unpleasant to deal with. Now that she's dead, it seems so petty."

"Unpleasant wouldn't be the way I'd choose to describe her," Vinnie said. "I think 'snotty entitled bitch' would be much closer to the truth."

"Tone it down, big guy!" Jack said. Both Jack and Vinnie heard the door to the hallway burst open, and both turned to see someone coming in their direction. It was Chet McGovern. He'd pulled on a surgical gown over his street clothes and was holding a surgical mask against his face. He walked right up to the table and looked down on the naked corpse.

"Nice body," he said. "What a waste."

"Oh, please," Jack complained at the utter inappropriateness of such a comment. "Let's show a modicum of respect for the dead, particularly a colleague!"

"Hey, loosen up," Chet said. "I was only trying to lighten the mood with a bit of black humor."

"I hope that was the case," Jack said. "But with a man of your off-hours reputation, who's to know?"

"Okay, maybe I crossed the line," Chet said. "I suppose under the circumstances it was out of place and out of line."

"You got that right," Jack said.

"Are you guys okay to do this case?" Chet said. "Having just worked with her yesterday, maybe you want me to find someone else to do the autopsy who hasn't had anything to do with her."

"We've got it under control," Jack said. "To be honest, Laurie specifically asked me to take care of it, and I said I would. But thanks for asking."

Once again, the door to the hall banged open, and all three men turned to see who it was. This time it was Marvin Fletcher, one of the mortuary techs, and he, too, came directly to table #1 and looked down at the corpse. "Holy shit, it is her! I heard about this and couldn't believe it. I had to come and check if it was just a rumor."

"It's certainly not rumor," Jack said.

"Obviously," Marvin said. "It's a shame, I guess, but I can't say I was charmed by her. I also heard that she still had the needle embedded in her arm, just like the case I did with Dr. Montgomery and her just a few days ago."

"That's right," Jack said. "We just removed the syringe, and as expected it tested positive for fentanyl. I assume you are talking about the Kera Jacobsen case?"

"That's the one," Marvin said. "We thought it meant she died really fast, probably with a big overdose of fentanyl."

"That could be the case here, too," Jack said. "Who knows, maybe they got the drug from the same source since they both worked at the NYU Med Center, and it contained more fentanyl than usual. Part of the overdose problem is that the concentration of fentanyl can vary, and as potent as it is, it doesn't have to vary too much to be lethal."

"We wondered the same thing," Marvin said. Then he added, "Hey, do you mind if I stay and add my two cents?"

"That's up to Vinnie," Jack said. Personally he didn't

care if Marvin stayed, but he knew there were some competitive feelings among the mortuary techs, and he didn't
want to be party to it. He knew that Vinnie, as the senior
tech, was sensitively possessive about his exclusive relationship with Jack, by far the busiest ME.

"Fine by me," Vinnie said.

"All right, I'm out of here," Chet said. "I'll be interested to hear if you find anything unexpected."

Ignoring Chet, Jack said to Vinnie and Marvin, "Okay,
you guys, let's knock this one out."

For a few minutes, Chet stood and watched the sudden burst of activity, but feeling cold-shouldered and a
twinge embarrassed at his attempt at black humor, he
soon left to prepare for the afternoon conference.

While Jack was doing the external exam, Marvin mentioned that there were other apparent similarities to the
Kera Jacobsen case, namely little or no evidence of dried
saliva around the mouth, suggesting there had been very
little foaming, which is typically seen with pulmonary
edema. Jack found this particularly interesting because
he was well aware that with fentanyl deaths, pulmonary
edema was almost always a primary finding and remnants
of foaming were invariably present. Also like with Kera,
there was no scarring from previous episodes as usually
seen with intravenous opioid, particularly heroin, overdoses. Although there was no scarring, there were signs
of other venous punctures, but they all appeared to be
new or relatively new, suggesting that Aria's drug use,
at least intravenous drug use, hadn't been a long-term
habit.

Once Jack made the usual Y incision and the internal aspect of the autopsy commenced, any strangeness that existed because of familiarity with Aria on a personal level vanished, and the team functioned with professional celerity. Since Vinnie and Jack had worked together so often, they could anticipate each other's needs, and often they could go for periods with no conversation. Sensing that he wasn't really needed, Marvin mostly stayed out of the way and functioned more as a gofer than an integral member of the team.

"My goodness," Jack said as he lifted both lungs and put them onto the scale. "These babies feel entirely normal." He then called out to Vinnie that their combined weight was 2.9 pounds.

"That is normal," Vinnie said, writing it down.

"Jacobsen's lungs were the same," Marvin said. "Dr. Montgomery felt that there was minimal if any pulmonary edema."

"I'd have to say the same with these," Jack said. He took the lungs from the scale, placed them on a cutting board, and made a series of slices to look at the interior. "Yup, minimal edema, if any. That's weird. The respiratory depression from the fentanyl had to be really rapid, almost like turning out the light. That makes me suspect we are dealing with a very powerful fentanyl analogue, like carfentanil or, even worse, the cis version of 3-methylfentanyl."

"Don't listen to him," Vinnie said, talking to Marvin. "He wants to impress you."

"Really," Jack said. He knew Vinnie was teasing him,

but he wanted to be sure the techs knew he was telling the truth. "Those analogues are up to ten thousand times stronger than morphine in all regards, including suppression of respiration. It's the potency of fentanyl analogues and their ease of manufacture that's the major cause of the rising opioid death rate."

As the autopsy continued and no pathology was being found, Jack's imagination began to be stimulated. Certainly, one of the ungodly powerful fentanyl analogues could explain Aria's death and the lack of pathological findings. There was no question in his mind. The same could be said about Kera Jacobsen's death, since no pathology was found there, either, as confirmed by Marvin. Could the same analogue be involved in both deaths? Jack thought the chances were high, so Toxicology had to bear the burden of making that determination. The drug Aria used and the drug Kera used had to be compared. If it was the same, the city authorities would have to be alerted to warn addicts. Such a situation of a particularly potent batch of drugs on the black market had happened in the past, resulting in a sharp uptick in the already high number of opioid deaths. The user community had to be informed.

This line of thinking plus the lack of signs of previous intravenous use motivated Jack to try something he normally wouldn't have done on an obvious intravenous overdose case, and that was to test the stomach contents for fentanyl. His thought was that maybe Aria had taken some orally and had been disappointed in the result before switching to the intravenous route. While Vinnie and Marvin were washing out the intestines at the sink, Jack took a small syringe, pulled out a fluid sample from the stomach, which was easy since the organ was in plain view after the intestines had been removed, and used a fentanyl test strip. He was surprised when it tested positive.

When Vinnie and Marvin returned to the table, Jack told them what he'd found.

"What does that mean?" Vinnie asked.

"I have no clue," Jack said. "Except it suggests that Aria ingested some fentanyl before injecting it."

"That doesn't make any sense to me," Vinnie said.

"Did the stomach contents get tested on the Jacobsen case?" Jack asked Marvin.

"I don't think so," Marvin said.

"Maybe I'll ask Toxicology to do it," Jack said.

The rest of the autopsy went quickly, especially since absolutely no pathology was found. At the very end, Jack thanked the two mortuary techs and left the autopsy room. Normally he would have stayed to give Vinnie a hand with the body and with cleaning up, but with Marvin there, he knew he wasn't needed. Instead he picked up all the toxicology samples and, juggling them with a bit of difficulty, took them up to the sixth floor. There he found the head of Toxicology, John DeVries, in his spacious new office.

Back when Jack had been a new hire, he'd had issues with John, as he was a cantankerous individual struggling to run one of the key departments of the OCME with inadequate space and an inadequate budget. For his investigations, Jack needed answers, and he felt he needed them quickly. When the toxicology results weren't forthcoming, he complained, and John's response was to passive-aggressively delay the results even more. It became thornier still when the chief medical examiner got involved. There was even a time when Jack and John nearly came to blows.

Things changed dramatically after the new high-rise was opened, and many OCME departments moved into the slick new space. Toxicology stayed in the old building, and instead of occupying a few cramped rooms on a low floor, it moved into renovated space, consisting of the entire top two floors. And the Toxicology budget was increased commensurably, changing John overnight from an aging, cranky, gaunt, and bitter man into a younger-appearing, happier version of himself. In contrast to the "olden" days, Jack enjoyed running into the man or stopping into his new office on occasion.

"What do you have?" John asked graciously when Jack appeared at the door.

Jack explained the situation and his concern that the OCME had an obligation to the city's addicted population to let them know if there was a new batch of particularly lethal drugs on the market. He explained the two cases of highly accomplished young women whose autopsy findings matched, making him feel that there might be a new fentanyl analogue out in the community, and that he needed to know if the two cases matched.

"We'll get right on it," John said, as he helped Jack unload his clutch of sample bottles from Aria's autopsy.

"I have one more request," Jack said.

"I would be surprised if you didn't," John said with a smile. "Ask away!"

Jack told him about his running the fentanyl test strip on a fluid sample of Aria's stomach and getting a surprising positive result. "I'm wondering if you might run a speed test for fentanyl on the stomach contents of the first case, Kera Jacobsen. She was autopsied several days ago."

"I'll be happy to do so," John said. He wrote down Kera's name. "Where will you be in the next half hour or so?"

"I'll be available," Jack said. "Just call my mobile number."

"I or Peter will be back to you shortly," John said. Peter Letterman was the deputy director of Toxicology.

As Jack walked out to summon an elevator, he had to smile. The change in John DeVries had been nothing short of astonishing. It was now a pleasure to work with the man, whereas prior to his metamorphosis it had been a battle.

Retreating to his office, Jack tried not to think about what was going on in one of the Langone Medical Center's hybrid operating rooms. He even avoided checking the time for fear he'd start worrying that he hadn't gotten the call to tell him the procedure was over and there was nothing to worry about. Knowing himself, he needed to keep busy to mentally survive. As sad as it was, the autopsy on Aria Nichols had done the trick, but it was now over.

The growing stack of unfinished cases beckoned as did all the histology slides that needed to be reviewed, but he quickly nixed the idea. That kind of busywork didn't require enough brainpower to keep him from thinking about things he didn't want to think about, like Laurie's biopsy being positive. He needed something else that was more demanding and used more parts of his brain, like the rarely used creative sections. Jack was totally aware that he was a man of action who needed physical exertion to keep himself focused, which was why he still liked to play sports rather than watch them.

Thinking about sports brought up the idea of heading home and getting in a bit of basketball despite his promise to Laurie. He felt his mental equilibrium trumped her worry that he might injure himself. He knew that a good run would surely take his mind off Laurie's surgery. Jack liked the idea more and more until he checked the time.

"Damn," he said out loud. It was 2:25 P.M., much too early for basketball. People didn't start showing up on the court until at least 4:30. Unfortunately, checking the time had the negative effect he feared and was trying not to think about, namely that Dr. Cartier had not called him. If Laurie's surgery had begun around noon, that meant it had been going on for more than two hours, not a good sign.

"Get a grip!" Jack voiced through clenched teeth. He knew he had to think about something else, and the only thing that came to mind was the autopsy he'd just finished on Aria Nichols. As a kind of mental game, he carefully, step by step, went over the entire procedure, forcing himself to remember all sorts of insignificant details from the external exam all the way through to the bitter end. Ultimately, he admitted to himself that the only significant finding was the lack of evidence of pulmonary edema, a kind of positive negative. Such a thought at least brought a passing smile to his face since he was a major fan of wordplay and double entendre, which the phrase *positive negative* surely represented. Remembering the lack of pulmonary edema reminded him of the apparent similarities between Aria Nichols's case and Kera Jacobsen's and what that might mean beyond the worry that both women possibly had gotten their drugs from the same deadly source. Was it just a weird coincidence or did it presage an even greater rash of overdoses in the city than what they were already seeing? He also found himself pondering the weird irony that Aria had participated in Kera's autopsy as a further association between the two cases.

The sudden ringing of his phone jarred him out of his thoughts. It was John DeVries. "The Jacobsen gastric sample was positive for fentanyl," he said. "Was that expected?"

"Yes and no," Jack said. "As I mentioned, it was positive on the case we did today and there were other similarities between the two cases. I don't know what it means, if anything."

"I just thought I'd ask," John said.

"Let me ask you a question," Jack said. "Is there a fast test for 3-methylfentanyl?"

"No, the rapid tests don't differentiate between the various analogues."

"That's too bad," Jack said. "The autopsies on these two women suggest they died very rapidly, which scares me to think it involved one of the super-potent analogues."

"We'll know as soon as we have our results from liquid chromatography and mass spectrometry."

"But that takes time," Jack moaned. "You know me, I want the results yesterday."

John laughed. "I can vouch for that, remembering our battles in the days of yore. Give me the case accession numbers and I'll see if I can speed things up."

"I only have handy the accession number of the case I did today," Jack said. "But I can get the other one easy enough."

"Don't bother," John said. "Just give me the names again and I'll look them up."

"Aria Nichols was today," Jack said. "Kera Jacobsen was the one done a few days ago."

"I'll see if I can have the results early next week," John said.

"Much appreciated, John," Jack said.

Marveling anew at John's personality change, Jack went back to going over the details of Aria's autopsy, and without knowing why, he started thinking about the autopsy he'd let Aria do on Madison Bryant. What came to mind was the vulgar tirade Aria had let loose the moment she'd seen Madison Bryant on the autopsy table, complaining about Madison avoiding helping her on the Jacobsen case by getting hit by a train and dying. At the time, it was Aria's obscene language and total lack of human warmth or empathy that had caught Jack's attention. Currently, instead of the profanity, he was stuck on how the three cases were interrelated.

Tipping forward in his desk chair, Jack put in a call to Bart Arnold. Thinking about Madison Bryant reminded him that he'd not seen the hospital chart that he'd called for after the autopsy yesterday. Besides, Bart had asked him to provide a follow-up with Aria's autopsy.

As was usually the case, Jack got Bart on the phone immediately. As the department head, he rarely did cases himself, with Aria's being an exception, so contrary to the other MLIs who were out on scene most of the day, Bart spent the vast majority of his workday at his desk.

After identifying himself, Jack said: "I finished Aria Nichols's autopsy. Except for a lack of the usual pulmonary edema seen in fentanyl overdoses, there was nothing striking about it."

"Thanks for letting me know," Bart said. "And from this end, the mother didn't add anything particularly relevant other than insisting she'd had no idea her daughter was a 'goddamn druggie.' Those were her words."

"Like mother, like daughter," Jack said. "What about the Bellevue hospital records for Madison Bryant? Any luck? I want to see them and not just the digital record." Jack made no effort to hide his frustration.

"I got the hard copy here on my desk," Bart said. "Sorry! I can have someone run them over to 520 within the hour if you'd like. Are you in your office?"

"I am," Jack said. "Send them over!"

"Any word from Dr. Montgomery yet?" Bart asked.

The innocent question felt like a stab in the back for Jack, who had been actively trying to avoid thinking about Laurie. He had to clear his throat to steady himself mentally. "Not yet, but soon."

"Give her my best when you speak with her," Bart said.

"I will," Jack said. As he hung up the phone, he felt suddenly irritable. He wasn't angry with Bart but rather angry that Laurie had had the bad luck to inherit the mutated BRCA1 gene. If that hadn't happened, at that very moment she would have been down in her office taking care of business instead of being on one of the NYU Langone Medical Center's operating tables.

"Hey partner, wassup?"

Jack looked up to see Chet's silhouette filling the doorway to the hallway.

"Not much," Jack said, purposefully avoiding the truth that he was desperately trying not to think about Laurie.

"I wanted to apologize for my flippancy down in the pit," Chet said.

"It's already been forgotten," Jack said with a wave of dismissal.

"Thanks," Chet said. "Find anything of note on Aria's autopsy?"

"No, unless you think finding no pulmonary edema on a fentanyl overdose is noteworthy."

"Since it is found in ninety-six percent of fentanyl overdoses, I'd say it is noteworthy," Chet said. "Interestingly enough, it was the same on the Jacobsen case. Are you aware of that?"

"Yes, Marvin reminded us," Jack said. "It makes me worry both were killed with one of the extraordinarily potent fentanyl analogues. I think the explanation for the lack of pulmonary edema is that both died so rapidly there wasn't time for it to develop."

"That's an interesting supposition," Chet said.

"As long as you're here, let me run something by you," Jack said. "There's an interesting association between the Jacobsen, Bryant, and Nichols cases."

"How so, other than Jacobsen and Nichols being overdoses?" Chet asked.

"There's a curious tangled web of sorts," Jack said. "Or at least there might be a tangled web. Jacobsen and Bryant were coworkers and fast friends. Nichols did the Jacobsen autopsy and, according to Laurie, was motivated to find the father of the unexpected fetus. Apparently, Bryant was going to help her but ended up getting hit by a train and dying in the hospital. All this happened over three days." Jack fell silent, staring at his former office roommate.

Chet shifted his weight. "Are you thinking that there is some underlying connection here?" he said.

"I'm not sure what I'm thinking or asking," Jack said. "To be honest, I'm uptight about Laurie and her surgery."

"Oh, right!" Chet said. "I heard that was happening today. How did it go? Is everything okay?"

"The problem is that I haven't heard boo," Jack said. "I thought I would have heard from the surgeon by now. The longer I have to wait, the more anxious I become. Of course, I don't know when the case started. I mean, there might have been a delay as Laurie's case was scheduled as a to-follow case. In that situation there are frequent delays. Anyway, to keep my mind occupied I'm obsessed with these autopsies on these three women and a possible association that I'm not seeing. To put it bluntly, I'm wondering if I'm missing something that ties them together."

"If you want my opinion, I think you're overthinking," Chet said. "To me, the associations you mention sound like just a couple of tragic coincidences rather than a conspiracy. As for Laurie's situation, would you like me to make some calls? I'm relatively certain I could find out what's happening with her surgery. My experience is that to-follow cases are always delayed because OR schedulers want the patients to wait, not the doctors, if you know what I mean. If I find out for you, you won't be sitting here stewing."

"Thanks, but I suppose I could call myself," Jack said. "But I'm hesitant. Stupidly enough, I'm superstitious about calling whether it's you or me. I know that sounds crazy, but what can I say."

Suddenly Jack's mobile rang loud enough to make him jump. "It's Laurie's surgeon," Jack said to Chet after taking a peek at the screen. Chet flashed a thumbs-up and left. Jack clicked on the call and put the phone to his ear.

"Hello, Doctor," he said, trying to sound upbeat while crossing his fingers. It was a throwback gesture to his childhood. He'd never met Claudine Cartier but knew of her by reputation. She was one of the busiest general surgeons.

"Hello, Dr. Stapleton," Claudine said. In his hypersensitive state, she sounded upbeat, which was encouraging. "I wanted to let you know that Laurie is in the PACU and is doing just fine. Everything went well, including the endoscopic oophorectomy."

"Fabulous," Jack said. "What was the result of the breast biopsy?"

"The biopsy was positive," Claudine said. "The preliminary path diagnosis is carcinoma with medullary features. It is not a common tumor, except with patients having the BRCA1 mutation."

"I see," Jack said, trying not to let his sudden disappointment and distress show. He'd hoped and trusted the biopsy would be negative or if it had to be positive that it would be a more benign, intraductal variety.

"There was also a microscopic amount of the tumor in the sentinel lymph node but none in the other of the half dozen or so nodes that were removed. I think that's very encouraging, especially considering the small size of the primary tumor."

"Did you do a total mastectomy on the involved side?" he asked.

"We did," Claudine said. "And what we call a preventive mastectomy on the other side. And with the help of Dr. Roberta Atkins, a superb plastic surgeon, we did bilateral breast reconstruction. I'm very pleased with the final result, and I believe Laurie will be, too."

"So, what's next?" Jack asked. He felt a little weak and supported his head with his free hand, elbow on the desk.

"I will leave that up to Dr. Wayne Herbert, the oncologist," Claudine said. "I believe he will be happy hearing about the small size of the primary tumor and the minimal nodal involvement."

"How long will Laurie be in the PACU?" Jack asked.

"That's up to the anesthesiologist," Claudine said. "I'd guess an hour or so. The anesthesia went very smoothly, and Laurie woke up quickly."

"Thank you," he said.

"You're welcome," Claudine said.

Jack disconnected the call and sat for a few minutes staring ahead. It certainly wasn't what he wanted to hear, but in retrospect it wasn't terrible news, and Claudine definitely sounded content. With a sudden need for human contact, Jack pushed back from his desk and hiked down the hall to Chet's office.

"The news wasn't terrible, but it wasn't great, either," he said, standing in the doorway.

"Come on in and tell me what you learned!" Chet said. He lifted a stack of case folders off his office chair and stashed them next to his microscope.

Jack stepped into the office and sank into the chair. He then summarized for Chet in a kind of depressed monotone what the surgeon had told him.

"I'd say that sounds like pretty good news to me,"

Chet said. "Come on, man! Buck up! Small tumor, one node, hell, that's child's play for today's oncologists. You should be glad it was found this early."

"I suppose you're right," Jack said, trying to rally.

"When will you be able to see her?"

"In a couple of hours or so, is my best guess," he said. "She just got into the surgical recovery room after a pretty lengthy anesthesia."

"You know what you should do?" Chet said suddenly with conviction. "You should get your ass out of here. Go home, see your kids, and then when Laurie is back in her hospital room, go and see her! That's what you should do. Otherwise you are going to drive yourself bananas sitting in that office of yours trying to keep your mind busy by looking at histology slides and filling out death certificates."

"Maybe you're right," Jack said. The idea of some exercise had a humongous appeal. So did seeing Emma and maybe even JJ, if he got home early enough. And there was always the chance of a bit of basketball. He stood up. "Thanks, Chet. I needed that."

"Don't mention it," Chet said. "I'm sure Laurie is going to be fine. Why don't you text her to give you a call as soon as she hooks back up with her mobile. She'll get it when she gets back to her room."

"That's another great suggestion," Jack said, and meant it. The fact that he'd not thought about doing it himself made him appreciate that he wasn't thinking normally.

CHAPTER 38

May 11th
3:40 P.M.

Never had Jack gotten better advice. For the next thirty-four minutes he didn't think about anything but the road and the traffic around him. With the air whistling through his bike helmet, he made great time riding north on First Avenue all the way up to 55th Street, where he turned westward. For a time, he even managed to hit the traffic lights correctly. Then when he finally entered Central Park where Sixth Avenue dead-ended into it, the ride was even more enjoyable. Since cars were no longer allowed in the park, Jack and the other bicyclists, joggers, power walkers, skateboarders, and even a few in-line skaters had the East Drive all to themselves. It was with reluctance that he exited the park at 106th Street and rode the half block down to his brownstone.

After climbing the ten steps up the stoop, he turned

around and looked over at the basketball court. As he expected, there was no game yet since it was too early, although there were two people working on their jump shots. If he wasn't intent on spending some quality time with the kids, he might have gone over and joined them. Instead he carried his Trek bike inside, then climbed the stairs up to his family's apartment.

Once inside the apartment and while mounting the flight of stairs leading to the family room and kitchen, he could hear the calm voice of Emma's speech therapist, Karen Higgens, whom he had met on several occasions. As the floor came into view, he could see Emma and Karen sitting at the dining room table having a snack while Caitlin was in the kitchen, doing the prep work for the children's dinner. Not wanting to interrupt the therapy session, Jack gave the table a wide berth to get into the kitchen. Caitlin was ostensibly glad to see him.

"How is Laurie?" she whispered to avoid bothering Emma and Karen. Her concern for Laurie's well-being was palpable. "Have you heard?"

"I did talk with the surgeon," Jack said, also keeping his voice down. "I was told the surgery went well and that Laurie was in the anesthesia recovery area." He didn't elaborate, thinking that Laurie could share what she wanted to share.

"That's a relief," Caitlin said.

Jack got a bottle of San Pellegrino from the refrigerator and a glass from the cabinet. He poured himself a glassful and then gestured with the bottle toward Caitlin. She shook her head.

Leaning his backside against the kitchen countertop, Jack turned his attention to Emma and Karen. It was apparent that Karen was using the snack as a teaching opportunity, and with great patience was teaching Emma a kind of sign language for the juice and for the cookies. What impressed Jack was that Emma was paying attention and making eye contact. There was no doubt she was making progress, not only with this particular activity but also in general. It was rewarding to see.

"Is this about the time that JJ usually arrives home?" he asked Caitlin, still using a hushed voice.

"It is," Caitlin said. "The bus drops him off at the corner right around four."

Jack's phone buzzed in his pocket. In his haste to get it out, it got caught momentarily in the fabric of his pocket. When he finally got view of the screen, he was pleased. It was a text from Laurie: Just got back to my room. Call when convenient XO.

"It's Laurie," he whispered to Caitlin, who responded by giving him a thumbs-up. "I'll call her from the study," Jack added.

Still trying not to intrude on Emma and Karen, he tiptoed out of the kitchen and then darted down the hall in his stocking feet into the study. With a few taps he put the call through and was much relieved to hear her voice, even if it was a bit hoarse.

"How are you?" Jack asked with urgency.

"I've been better," Laurie managed. "Sorry about my voice."

"Not a problem, believe me," Jack said. "I'm glad to hear it."

"Where are you? Are you still close by at the OCME?"

"No, I came home to briefly see the kids although JJ has yet to get home from school."

"And Emma?"

"She's doing fine," he said. "I have to give your mother credit. These therapists she's arranged are doing amazing things. While I watched, Emma was learning to sign for cookies and juice."

"I'm glad you're home," Laurie said. "This morning I could tell that JJ was upset about me having surgery despite his seeming nonchalance. Be sure to reassure him that everything is hunky-dory when he gets home."

"I'll be happy to," Jack said. "How do you feel? Do you have much pain?"

"I feel pretty damn good considering," she said. "How much of that depends on drugs, I haven't a clue. I have my own pain med source piggybacked onto my keep-open intravenous line. At the moment it's mainly my throat that bothers me, probably from the endotracheal tube. Still, it's minimal and getting better. I also get a twinge from the tiny abdominal incision when I move suddenly or when I cough or laugh. But other than that, I feel good. I'm even hungry if you can believe it, although I'm still being restricted to fluids."

"Hearing that you're laughing is music to my ears," Jack said. "Are you up for a visitor?"

"Of course," Laurie said. "But it's not necessary if you

want to stay with the kids. I'm doing fine and will be even better when they allow me to eat. I also plan on taking advantage of the sleep meds Dr. Cartier suggested."

"I want to see you," he said. "As soon as I get a chance to talk with JJ and maybe even grab a quick bite to eat, I'll be on my way."

"If you insist on coming, I want to ask a favor," Laurie said.

"Sure, anything," Jack said. "What is it that you want? Did you forget your laptop?"

"No, I have my laptop," she said. "What I want to ask is that you use a rideshare and don't ride your bike down here."

Surprised by this request coming out of the blue, Jack paused before answering. His mode of transportation hadn't even occurred to him. "Do you really care that much?" he said while he winced at the idea of sitting in a car in stop-and-go rush-hour traffic.

"I always care," Laurie said with a touch of annoyance. "But I care particularly because I'm stuck in the hospital, and for our kids' sake I don't want you to be in here as a patient at the same time, leaving them parentless. Humor me!"

"Okay, okay," he said. The last thing he wanted to do was to get Laurie riled up in her present condition.

"Thank you," she said. "It will be one thing less for me to worry about. Now tell me, how did the autopsy go on Aria Nichols and did you talk with Carl Henderson?"

"The autopsy went fine," Jack said. "Marvin Fletcher lent a hand and remarked that it was a mirror image of the Kera Jacobsen case with very little pulmonary edema."

"That's interesting," Laurie said. "My thought was that Kera Jacobsen died very rapidly, not the somewhat slower death from progressive respiratory depression as seen with most fentanyl overdoses."

"That was my feeling as well with Aria Nichols," Jack said.

"I wonder if they both got their drugs from the same source," Laurie said.

"Well, it seems we are on the same page; that's my concern, too," he said. "They could very well have had the same supplier since they both worked for the same organization. I have John up in Toxicology going to let us know if they both had the same fentanyl analogue. I certainly hope we don't see a flood of overdoses with other medical center personnel."

"I hope so, too," she said. "On a happier note, what time can I expect to see you?"

"Why do you ask?" Jack questioned playfully. "Are you going to have to squeeze me in among your flood of visitors?"

Laurie let out a suppressed chuckle. "I told you it hurts when I laugh," she complained. "But your sarcasm is good to hear. Now you're sounding like the Jack I know and love."

"Let's say an hour from now," he said, becoming serious. "Is there anything you'd like me to bring?"

"Just your humorous self will be most welcome," Laurie said. "It will be fun to show you the room they put me in. It really is the height of luxury."

"I'll look forward to seeing it," Jack said. "But mostly I'll be looking forward to seeing you."

CHAPTER 39

By four o'clock, Carl had finished his last scheduled meeting of the day. Appropriately enough, it involved the first meeting of the Pathology Residency Program Acceptance Committee. The matching results for the NYU Pathology program were released on the third Friday of March of each year, as were all residency matching results for all US academic programs in all specialties. Getting to that point represented the culmination of a lot of work by the committee, who had to review all the applications, interview the prospective residents, and put together the list in the order of preference.

As head of the department, Carl had a seat on the committee. Since the death of one of the program's third-year residents, Dr. Aria Nichols, was already common knowledge, he had taken the opportunity to speak

up about the inappropriateness of her original acceptance. The point he wanted to make was that the committee needed to place as much emphasis on the
personality of applicants as they did on medical school
grades and graduate medical exams to avoid the kind of
problems a resident like Aria Nichols created.

After the meeting, Carl made it a point not to go directly back to his office. Instead he'd taken the opportunity to walk over to the corner of First Avenue and 34th
Street and enter the Kimmel Pavilion. A short time before, he'd used his access to the medical center's database
to check on Laurie Montgomery's room assignment to
make sure it hadn't changed. It hadn't. It was still listed
to be 838 in the Kimmel Pavilion.

As always, particularly in the late afternoon, the Kimmel lobby was full. Carl was counting on that being the
case, as he wanted to blend in with the crowd although
not completely. He was, as usual, in his professorial doctor outfit with a long white coat. Dressed in such a fashion, and with his medical center ID in plain sight, he
wasn't bothered by any of the uniformed or plainclothed
security personnel. Even the elevator was completely full
as he rode up to the eighth floor, and he was pleased
when at least a half dozen or so people got out along
with him. As far as he was concerned, the more the mer-
rier.

Passing the eighth-floor central desk with several ward
clerks busily manning the phones, he continued down
the long hallway. As he passed patient rooms on both the
right and the left, he saw many obvious visitors. He also

saw many nurses, nurses' aides, and orderlies. It was a busy time for them as well since they were the evening shift, having just come on duty at three P.M. and needing to familiarize themselves with the status of all the patients.

Without so much as altering his stride, he walked all the way down to room 838 and stood for a moment in the doorway. He didn't go inside because he didn't need to. He could see all he needed from where he was. The most important observation was that the patient was indeed Laurie Montgomery. He'd reviewed what she looked like with all the PR the OCME put out, which included multiple pictures of the chief medical examiner. The second crucial observation was that she indeed did have an intravenous line in place, and since she'd just had major surgery, Carl knew it would remain in place for at least twenty-four hours post-surgery. From his experience, that was typical. Without it he couldn't do what he needed to do.

Since there was no one else in the room but the patient, which he didn't expect, he felt a little disappointed that he hadn't brought the syringe already loaded with the deadly potassium chloride that was waiting in his desk. Had he brought it with him, and used it, it would have meant that the mildly stressful task would already be over. As good as that sounded, he still thought it was best to wait until 3:30 A.M., during the graveyard shift. He smiled at the appropriateness of that name given to the eleven P.M. to seven A.M. tour, and he knew why. It was in the early-morning hours that the vast majority of hospital deaths occurred, for reasons both known and unknown. Of course, the biggest benefit for him was how easy it was going to be to just disappear in the middle of an attempted resuscitation, whereas at that moment there were people and potential witnesses all around.

"Excuse me, Doctor," a nurse said as she materialized out of nowhere and squeezed past Carl, carrying some kind of medication for Laurie. He watched her go into the room and begin a conversation, and he smiled. The nurse's sudden appearance was a corroboration of why he needed to wait until 3:30 A.M. to do what he needed to do. The chances of a nurse or nurse's aide suddenly appearing at the exact inopportune time were almost non-existent. "I'll be back," Carl mumbled to himself using an Austrian accent, recalling the famous line in the *Terminator* movie. As he walked away, he had to suppress a smile. By this time tomorrow the nightmare would be over, as there weren't any more dominoes that could possibly tip over and implicate him.

CHAPTER 40

hank you," Jack said to the Lyft driver as he alighted
from the black Honda Accord at the entrance to the
main lobby of the Kimmel Pavilion. It had been an
uneventful and pleasant enough ride, but just as long as
he feared, and he would have much preferred to have
come on his bike as it would have been a hell of a lot
faster. For Laurie's sake, he'd taken the rideshare as he
had agreed. Eager to see her, he pushed through one of
the revolving doors and quickly headed for the elevators.

JJ had come home while Jack had been on the phone
with Laurie, and when Jack had returned to the family
room, he'd found his son playing *Minecraft*. He was sitting on the couch, feet on the edge of the coffee table
and his laptop balanced on his knees. Jack took a seat
next to him and asked him about his day.

"It was fine," JJ said.

"Mom's surgery went well."

"I know." JJ's hands never paused, playing across the keyboard with surprising rapidity. Although Jack wasn't happy about the amount of time JJ spent playing computer games, he couldn't help but be impressed with the child's hand-eye coordination that had developed.

"How did you know the surgery went well?" Jack said. For a moment he'd thought maybe Laurie had called him and hadn't mentioned it.

"Caitlin told me."

"Mom will probably be home in just a few of days."

"Okay, good," JJ said after a pause. He clearly had been distracted by his gaming.

"Could you stop playing your computer game and talk to me for a moment?" Jack said with a touch of exasperation.

JJ rolled his eyes but reluctantly did as Jack asked.

"Were you worried about her today at school?" Jack asked, ignoring the eye-rolling.

"A little, but it was okay."

"I'm sorry I didn't call you today like I said I would," Jack said. "What happened is that I didn't hear anything until really late. I thought I was going to hear earlier. Did that concern you?"

"No," JJ said.

"Do you want to ask me any questions about anything?"

"No. Except can I go back to *Minecraft*?"

Jack smiled when he recalled the conversation. In

many ways it was typical, at least since JJ had been in the fourth grade. Getting any information out of him was becoming progressively difficult, especially when he was on his computer.

The elevator was crowded, so much so that Jack was pressed up against the back wall. When the car stopped on the eighth floor, he had to excuse himself and push his way out. As he walked down the corridor, he saw that most of the rooms had visitors. When he got to 838, he paused at the open door. Laurie was asleep in a typical hospital bed with the side rails up. To Jack she looked as beautiful as usual, with her face framed by dark hair that she had obviously taken the time to comb.

Silently Jack stepped inside and glanced around at the rest of the room's interior. As Laurie had suggested, it was impressive indeed, with an expansive view out over the East River. A good portion of Queens and Brooklyn was plainly visible. The bed was oriented parallel with the large window and faced the wall to the right that contained a strikingly large, built-in flat electronic screen. A news show with talking heads was playing without sound. The rest of the furniture included a bedside table, a love seat, a desk, and some built-in drawers. There was an open door leading into a bathroom, as well as a closed door that Jack assumed was a closet. Jack had to smile to himself at how different it was from any hospital room he'd ever seen when he was in medical school or when he was a resident.

Silently, so as not to wake Laurie, he tiptoed over to the bedside. Mounted into the wall behind the head of the bed were several flat-screen monitors capable of displaying her vital signs. Only one was functioning, with her ECG playing across the screen in a monotonous but reassuring repetition. The sound associated with the ECG was an equally repetitious, faint beep announcing each heartbeat. The only other noise in the room was the muffled voices drifting in from the hallway.

Jack was confused as to what he should do. He didn't want to wake her, yet he wanted desperately to talk with her. As he was about to tiptoe over to the couch and wait for her to awaken, one of her eyes popped open. As soon as she saw him, the other one opened as well. Then she managed a smile. They exchanged endearments and he gave her a gentle kiss and a tentative hug, being careful to avoid putting any pressure whatsoever on her chest. Then he brought over a chair to put next to the head of the bed.

"Thanks for coming in," Laurie said. With some effort she pushed herself back against the head of the bed to assume a semi-upright position. She winced as she did so.

"My pleasure," he said. "I must say you look terrific despite what you've been through."

"That's nice of you to say but I don't believe it for a second," she said, managing a smile. "Did you get to talk with JJ?"

"I did, and I'm happy to report that he's acting totally like his old self," Jack said. "It was hard to get him away from his computer screen. I think he's taken his mother's having surgery in stride."

"I'm not surprised," Laurie said.

"Do you want to talk at all about your procedure and what was found?" Jack asked. "I'm sure you've been told what Dr. Cartier told me."

"Thank you for asking," Laurie said. "But to be honest, I'm trying not to get too hung up on the details until I get to talk with the oncologist."

"I think that's wise," he said. "And, if you don't mind, I'll follow your lead."

"At the same time, I'm truly glad and thankful it was found as early as it was, considering its small size, and that there was only a microscopic amount in one lymph node."

"I was thrilled about that, too," Jack said. He noticed she avoided the term *cancer*, so he did as well.

"On a happier note, what do you think of this room?"

"It's pretty amazing," Jack said, letting his eyes roam around the room again. "Is that a sleeper couch?"

"It is, but don't get any ideas," she said with a laugh. "I want you home with the children."

"Aye, aye, captain," he said, raising his hands in surrender.

"Let me show you something else amazing," Laurie said. "Hand me that tablet from the bedside table."

Jack did as he was told, and Laurie proceeded to demonstrate how she could use it in conjunction with the monitor to order meals, watch TV or streaming services, adjust the window shades, or change the lighting and even the room temperature.

"Wow! If it can also put out the trash, I want one for

our apartment," Jack said, causing her to laugh hard enough to evoke a twinge from her endoscopic incision.

"Is everything copacetic at the OCME?" Laurie asked after resettling herself in a more comfortable position.

"Surprisingly enough, it's still standing," he said, trying to be funny. "Actually, it was a slow day in the autopsy room other than the Aria Nichols case. But let's not have you worrying about work. I'm sure George will be able to handle any problems over the weekend."

"Did you call Dr. Henderson back after you finished poor Aria's autopsy?" Laurie asked.

"I didn't," Jack said.

"Why not?"

"For two reasons. One, he didn't ask me to, and two, because there wasn't much to report. Besides, when I spoke with him before the case, he didn't seem to be all that concerned. And frankly he ended the conversation rather abruptly."

"That's odd," she said. "He was very concerned about hearing what was found with Kera Jacobsen."

"I think it has something to do with pressure he's been getting or not getting from Vernon Pierce."

"You're probably right," Laurie said.

―――――――――

A little while later, Laurie was eager to mobilize. She'd done it earlier, before Jack's arrival, but wanted to do it again. He was all for it as both knew how important it was after having surgery and general anesthesia. After disconnecting the monitor leads and with the help of an IV pole on wheels, the two of them strolled up and down the lengthy hall several times. Later they returned to the room to watch *PBS NewsHour* while she had a light meal. When *NewsHour* was drawing to a close, a nurse named Teresa Golden came in with the sleep meds that Dr. Cartier had ordered.

"I can leave them here on your bedside table," Teresa said, seeing that Laurie had company. "How is your pain? Do you think you need any more pain meds beyond what you're giving yourself with the IV piggyback?"

"I think I'm doing okay," she said.

"If not, just let us know," Teresa said brightly as she checked Laurie's surgical drain. "Very little drainage. That's terrific."

After Teresa left, Laurie commented on how warm and professional the nursing staff was, which was making the experience far more tolerable than when she'd had surgery at the Manhattan General years previously.

Following *NewsHour*, a show called *NYC-ARTS* came on. She and Jack watched it with half an eye, as they continued to do with the next show, which dealt with NYC metropolitan news. Mostly they talked about Emma's progress and JJ's upcoming psychologist evaluation, as well as their mutual concern about the amount of time JJ was spending playing computer games. A little after nine, Laurie began to feel exhausted.

"I'm afraid I'm running out of steam," she said as she switched off the monitor. She took several deep breaths, as she was doing frequently, knowing how important it was.

"Are you sure you don't want me to stay?" Jack said.

"I'm positive," Laurie said. "I'm doing just fine. With my pain meds, these sleeping pills, and having had general anesthesia, I'm going to sleep like a baby."

"When do you think you might want to come home?" he asked.

"I'm going to leave that up to Dr. Cartier," she said. "She said she'd be making early-morning rounds. I'll text you as soon as I see her and we talk about it."

"Fair enough," Jack said. He stood up, handed her the paper cup containing the sleeping pills. He poured her a glass of water and handed that to her as well. When she was finished, he took both back and replaced them on the bedside table. He then bent over and gave her another tentative hug. She hugged him back but winced with the discomfort caused by using her arms.

"I'll keep my phone with me all night in case you want to call or text for any reason," Jack said. "Try to have a good night's sleep."

"I'm sure I will." Laurie managed to give a little wave before he turned and headed for the door.

CHAPTER 41

To avoid the crowds waiting for cabs and rideshares outside the hospital, Jack headed south on foot. As he approached the OCME building, he remembered his call earlier to Bart Arnold. He'd been open about expressing his frustration over not having gotten Madison Bryant's Bellevue hospital records, but then had left before they had most likely arrived. Realizing there was no reason to rush home as the children would be already in bed, Jack decided to go up to his office. With everything that had happened that day, he felt jazzed up and knew it was going to be a long time before he'd be able to fall asleep.

He entered the building through the 30th Street receiving dock where bodies were brought in, waved to the guard manning his security desk and then to the two evening-shift mortuary techs in their office. Taking the back elevator, he went up to the floor where he and the rest of the medical examiners had their offices. As he descended the hallway, the sound of his heels echoed loudly. Except for the basement and the radio the guard had, the building was deathly quiet and seemed completely deserted.

The moment he turned on the light in his office, he saw the hard copy of Madison Bryant's Bellevue hospital records front and center on his desk. As usual, Bart Arnold had been true to his word. Sitting down, Jack opened the record and started reading. There was a lot of material, beginning with transcripts of the EMTs' communications with the Bellevue trauma team when they first arrived on scene at the subway station. Again, Jack was impressed with how lucky Madison was to have survived the initial fall onto the tracks and being passed over by the train, as well as to have avoided any contact with the highly electrified third rail.

What he was searching for in the records was any hint of cardiac problems, but there were none, not in the ambulance on the way to the Emergency Department trauma center or while in the Emergency Department itself. There were several electrocardiogram, or ECG, tracings from the time in the Emergency Department as well as in the OR when the stump of her leg was revised and sutured closed after the foot had been dismembered by the train.

The next part of the record documented her arrival and stay in the intensive-care unit. Jack carefully read all the entries by intensive-care hospitalists, doctors who specialized in intensive care, as well as intensive-care nurses. There was a lot of material, as was usually the case. Once again there was no mention of any cardiac abnormalities whatsoever that might have been a harbinger of the ventricular fibrillation that abruptly occurred and had not been at all amenable to treatment even though the treatment was started within seconds. Turning to the lab values for her blood work and chemistries, Jack was curious to see if there was any recording of her electrolyte values prior to her heart attack since wide swings in electrolyte levels were well known to cause abnormal cardiac function, including ventricular fibrillation. However, all the values he saw were within the normal range.

Just when Jack was about to give up, thinking he was not going to find anything of note in Madison Bryant's hospital record, he got another idea. With the enormous uptick in digital storage capacity, combined with the iCloud, Jack had in mind to see if there was any continuous recording in existence of Madison's vital signs, including her ECG, prior to her fatal heart attack. Using his ability to log in to both the NYU and Bellevue databases, he looked up Madison Bryant's record and was rewarded to find exactly what he was looking for: namely a record of her vital signs during her entire stay in the ICU. From the chart he knew the exact time of her cardiac arrest and was able to find that section without difficulty. As he had been told, the change was startlingly dramatic. The ECG was entirely normal until there was a sudden appearance of the erratic, sinusoidal, ventricular fibrillation when the heart's conduction system went berserk. Going back and looking more carefully at the tracing, starting an hour before the fatal event, he searched for any changes, even subtle ones. Usually in such cases there were a few progressively aberrant heartbeats or other evidence that the cardiac conduction system was under stress from myriad possible sources, either structurally in terms of the coronaries or the heart valves or chemically from drugs or electrolyte changes. But there was nothing. There was absolutely no indication of the coming disaster, as Jack scrolled through the record. That was the case until the fibrillation suddenly erupted. Magnifying the tracings, he stared at several heartbeats just seconds before the final event, and when he did, he noticed some possible subtle changes. At first, he thought that maybe it was artifact, but he became more suspicious it was real when he watched the tracings a number of times in a row, particularly the three beats just prior to the onset of the fibrillation. By stopping the tracing to freeze-frame the heartbeats in question and then enlarging the image, he was able to study them, allowing him to measure the heights and the widths of the waves. Then moving the tracing to a normal earlier section, he compared the measurements. What became clear to him was that there was a progressive but subtle peaking of the T wave and a similarly subtle flattening of the P wave in the three beats before fibrillation started.

"Good Lord," he voiced out loud. The slight but progressive changes he was seeing were reminding him of a case he'd been involved with along with Laurie more than a dozen years previously. It involved a nurse named Jasmine Rakoczi, who had been a serial killer at Ameri-Care's Manhattan General Hospital. She had been hired by an organization employed by a health insurance giant to kill off patients with inherited tendencies to develop expensive, serious diseases. As diabolical as the situation turned out to be, it had not totally shocked Jack or Laurie as they knew, like most health professionals, that health insurance companies love to collect premiums but hate to pay claims. Killing off clients destined to become seriously ill with chronic disease made a certain amount of sick sense to the company's bottom line.

What was reminding Jack of this notoriously depraved case was that the nurse had employed a demonically clever way to kill the victims, namely by using potassium chloride injected intravenously in a large bolus. The effect was to cause ventricular fibrillation, just as he was seeing on Madison Bryant's tracing, and it was preceded by the same subtle changes. To be sure his memory was serving him appropriately, Jack used the Internet to look up potassium chloride and the changes it caused to the ECG. Quickly he ascertained that it was as he remembered.

Going back to Madison Bryant's ECG tracing, he watched it several more times in a row, confirming to himself that a bolus of potassium chloride could have been involved. It certainly didn't prove the existence of KCl in this instance, but it suggested a definite possibility. That led him to question whether a health insurance company could have been involved as it had been in the Rakoczi case. But he didn't think so. Except for having lost her foot, Madison Bryant by all accounts had been doing well and wasn't going to be a lifetime healthcare burden. Thinking it had to be something else and not a random event, Jack went back to his previous thoughts of an association between the deaths of Kera Jacobsen, Madison Bryant, and Aria Nichols. What if they were all connected, and the overdoses were staged and not real? Although opioid deaths were so common and occurring on all strata of society, there was reason to suspect that Kera's and Aria's deaths could have been staged, especially when it seemed that neither one had been using IV drugs very long. And considering Madison's death, maybe whoever pushed her in front of the train had something to do with her death in the ICU?

As he thought about these possibilities, he felt his heart rate pick up. If Madison had been purposefully given a bolus of potassium chloride, it had to have been done in the intensive care unit by someone in the healthcare community, like the nurse he and Laurie had exposed, or by an orderly, or by a doctor. People were always coming and going in the ICU, and although oversight of patient care was relatively constant, for those patients doing well, there were times when they were not being monitored by personnel but more by technology equipped with alarms. What that meant was that there were times when someone could administer a bolus of potassium chloride and get away with it.

"Oh my God!" Jack said as he raised his gaze to stare

at his office wall with unseeing eyes. A new horror and new worry were taking form in his brain. If the three deaths were somehow connected with Bryant and Nichols being killed possibly to cover the death of Jacobsen, Laurie might very well be at risk since she had done the autopsy on Kera Jacobsen and had been supervising Aria Nichols's investigation of the case. And the really scary part of that idea was that because of unfortunate timing, Laurie was now an inpatient in essentially the same medical center with an intravenous line in place in a private room, meaning she, too, could be at risk far more than if she were in the Bellevue ICU.

With a sudden sense of panic, Jack leaped up, turned out his office light, and then ran down the hallway to the front elevators. He had no idea of the veracity of his rather wild and possibly paranoid suppositions, but there was one thing that he was absolutely sure of. Despite Laurie's objecting to his staying the night in her hospital room, he was going to do it anyway. If there was any risk whatsoever, he wanted to be there to make sure it didn't happen.

Retracing his steps by heading north on First Avenue, he power walked the length of the NYU Langone Medical Center, noticing that most of the visitors had left from the Tisch Hospital as there were far fewer people, taxis, and rideshare vehicles clogging the entranceway. It was the same at the Kimmel Pavilion. Even the Kimmel elevator was distinctively less crowded. Same with the hallway on the eighth floor. Although there were still a few family members in some of the rooms, thanks to the hospital's very tolerant position on allowing visitors pretty much twenty-four/seven, it was relatively quiet.

When he reached the door to 838, he noticed it was only ajar by three or four inches. Quickly but quietly, he pushed it open just enough to step within and then close it behind him. Inside the room it was quite dark with only a tiny bit of light spilling out of the slightly open door to the bathroom, where there was a night light. The only other illumination was from the monitor behind the bed still dimly displaying Laurie's ECG. The beeping had been turned off. All the window shades had been lowered.

Approaching the bed on his tiptoes, Jack looked down at Laurie's sleeping form. She was on her back with her face mostly lost in the shadow of her framing hair. In contrast to that evening when he had arrived, she was now quietly snoring and seemed the picture of total repose, thanks to the sleeping pills, the pain medication, and the remnants of anesthesia she'd had that day. A definite sense of relief spread over Jack, seeing that she was safe and that nothing had happened to her since he left and had conjured up the possibility she was in danger because of her association with Kera Jacobsen and Aria Nichols. Watching her calmly sleeping made him question the validity of his fears and whether he was suffering from paranoia to have imagined such a scenario.

Reversing course, he made his way over to the sleeper couch positioned directly under the huge monitor that was now as black as night. After lifting one of the pillows to make sure it was a foldaway bed, he stood up and tried to decide whether to open it. The concern was that if he wasn't careful, it might make a considerable racket and possibly awaken Laurie. Wanting to avoid that at all costs, he abandoned the idea. Instead, he turned around and merely silently lowered himself into a sitting position. Looking over at Laurie, who was about twelve feet away, he was relieved she hadn't stirred. His plan was to stay there and keep watch all night.

After only a few minutes sitting in the dark, Jack sensed how tired he was. It wasn't surprising, considering he had awakened before five that morning and had had a busy and emotional day. And as quiet as the hospital room was, he began to worry about falling asleep. Such a thought made him seriously question whether his presence alone could protect Laurie, given the rapidity with which potassium chloride was capable of eliciting a fatal ventricular fibrillation. Such a thought begged the question of whether someone could come into the room and inject Laurie even while Jack was there. The fact that he'd apparently proved that Madison Bryant had essentially died after three heartbeats was a dramatic confirmation of these fears. He had to think of something, but he had no great ideas. Could he stay awake somehow all night? He didn't know that, either, but being realistic, he doubted it. The real problem was that he had no way of judging how probable his suspicions were or whether they were a distorted product of his overtired, emotional, and paranoid mindset. Maybe he should have a talk with the nursing supervisor when she came on duty at eleven or . . .

. . . five minutes later Jack shocked himself by being jolted awake after having slowly crumpled against the right arm of the small sleep sofa and then falling off onto his hands and knees on the floor. As quietly as he could, he scrambled to his feet, furious with himself. He'd worried about falling asleep, and now he had proved it was a real concern. Once again, he looked over at Laurie's sleeping form in the half-darkness. Luckily, she was still quietly snoring and obviously still fast asleep despite the noise he'd made plopping off the couch onto the floor. He had to think of something before he really fell into a deep sleep and wasn't lucky enough to fall off the couch in the process. Jack was well aware that he was a heavy sleeper, which probably had something to do with the amount of exercise he got on a regular basis. When Jack was really tired, even coffee wasn't helpful. In medical school he'd been able to fall asleep standing up on occasion. Was there anything he could think of or do to make sure Laurie was safe? Was she really in jeopardy or was his imagination working overtime? There were many questions. Trying to think, he slowly sank back down onto the couch and leaned his head against the cushion. He could feel sleep threaten, and to avoid it overtaking him, he opened his eyes to their limits and took a deep breath . . .

CHAPTER 42

The alarm on his phone went off at exactly 3:05 A.M., and Carl turned it off. He hadn't needed it to awaken him as he was already awake and pumped up about what he had to accomplish in the next half hour or so. On the previous occasion, when he was finally ready to take care of the Madison Bryant threat, he'd been apprehensive. But not on this occasion. In keeping with the adage "practice makes perfect," Carl was confident that he would be able to eliminate with equal ease the even more worrisome threat Dr. Laurie Montgomery posed. His previous, hypothetical belief that a large intravenous bolus of potassium chloride would be the perfect surreptitious method to eliminate a human being had been proven beyond any doubt with the way it had worked with Madison Bryant. Even with the woman as a patient

in an intensive care unit surrounded by intensivist doctors and nurses and her body later being subjected to an
autopsy by forensic pathologists, no one had had any inkling of what had actually transpired. And tonight, with
Laurie Montgomery, it was going to be a breeze with
her being in a private room instead of the busy ICU. In
many respects it was going to be too easy, without the
intricacies of the challenge the Madison Bryant situation
presented.

Despite his confidence, he did not shortchange himself on his disguise. He made the same amount of effort
with the black wig, dark heavy glasses, and long white
doctor's coat complete with a hemostat, a pair of scissors,
a penlight, and several pens on prominent display in the
breast pocket. The KCl-filled syringe was nestled in
the depths of his coat's right-side pocket. Once he was
ready, he made one last check in the medical center database to confirm his destination. As he suspected, Laurie
Montgomery's room was still listed as 838. Thus prepared and after a final check on his disguise using his
full-length mirror to make certain no one would recognize him, he left his office.

Although he could have gotten to the eighth floor of
the Kimmel Pavilion any number of ways through the
labyrinthine medical center that stretched nearly from
34th Street in the north to just shy of 30th Street in the
south, he chose to walk outside. Despite his confidence
in his disguise, he preferred not to run into anyone he
knew, which was always a possibility within the well-
lighted main corridors. As a major medical center with

surgery going on around the clock, surgeons in particular were often in the hospital at all hours. Since Surgery
and Pathology often had to work in tandem, he was acquainted with a number of them. Carl also avoided entering through the main Kimmel Pavilion lobby entrance
for fear it would be too quiet, and he might attract the
attention of one of the security personnel who might feel
obligated for some unknown reason to check his med
center ID. Instead he entered back into the medical center through the Emergency Department, where there
was more activity twenty-four/seven.

Arriving on the eighth floor, Carl was immediately
encouraged by the general peacefulness as he walked
quickly and silently down the long, dimly lit hallway. At
that moment on that particular floor it was as if the hospital was deserted, save for an occasional nurse or aide
coming out of one distant room and then quickly disappearing into another. Most of the rooms he passed were
silent and dark, although there were a few where the
lights were on and even a few where the quiet sound of
the TVs drifted out into the corridor. Near the far end of
the corridor he could plainly see the nurses' desk because
it stood out starkly as the only area brightly illuminated.
Behind the counter-high barrier, he could just make out
several heads either of nurses, aides, or clerks, who were
most likely busy with data entry or paperwork.

Slowing down and then stopping when he came
abreast of room 838, he noticed the door was nearly
closed with but a half-inch gap between the door and the
jamb. Pausing for a moment, he reached into his pocket

to fondle the syringe loaded with the KCl just to reassure himself it was there waiting for him. After glancing up and down the hallway to make sure the coast was completely clear and his presence hadn't attracted any attention, he used just the tips of his fingers to push gently against the door, slowly and silently opening it. Progressively the darkened room came into his view and ultimately the hospital bed. What caught Carl's eye first, in addition to the dark-haired woman sleeping in the bed, was that her ECG was being continuously displayed on a monitor mounted in the wall behind and above the head of the bed. He thought this was convenient as it would immediately reflect the ventricular fibrillation and sound an alarm. Carl liked the idea of an alarm being involved as it would provide an explanation of why he had dashed into the room, if anyone were to ask. The other important thing he noticed was that there still was an intravenous line snaking into Laurie's arm. If that had been removed, he might have had to scrap the entire plan and come up with a new idea. But he had been confident it would be there as normal protocol dictated it.

With a final glance up and down the corridor, he pushed open the door enough to allow him to step silently into the room. Pausing for a moment to allow his eyes to fully adjust to the relative darkness, he glanced around at the rest of the interior. Suddenly he froze. With an unpleasant sense of shock, he noticed a second occupant in the room. Curled up in a fetal position on a small couch was a man who Carl immediately assumed was Laurie Montgomery's husband, Jack Stapleton, with whom he'd spoken on the phone that afternoon.

Carl's first inclination was to immediately flee as this was an unexpected and unfortunate change in the circumstances. But he hesitated, silently telling himself that perhaps it wasn't quite as bad as he had initially feared and might actually help to deflect attention once the feverish activity of the resuscitation attempt was initiated. On top of trying to save the patient, the resuscitation team and the floor nurses inevitably would have to deal with the aggrieved husband.

What had brought all this to his mind after the initial concern was recalling how rapidly the fibrillation would occur. Just like he had done in the ICU, Carl would start resuscitation immediately. By the time the husband would wake up, orient himself, and get over to the bedside, Carl could already be giving external cardiac massage, saying he'd heard the alarm while passing by in the hallway. If anything, the husband, as a physician himself, would surely participate, perhaps by giving mouth-to-mouth respiration. Suddenly Carl was so confident, he found himself smiling at the mental image of him and the husband trying to save the doomed Laurie. Carl knew full well that once the bolus of KCl was in her system and wasn't immediately reversed, there was no way for the cardiac conduction system to function, no matter what any resuscitation team tried to do.

For another minute Carl continued to stand in the middle of the dark room as he rethought the entire scenario. When he did so, he was even more convinced that having Stapleton unexpectedly present actually afforded a way around the problem of his getting away after the deed had been done. It had worked like a charm in the ICU, but that was because there were so many people involved. Here on the private floor there would be far fewer people, particularly fewer staff doctors since the entire resuscitation team was composed of residents, mostly in internal medicine, and Carl's presence would stand out, especially if someone questioned whether he had any private patients on the floor. As for Jack Stapleton recognizing him, he thought the chances were essentially zero. He doubted they had ever met, but even if they had, with his wig and dark glasses, Carl didn't even recognize himself.

Fully reassured of his plan, he silently advanced up along the right side of Laurie's bed. For a moment, as he listened to Laurie's regular breath sounds in the darkness, he glanced up at the ECG as it metronomically traced its normal squiggle across the screen. He inwardly smiled as he anticipated that in a few seconds the tracing would suddenly change into the sinusoidal jumble of ventricular fibrillation, meaning the entire heart's electrical conduction system had devolved to pure chaos.

Carl pulled the loaded syringe out. The meager light coming from the bathroom was just enough to make sure it was still entirely full. Using his teeth, he pulled off the plastic protective cap from the large-bore needle. After one more glance back at the sleeping husband who'd not moved a muscle or made a sound, Carl picked up the

IV line with his left hand so that with his right hand he could insert the needle into the IV port. Holding the syringe in both hands, with both thumbs on the plunger, and after one more quick glance at Jack Stapleton's sleeping form, he rapidly injected the entire contents into Laurie's intravenous line. As with Madison Bryant, the level in the drip chamber rose suddenly as a bit of the KCl traveled retrograde. In the next instant he opened the IV line completely, letting it run free.

As he had anticipated, almost simultaneous with his withdrawing the syringe, he saw the initial changes appear on the ECG tracing that included a dramatic upward shift of the T wave. With the very next beat it was worse. Two beats later the entire normal ECG complex disintegrated into a kind of chicken scratch or child's scribble to reflect that the heart had stopped beating and had become a quivering mass of muscle. At the same time the cardiac alarm went off to shatter the room's silence, causing Carl to start despite his fully expecting it.

Vaguely aware of the figure on the couch leaping up, Carl quickly pocketed the empty syringe and then collapsed the safety rail to facilitate his climbing onto the bed to start closed chest massage. He couldn't have been more confident and more content. For him it was a kind of confirmation of the scientific method as things were going like clockwork. He knew full well that first one of the nurses, followed by one of the hospital's on-call resuscitation team, would be rushing into the room in a matter of seconds to take over what would turn out to be a hopeless task.

Jack initially tried to avoid waking up because he was in the middle of one of his favorite dreams. He was playing basketball, but he wasn't playing the way he normally played in real life. He was playing a type of basketball where he was capable of jumping so high that he could hang in the air and easily dunk. Even when he'd been at his physical peak somewhere around age seventeen, although he could manage to touch the rim with ease, he could never dunk because he couldn't palm the basketball. Yet despite the enjoyable high the dream engendered, the raucous sound of the ventricular fibrillation alarm, which he initially had incorporated into his dream, finally yanked him into full wakefulness. Becoming oriented to time, place, and person, he leaped off the couch.

The first thing Jack saw in the half-light was a man dressed in a long white lab coat struggling to put down the hospital bed's safety rail, and the sight propelled Jack into action. He knew what the alarm had to signify, namely that this shadowy individual had knowingly injected Laurie with KCl in order to kill her, and the realization infuriated him as much as he could remember anything angering him. It seemed as if every bad or terrible thing that had happened to him in his whole life coalesced into this one horrible act. Seeing red and instead of running up alongside the bed's free side, Jack ran up behind the man who was now kneeling on the bed. From the back he grabbed a handful of the man's white coat and pulled as hard as he possibly could. Since the man was essentially teetering on the bed's edge, Jack's fearful yank caused him to completely lose balance, falling over backward onto Jack. In the process, his flailing arm swept off the water pitcher, the telephone, and some of Laurie's personal items from the bed's side table, creating a gigantic clatter.

For a few moments in the semidarkness a violent struggle ensued, trapped between the confines of the bed and the wall to the bathroom. It involved floundering legs and flailing arms all tangled in a confusing mass. It wasn't until the mystery man, who was splayed on top, managed to roll off Jack into the center of the room that both were able to scramble to their feet and face off. "What the hell?" the man yelled. He frantically pointed back toward the hospital bed. "The patient's in ventricular fibrillation! She's going to die!"

Jack didn't answer but in a singular fury lunged forward with the idea of retackling his adversary, but the man, in a purely defensive move, stepped to the side and deflected Jack's outstretched arms. In his uncontrolled rage, Jack bounced off the wall that had the large-screen TV.

"What are you, crazy?" the man yelled in bewilderment as Jack immediately regrouped and came at him in a headlong rush for a second time, forcing him to again step to the side like a matador dealing with an enraged bull. "The patient is in extremis!" the man cried. "We have to start CPR!"

On this occasion Jack collided with the sofa he'd been sleeping on and his momentum bent him over the couch's

back, forcing him to thrust out his arms and hands to
keep from somersaulting over it. With a few seconds' re-
spite, the man abandoned any hope that Jack's attention
would be dominated by the need to save Laurie's life, and
in a pure panic he opted to flee the scene while Jack was
regaining his footing. Wrenching open the door, the man
dashed out into the corridor and disappeared.

A moment later Jack burst out of the dimly lit hospital
room into the comparatively well-illuminated hospital
corridor in pursuit of the man he now strongly suspected
was a serial killer. It took him only a split second to determine that his adversary had run to the right toward
the elevators and not back toward the nurses' station,
and he guessed why: Several nurses were rapidly approaching from that direction in response to the cardiac
alarm that was still raucously blaring.

Ignoring the nurses, Jack took off like a sprinter in hot
pursuit of the fleeing man, but the mere sight of the
nurses had finally awakened the rational, thinking part
of his brain, which then wrested control from his more
primitive, aggressive, flight-or-fight reptilian center that
had been in command from the moment he'd been
rudely awakened by the fibrillation alarm. The first thing
he noticed was that he was rapidly gaining ground on the
man, suggesting Jack was ostensibly in better shape. The
second thing was seeing in the distance a resuscitation
team of four resident physicians in scrubs pushing a four-
wheeled crash cart rushing toward them on a collision
course.

Jack slowed. Ahead the man had collided with the

team, roughly shoving aside the bewildered residents and commandeering the cardiac resuscitation team's sizable crash cart. Getting on the opposite side from Jack, he forcibly wedged it sideways in the corridor, blocking Jack's way. In the process many of its contents noisily crashed to the floor. The man then recommenced running down the corridor toward the elevators and the stairs.

"So sorry!" Jack yelled to the totally perplexed residents as he struggled to free up the crash cart to get by. Behind him he caught a glimpse of nurses ducking into the room he'd just left.

As soon as he could, he recommenced running. Bursting into the stairwell where he had seen the man disappear, the first thing Jack did was determine whether the man had gone up or down. It wasn't difficult. Jack managed to see glimpses of the man's white coat flapping in the breeze and hear his thundering footsteps pounding on the metal stairs several flights down as he was descending as fast as he possibly could. It was the type of stairwell that had two flights of stairs and a landing between each floor, creating a kind of rectilinear spiral. It was also possible to lean over the railing and see all the way down to the basement level nine stories below. He started down, and once again and rather quickly he could tell he was gaining on the individual.

Jack's anger had not abated, but with his cerebrum having kicked in, he was recognizing he was chasing someone who wasn't defenseless but rather a sizable, muscular opponent who seemed reasonably athletic. The man had done an acceptable job parrying Jack's headlong attacks in the hospital room despite being hampered by being dressed in a long doctor's coat whose pockets contained surgical instruments and other medical paraphernalia; he had heard them when they had noisily clattered to the floor during their brief tussle. With these thoughts in mind, Jack began to worry what else his adversary might have on his person, such as a scalpel or sharp surgeon's scissors. Accordingly, Jack slowed to a degree to avoid catching up with him in the stairwell yet fast enough to keep pressure on him in a manner similar to how an experienced angler plays a large sport fish. It was his belief that unless the man indulged in the kind of athletics akin to the basketball Jack played or rode his bike like Jack, which Jack seriously doubted as few people did, he was confident the man would soon seriously tire from the amount of energy he was expending in his breakneck flight.

By the time they passed the building's second floor, Jack could tell his plan was already working. It was becoming obvious that the man was clearly in trouble from the monumental exertion the panicked descent demanded. Upon passing the first floor, the loud, rapid, and repetitive drumbeat of the man's footfalls had slowed significantly, particularly on the final flight. As Jack passed the ground level and started down the last two flights of stairs, all he could hear was the man's labored breathing, particularly on the exhale. As Jack rounded the landing and started down the final flight of steps, he could see that the man was stooped over, hands on his knees, struggling to catch his breath. His coloring was ashen, his mouth slack. It appeared that he didn't have the energy to open the heavy fire door from the stairwell into the basement.

Jack slowed as he descended the last few stairs, warily keeping his eye on the man as he approached, wondering if the individual's distress could be a ploy and whether he might suddenly brandish a weapon of some sort. Now only five or six feet away, Jack could see that the man was wearing a wig, as it was askew on his head. Also, his glasses were crooked with one of the temple pieces bent at a right angle.

Jack reached the basement level and stepped off the last step onto the concrete floor. In contrast to his opponent, his breathing was deep but not labored, particularly not to the extent of excluding any other activity. He could see that the man was watching him with his bloodshot, pained eyes. In obvious fear of Jack's tight-lipped expression and his relentless approach, the man straightened up with great effort and stumbled backward to press his back against the closed door.

Without the slightest hesitation once in range, Jack balled his right hand into a tight fist and smacked the man directly in the nose, sending the heavy-framed eyeglasses flying. The man's legs buckled as if they were made of rubber, and he collapsed into a sitting position with his back against the door. He was still fighting for breath.

"Stupid bastard," Jack said as much to himself as to his adversary, while he wildly flapped his hand in the air to counteract the sharp pain he felt in his knuckles. He hadn't planned on striking the man. It had been an irresistible spur-of-the-moment urge to give vent to the roiling anger that he still felt. Next, he reached down and grabbed the wig and yanked it off the man's head. Tossing that aside, he looked at the individual's face. Although the man looked vaguely familiar, Jack couldn't place him. Next, Jack lifted the man's ID that was hanging around his neck on a lanyard and glanced briefly at the picture. Only then did he read the name.

"Carl Henderson?" he cried in astonishment. With disbelief he again looked at the photo laminated into the ID and then back down at the man sprawled out against the fire door. The image and the person matched. "Are you really Carl Henderson?" Jack asked in disbelief.

The man didn't answer. Instead he closed his eyes and let his head slowly fall back to lean against the fire door as he continued to try and desperately catch his breath.

Standing over the downed man, Jack reached into his pocket and pulled out his phone. With a couple of pokes against the touchscreen, he pulled up Lou Soldano's information from his contacts and put in a call to the Homicide detective. Despite the hour, he knew Lou would answer. He was, after all, one of his best friends and an admitted workaholic.

EPILOGUE

May 12th
9:15 A.M.

Knock, knock," Jack called out as he pushed his head through the half-open door of room 821 of the Kimmel Pavilion.

"It's about time," Laurie said, with barely concealed frustration. "Where have you been? I've been texting you since early this morning."

"It's been an interesting night," Jack said sheepishly. He walked over to the bed and gave her a peck on the cheek. She allowed it, but just barely.

"What is an 'interesting night' supposed to mean?" Laurie demanded. "That sounds to me like more of an excuse than an explanation."

"It's a little of both," he said as he dragged over a chair to sit down next to the head of her bed. "Before I get more specific, how are you doing?"

"I'm doing remarkably well," Laurie said as if angry. "Dr. Cartier was in here at the crack of dawn and couldn't be more pleased. She even removed the drains as there had been so little discharge. She's going to leave it up to me when I want to go home, including today if I choose."

"That's terrific," Jack said. "Really terrific. What do you think you want to do?"

"I want to see exactly how well I can use both arms before I decide," she said. "But considering how I feel now and with what I've been able to do so far this morning, I think there's a good chance I'll elect to come home today, but if not, tomorrow. I'll still need considerable help with some common activities if you are up for that?"

"Absolutely," Jack said. "I'd prefer you to be home."

"Okay, good, and now with that out of the way, I want an explanation," Laurie said with continued annoyance. "When I woke up this morning, I found myself occupying a different room, and one that was without the view that I was enjoying yesterday. When I asked the nurses why I was moved in the middle of the night while I was asleep, their answer was that I needed to ask you because it was your doing. Why, in heaven's name, did you have my room changed while I was asleep?"

"Strangely enough, if you want to know the truth, it was your fault," he said, allowing himself a slight smile.

"And what does that mean, my fault?" Laurie demanded. "Come on! No riddles or games! Just tell me."

"I can't help sounding obtuse," Jack said. "I'm in kind of a daze. It's all been so . . . what should I say . . . unexpected."

"You're teasing me, and I don't like it," she complained. "Out with it! Why did you change my room?"

"I'll give you a hint," Jack said. "I moved you because, incredibly enough, Aria Nichols was right in pursuing her investigation about the father of Kera's fetus, and you were right for encouraging her."

"So, this is all a big riddle, is that what you're trying to tell me?"

"I suppose," he said. "I could just out-and-out tell you, but somehow it will mean even more to you if I allow you to understand the dilemma I felt last night coming late to what you and Aria had essentially figured out even if you didn't realize it. The bad guy in all this actually turns out to have been the father of the fetus, just as Aria suspected. What seems to have happened, as it is now being properly investigated, is that both Kera's and Aria's overdoses were staged. Apparently both women were either killed or rendered helpless with fentanyl in alcohol, or at least that's what it is now assumed to have happened. Once they were unconscious, they were injected with a fentanyl-heroin mixture to make it look like an overdose. Now, all of this has not been entirely proven as of yet, but at the moment that's what is being hypothesized."

"This sounds extraordinary," Laurie said. Her voice had lost all its edge. "Who's looking into all this?"

"Lou Soldano," Jack said proudly.

"Really?" she questioned. "How on earth did he get involved?"

"I called him in the wee hours of the morning," Jack

admitted. "When I suddenly discovered the identity of the bad guy, I knew Lou was by far the best person to take over what was undoubtedly going to become a major scandal."

"When did you find out the identity of the quote-unquote bad guy?" Laurie asked. "Was it before or after my room got changed?" For self-preservation and to maintain her composure, she was forcing herself to participate in his convoluted storytelling.

"It was a number of hours after," Jack said. "Okay, I can tell I've tortured you enough. Here's the story: After I left you around nine last night, I ended up going back to my office because it was so close by and because it was too late to catch the children before they went to bed. The reason I wanted to go back was remembering that I had failed to look at Madison Bryant's hospital record, which I'd given Bart Arnold some heat to get. When I looked at the record, in particular Madison's ECG when her fatal fibrillation started, I had an epiphany. The changes that occurred in the last three heartbeats reminded me of a case you and I were involved with years ago about the nurse serial killer in the Manhattan General Hospital who was knocking off patients destined to be economic drains on their health insurance company's bottom line. She used intravenous KCl. Do you remember?"

"Of course I remember," Laurie said. "Jasmine Rakoczi. I'm never going to forget that horrid individual. That was back when I had my ectopic pregnancy."

"My epiphany was that possibly Madison Bryant had

also been killed with KCl, which immediately begged the question of why. When I asked that question while associating Kera's, Madison's, and Aria's deaths all at the same time, it made me terrified of you being in the hospital with a keep-open IV. If perchance the father of Kera's fetus had indeed killed her, and Madison, and Aria, you, with your connections to the case, were potentially in the crosshairs for the same reason."

"So, you moved me to protect me," she said with a combination of astonishment and appreciation. "And then did you have confirmation that my life was indeed in danger?"

"Yes and, I'm afraid to say, yes again," Jack said. "But when I moved you, I was far from convinced I was right and truly thought I might have been suffering from anxiety-induced paranoia. I really had no idea what to do besides try to stand guard all night. I wasn't even sure enough to involve any of the hospital authorities, or to call and ask Lou's opinion. I was truly at a loss."

"So, after you moved me, what did you do?" Laurie asked. "Did you merely wait in ambush for someone to show up? I mean that wouldn't really work unless I was there, and he tried something."

"Exactly," he said. "If someone used KCl in the ICU to take care of Madison, it had to be a healthcare worker of some import, like a nurse, or an aide, or a doctor. Otherwise, they wouldn't have gotten in there. After I'd safely stashed you in one of the vacant rooms, which turned out to be this room, I took a patient gurney down to the medical school simulation center and borrowed

one of the computerized high-fidelity simulation man-
nequins that are used to teach students how to respond
to critical emergencies. You know, the kind that are pro-
gramed to respond physiologically just like a live human.
I then brought it up to 838 and set it up with the ECG
going and covered it with a blanket. I mean, it was terrific, especially in the dark. Even the breathing sounded
entirely normal."

"So, it was a kind of a trap," Laurie said with amazement.

"Exactly," Jack said. "And it worked like a charm.
When the bad guy came in somewhere around three
thirty, he obviously thought for sure it was you and was
probably hyped up enough not to check. To tell you the
truth, I was sound asleep at that point and didn't wake
up until he caused the simulator's alarm to go off by injecting the damn KCl."

"My good Lord!" she said.

"It's appropriate to invoke his name," Jack said with a
smile. "In retrospect, he had to have been involved in
how everything turned out."

"Maybe you better not tell me the details of what happened after that," Laurie said. Knowing him as well as
she did, she could imagine he'd transformed into a wild
man, possibly putting himself in danger. Her only con-
solation was the idea that the individual was most likely
a healthcare worker and probably not armed.

"It wasn't pretty," Jack admitted.

"All right, enough evasions," Laurie said. "Now I'm
ready for you to tell me the identity of the bad guy. From

your description of him as a *bad guy*, plus mentioning that you wanted Lou involved early because you feared a scandal, and finally your sense it had to be a healthcare worker, I'm fully prepared to be shocked. Who is it?"

"Dr. Carl Henderson," Jack said.

"Oh. My. God!" she exclaimed, pronouncing each word separately. She was totally stunned. It took her a moment to gather her thoughts before saying: "Who would have guessed? He's about the last person I would have suspected. It's all such folly and such a tragedy on so many levels . . ."

"Let's look on the bright side," he said.

"I'm having trouble seeing a bright side," Laurie said.

"It seems that you and Aria Nichols have added genetic genealogy to the forensic grab bag of tricks to make it possible to construct a perpetrator's genome. If that's not a bright side, I don't know what is."

ACKNOWLEDGMENTS

In alphabetical order I would like to thank Mark Desire, Assistant Director of Forensic Biology, Office of the Chief Medical Examiner, New York City, and Mark Flomenbaum, M.D., Chief Medical Examiner, State of Maine. Both were generously willing to answer multiple questions. I would also like to acknowledge that Blaine T. Bettinger's *The Family Tree Guide to DNA Testing and Genetic Genealogy* and Tamar Weinberg's *The Adoptee's Guide to DNA Testing* provided valuable insight into the new frontier of genetic genealogy.

ROBIN
COOK

"Master of the medical thriller."
— *The New York Times*

For a complete list of titles and to sign up for
our newsletter, please visit prh.com/RobinCook